I0733132

DREADKNOT

ALSO BY THE AUTHOR

THE STARSTRUCK SAGA

Starstruck

Alienation

Traveler

Celestial

Starbound

Earthstuck

Inalienable

Dreadknot

AIX MARKS THE SPOT

NOVELLAS AND SHORT STORIES

Miss Planet Earth (Pew! Pew! - The Quest for More Pew!)

The Horrible Habits of Humans (Pew! Pew! - Bite My Shiny Metal Pew!)

Miss Planet Earth and the Amulet of Beb Sha Na

Head over Heels (Starstruck Halloween Short)

Lasers and Tiaras (Starstruck Short)

Study Night at the Museum (Unbound: Stories of Transformation, Love, And Monsters)

BOOK EIGHT OF THE STARSTRUCK SAGA

DREADKNOT

S.E. ANDERSON

BOLIDE

DREADKNOT

© S.E. Anderson 2022
Cover design by Sarah Anderson
Editorial: Michelle Dunbar, Madeline Dyer, Cayleigh Stickler, Anna Johnstone

All rights reserved. No part of this publication may be reproduced, distributed, or transmitted in any form or by any means, including photocopying, scanning, uploading to the internet, recording, or other electronic or mechanical methods, without the prior written permission of the publisher and/or author, except in the case of brief quotations for reviews.

This is a work of fiction. Names, characters, businesses, places, events, and incidents are either the products of the author's imagination, or used in a fictitious manner. Any resemblance to persons, living or dead, or actual events is entirely coincidental.

First published in 2022 by Bolide Publishing Limited
Bolidepublishing.com

ISBN: 978-1-912996-34-6

TO EVERYONE STILL HANGING ON
KEEP HANGING ON.

ONE

POST-PANDEMIC SHOPPING VIBES

THE FIRST PROBLEM WITH TIME TRAVEL IS IT technically constitutes as tax evasion. The second is the relativity of time itself—relatives tend to hate the jet-setting camp of being lost in time and space.

Three years on Earth were a lot to miss, especially when two thirds of them were a dumpster fire. Just when I thought I was caught up on every facet of the pandemic, nothing prepared me for dealing with family drama. It turns out a parent's hospitality wears out the second their relief at seeing their daughter alive is replaced by the dread of living with her kidnappers-but-not-really. In our case, the honeymoon phase lasted all of two days before my parents were already tired of me and my delinquent friends lazing about their living room. When you plead the alien defense in court before breaking out of an institution while your psychiatrists were being arrested then hold their daughter hostage for three years in the process, you don't make a good first impression.

It was all time travel's fault, but telling them that was a big, fat *no*.

But we were on Earth. Home. We should have been relaxing. We'd come up against the Alliance and won; true to their word, they'd ordered the Agency to stand down and drop their charges. New evidence had come to light showing our innocence. The story that hit the media was vague—the Agency had been too lazy to write clever cover stories—but we were *free*. Well, free from the Agency, not free from the journalists hounding us for an interview.

So, we hid in the house, curtains drawn, the TV filling us in on what we'd missed. We'd been like this for a week, trying to catch our breath, though each story was worse than the last. I'd given up on the internet at this point. After all we'd been through, even cat videos seemed unsettling and morose.

"Does Earth feel… different since we've been back?" I asked, after the third breaking news story in a row.

Blayde looked up from her journal and cleared her throat, all cozy in mom's old Minnie Mouse sweatshirt. Everything I owned had either been taken as evidence or was in the storage locker my parents had been forced to get when my landlord evicted me for not paying rent due to being on another planet. Even my trusty duffle bag was still buried under a mountain of procedure. I hadn't realized I'd miss it until it wasn't there waiting for me when I got back, but now my shoulder felt empty.

Blayde looked at me. "Hate to break it to you, but your planet has always been a"—Zander nudged her in the ribs—"adorable little hovel."

"Wow, thanks for that." I shifted closer to Zander on the couch and he put my arm around me, pulling me in tight. We hadn't had time to ourselves since we'd gotten back, not a moment to comfort each other after the events of Pyrina. "Something's off, though. Can't you feel it? Like we're home, but not really. We can't travel to parallel universes, can we?"

Galli snorted from her bed by the kitchen. My family dog had changed color while we were gone, more white in its fur than when we'd left, and had gained a passive-aggressive streak to rival the rest of us.

"This is what happens when you live it up on Pyrina." Blayde shook her head. "You can never go back to dumpy little worlds again."

I frowned. Pyrina had been a letdown. Despite its vibrant patchwork of peoples, the political fabric had been stretched thin. And with multiple rebel attacks—including our own—on the president on the same night, I'd expected better from the Alliance capital.

"We need food."

Dad stood in the doorway, one hand on his hip, the other taut and holding a shopping list out to me. Since we'd gotten back, he'd been treating us like we were teenagers caught underage drinking and was understandably sulky.

I plucked the list out of his hands. It was as long as my arm. "Jeez, how many people are you trying to feed?"

"Be sure to check the brand," he said. "After the consumer wars in early November, stick to what you know, Sally."

Was he trying to get rid of us? Every conversation with my parents since we'd gotten back had been like fixing a warp core; one misstep and your arms would end up hugging opposite ends of the galaxy. Sure, they had good reason to hate us, but it was hard to catch one's breath when the air was this thick with tension. Dad practically shoved the car keys into my hand and pushed us out the door.

Our drive to the grocery store was silent and cold, like most everything since the ball. And inside, Publix was worse still. There was a certain chill in the air, like the drop of pressure before a storm. Not from the cosmobeat blasting through the PA system—a whole new musical genre we'd missed, which sounded like the universe was trying to bathe a cat. Maybe from the way people seemed to be avoiding not only us but each other too.

Anxiety appeared to be catching.

"I got the ice cream," said Zander. "Not sure if your parents even have a freezer big enough for it all."

Seeing him there with a metric ton of ice cream just made him all the more beautiful. Perks of his sturdy arms were that he could carry a dozen containers at once as well as beat up interstellar fiends. He dropped them unceremoniously into the cart.

"Air conditioner problems?" I rubbed the goosebumps on my arms. "Where's Blayde wandered off to? We should find her before she stumbles upon a quest in the dairy aisle. She was ranting about needing purpose again."

I couldn't imagine Blayde being happy with our current pace. We made our way to the checkout and saw Blayde in deep conversation with an older lady in the bookstore corner.

"They only published the manuscript now?" Blayde was either truly interested or a brilliant actress. "Fascinating. I've been to your seventeenth century and don't think I know this specific Desmond, but I can go back and check."

"It's a free country," said the woman, before stomping away.

"We're done." I waved Blayde over to the cash register. It was a lot more polite than screaming *Earth is not ready for time travel!* We'd only just gotten out of a mental institution, and I wasn't aiming to be put back in one.

"We leave your planet for three years, and *that's* when things get interesting?" Blayde grimaced as she joined us, tossing a paperback on top of a tub of mint choco-chip. So many uber-specific, niche brands of chips, along with vegetables we'd had to measure and compare against a chart.

My phone vibrated in my pocket—Dad, probably wondering what was taking so long. I handed Zander the credit card and stepped away, pressing the phone to my ear.

"Dad?"

"Sally, is that you?" he asked, breathless.

"What happened?" The hair on the back of my arm rose like zombies from the grave. "What's wrong?" I paused. "Dad, is Mom okay? Is anyone hurt?"

"No, Sally." His voice was thick with tension. "But you'd better get here soon. It's—"

The phone fizzled out, and so did my thoughts. I stood there, frozen, my phone still pressed to my ear. After all the Agency promises that my parents would be safe…*no*.

"What happened?" asked Zander, pushing the cart past checkout.

My mind snapped into action, screaming at me that everything Foollegg had threatened me with was now coming true. That my parents would pay for my supposed crimes with their life. Or maybe a worse threat than the Agency had gotten to them first. "Something's wrong. We have to go. Now."

Everyone you love is in danger because of you.

A scream burst my eardrums, and I spun to see the checkout aflame, a column of heat reaching up to the ceiling. White-hot fire all around the… the *person*. Our clerk, a woman I'd seen alive and smiling a second ago, was now consumed in flames. The column fell just as quickly as it had appeared, leaving the charred body of our cashier seared into our eyes before it, too, crumbled.

Zander's hand grabbed mine, tugging me away, but I couldn't move. My feet were rooted to the floor. She had been there, then on fire and—

"What the hell?" I shrieked, as the grocery store erupted into screams. I'm pretty sure people didn't just start bursting into flames since we'd left. If there was a new side effect to working in the service industry, I'm sure somebody would have told me about that by now.

"SHC!" Blayde answered. "Don't talk, run!"

We bolted out of the store to the car, screams ringing in my ears. Zander spilled the shopping bags into the trunk, loose fruit rolling around as he slammed it shut. I peeled out of the parking lot. We couldn't be anywhere near the incident, not when we'd been criminals just days ago. And we weren't just driving away; we were driving toward—toward my parents and whatever had happened to them.

"S-SHC?" I stammered. The woman had been alive and then… gone in such a horrific instant. I could still smell the sizzle of skin. Could the same thing have happened to—

"Spontaneous human combustion," said Blayde.

"Wait, I thought that was an urban myth! People just bursting in flames? That doesn't happen. Does it?"

"It's a safeguard for Agency operatives," said Zander, his voice impossibly steady. "When their cover is blown."

"The Agency has infiltrated Publix? Is nowhere sacred anymore?"

"It *was* a safeguard," Blayde corrected. "The whole system was terminated centuries ago. After the locals started getting…inspired."

And here I thought Agency tourism was a recent thing. How long had we been entertaining off-world guests? I clenched the steering wheel. "They *ignite* their own agents?"

"There're meant to be protocols in place." Zander's head spun around, checking every mirror. "It must have malfunctioned."

"Sabotage?" said Blayde. "The only reason it would activate now is—"

"If someone is trying to send a message to the Alliance." I gasped. "The Agency would never allow themselves to be this sloppy in the smartphone era. It'll hit the internet immediately, no matter how far the Agency reaches. People will panic."

"She's right. Zander, I can't believe I'm saying this, but Sally's right. Someone wants the Agency to notice them. And we've officially been exonerated for one day, so this can't be a coincidence."

My heart clenched. Here I thought our ordeal in Pyrina had accomplished something.

There was something more than wrong happening here. I could feel it deep in my gut and deeper still. It wasn't just that familiar feeling of anxiety. No, there was something more, something in the air reflected in the glares at the supermarket. Something toxic and growing stronger. Because under everything, there was something bigger, a gut-clenching feeling of dread.

Trust me, I know my anxiety. This was different. It had been waiting for us when we'd returned from the presidential ball, suffusing the air of this time. Maybe it had been on Pyrina, too, but my usual baseline panic had covered it up.

Dread. Deep, dark *dread.*

There was no room to park in my parents' driveway. It was taken up entirely by a gigantic black SUV, with more cars up and down the street on both sides—way more than there should be. The zombie-stiff hairs on my arms grew stiffer. Agency operatives?

I pulled to the curb three houses down and practically fell out of the car. Despite my beatless heart, I felt a phantom pounding in my chest. I ached to rush inside the house, but Zander took point and I was forced to follow his slow, methodical lead. I looked back and Blayde was gone—flanking the house maybe. My trembling legs carried me to the already open door, which creaked as he pushed it in, my guts twisting.

The instant Zander's foot crossed the threshold, lights illuminated the room, and before I could focus my eyes, a single cry rose to the heavens.

"Surprise!"

People burst out of everywhere, my parents front and center, alive and smiling. And standing between them, Marcy and Dany. My world was thrown upside down as I was wrapped in a massive hug, complete with tears in my hair.

"Oh god, Sally, you're alive!" Marcy shrieked in my ear. "Don't you ever run off like that again, understood?" She grabbed me so tight I probably wouldn't have survived if I wasn't immortal. I sobbed into her familiar shoulder, her familiar sweater, her familiar scent.

The other guests were Dad's truther buddies and Mom's MMA bubble. It turns out when you've been missing for three years, absolutely anyone will have an excuse to miss you, though I'm pretty sure the older crowd was more moral support for my parents rather than here to celebrate.

"What is this?" asked Zander. "Oh Veesh, is this an intervention? Look, if you need me to stop with reality television—"

Marcy let go of me, only to step back and turn to him, shooting daggers with her eyes that were sharp enough to turn him into Swiss cheese.

"I would slap you, but there's a crowd and my wife is against violence of any kind," she spat.

Blayde took a step closer to her brother, positioning herself between him and Marcy. I'm not sure how she even got there—not enough screaming for her to have jumped.

"There are people here," she hissed. "What are people doing here?"

"Stand down," I said. "It's a party. For *us*."

"Party? Well, this explains the excessive amount of ice cream we currently have melting in the car."

"I thought they were all for me?" said Zander. Marcy's glare was unwavering, and he swallowed loudly. "I'll … be right back." He darted out the door.

So, the timing between the SHC and the phone call *had* been a coincidence, rare as they were. The call had only been a ruse, a way to get us to hurry back. Perhaps the near heart attack was retribution for the way I'd left. But explaining to the guests that we had to cancel to discuss why our cashier had gone supernova on us… big party foul. We'd just need to smile and pretend everything was hunky-dory for a few hours and make sure no one turned on the TV. I had to talk to Zander about what we'd just seen. There had to be a reason for it, some reason our cashier… I held down vomit as the scene replayed behind my eyes.

"So, what do you think?" asked Marcy, gesturing at the room. "We didn't have much time to decorate, but…"

Dany tugged on a string, letting the banner down.

Blayde snorted. "Lovely. *'Congratulations on NOT being murderers.'* Simple. To the point. Well, what can I say? I'm flattered." She grinned that smile of hers, the kind that could blind airline pilots if the sun hits her teeth just right. "What I don't understand is why someone covered up the word *'boy'* so that all your paper plates now read *'It's an Innocent!'* Is innocent a gender now? I'll add that to the list, but I'm not sure where on the spectrum I should place it. Probably outside the visible wavelengths."

"Thank you," I said, trying to expel that phantom feeling of danger that filled the room. "You are…simply the kindest."

I couldn't hold back the tears any longer. It was almost comical to hear the crowd swoon at my overflowing feelings. Would they be *ooh*ing and *ahh*ing if they knew most of the tears were from the most gruesome death I had ever seen?

But…I was home.

Despite the party now officially underway, the tension in the air was still palpable. The older crowd kept my parents occupied, occasionally shooting me a glare or two, which I probably deserved. The five of us young'uns—let's forget for a second the thousands of years Zander and Blayde had under their belts—banded together for conversation and to raid the dinner table. Galli waited by our feet for us to accidentally share.

"I see chicken." Zander smacked his lips. "You know, of everywhere I've been in the known universe, chicken has always been the comforting, always present, *ultimate* constant. Anywhere. Okay, sure, not all like Earth chickens. I mean, they've evolved differently to adapt to their environment, but they *always* taste the same, gills or no gills."

"No gills here." I sipped my beer.

"Wonderful. I was being polite. Chickens with gills are the *worst*."

I glanced past Blayde to where Marcy and Dany were shoveling macaroni salad onto their festive paper plates. They were discussing something in hushed whispers that even I couldn't follow, Dany having to fold practically in half so Marcy could reach her ear. It instantly sent my gut into a Boy Scout knot lesson all over again.

"What did I do to her?" asked Zander, indicating to Marcy with a jut of his chin.

"I'm pretty sure our disappearing act was a shitty friend move." I didn't want to linger on the drama of time travel. "She's probably taking it out on you because you're the only one she can."

"Do you even celebrate birthdays at this point?"

Her voice hit me like a spaceship in warp. Agent James-freaking-Felling stood in my parents' living room with a red solo cup in hand, her smile so radiant I'm sure it would have ignited a sun when combined with Blayde's. My relief at seeing her instantly undid all those frustrating gut knots. Unless…was she here because of the fire?

Blayde picked her up and swung her around by the waist. "You came!" she squealed, and James looked about as excited as one could be when sprung into a sudden bout of dizziness.

"Of course I came. Now put me down before I barf all over you."

Blayde plopped her down.

"It's good to see you, Agent." Zander shook James's hand. "Sorry for being incommunicado."

"You have a lot of explaining to do." James's jaw clenched. "Hal and Laurie invited me tonight. And yes, we're on a first-name basis now, seeing as how I spent the better part of the past three years trying to reassure them you were coming back."

I took a breath. My parents had invited her here. Nothing to do with SHC. Still, I dropped my eyes to the ground. James was far less passive aggressive when I'd left her.

"Oh, hey, James," said Marcy, joining our little circle of confusion just as Blayde ducked out. "How was Cancun?"

"You two know each other?" With all this sputtering and stammering, I was probably getting spittle all over everyone. I guess this was why they called them surprise parties; I was jolted into different states of shock every few words.

"She set up the group text after you three vanished," said Dany. "She even named our cat."

"You have a cat now?"

"Oh, lovely. This is the girl from the Cross case, isn't it? Good god, Felling, what is wrong with you?"

The stranger who had appeared at James's side was the dictionary definition of beautiful, with angelic waves of golden hair framing a factory-fresh face. She was a whole head taller than James and wore heels with the grace of a ballerina.

"It's a long story," she replied. Then, turning to me, "Sally, meet Perenelle Johansen, my new partner. Perry, meet Sally Webber."

We shook hands, though the corners of the woman's lips failed to rise to even the fakest of smiles.

"Perenelle, what a lovely name," I said.

"Sure." She gave me such a dismissive look that my anxiety immediately rose a few octaves before she turned back to James. "Felling, I can't believe you. Does that mean the case down here is a bunch of hogwash?"

"Well, I might have exaggerated the authenticity of the source, but I'm still looking into it. Call this night a… social detour."

"So, the astronomer who spotted strange lights over Tampa Bay—"

"Is less of an astronomer and more of a… podcaster?"

"I can't believe this." Johansen looked like she was about to be sick.

I suppose I might be, too, if I had been expecting a lead and ended up at a surprise party for an ex-con. The latter held out a hand to shake hers.

"I would say nice to meet you, but I thought we'd closed the Cross case and your change of circumstance has put me in a tight place."

"Alexander Smith. Pleasure," said Zander. She ripped her hand back from their handshake, stuffing it in her pocket. "Trust me, my life isn't as glamorous as my wanted poster makes it seem. Look, I hope you don't mind me stealing James for one minute?"

"You know what? Yes, let's all go outside and clear some things up," said Marcy, grabbing Dany by the hand. "You. Me. Outside. James, you're free to join."

"What's going on?" I asked.

"No, you stay here, dear. Turn the music up loud."

Now I was alone with Johansen. Lovely. I would much rather be outside attending the small screaming match than with this stranger. She gingerly rubbed the raw, red skin of her hand, frowning.

"Do you need some cream for that?" I tried to show the hospitality that was expected of me. *Be the bigger woman, Sally Webber.*

"No, I'm fine, thank you. Just eczema."

"Who's this?" Blayde asked, seemingly appearing out of nowhere again. Always there when I needed her to defuse a situation, thank goodness.

I was tired of making so many introductions, but at least her name was fun to say. "Blayde meet Perenelle Johansen, James's new partner."

"So that's what you're calling yourself now?" Blayde let out a razor-sharp laugh. "Wow. And don't think I didn't see your hand. Felling has the absolute *worst* luck."

"Blayde, stop this," I said.

"Look at her palm. I mean, seriously, look at it."

"Eczema. So?"

"You're such an Earthling. Have you learned nothing from Zander or me?" She held up a saltshaker. "Well, thank your mom for putting salt on the table, and thank Zander for not being an idiot when meeting the new partner of a friend who's already been conned by an Agency agent."

All that was left of Johansen was the wind from her dashing outside, Blayde at her heels, the back door slamming shut in their wake.

Skin wraps. I swore under my breath. Whatever they're made of couldn't handle concentrated sodium chloride. Which meant whoever I was just speaking with wasn't even human.

Shit. How long had she been assigned to James?

I rushed outside to the dark beach, where Blayde had Johansen pinned down in the sand under the porchlight. I made a beeline for them before realizing we weren't alone. *Oh no.* Zander's chastising team was frozen mid-shout, Marcy's tiny first grabbing his shirt so tightly I thought she was going to rip it right off him. Dany was struggling to hold her back, and James—well, James was the only one who had moved from the tableau, sprinting across the beach toward her partner.

"What the hell, Blayde?" she shouted.

"She's Agency." Blayde's face was as neutral as Switzerland as she flipped Johansen over. "Come on, I thought Zander was telling you."

"I was getting to that!" Zander turned to Marcy. "Seriously, I was getting to that part. You see? Despite what you think, I *do* care about your feelings. I just wanted you to get your catharsis first."

"Stop trying to be everyone's bestie and help me hold her down," Blayde ordered. "She's stronger than she looks."

Zander grabbed Johansen's other arm. Between the two of them, she wasn't going anywhere.

"Oh, come on!" James screamed. "This can't be happening. Not again. I had been so careful. Who even are you?"

"I'm Perenelle." She flailed in the siblings' grasp. "It's Perry! Help me!"

"Who are you, *really*?" Zander grabbed her hair and started to drag her down the beach. Marcy let out a small gasp from behind us.

Marcy was watching this.

In that instant, my reality shattered. I could never keep these two parts of my life separate anymore. Marcy had seen—she had actually *seen*—the other side of Zander. My mind spun into overdrive trying to figure out how to twist this, but it quickly overheated and threw up some interesting warning signs.

"You know where I'm taking you?" he said. "An ocean full of water—and *salt*."

Johansen squirmed harder, like an octopus seeing its name on a menu. She lifted her hands and tried to pry his fingers from her hair, but he wasn't giving even an inch.

"James," she begged. "Help me!"

She started to cry, full jet-powered sprinklers. Marcy raced past me, and I instinctively grabbed the back of her dress.

"Let go of me!" she spat. "What are you doing? He's hurting her!"

"He's not!" Was it a lie? I didn't know. Johansen was full-on sobbing and thrashing in Zander's grasp, and I almost believed Marcy.

"Think of it," Zander continued, drawing Johansen ever closer to the sea. "Salt—that pain that was on your hand for a second, but burning your every pore, in your mouth and nose. Imagine as it hits your lungs, as your every breath begins to burn…"

I drew back. This was a side of Zander I never wanted to see, no matter how necessary. I had to keep convincing myself this was just an act, that he wouldn't *really* torture—

"Let go of me, Sally!" Marcy struggled to pull free, but I was so much stronger now. Effort was a tiny sting in the depths of my mind. "Dany! Help me stop him!"

But Dany wasn't coming. Dany's feet were planted on the beach, the perfect rendering of a tree.

"Last chance," said Zander, stopping at the edge of the water. "Tell us who you're working for, and maybe I won't hold you down under the waves."

"James?" Johansen pleaded.

"Identity theft is not a joke, *Perry*," said James. "If you knew me at all, you'd know I take that personally."

Johansen sighed, leaning into Zander's grasp, and gave him a dry half-smile. "Have we come to this? You know me better than that, Zander. You wouldn't hurt me. Not silly old me."

"Wouldn't I?" he growled. "I don't know you."

"You sure? Look into my eyes and see for yourself. They say the eyes are the only real thing of yourself that can be seen through the wrap. I wonder if that's true?"

He stared into her eyes as she scowled back, moving closer, until the glare turned to confusion then comprehension, then confusion yet again, his brows swinging together and apart like a ballet about forbidden romance.

"Foollegg?"

"Looky here, the Sand's got a brain after all." She smiled. "Good to see you, too, Zander."

Foollegg. The director of the Agency, the one who had threatened my family, who had forced us into hiding. My breath caught in my throat. It was meant to be over with her the moment we got our pardon, yet she was here—as James' partner. If she was here…

The fire. We'd been set up. The Alliance must have wanted an excuse to arrest us, used the Agency to frame us for the crime.

In my shock, I let go of Marcy, and she flew at Zander in a fit of rage-induced justice or justice-induced rage. Zander let go of Foollegg, who sprang to her feet just in time for Marcy to collide headfirst into her. This, of course, sent Foollegg and Marcy crashing into the sea, only for Zander to dive in between them and the waves. The three of them tumbled into the spray, screaming a whole universe of obscenities.

"What the hell is wrong with you?" shouted Marcy, swinging a fist at Zander, who dodged out of the way while her momentum sent her sprawling.

Foollegg was busy pulling herself from the water, clutching her now-dissolving face as her skin wrap melted in the sea. She took a step onto the shore and wrung out her shirt, her human chin giving way to pearlescent skin.

"Well, that's one way to say hello." She wiped off gobs of melted silicone-like goop with a flick of her hand. Where had they stored her serpentine neck? "Well, hello there, Miss Webber. So lovely to see you again."

I thought Dany might try to intervene, but Marcy was holding her own—Zander wasn't exactly fighting back—and she was letting everything happen, just standing there. This left Blayde and James and me to alternate between watching the fistfight between my best friend and boyfriend in the waves and the goop running down Foollegg's face. James hadn't yet picked her jaw up off the floor, and Blayde, well, she was happier than I'd seen her in ages, watching the beach fight the way I might watch a puppy parade.

Okay, so I was the only one who was going to make conversation with Agent Melty Face. Lovely.

I crossed my arms over my chest. "I see someone has been demoted to Earth duty."

"All thanks to you," she glowered, staring at Blayde, James, and me in turn as if we were insolent children that she was intent on disciplining. "You disappeared on my watch. *Mine*. So I get pinned up with James 'Juxley' Felling here. It's almost embarrassing, but then I remember that it's better than having been the-woman-who-had-the-Iron-and-the-Sand-for-a-minute-and-let-them-go running the Agency."

"Juxley? Who the hell is Juxley?" asked James.

"It's from a show," said Blayde. "I don't think you'd like it."

Foollegg was starting to look like herself again. The long, spindly neck neatly unfurled from the constrained human one, large doe eyes waiting patiently under the small European ones, taking their turn to shine.

James gasped, finally out of her state of shock. "Who—who are you?"

"Right, introductions," Blayde said. "James, meet Foollegg, former head honcho of the Earth Agency. Foollegg, I take it you were assigned as her partner in hopes of catching us?"

"You say that like it's a dumb idea," said the agent. "But look at me, I caught the terrorists who assassinated President Straiddies."

If I had been drinking a glass of water, I would have done a spit-take. "We did *what*?"

From behind us, Dany's voice rose above the fray. "Father is dead?"

The fighting in the sea stopped in an instant. Marcy pinned down Zander in the waves with a kick of her heel, spinning toward Dany. Dany, who was closer than ever. Dany, who stared at Foollegg not with surprise, but with heartbreak. Dany, who Foollegg was now bowing to.

"My—" Foollegg started, but Marcy was up the beach in a flash, rushing for Dany.

"The Alliance knows!" Marcy screamed. "Run, darling, run!"

But it was too late. The only person who would have liked the next part would have been my dad, had he been watching. He does love a good tractor beam.

TWO

CAN'T THE UN HANDLE INTERSTELLAR DIPLOMACY FOR ONCE?

FUN FACT ABOUT TRACTOR BEAMS: WHEN THE technician manning it is in a rush and doesn't have it fine-tuned, it picks up everything—and I mean everything—in its field. So, if you're lifted from the beach, you're basically in a tornado of sand and saltwater until they finish reeling you in.

"Frash this!" Blayde spat as she swung around in the air, thwacking me in the shins, while some very confused crabs pinched whatever skin they could find for dear life. "Who's the asshole with the ship?"

"Stay calm," said Foollegg, drifting up along with us. "This will all be over soon."

Stay calm? There were so many things to *not* be calm about right now. A cashier burst into flames, the Alliance thought we killed their president, and perhaps the most terrifying point: *Marcy knew about the Alliance.*

Oh, and Dany calling dead-president-emperor-dude her *father?*

All these thoughts swirled in my mind as I tried to avoid the swirling outside it. Partly because I didn't want to get dizzy—and, as a result, nauseous, making the sand-sea tornado a sand-sea-sick tornado—but also because *hello*, I'm still not a fan of heights in general. The mind-swirling was thankfully a good distraction from the distance of death beneath me.

Yes, I know I'm not going to die from great falls anymore, but that anxious part of my brain wasn't gone yet. Cut me some slack.

The beam's brightness intensified until it was blinding. It then promptly shut off, dropping us unceremoniously on the floor of a cargo bay. The accidentally abducted crabs skittered in all directions. With all the white walls and borderline lens flares from every light, it was easy to know who'd taken us. The Alliance.

Marcy's voice filled the hold. "Step back, all of you!"

She clung to the sharp heel of her once fabulous shoe, wielding it like a dagger. I was still trying to pull myself up onto my feet while she was already on hers, barefoot and weaponized, putting me to shame. It couldn't be her first rodeo with them.

What the hell, Marcy? I wanted to scream. Where was Felling? And why weren't the siblings doing anything? I was waiting for their signal, but they were completely still.

"Put the heel down," said Foollegg. "No harm will come to you."

"Screw you," Marcy spat. "Put us back on the beach. You want the Iron and the Sand, not us. We've done nothing to bring attention or harm to the Alliance."

"It's ok, Dove," said Dany, placing a gentle hand on her wife's shoulder. "If Father really is dead…"

Father. The president-emperor of the Alliance was Dany's father. How had I not seen this before? The way we'd met, with her bursting into Marcy's party ranting about bodyguards, those mercenaries talking about the lost prince…

"Then they shouldn't be hunting you." Marcy kept her eyes on Foollegg. "Let me, my wife, and Sally go unharmed. We won't be trouble. I swear."

"I'm afraid I can't do that," said Foollegg. She stood to her full height now, towering over all of us with her head-on-a-stilt. When her gaze landed on Dany, her eyes glazed over, soft and gentle and adoring. "We thought you were dead, my prince—" Dany winced. Marcy clutched her hand, rubbing her arm with the other. "—princess, sorry. No. Empress."

"Not your frashing empress." Dany spat on the floor. Marcy frowned. "Eww. I know we're on an enemy spaceship, dear, but the janitorial staff shouldn't be punished for it."

"Well, this reunion is beautiful and all, but we need to bounce," said Blayde, one hand extended for me, the other already gripping Zander's. He was reaching for

Marcy, but she kept swatting him away. "I don't think you've noticed, but you've basically crashed our party, and I'd like to go back before all the chicken is gone."

"Not this again," said Foollegg. "We have more important matters to discuss."

Without hesitation, she whipped out a pistol and shot each of the siblings in the head. No jumping away when you're dead.

Marcy let out a blood-curdling scream. I did too. As many times as I'd see them die, I wasn't getting used to it happening so suddenly. Or violently. That brain splatter alone was going to fuel nightmares for a while.

"Please, tell your concubine to calm down," said Foollegg, her gaze still riveted on Dany. "We mean you no harm."

"*Concubine?*" Marcy's eyes went so wide they rivaled Foollegg's.

"We don't have time for this. Put them in the room until Director Stook is ready."

The room was just a room: six sides, no windows, and a single door, with a turtle sitting in the very center.

Marcy and I stared at it. I'm not even sure how much time passed until she sneezed—spaceship air conditioning was just as bad as Florida's—breaking us both out of our trance. It was only then I realized were alone, except for Zander and Blayde, who were unceremoniously piled in a corner like a couple of lifeless dolls, staring at us with wide, open eyes. The gaping holes in their foreheads were closing oh-so slowly.

"Where's Dany?" asked Marcy.

I wished I had an answer for her. All I knew was the reptile had stolen precious time.

"Don't look at the turtle," I said as assertively as I could muster.

"I think it's a tortoise?"

"In all honesty, I don't think it's either. It's probably not from Earth."

"It's giving me the creeps."

"Same."

We kept our backs to it to avoid any more unforeseen trances. Instead, we stared at my space buds as their skin knit itself back together. It's a pretty fascinating process when you have the time to fully appreciate it.

There was no way to avoid an awkward situation, so I leapt into it, which was becoming a signature move of mine. "Um, Dany…?"

"Oh, come on," Marcy scoffed. "Don't tell me you didn't know."

"Know what, specifically?"

She rolled her eyes. "That aliens exist, that Earth is a tourist hotspot, who I married, and so on. That stuff."

"Best two out of three?"

"Which two?"

"I'm up to date on the alien stuff. Just not Dany's stuff."

"I thought Zander told you?"

"Told her what?" Zander's eyes blinked open, and he rolled out from under his sister's corpse, who evidently wasn't a corpse anymore, since she let out a gasp as she fell off him. "Oops, sorry."

"You knew?" I asked.

"Knew what?"

"Whatever there is to know about Dany!"

"Oh, you mean Danirshna?" Blayde pushed herself to her feet. "Frash, Zander, *they have a riveting tortoise.*"

"I *told* you it's a tortoise," Marcy said to me, smugly.

"Well, you could have told me a whole lot of things!" My head was spinning. It wasn't the right moment to get mad, but I had a right to be pissed. I'm Marcy's BFF. I was at her wedding, and yet I'm the last one to know she married into interstellar royalty? At least this explained a lot about those cousins. This was way too much information for one night, and I hadn't had anywhere near enough beer for this. That, and staring into the tortoise's eyes for so long had given me a hangover.

"When did we have the time? You were off on an intergalactic adventure for the past three years!"

"Will someone deal with the frashing tortoise?" said Blayde.

"It's fine, I'll get it." Zander tossed his coat over the small reptile, which let out a mournful croak. Noting my confusion, he launched into explanation. "Riveting tortoises evolved to be so incredibly fascinating no predator can look away. The Alliance probably figured out it could keep us entranced. Can't jump away if we're staring at a riveting tortoise. Anyway, where are we, what are we doing here, and how do we get out? As much as I'd love for us all to catch up, doing so in an Alliance stronghold with a riveting tortoise is not my idea of a rewarding social gathering. And where's Dany?"

As if waiting for her Hollywood moment, Dany burst into the room and rushed straight for her wife. Foollegg followed, flanked by the man whose name my brain had only just processed: Director Stook. The last time I had seen him, he'd been vying for the glory of apprehending the siblings in the Great Terminal Manhunt. The door slid shut behind them, sinking back into the wall with a pneumatic hiss.

"Did they hurt you?" asked Dany, and Marcy shook her head. They clutched each other's hands like lifelines.

"My liege." Stook bowed dramatically to Dany. He beamed as brightly as the walls. "Where do we start? Finding the siblings mere days after their heinous regicide, about to strike at the next in line?"

"Please," said Blayde. "You think we'd still be here if we didn't want to be? You *killed* us."

Stook's smile dropped to a frown. Despite his nose being nothing more than slits, it looked like he had turned it up at us. "You look fine to me."

"Well, we got better."

Foollegg stifled a laugh. It was strange to see her so silent, standing on the sidelines rather than taking control. Knowing her, she was just biding her time, waiting for Stook to slip up.

"If you truly thought we were a threat to your heir," I said, my hands in fists at my side, "then you wouldn't have us all in the same room together."

"She demanded it, actually."

We all turned to Dany, who took a deep, measured breath. But she said nothing.

"What do you want from us, Stook?" I asked. "We were pardoned. I have the document to prove it, signed by the president's own hand. Why would we have killed him?"

I didn't want to think of the repercussions his death would have on the Alliance—or on us. We'd gone through the gauntlet to get his pardon. All for nothing.

"I believe you," said Dany, nodding at me. "If you vouch for your friends, I believe them too."

"I trust them with my life," I said, before it hit me that I was going to have to reword that. When was the right time to tell your bestie you're immortal?

Stook's frown deepened. "We have witness testimony from the ball—"

"What witnesses?" asked Dany. "I know your methods for gathering testimonials, and I trust these so-called criminals more than your inquisitors."

The ball. What had happened to Kork and Sekai after we'd left? They were supposed to be safe. The journalist had enough blackmail material to keep the president in line, after all. Picturing them undergoing the Alliance's methods of questioning made me shudder.

"My liege," said Stook. "Please let us do our job."

"Then *I* pardon them!" Dany shouted. "As president, I hereby grant them pardons for all their crimes, proven and unproven. How's that? Is that what you wanted me to say?"

"Darling, they're not worth it," Marcy said, her voice barely a whisper as she clung to Dany's arm. "We have to go."

"We need them," said Dany. "I know this isn't what we wanted. Not this soon. But we have to gather all the help we can get."

I felt like an extra in my own life, watching as history was being made. I could have left, should have left, but my body wouldn't let me.

Dany let go of Marcy's hand and stepped forward to meet Stook head on. The director flinched, as did Foollegg, still silently flanking him. How could I not have seen it all this time? How could I have missed Dany's regal disposition, the way we all bent and swayed to her? Unlike Zander and Blayde who conveyed a sense of strength, Dany radiated control. She was a leader, a peacemaker.

My best friend's wife was a—hopefully benevolent— alien overlord.

Cute.

"Make me your matriarch," said Dany, staring Stook straight in the eye. "And heed my decree. By presidential order, the former criminals known as the Iron and the Sand are now our allies."

Zander's eyes went round as the ship and wider still while Blayde full-on choked on her own saliva. Marcy's face lost all color, but she said nothing.

And me? I'm not sure what I did. I was still frozen, a distant observer, in dire need of popcorn.

"Hello? Did we walk into a parallel universe here?" Foollegg burst into hysterics, sounding like my sink disposal gaining sentience. She folded over, clutching her gut, her spindly neck barely keeping her head up. "The siblings? Working for the Alliance? In what world…?"

"*With* the Alliance," said Dany. "It's up to you. The Alliance needs a figurehead; they need hope. They need *me*. But I come with a price tag. I need *them*."

"Whatever for?" asked Stook. "What is so terrible we need to turn to terrorists?"

"Is this about who burnt your spy to a crisp at the supermarket?" asked Zander.

Ah. With all this back and forth about secret identities, I was half hoping they had forgotten about that. I sure hadn't, not with the smell of burning flesh still seared into my nostrils. I didn't want to be framed for another crime. Why did Zander even bring it up?

"How did you know about that?" Stook whipped his head around. "Did that sound like a confession to anyone else?"

"Confession, my *lobe*," he said. "We saw one of your operatives publicly go up in flames. I assume that wasn't intentional?"

"It's happening everywhere." Foollegg lowered her head. "Almost four hundred years without a glitch, and this week alone we've had *five* combustions. If it wasn't you, then who?"

"This is bigger than the SHC system being sabotaged." Dany took a deep breath, loud enough to silence us all. "You must be feeling it, too, haven't you? The wrongness in the air."

Zander and Blayde exchanged pregnant looks that must have carried triplets. Their eyebrows began to dance, deep in private conversation.

"Even if we do," said Blayde, turning back to Dany, "it's nothing new, kid. Trust me. We've been in this universe quite a long time, and inherent *wrongness* is about as much of a constant as we are."

"But it's more than that, isn't it?" Marcy stepped forward. "Every prey species in the universe has evolved to sense oncoming danger. And we're all feeling it now. Something's coming. Something toxic and growing stronger."

"I've been feeling it for months now," said Dany. "Like…a claw is trying to get my soul. I'm afraid of the dark again. More than afraid; I'm terrified. I can't eat. I get more and more tired every day. I worry one morning… I just won't wake up. I thought I was going insane until we found the reports."

I shuddered at the memory of days, months I felt that crushing fatigue. I wouldn't wish it on my worst enemy, and yet, it seemed, everyone would soon know how it felt too. Did everyone feel the deep-set dread that only medication could shake?

"Something in the air and the space in between," I agreed. This could explain all the scowls, the tension everywhere we went. "So, the bad vibes I've been feeling are actually severe psychological distress? I know the anxiety epidemic is a problem, but…"

Blayde shot me a glare, and I closed my mouth. Maybe I shouldn't be feeding into this. The Alliance was their enemy, after all. But what Marcy and Dany were describing, I used to feel most of the time, and it sounded like it was catching. They were right; it was bigger than all of us.

"You wouldn't be here if you were feeling this alone," said Blayde. "Who else?"

"It's not just this world: It's *everyone*. Everyone is on edge, until they snap. It's not only in the air; it's crossed the voids between planets, spreading like a disease. Like Sally said, it's an epidemic but on a galactic scale. Maybe more."

"We've been seeing it all over Alliance worlds and trade partners," said Foollegg, earning a brow-beaten frown from Stook. "It started months ago back on Pyrina and has been escalating ever since. We've been treating who we can with everything we have, but it's more than a plague. The dread they feel is *real*. The rebels who attacked the ball? Those arrested admitted to having acted on some strange, self-preservation instinct, as if it would be the last thing they would ever do, and they would go out with a bang. Many physically succumb to it. There's reports of people... giving in. Worlds have gone silent."

"Silent?" I gawked at the others, who all looked at their feet. "What do you mean?"

Stook grabbed her arm, and she shook him off.

"Then there was... a research outpost," Foollegg continued, steadfast. "Out on the border of

Consortium space. We missed the first signs: the messages that staff was losing motivation, that they wanted to come home, a general dissatisfaction that their mission was futile. But then we received requests for more security, that the tensions between sectors were growing at an alarming rate, or contradictory statements about missing resources. Then they called for the army. When we attempted to respond… nothing. They'd engaged their own self-destruct. Twenty thousand souls—gone. No survivors."

A shiver ran up my spine. The air in the room was heavy and cold, as if death stood beside us. What horror could have been so terrible it drove twenty thousand people to destroy themselves?

"We first assumed this was a weapon from the Consortium," said Stook, his frown deepening until his lips touched his chin. "But when we investigated the border, all we found was death. Whatever this is, it targets us all with impunity."

"And what is *it*?" asked Zander. "Are we engaging some old prey sense? Symptoms of a disease?"

"Maybe, but I have a theory it doesn't just affect organic life," said Foollegg. "That the dormant SHC wasn't awakened by sabotage… but by the influence of this Dread on our systems."

Stook was positively boiling now, his face redder than I'd ever seen it, which in his case was a gentle rose blush. I wasn't a fan of Foollegg, but compared to Stook, she seemed to care much more about solving this problem rather than sweeping it under the rug until it was too late.

"Please. We'll do anything." Dany dropped to her knees. "I'm not bringing you together to talk. I'm asking you for your help. No, I'm pleading. Help us. We'll give you anything, anything you want. You want a planet? We'll give you a planet. Just…help us."

"Uh, we can't just—" Stook started.

"Look," said Zander. "We have no intention of doing anything for the Alliance. Why would we? You've tried to have us captured more times than I can count."

"Zander, please," said Dany. "I'm giving up my independence to become a dictator to the fucked-up world I fled"—Stook scoffed at this—"just so that I can beg for your help. This is bigger than all of us."

Blayde threw up her hands. "You're out of your *frashing* minds. If something is going to take over the Alliance, then let them do it. What's that saying? The enemy of my enemy is my new bestie?"

"I should be arresting you this instant, but I'm not," said Stook. "Shouldn't that be enough to prove our determination to solve this?"

"You're not arresting us because your *liege* told you not to," Blayde scoffed. "All you have is a feeling. *Dread*, that's it."

"I think we can work something out," I said.

I could sense all their eyes on me, but I didn't care. The feeling Dany was describing was one I didn't wish on my worst enemy, and now entire *worlds* were feeling it. Succumbing to it. Shattering. I had to do something.

But I'd learned my lesson; I don't work for free.

"Sally," Blayde seethed, "you don't speak on our behalf."

"No. I'm speaking for *me* alone, and I'm speaking for my planet." I turned to Stook. "We can't have people bursting into flames all over the globe. I want the Agency to do its job: protect the pre-contact state of the Earth and defend the planet with everything you've got, as you should be doing already. In return, I'll defend you. Fight for my planet, and I'm yours."

"Oh great," said Blayde. "We give you immortality, and you sell yourself to the first buyer on the market?"

"At the very least, negotiate with other interests," said Zander.

Blayde slammed a fist into his kidneys, earning her a grunt.

"You made her *immortal?*" Marcy gasped.

My gut dropped like a stone in the ocean. That was my secret to tell, and here it was, blurted out in the heat of the moment when I was far from ready to have this discussion. So many secrets thrown out tonight like they were nothing. My stomach was a wretched sea of bile.

You really are poison.

"It's a very small price to pay for my help, really," I continued, knowing it would cost me later. "Enforcing a border check on every visiting ship in exchange for finding out who's lighting your people on fire—oh, and fighting anxiety incarnate."

Dany nodded at Stook. "Make it happen."

"Take your time," said Zander. "Just know that we'll only start helping once all this is down in writing. Contracts are our bread and butter, these days. We never did get paid for the whole Cross affair."

"It's settled then," said Dany. "In exchange for your help finding the source of the Dread, we'll enforce the protection of Earth." She turned back to Stook. "And I'll return to Pyrina and take on the leadership of our *glorious* empire."

Despite Stook's snarl, Foollegg was beaming. I could only imagine how grateful she was to not be acting director of the Agency right now.

"You know," I said, "sometimes I wish I could just once—*just once*—have a casual night with my friends without one of them suddenly telling me they're an alien and that the universe needs saving. Next time, we're doing a movie night, okay? And no weird stuff."

"You might have to wait a little for that," said Dany. "But, yeah, movie night sounds fun."

"You had better solve this." Marcy's eyes finally landed on me, and I felt a shiver run through me, colder than the void of space. "Dany gave up everything for you. Everything. You don't know how much you cost us, you cost me. *I* gave up my family, my future here so that we could get your help. Don't let us down, Sally Webber."

Tears welled up. Shit. I hadn't thought of her at all. Look in the dictionary, and you'd find me under the definition of "bad friend," along with Brutus and Scar. I forced the tears back down.

"Marcy, I—"

"Save it," she said, "We both kept things from each other that we shouldn't have, and now we're facing the consequences. I'm a space princess."

Stook unceremoniously dropped us off back on the beach, keeping Marcy and Dany for their greedy selves and leaving me caught between a glaring pair of eyes and some extra crabs who would spend the next years of their lives spreading abduction stories on the crab equivalent of the dark web.

THREE

TENSION IS A FORCE YOU WON'T FIND AN EQUATION FOR

"DOES THIS MAKE SALLY OUR AGENT?" BLAYDE wiped sand from her leggings. "I mean, if she can dictate what causes we're going to ally ourselves with without any kind of consultation whatsoever, that's the only reasonable explanation."

I felt like I was still bobbing around in the tractor beam. Shit. I really didn't want to do this right now. After everything that had just gone down, I needed to sleep, to process, not have another argument.

Oh god. The party.

"I did what I had to do to get us all out of there," I said. "And, look, we're all out of there. None of us have been arrested. Neither of you are in Alliance custody."

"And you thought your five minutes of interstellar experience were better than our lifetimes of handling the Alliance?" she snapped, "How deluded are you? You don't speak for us. You're not entitled to our services just because you're boning my brother."

My skin went cold all at once and I stumbled back, hands flying to my face to cover my slack-jawed mouth. Even Zander recoiled at her words.

"I was trying to help—"

"Stop trying!" she said. "Just…stop. We've already made too many adjustments for you. We could have left the instant the tractor beam hit, but we didn't. Why? Because you're part of the team. But that doesn't mean you have a monopoly on our services. We draw the line at being the Alliance's lapdogs, something you should know by now—and we're not changing that for a single backwater planet."

I found myself reaching for Zander, but he was standing too far away. And he wasn't reaching back, his hands instead plunged deep into his pockets.

"I was trying to help," I squeaked. "I told them I would help—*me*, not you. This agreement is between the Alliance and *me*. If you want to help me, fine, but you don't have to. I can handle this."

Zander's lips quivered, brows tight, but still, he said nothing, avoiding my gaze. But Blayde? She didn't hold back an ounce of laughter.

"You? Solving an interstellar—perhaps intergalactic—crisis on your own? Come on. You knew Zander wouldn't let you go without him. And I don't go anywhere without Zander. You're manipulative, Sally. You either assumed we'd be there or knew we'd be stuck helping you *again*. Because *of course* we are. Especially for a crisis of this scale. But you made the negotiations, and you took away our voice. Never do that again. Zander, back me up here."

"Oh, now you want to hear what I have to say?" Zander's face was red. "All this about taking away your voice, and you haven't given me a breath in which to speak."

"Oh, please. I've known you for lifetimes. I know what you're going to say before even you do."

He threw his hands in the air. "I'm tired of fighting. I'm tired of crisis after crisis, all the secrets and lies. I'm tired of you assuming you know what's going on in my head, Blayde. And, Sally, I'm tired of the expectations. Blayde is right. Whether consciously or subconsciously, you're forcing our hands here. I know everything with Marcy and Dany took you by surprise—"

"You knew," I spat. "You knew for *years* who Dany was, and you never told me!"

"Stars, Sally, I wasn't going to expose her identity to you. How would you have liked Felling to have told your parents everything while you were gone? I know Earth is important to you, but you're being incredibly self-centered right now."

"Me? Self-centered?" I crossed my arms over my chest. "I haven't had time or freedom for years! I've been putting out off-worlder fires since the first day we met, Zander, and haven't had a moment's peace since. Grisham, the Leechins, Tallagans, Kranyonites—it never ends. It's cost me my job, my friends, and maybe even my family. You have no right to call me selfish."

"Two years is nothing," said Blayde, baring her teeth. "We've been at this game for centuries."

"We're not turning this into a contest over who has sacrificed the most," said Zander. Our eyes met before he ripped his gaze away. We knew—we *knew*—this argument would go nowhere. I'd given up my mortality for him. In return, he'd given up his only hope of finding his past for me. "We're all tired, and not just from tonight. We need to calm down, reassess, and figure out how we're going to tackle the Dread. Because guess what? I'm pretty sure we wouldn't be fighting like this if our anxiety wasn't peaking."

I swallowed hard. He was right. I could feel the pressure on my chest, the oncoming onslaught of panic. There was blood in my mouth; I had been chewing my cheek without conscious thought. The feeling was so familiar I hadn't realized it could be alien.

"Frash, you're right," said Blayde. She took a deep breath—then three more. "I should have more control than this. How long for you?"

"Since Pyrina." Zander wiped sweat from his brow. "Sally?"

"Yeah, since before the ball." I had to pinch my lips to keep them from trembling. "I mean, I've been struggling to manage all the new emotions since I…changed, but I had just assumed the anxiety came from faking an assassination attempt on the president of the Alliance. When we got home—"

"Why didn't you say anything?" asked Zander.

"Why didn't *you*?" I pushed my flip flops into the sand, feeling it crunch under my toes. Just because their brain chemistry was off, it didn't make what they said any less true or any less painful to hear.

It didn't excuse the crap I'd said either.

"I'm sorry," said Zander, his voice a warm and welcoming blanket. "Can we all just say sorry?"

We did. Not that it made anything better, but it defused the situation for a while. When my anxiety had been at its worst, it had rendered me silent, but now that the whole universe was feeling the same, it was as thick and syrupy as truth serum.

"We should get back to the house," said Zander. "Sleep this off. Start fresh in the morning. Do you think there's any chicken left? All this misplaced anger has made me hungry, and if we're going after this Dread thing, we're going to need some sustenance."

"You know one thing I like about Earth?" said Blayde, skipping down the beach ahead. "The ice cream. Sure, loads of planets make ice cream, but you're the ones that do it right. It's wonderful."

And, in the silence of her departure, I couldn't help but agree. If I was going to help save the universe from an unknown psychological torment, then I needed a good hearty scoop of Earth-made ice cream. Preferably with brownie chunks.

"Hey," said Zander, finally taking my hand. The warmth of his presence was instantly reassuring, an anchor in the tumult. I sank into it, letting it overflow. "I shouldn't have spoken to you like that. I'm sorry."

"Me neither," I said. "I'm sorry too. You're right."

"Whether I was or wasn't doesn't matter. I love you. And we'll solve this thing together."

"I love you too." I nodded, grasping his hand tighter. I was too exhausted to say anything else. His shoulders dropped, then rose again, steady and strong. I needed him, needed to ground myself in his steadiness, needed… all of him.

I'd panic about everything when I processed it later.

· · · · · · · · ● · · · · · · · ·

JAMES WAS BEYOND PISSED WHEN SHE SHOWED up the next morning, and to make sure we felt the full brunt of her annoyance, she knocked at 7 am sharp. Seeing as how we'd spent most of the evening on a spaceship, we hadn't gotten much sleep.

"You left me," she said, as I opened the door. She glared at me over the thick stack of papers in her arms, and burned holes into my soul. "Again. You never invite me to the interesting stuff."

"We weren't exactly *invited*," I replied, stifling a yawn. It left my chin trembling. "Had I known we were going to get abducted, I would have asked to bring you along."

You're poison, said the old voice in my head. *Everyone who tries to help ends up dead or destroyed.*

"What is it this time? Another invading alien ship? Or will another of my partners turn out to be an ET? Who will I be assigned to next? Alf?"

"The anxiety epidemic?"

James grunted, pushing her way into the house. My cheeks were hot, and I bit my lip to keep myself from saying anything I might regret. I hadn't even thanked her for her *three years* of covering for me. Too much had happened last night, let alone in these past few months. But angry as she was—and boy did she have a right to be—she was still *here.*

"Oh, don't worry. *Perenelle*—Full Egg, whatever— filled me in this morning. My alien partner, remember?"

The tension was so thick I doubted I would have been able to saw through it with a laser saber. At least I knew the familiar anxiety knot in my gut wasn't *entirely* mine to begin with.

"I'm really sorry," I said. "They dropped us off, and everyone was already gone—"

"You could have called! I had to learn everything from *her.* Now she's running damage control on the Costco incident, trying to cover up the whole thing. The only reason I'm here is because I already know how to fill *these* out."

She shook the papers in my face, all the while glaring at me with her cold, tight eyes. I wanted to crawl back into bed and skip this whole day. What lengths was

Foollegg going to, to wipe the SHC incident from existence? That poor clerk… all those people watching…

You should have helped her. What good are you to anyone if you can't help a single person?

"James, I'm sorry." I couldn't meet her gaze, so I stared at the linoleum instead. "I really, truly am. And I'll do everything I can to make it up to you. I was blindsided, too, last night. We all were."

Her shoulder dipped just a little. She clutched the papers to her chest.

"I know it's not your fault, but I can't help but feel like I'm the one who's always left behind cleaning up after you. Three years, Sally, three *years* I've kept this secret from your parents, your friends. And all for *nothing.*"

"No." My head swam. "Not for nothing. You were there for my parents when I couldn't be. I can never repay you for that. I'm going to have a normal life with my parents for a little bit longer, all thanks to you."

"You're going to have to tell them, eventually," she said. "You know what you've done to them?"

I did know; I knew exactly what I'd done to them. Zander had done the same thing to me, leaving for two unscheduled years, but at least I'd known *what* he was and had had the promise he'd return. My parents had seen their only child completely disappear.

I could tell both of them everything, barring no detail, as I should have done the second I walked through their door a week ago. Should have tried harder to explain to my parents why I had been gone so long, what had happened to me. *Hey, Dad, have you heard how I can't die?* I was selfish, clinging to the illusion that I could have it both ways: have a normal human life *and* the adventures and responsibilities of whatever I was.

Zander and Blayde were waiting for us in the breakfast nook. Blayde smiled at James in a very un-Blayde-like way, so wide and beaming and beautiful that I couldn't help but shiver. James dropped the papers on the table and spun on her heels before marching to the kitchen and pouring herself a cup of coffee. She grabbed the milk and sugar, totally at ease in my parents' home.

She's been more of a daughter to them in the past three years than you have. They don't want you back.

I was too tired to say anything. I wasn't even sure if I could be trusted to say anything. What anxiety was mine, and what was the Dread?

Zander's eyes slid to the paperwork, but instead of turning away, he beamed. "James! You brought us forms! Is this because of the men watching the house?"

"That I did, yes." She split the papers into several stacks. "We have NDAs for the Webbers and the *official* official secrets for Sally, since you're still a citizen of Earth and bound by its laws, like most of us. Then we have a whole pile about the sharing of information and so on. There's more, but we'll start with this cocktail for now."

"Back up. What men watching the house?" I asked, glancing through the living room window, as if I were going to spot them that easily.

"Oh, you mean Secret Service?" said Felling. "They need to make sure this place is secure first."

"First? Before what?"

James let out a heavy sigh. "Before they bring the president, silly."

Three men in black suits let themselves in through the front door, marched through the living room, and threw every couch cushion in the air.

A scream. *Ah, so Mom was up.*

"Get out of my house!" she shouted from the top of the stairs. "Hal!"

"Secr—"

But the Secret Service agent didn't have time to finish. She had already leapt from the stairs and come at him like a bullet released from its chamber. Her flying kick got him square in the sternum.

Shit, her MMA class was legit.

"My daughter is *innocent*," she said, turning him on his back. His colleague didn't move, keeping both of his hands visible in the air. I wondered what his superiors had told him about my family; he wasn't exactly fighting back. "You leave her alone!"

"Mom!" I cried as I rushed into the living room. "He's Secret Service!"

She turned to me, frowning so cold I took a step back. I would never forget the look on their faces for the rest of my life, like I was a stranger, a trespasser.

What a disappointment I turned out to be.

I shook the thought out of my mind. *This isn't me; this isn't me.*

"Secret Service?" she asked, just as Dad appeared at the top of the landing, brandishing Grandma's country lamp. "Hal! That's an heirloom!"

He put it down oh-so slowly. If an heirloom were to go, I don't think he would have been unhappy if it were that one.

"Ma'am," said the man in black, surprisingly calm despite having been kicked down by a woman half his size. "We need to clear the area—"

"The area?" she said, incredulous. "You mean my living room?"

"Uh…" I glanced down at Mom, up at Dad. Was he glaring at me too? "Who wants a spa day?"

At least that surprised them long enough for Mom to release the Secret Service man, who joined his colleagues and James, who had rushed onto the scene to do damage control. Dad raced down the stairs to Mom.

"Sally," she said, crossing her arms over her chest, "what is this about?"

I took a deep breath. It was time for the truth, wasn't it? But then the Secret Service man caught my gaze and shook his head, like he knew. *Shit.* Even the US government wanted me to keep this secret. I hadn't even signed James's fancy forms yet.

"It's about the…manhunt for us," I said, spit balling. "We need to…make amends."

Mom's frown deepened. "In my living room?"

"Yeah. Which is why I want to send you all on a spa day."

"You left. *Again*." Dad put an arm around Mom's shoulders, the sure sign of an allied front. I felt like I was fifteen all over again. "Not a word. Nothing. Do you have any idea how worried we were?"

My words stuck in my throat. And here I thought we wouldn't have to talk about last night. That we'd get over it, get through it, but I couldn't say anything. Tears streamed down my cheeks.

"You can't just come back here and expect things to return to normal," said Dad. "We tried that already, tried to give you the time and space to talk to us, even tried to have a *party* to show you how happy we are that you're back—but it's obvious you don't respect us." He waved at the Secret Service men behind him. "This isn't normal."

"Dad." I opened my mouth, found once again that I couldn't find the courage to say the truth, and closed it again.

Say it. Say it now, I begged myself. But I couldn't. Whether I told the truth or kept it to myself, it was too late. Of course someone was going to get hurt. Everyone was going to get hurt.

And I couldn't blame it all on the Dread.

"We tried, Sally. We really tried." Dad sighed.

Shit, I couldn't do this. Zander put an arm around my shoulder, giving me strength. I took a deep breath and then another. I couldn't give them the truth, but I could give myself time.

"I screwed up majorly." I reached up for Zander's hand, clutching it. "But we're trying to make things right. If you give us the living room for a few hours, then we have a chance of making it better."

"Fine." Mom's lips pursed so tightly they were a thin, white line. "But when we come back, we either want the truth or nothing at all. You were resourceful enough these past three years. We trust you'll find someplace safe tonight."

I swallowed hard, handing them my credit card. Hopefully the spa would soften them in more ways than one. I got one small relief: a thumbs-up from the Secret Service agent my mom had assaulted. Was he one of ours or one of the Agency's? Either way, I was doing right by somebody.

If I wanted life to carry on as we knew it, I was going to have to play by the rules—but whose?

FOUR
SECOND CONTACT HAS MUCH MORE PAPERWORK THAN THE FIRST

PRESIDENT ROBERT TURNER ARRIVED THAT afternoon in a plain, black town car. His men shuffled him in, seating him on the couch and flocking around him protectively. A film crew was already setting up cameras and adjusting the lighting, Galli frantically weaving through their legs and almost tripping them in her quest for pets. And here I was, putting dishes away, still in my parents' hand-me-down sweats and jeans.

This is how the history books would remember us.

I glanced into the living room, drying a plate that could have rivaled the Sahara about a minute ago. "I should probably tell my dog to leave the president alone."

"He'll manage," said Zander, as he put the last of the mugs away. Blayde sat on the counter beside him, decidedly not helping. "Plus, I heard Terrans have a thing for therapy dogs."

"Why is the *American* president here, exactly?" I asked. "He only learned about the aliens after the Youpaf attack. It's not like he's well trained in interstellar diplomacy."

"He was closest," said Foollegg. She had somehow obtained a fresh skin wrap and strode in on sunshine, looking like a grown-up Elle Woods. James stood warily by her side. "Alliance procedure dictates we need three parties present during any political negotiations: the two writing the accord and a neutral third party. President Danirshna insisted we keep everything local and quiet. She said she preferred an excuse to meet Trudeau, but then her wife got angry about something she calls a *free pass...*"

I stashed that information away for the next time I got a girls' night with Marcy. If we ever got a chance to talk any of this over.

"Well, we'd better get situated," said Foollegg. "Don't you have anything better to wear?"

"This is traditional American garb," said Blayde, indicating the face of Minnie Mouse blazoned on her chest. "It would be offensive to ask us to change."

"Well, I don't want to be accused of cultural appropriation," she replied.

"Fair point."

One of the camera crew guided her to the sofa, and then beyond, until her sweatpants were perfectly hidden behind the seat. I was made to sit at my mom's usual place—all of two feet from the President of the United

States, white-faced and clutching mom's favorite flowery cushion. He glanced up as I took my place, eyes widening.

"Not you too," he said.

"Um, hello, Mr. President. Long time no see?"

The last time I'd had any interaction with the man, we were having an undercover luncheon at a sushi bar as the Youpaf ship barreled down on D.C., and I'd accidentally made myself alien bait. That was over three years ago now, and he was nearing the end of his second term, evident by the shock of white hair that had taken over his scalp. The dark circles under his eyes were more pronounced, a sign of the times.

"This morning," he said, "an *alien* pops up into my office and hands me official papers dated as far back as the forties, interrupting me from the Cincinnati protests. Anything to do with you?"

"It's a long story."

He probably expected me to tell a long story, but since I didn't know anything beyond drunk-driving aliens, I was at a total loss.

"I suppose I should apologize," he said.

"What for?"

"Remember that incident with the ship that was trying to roast us?"

Oh, no, I *totally* forgot the time the USA picked me as a human sacrifice. "Yes?"

"I never got time to thank you. To tell the truth, I thought you were dead until you were wanted for murder. You did your country a great service that day. With the planet saving, not the murder."

I brushed a strand of hair behind my ear. A thank you was the last thing I'd expected. "Just doing my civic duty, sir."

"You owe her much more than just thanks," said Blayde, making the president shuffle deeper into his cushion. "She's putting a lot on the line for your puny country."

"Who are you?" He twisted his neck farther back than it probably should have gone. "What are you doing here again?"

"Oh, excuse my manners." She flashed him a pearly-white smile. "I'm Blayde. Pleasure."

"Blayde? Is that Australian?"

"If you'd like. As for what I'm doing here, apparently the entire universe is experiencing simultaneous Dread, and we have to figure out why. Why us? Because Sally's going around making deals with people she shouldn't be messing with. What kind of deals? Well, if she solves the riddle, then Earth will get a full defense force protecting it from alien invaders. That's something you can get behind, right?"

President Turner furrowed his brows. "I thought that was the whole point of the Agency's existence?"

"And what a great job they've been doing of it," I said, letting out a heavy breath.

"We're here to make sure the Agency keeps up their side of the agreement," added Blayde. "They want good diplomatic connections with you in case we go rogue."

He shuddered. And too bad for him because his economic policy wasn't all that great to begin with, so I wasn't going to comfort him.

"Don't stare at the neck," she instructed. "Look them in the eye. They're incredibly self-conscious."

"Who?"

As if to answer his question, the room fell silent, a strong electrical hum filling the small space. An instant later, Stook fully materialized on the coffee table. His head immediately collided against the ceiling lamp, and he swore as he rubbed his bowling-ball scalp, stepping off the table toward the president, who hadn't noticed anything beyond the fact that an alien was standing before him.

Then *she* arrived.

As human as she was, Dany was more otherworldly than even Stook. She alighted on the coffee table dressed in a military uniform so white and crisp I would have thought she was Origami . She had shorn off her long blonde hair, leaving it tapered short at the back of her neck, dipping forward with a razor-sharp edge. What had once been her signature side sweep was now a short, diagonal bang, the longest hair casually sweeping her perfectly shaped eyebrow. Medals dripped down her chest like she had been dipped in gold.

Marcy didn't show. I pressed my lips tight. I don't know why I expected her to be here, but seeing Dany without her made my breath hitch.

"With everyone here, I guess we can start," said Stook, dropping himself into Dad's La-Z-Boy.

"Indeed," said Dany—should I be calling her Danirshna? Dany doesn't seem to convey half of what she was—as she turned.

Not toward Zander or Blayde.

Not toward the president of my home country.

Toward me, to shake my hand.

It was then that I realized—too late, perhaps—that this was *my* negotiation.

Oh shit. After all this talk of being their point of contact, of keeping Zander and Blayde out of this, I still believed they'd be dealing with them instead of me. Maybe Zander was right—that I was putting all these expectations on them—but they were the leaders, the fighters, and I was just the glorified intern trying to learn the ropes.

I took a deep breath. This time, I had to be enough. For my people, for my planet.

"We have drafted the agreement between our two parties." Dany handed me a tablet. I scanned the document, trying to decipher the jargon stuffed in each line. This wasn't software terms of agreement I could just check off without reading.

"You say here you retain the services of the Iron and the Sand." There was a wobble to my speech, and I reached for a glass of water on the table. Great first start.

"Yes."

"You don't. This agreement is just with me. They're just… consultants. If they want to help me, they can, but they're not part of the package."

Dany's brow furrowed. I had to see her not as my friend but as the leader of billions, someone who held the future of my planet in her hands. She wasn't impartial. But if she was working with me, she would be working with *me*.

"Then the blanket pardon would only apply to you," she said coolly.

"I thought you said you trusted us. They are guilty of nothing and need no records expunged."

Dany kept her face stern. "We don't know how *you* operate. We can't offer as much for such a small asset."

I tried not to take that personally. "Do you want help or not?"

We were the only ones to speak for the next hour, arguing the finer points of the treaty. The extent of my help and of the Agency's. If they wanted their Disney World vacations, they would have to play by the rules and fully defend Earth against invasion rather than sit back on their asses. I fought for clauses for feeding, reminding everyone of what happened the last time beings used Terrans for food unchecked. Twice, in the same month, in the same country, I'd had to step in. Who knew who else was running rampant.

In exchange, they wanted more of me. Ways to reach me and, by extent, the siblings. Control over them I would not let them take.

I would be their buffer.

We wrote the treaty and signed it in blood. And in spit. And in hair. There were a lot of biometrics involved, and they weren't the fun kind.

Almost the instant the new deal was settled, the president was whisked away by his Secret Service agents without so much as a goodbye. Then went the Alliance film crew. Secret Service tried to keep their cool as they shook hands with Agency men in skin wraps, some looking less surprised than others. Stook gave us each a stern glance before fizzling out, leaving the room quiet.

"So, what are you going to do next?" Dany asked, taking a drink of her water. The subtle shift in tone was enough to indicate our old friend was back, despite the lingering security guards who flanked her.

"We've got a contact who might be able to help us find out what the Dread really is," I said. If I was in charge of this investigation, then we'd be turning to the only contact I knew, Meedian Gray. Our future selves were buddy-buddies with his past self, and he'd helped us with the Cross case when our timelines finally aligned.

"Though, no offense, we're not open to discussing them with the Alliance." Zander shot me a glance, and I shot him one back. Did he really think I would reveal our friend to the very people he was hiding from? He couldn't possibly think I was that stupid. I suppose he wasn't going to let me run this without training wheels. They say never mix work with pleasure, and I get it now.

It was hard to feel butterflies from my sexy boyfriend when he was acting all high and mighty and planet save-y at your expense.

Dany shook her head. "I'm sorry for... *this*."

And, just as suddenly as she arrived, she was gone. Whatever teleportation technology the Agency used to reel her in left the air sizzling where she had stood.

I stared down at my hands. I'd just signed myself away to them, sealing my future and the future of my entire planet. I could have really used Marcy by my side, but they had kept her from me. I turned to Zander for reassurance, but Foollegg was already hounding him.

"When do we leave?" she asked, her lip quivering with anticipation.

Oh no. She couldn't be coming with us, could she? After everything she'd put us through? I bit my tongue to contain my outburst.

"You can't come with us," said Zander, saving me from being the bearer of bad news. "Our contacts won't appreciate being outed to the Alliance."

"But you work for us now," she said, her mouth a wobbly O. "We're meant to be investigating this together. For the good of all of us."

"*With* you," said Blayde. Her tone cool and even. "We can keep you apprised of our progress, but we can't bring you with us."

Foollegg blinked. "Tell you what, take Felling. She's not part of the Agency, but she's still my partner. Isn't that right, James? You'll keep your dear partner up to date with their actions, won't you?"

"I'm not a pet for you to discuss custody of," James spat. "If I go with them, it's because I want to."

"And do you?"

"Oh, hell yes."

"Then it's agreed. Felling will go with you."

"Hey, wait, don't we get a say in this?" said Zander. "It's not like we need an extra pair of hands. She's going to—"

"I vote we take her," said Blayde. All eyes turned to her, as if to check this was the real Blayde. "No, I mean it, Zander. It'll be useful to have a connection to the Agency without actually having to take an *agent* with us. Plus, we've worked with Felling before."

My gut could have won gold at the Olympic diving event. James was going to come with us. *James.* It made sense for her to join us, but the fact that Blayde was the one to suggest it made me queasy. She barely wanted me around, and now she was inviting others?

James is just better than you.

I shook my head. Where had that thought come from?

"Keep your bills, and I'll reimburse you for travel costs," said Foollegg. "I'd best be off then. I'll see you all soon, all right? James, you know where to reach me."

"Don't worry about us."

"Never have."

With that, Foollegg poofed out of existence, leaving the four of us to save the universe.

"So, where exactly *are* we going?"

Despite both of James's feet being firmly planted on the floor, there was a bounce to her words. I took a deep breath. For all this talk of this being my investigation, Blayde was going around building our team. It's not that I didn't want James with us, but I knew how dangerous this could get and I didn't want a repeat of Nim. Just the thought of him—I shuddered. Even knowing he survived, I couldn't forget the dark cloud that had hung over us after his loss.

We couldn't lose James too.

Blayde turned on the stereo. The playlist from last night's party filled the air with the chirpy shrieks of teenage glee, all grated on by a deep rumble, enough to cover our voices in case the Agency had taken the opportunity to bug the house.

"First of all, Felling, we're only bringing you along because we know you won't blab," she said. "You tell anyone, and they'll be the last person you'll ever talk to. Fair?"

"Shall I list how many secrets I'm keeping for you already?"

"Great!" Blayde now turned to me. "So, where are we going?"

"Meedian's." At least he was on Earth and getting there was low risk. I turned to James. "He's an off-worlder with off-world connections—if you pay, of course. He might be clued in to the underworld chatter about the Dread or whoever is tampering with the SHC."

"Can he be trusted? How long have you known him?" she asked.

"We met him while we were helping you out with that Cross case," I said.

James raised a brow. "So, like, a week ago—for you."

"Well, our *future* selves trust him," added Zander. "Told him everything there is to know about us. And, at this point, with the great library completely destroyed, he's the only person we know who'd be able to help us track down this so-called Dread."

"Explain to me how we are getting to Malaysia?" Blayde crossed her arms, staring intensely at me. Her eagerness for answers seemed to be currently at a lower priority than her need to glare. "We can't exactly borrow an Agency shuttle without tipping them off to our location, legally or illegally."

"And security's been upped at Area 51 after your little stunt, so don't even try pulling that shit again." James glared at us each in turn. We deserved that for screwing her over and costing her her credibility within the not-FBI. I should have bought her a gift basket to apologize.

"Need some dental work on those molars, James? I can hear them grinding from here." Blayde's grin stretched ear to ear. "I'm really good at it, you know. I was in deep cover for almost twenty years as a small-town dentist on Panga. Sure, most of my patients had been a little on the feline side—"

What was she going on about? Blayde was never this chatty; it was almost Zander-level. I shook my head, trying to focus. Even as we talked, I could feel the tug of Meedian's compound like a butterfly's kiss on my cheek. I could jump there in a heartbeat, the same way I'd reeled us all home after the ball. It was so easy for me, but not for the siblings, who had been jumping for centuries, millennia even. How could I do what they couldn't? How could I find my way around the backstage of the universe while they stumbled around in the dark fumbling for a light? Maybe Cross really had messed with my brain when he had crawled around inside my head. The thought churned my stomach.

Zander wrapped a protective arm around me, maybe sensing my nerves. I could tell him, couldn't I? I could tell him right here and now that I was different, a freak among freaks. But I couldn't tell him for the same reason I couldn't tell my parents the truth: I was clinging to any shred of normalcy I could still get.

"What about commercial flight?" said James. Blayde made a retching motion into my mom's fichus. "Foollegg did say she'd reimburse us for travel expenses."

"She'd then be able to track us right to our source," said Zander. "We can't put Meedian in danger that way."

"Then just swim while you're at it," said James. Zander glanced at Blayde, lifting an eyebrow. She shrugged. "No, no. I didn't mean it."

At least one lie was still running smoothly. I took a deep breath. If I was meant to save the universe, then I was going to have to put all my cards on the table.

"I should be able to find the place," I announced. "If we spent as much time there in the future-past as Meedian says we have."

"Maybe," said Blayde, nodding. "You *did* manage to bring us back here and not get us lost in the fabric of time. Still not sure how you pulled it off."

"I guess I love my parents as much as I love Zander?"

I knew it was the wrong thing to say the second I opened my mouth. Her upper lip twitched ever so slightly. *Shit.*

"What does love have to do with anything, exactly?" asked James.

"How much do you know about our jumping?"

Zander pulled me tighter to him. Protective. James shrugged.

"The long and short of it is that our jumps are random. It wasn't a problem when Blayde and I were on our own, but now—"

"Now that Zander has certain *attachments*, we can't allow ourselves to go just anywhere. Especially now we know the time-travel variable is thrown in. But Sally seems to have hacked the system 'cuz she *lurves* Zander oh so very much."

She made a kissy face at us, and I looked away. All this walking on eggshells, and I'd still managed to rile her up. Love might have brought me to Zander the first time I jumped, but it was just an excuse for the precision of every jump since. I couldn't keep using it, not when I was accidentally insinuating she didn't love her brother enough to follow him to the ends of the universe too.

"We can try," I said. "Like I did when we left the ball. Find a Past-Zander's location but keep us steady in time."

"No," said James, her jaw set. "We can't take that risk. If you leave Hal and Laurie again, Sally, I swear…"

"I can keep us steady. I promise." I couldn't imagine the alternative. "And if worse comes to worst, I reel us right back here."

"So, what do we tell them?" James nodded her head toward the door. My parents. "This can't be like last time."

I rubbed my fingers against my temples. *Think, Sally, think.* If I wanted to keep the two parts of my life separate from each other, I'd have to get better at balancing them. But as much as they deserved honesty, it was the wrong time for the truth.

"We'll tell them it's an incredibly complicated community service program?" I said, grabbing my phone. "I mean, a three-year manhunt has to have some repercussions."

We waited until they got home, and I sat them down on the couch, all signs of the president ever being here wiped from its surface. With James in the room, it made things a little easier; they trusted her a lot more than they did me right now. Not to mention that she was a whiz at weaving alibis. The forms she handed them were more convincing than my smile.

"It's like *Scared Straight* meets Teach for America, with a touch of DARE," she explained, adding her special touch to my dismal attempt. From their furrowed brows, I could tell they didn't believe me, not entirely. Their lips were pencil lines.

"I really wish I could stay longer," I said. "I know, I know we need to talk. But we need to fix our mistakes, and this is part of making things right too."

And I meant it. I would tell them the truth. I would be ready.

"Well, now we have something special to add to the family Christmas newsletter." Mom gave me one of her patented extra big hugs, her cheek wet against mine. "Our daughter was exonerated and moved to Malaysia in the same week."

"This is the right thing to do." Dad's hug was looser, but longer. Between the footage he'd seen of me under the overpass and everything I'd said in court, he knew more than he was letting on. "A little space will be good."

"I'm sorry," I said, clutching him to me, feeling the warmth of the heartbeat that had carried me through all my heartbreaks. "I'm still processing what we've been through. But this is a good thing."

"It's a good thing," he agreed. "Just promise me you'll come back."

"I promise," I said, and I was going to stick to it.

The last thing we did was return James's rental car before we marched out into a swamp, grabbed hands, and thrust ourselves into the void.

FIVE

TRUST CATS TO KNOW A SOLID INVESTMENT

THERE'S NO MORE LIBERATING FEELING THAN letting yourself dissolve into the universe, knowing the entirety of it—past, present, and future—is at your atom-tips. Meedian's compound called to me like a flame to a moth, except less crispy at the end. Even the added presence of James didn't stop me from bringing us into the morning light of the Malaysian sun.

I remembered my first jump, the nausea that had kept me unconscious for ages. James looked, well, like James. Just a very happy version of herself.

She turned her wide, sparkling eyes on me. "That was…"

"Fancy that," said Blayde, slapping her hard on the back. "Not only are we here on time, but the agent's keeping her guts down."

"Incredible," James said, never unlocking her gaze from mine. "Holy shit, I want to learn to do that."

"Felling, get your act together," Blayde ordered. "We have a long walk ahead of us."

"No, we don't," said Zander, already on the road. "Amazing, Sally. We're right here."

Yeah, I know it. I'm fabulous. Only problem is this skill shouldn't be mine to begin with. This really shouldn't have been so easy for me. I kept my mouth sewn shut, joining Zander up the road. The Apothecary was less than a hundred meters away. I really was this good.

Good at putting your friends in danger.

The apothecary hadn't changed in the three years since we'd last been here, the madness behind the glass just a different flavor of strange. I could buy mac-and-cheese or the severed head of what could only be described as a man-gull for about the same price. How Meedian could even afford to stay afloat at these rates, I hadn't a clue.

"Meedian?" Blayde called, ringing the small bell on the counter. "Sunan? It's us. You in?"

James scanned the room, frowning. As far as an alien's hideout went, it was as inoffensive as a kitten. Even with a pack of Pokémon cards laid out on the counter like tarot.

There was movement in the back room, the sound of keys turning, and finally Meedian made his appearance. While his store hadn't changed, he sure had. His human face was ashen and pale, aging him twenty years rather than three. His glorious robes were draped a little too loosely, much of them dragging on the floor. Odd, as they were just the shell he used to cover his true alien form, the strangely unsettling baby. The top of his bald head was covered in blueish spots.

He glared at each of us, panting. "I told you very clearly that I don't want you dragging in strays."

"Ahem," Blayde intervened. "Agent James Felling. A friend."

"*Agent?*" Meedian recoiled. His face fell, making the bags under his eyes even more pronounced.

"Earth agency, not Alliance affiliated. FBI, I think?"

"*Basically* FBI," said James.

A smile climbed up his face. Not enough to chase off the shadows. "Oh, I just can't stay angry at you for long. Darling Blayde, welcome back."

"Good to see you too, Meedian," she replied. And with that, he scooped her up in a bear hug. She squeezed him back with far less gusto.

"Zander, you're looking well," he said as he put her back down.

"As are you," Zander replied. Boom, bear hug.

"And Sally, as beautiful as ever." He wrapped his arms around me and I squeezed back, surprised at how familiar the gesture felt.

"You're too kind, Meedian."

James braced herself for her own hug, but it never came.

"Good." Meedian sighed, returning behind his counter. "So, where are we on timelines?"

"Second time meeting you," said Zander. "When we last spoke, you loaned us transportation. Did it get back here okay?"

"It did, thanks for asking. That was the last I saw you as well—in person, I should say. Saw you on the news from time to time. Murder, eh?"

"Which we were pardoned for," I squeaked.

"So, that's not why you're here today?" Meedian asked. "I just got a new shipment from Veen. Nice, clean Haqq, right from the Troq planets. They sent along some Spice as well, but you don't want any of that, do you?"

"Not today, Meedian," said Zander.

"But"—Blayde started—"I mean, it's *Haqq*, Zander."

"We're here for information," I said.

"Information?" Meedian leaned over the counter to look me in the eye. My breath caught in my throat. His iris, once a vibrant orange, was black as the pupil. "What kind of information?"

"We're hoping you can help us figure out what this *Dread* is," I said. "You must have felt it?"

"Who hasn't?" He took a deep breath, then exhaled, slowly, through a bit lip. "The whole universe has, from what I've heard. Doesn't end well. Hasn't hit Earth all that hard yet. I just have this persistent migraine. Oh, and the near-crippling sense my investors are going to murder me in my sleep."

I nodded. "We're trying to find the source of it. To stop it before it gets worse. We thought you would have some info."

"If I had, wouldn't I'd have found a way to stop it? I'm not a memory bank here!"

"But you have books."

"And what would make you think my books will help?" he snapped. "Oh! I know what you're thinking, but no. Future you has not given me books on this."

"Because this Dread is different," said Zander. "We're hoping your books are old enough to have a similar account of what it was and maybe help us deal with it now."

That, and it was my only original idea, so I was hoping it would pan out to something.

"It can't hurt to take a look, right?" I said. "We're trying to save the universe. I personally would like to get to it sooner rather than later."

"Fine, fine," said Meedian. "My library is your library and all that. You can stay as long as you need."

Meedian ushered us through the storeroom and out through the back. My jaw dropped as I stepped outside onto a covered veranda extending left and right, with steps leading into a fanciful garden. Gravel paths twisted around a variety of stunning plants and old trees that looked like they had been standing there for centuries. I could even hear rushing water in the distance—a waterfall? The last time we'd been here it had been so dark none of it had registered.

"If you see a cat, don't pet it, all right?" said Meedian. "They're my visiting investors."

There was a sound like fighting to our left, and the closer we got to the source, the more cats we saw, perched on anything large enough to fulfill the "if I fits, I sits" rule.

"Cats are aliens?" James whispered as we began to walk.

"Not all of them," Zander explained. "Many of his clients and investors must work outside of Alliance's reach, so they can't risk coming in person. If you have money, you can mind-swap with a willing volunteer. It's basically Skype with four legs. If you don't—"

"You mind-swap with a cat?" James snorted.

"Sure. Cats are easy. Creepy, but easy. Hey, you didn't really think that the Ancient Egyptians were venerating plain old, common, everyday cats all those millennia ago, did you? I mean, some of them were."

"You're meaning to tell me that aliens mind-controlled some cats to rule a civilization?"

"And the Earthling gets it," said Blayde.

"Hold on, how do you know so much about Meedian's business?" I asked, struggling to keep up. It was hard to walk with so many cats strewn all over the place.

"It's the same with any kind of legitimate businessman with access to that kind of tech."

Meedian, an alien godfather? I suppose it wasn't that hard to believe.

"He doesn't look very alien," whispered James.

"Well, I don't strip for just anyone." He turned around and flashed her a winning smile that turned her face bright red.

Zander gasped, rushing up ahead. "Wait, is that what I think it is?"

We had reached the end of the path, and after a sharp turn to the right we could finally look over an even lower tier to the complex. The sun beamed down on the immense park, flooding the earth with soft white light, showing all the different sand pits and strange markings on the ground. Two fighters circled each other in the central pit, dressed in black wetsuits with long metal pipes snaked up their arms.

"The training center," said Meedian with a sweep of his hand. "You called me away from my weapons demonstration."

The ground was entirely covered in cats now. Hundreds of tiny fluff balls had arranged themselves in a circle around the pit, watching the spectacle below with…well, it's hard to tell a cat's expression. But there was a lot of tail twitching going around.

I choked as flames erupted from the fighters' arms.

The cats let out a long, simultaneous yowl. Impressed? Before we had time to admire the flames, one of the fighters leapt over the other, blasting a jet from their right hand. Their suit caught fire at once, flames covering their entire body, and they rolled over, quenching the fire.

"Flame-throwing exoskeleton suits," said Meedian, the side of his lip curling up. "A little project of mine. You showed up right in time for my demo."

Zander whistled a long note as the audience cheered. "I want one for Life Day."

"We are so trying these tomorrow." Blayde nudged him in the ribs.

"Your rooms are down this way." Meedian indicated the next stretch of path and handed us each a room key with fancy tassels. "Supposing you've forgotten, the pool and spa are only open between 3 p.m. and 6 p.m., and Yu will be serving lunch at noon. Just follow the signs to the dining hall."

"I have a room." Zander sighed, so quietly I almost didn't hear it. Our keys had the same number, and my heart fluttered, having found a reason to beat.

"What is with this place?" James muttered.

"I guess we just know how to pick our friends," said Zander, closing his fist tight around the keychain and pressing it against his chest.

"Seriously, what is this place?" James whistled, scanning the complex. "I thought this was going to be just some underground lair, but it looks like a resort."

"A man can live, can't he?" Meedian scoffed. "Ah, we're here."

The library clashed terribly with the elegance of his resort. Meedian wasn't just a collector; he was a *hoarder*. If there were shelves, they were completely lost behind vertical stacks. Some might have been holding the ceiling up for so long that taking a book out might ruin the building's structural integrity.

We'd be leaving those for last.

"Look for anything that could create anything even comparable to the Dread," said Zander. "We're talking fear amplification, emotional manipulation, any kind of broadcasting device with massive range—or all of the above. Maybe the biological route: some kind of parasite or infection that could spread on this scale."

"Or some beasty so big it reminds us we were built to panic," said Blayde.

"I, personally, have never heard of anything capable of that," said Meedian. "But then again, I never heard of immortal teleporters before I met you either, so hey, there's still a chance we'll find the truth." He paused, scanning over the piles of volumes surrounding him. "Some of these are centuries old. And now that the library's gone, they may be the last copies in the universe. Whatever you do to them, I do to you. So don't break their spines."

I gulped.

"If you don't find what you're looking for in this room, my non-corporeal book collection is a little more organized," Meedian said, puffing out his chest and ruffling his imaginary feathers like a peacock. "Just harder to read. That, and the edible ones are limited resources."

With that, he turned and left, abandoning us to his hoard. I stared the stacks up and down in a dread entirely my own. I thought I liked books, but this was terrifying.

"All right, pick your books," said Zander. "We can't get to universe saving until we know what we're up against. Stack all the ones in English over by James since she doesn't have a translator."

The problem with my own translator was that everything *looked* like English to me. I found a collection of little blue books and held up the first one to James, who gave me a thumbs up. She was already proving her usefulness.

Blayde got comfortable on the sofa, lifting a book gingerly off the large stack behind her. She sneered at the cover. "*A Detailed Exploration of the Flora and Fauna of the Casterberus System.* Surely, a thoroughly gripping read."

Half an hour later, she placed it back on the table and let out a sigh about twice as large as her tome. "I was wrong. Dull, dull, abysmally dull. I guess we can scratch off the Casterberus system. There's nothing to see there but giant lemurs. Dead society, too, but nothing on the scale we're looking at."

Zander tsked. "*The Encyclopedia of Ancient Species* seems to be written from a more modern standpoint and relies mainly on a single experience the author had with mushrooms. Even so, no hint about the Dread."

"Nothing here either," I said. "This explorer found a civilization capable of making everyone get down and boogie, but it's less of a diabolical machine and more of a good sound system."

"I think this translation is bad." James rubbed her hands down her face, sighing heavily. "Unless there really was a cosmic slug convention?"

Zander and Blayde exchanged glances.

And so I read. And read. And read. A job we had first thought would take only a few hours went on forever. We read book after book after book, pulling more off the shelves when our stacks reached their end without avail.

I fell into the scratch-and-sniff memoirs of some great cosmic adventurer, hours passing as I flew through the volumes, learning about the inhabitants of Jacussia and their traditions—all based around the magic and thrill of accountancy—the creatures that plagued the sixth moon of Hiroy—pretty sure it was just pollen—and the beast that terrified a tiny continent on some planet that's name always escaped me, though sounded a whole lot like Trader's Joe's. By volume five of this hero's adventures, there wasn't much going on but him ranting about old age and his three wives not getting along. The only Dread he felt was the dread at the idea of his wives finding about his mistresses.

Needless to say, we found nothing in the books that day except far-flung stories and sinking expectations.

"So, we've gone through ten together." James stacked her books. "With how fast the siblings read, that's thirty today. We'll have finished the library in a month!"

A month? My chest tightened. Not fast enough. Maybe I really wasn't cut out for this leadership thing. My one idea was costing us precious time. At this rate, we'd find our first lead right as the Dread engulfed us all.

· · · · · · · · •• ● •• · · · · · ·

IT WAS NEAR MIDNIGHT WHEN WE WENT TO BED, and not too long after that I got back up, covered in sweat. All my dreams were twisted and sour. When I saw my parents on the Alliance ship dressing the riveting tortoise in my old baby clothes, I finally gave up on the concept of sleep.

I needed space to think, to clear my head. I slipped out of my room, closed the door silently behind me, and tiptoed away from the main compound, shoes in my hand, until I reached the end of the boardwalk where I put them on. Then I made my way through the garden.

Meedian had an incredible green thumb. That, or he hired people with green thumbs. This garden was magnificent; large, old willows led me down to a stream where bright blue flowers glowed in the moonlight.

And there, up the stream, was a waterfall. It wasn't particularly large or impressive, but under the full moon, the water sparkled like sapphires. I dipped a bare toe, relishing in the cool water of the plunge pool, my passing making ripples in the smooth surface. Yes. This was perfect.

I eased out of my pajamas and slipped into the stream. The water was cool on my skin, reminding me that I was alive, alive, alive. The rocks sliced deep shadows in the flow, leading me up to the curtain of water, my muscles awakening as I fought my way through the current.

Blink, and I was on top of the waterfall, balanced on the rocks right before the sheer drop. I stared down ten, twenty meters of rock and water. Still, I wasn't scared. Tonight, all vertigo had gone. I was as calm as any one person could be, my breathing deep and even, just like my therapist had taught me. There—clear mind.

In that moment, I could hear it: an anxiety that wasn't mine.

A dread that ran deeper than thought.

Do it. End it. Make it easier on everyone else.

A faint, persistent murmur, a ceaseless string of fears. A voice I knew so well but no longer sounded like me. Where was it coming from? Was it my voice, or something… else?

Shut up, I replied. *You're not welcome here.*

I dove off the cliff, breaking the surface of the water without so much as a splash. Cool, perfect water surrounded me, washing through my hair. For seconds, I lay under the smooth surface, in the peace, in the silence. My lungs didn't burn as the oxygen depleted, but my mind got murkier, slowly and surely murkier.

What if you come up and everyone else is gone? What if they left you, like Zander left you?

What if the sun is imploding this very minute, and you won't know until it's too late?

Too soon I broke out of the silent realm, reflex taking over as I gulped a huge lungful of air, rolling on my back and letting the water carry me downstream. I focused on the ripple of the water against the rocks, drowning out the voice.

I thought I was free of these thoughts, but they were back to living rent-free in my head. Were they even inside or just on the outside, slithering in? Was this the Dread? A voice that sounded like your own, telling you what you most feared? My stomach boiled. If this was the Dread, how could we defeat it? How could we go up against intangible thoughts?

"Couldn't sleep either, could you?"

I gasped and spat water. The voice came out of nowhere, and it was real, so much louder than my internal monologue. I ran a finger through my ears to dislodge the water there. I scrambled to find the source, but I couldn't see anyone on the banks. The moonlight only did so much to help.

Who on earth would be up at this hour?

Well, then again, I was up at this hour too.

"Up here," said the voice. Zander. Calm and eager at the same time, as if as relieved to see me as I was to hear him.

I pushed my wet hair back over my head as I scanned the tree limbs, and there he was, leaning back against the trunk of a massive tree, balanced precariously on one of the branches, completely at ease.

"What are you doing up?" I asked. "Up as in awake. Not up as in…in the tree."

He shrugged, though his perfect balance was undisturbed. "Both are because it is impossible to sleep here. And by here, I mean at Meedian's in general, not the tree."

"Do you mind if I join you?" I asked. He nodded. I slipped my PJs back on, soaking them through, and I focused my jump, landing on the branch above him, and climbed down. He wrapped his arms around my waist so we could both look down at the pool, the surface having returned to its mirror-like state. He rubbed his hands down my arm, trying to warm me, though I wasn't cold. I wasn't going to tell him to stop, though.

We hadn't had a minute to ourselves since… No, not since being back on Earth. Not since the ball. Had it really been since our stolen kisses in the Pyrinian apartment? Every waking moment since then had been either public or a terrible crisis. A few awkward moments in my parents' house, the Dread seriously killing the mood, though we hadn't had a word to call it yet.

"And you? How come you can't sleep?" he whispered. I leaned back into him.

"Just too much going on." I sighed. "The Dread, I suppose. You?"

He didn't answer right away, as if trying to figure out how best to say an uncomfortable truth. Eventually, he simply spat it out, as casually as he could. "There's something. In my gut," he said quietly. "I can feel it. A little hard ball of… I don't know."

"Anxiety? Is it the Dread?"

"It feels more than that. It's like"—he paused—"I have this feeling that things are about to change. Dramatically. That there's going to be change and no way to turn back."

"That sounds like the Dread talking."

We stared into the pool, my head on his shoulder, his cheek pressed against my soaking scalp. He couldn't have been comfortable, but he pulled me closer anyway. I snuggled deeper into him, welcoming the warmth of his arms.

"You'd think I'd be used to change by now," he said, his voice oh-so quiet. "That being the only true constant in the universe."

"I don't think anyone can. Get used to it, that is. Dealing with it is always pain, and how you do defines you. It makes you who you are. If there was no change, there'd be no growth. Right?"

"Then why am I afraid of it?" He shivered, sending ripples through my body. "I don't know what thoughts are mine or this Dread's right now. And I don't like not knowing. I'm just…out of sync."

"What?"

"You know, like…waves." He pointed at the pond, making a dolphin movement with his hand. "So much of how we experience the universe is in waves. The light we see. The sound we hear. We catch a wave and translate it into our reality."

I leaned my head against him. There was something soothing in the way he spoke. Grounding. The only man I knew whose hand I could grip like a vice and who could squeeze mine back with the same force, reminding me I was here, now.

"When waves are in phase, they build each other up," he continued, "making each other bigger, stronger."

"Like us?" I said.

He laughed. "Yeah, like us. But right now, I feel…out of phase from the rest of the universe. The waves are cancelling each other out."

I shivered. The thought chilled me to the core, but he was right. No wonder I felt so on edge. We were going up against an enemy that was about as vague as gossip and just as deadly. Evident only on the macro scale, but to the self, an intangible feeling. Everything was out of sync, and so was I.

I needed to remember who I was.

I turned my head upward, kissing his chin, searching for his lips with mine. He found me instead, one hand rising to cup my cheek, the other holding back my hair. We were twisted like a pretzel, but the touch was real, louder than anything else. My head spun with delirious, deafening love, too dizzy to think, to let the bad stuff in.

"Now, what are you thinking?" I pulled back only far enough to breathe.

"That my thoughts are entirely my own," he whispered against my lips. "But somehow, you still know them."

I twisted myself around in the tree so that I could hold him, my hands pulling his face to mine. His arms looped back around my torso, but they were burning hot now, pulling me closer and closer until I didn't know where I stopped and he began. Kissing him was like kissing the sun, hot and explosive and all-consuming. I didn't want it to end.

And as an added bonus, kissing Zander eclipsed all other thoughts—mine and others.

I gently slipped my hand under his shirt, feeling the wonder of his skin and hard muscles waiting there for me. His odd-numbered abs, the out of place number nine. He shivered as I traced a finger up his back, exhaling sharply.

"You don't know what you're doing to me," he breathed.

"Oh, I know exactly what I'm doing."

I closed my eyes and leaned deeper, soaking up his presence, filling myself up. My nostrils flared. It had been too long since we'd had any time to ourselves. The night was ours. My skin was already slick with sweat.

"It's hot," he said.

"I'm not—"

"No, don't you feel that?"

We pulled apart, and I caught my breath, one full of flame and heat. Smoke in the air. In the few minutes I'd been in Zander's halo, I hadn't seen the garden go from blue to orange. And it was far too early for sunrise.

We dropped out of the tree and raced back toward the rooms. But it was too late; they were already aflame.

Ten cats in a flamethrower suit would do that.

SIX

FIFTEEN REASONS CATS AND FLAMETHROWERS SHOULDN'T MIX

I'D NEVER SEEN CATS COOPERATE BEFORE, LET alone operate a flame-throwing exoskeleton. Three for each leg, two for the torso, and one for each arm, holding their shape by tooth and claw. From a distance, it was a walking headless armor. Just ten meters away, a furry horror show. The arm operators screamed and yowled with glee as they unleashed their terrible fire, burning the bench bordering the garden. The flames devoured it in seconds before catching the tree behind it.

The compound was on fire.

Zander didn't hesitate. He flung himself at the cat monstrosity, knocking the exoskeleton to the ground. But the cats didn't scatter; they climbed on top of him, scratching and biting and howling bloody murder.

My breath hitched in my throat. They had Zander. Oh shit, they had Zander. The sight of him struggling beneath so many cats—shit, more were still flocking to him—sent my gut twisting.

This is your fault, you useless waste of space. You should have stayed under water until you drowned.

"Run, Sally, run!" Zander screamed.

I wasn't going to let them eat my man or whatever mad cats do. Without thinking, I ran right at them, waving my arms wide and screaming like a deranged hen. They didn't scatter. They were eating him alive.

So, I kicked a cat. It went flying like a football.

But there were more cats now, over a dozen and maybe more. I didn't have enough legs.

A brown tabby at the right arm yowled as it slammed a red button. A flame burned off my arm in a single burst.

I screamed in shock at seeing my arm reduced to ash. I'd died before, but never lost a limb. The lack of it sent my mind screaming. I didn't know how to deal with the loss or the lack of pain that should have come with it, and my mind decided to interpret the sudden lack of nerves as a craving for chalupas.

I kicked the cat, sending it flying. Just trying to swing my leg was hard; my balance was so off. The cat crash-landed a few meters away, rolled back to its feet, and rushed us again.

"What is happening?" I shouted. My arm was growing back, but too slowly. Right now, it was the size of a newborn's. "What is this?"

"Cats—*mff*—Dread!"

"What?" The Dread? How? I thought it was just the voice.

Except…if the cats were connected to people light-years away, maybe it was stronger there?

Zander could barely speak; the cats kept going for his eyes and mouth. I had to get him out of there. My baby arm was about the size of a toddler's now, but the other was enough to grab the scruff of his shirt and pull him away from the cats. With Zander freed, they flocked toward the exoskeleton again, and seconds later they were walking, horrofic flames wielded by tiny devils.

"It's too late," Zander panted, covered in small, rapidly closing red bite marks. "The whole compound is on fire."

It wasn't just our rooms. The flames were all around. Smoke wrapped its tendrils around us, turning the cat monstrosity into a beast of mythical proportions.

"*The library,*" said Zander. "Oh stars, the library."

"Where's Meedian? Where's James?" I wanted to scream, but my only hand was busy covering my mouth. The other was too busy going through puberty.

The cats marched in unison, following their exoskeleton overlord down the fiery path. In the distance, a second exoskeleton loomed, piloted by other crazed felines.

"Wh-why would… they d-do this?" I sputtered through rasping breaths. "I-I thought they were… investors!"

"I don't think they're in control," said Zander. "With the Dread, the psychic link between investor and cat must be decaying!"

We didn't have any time. If the Dread was this strong this soon on Earth, then it was escalating much quicker than anyone could anticipate. We had days at the most, if we were lucky.

"We have to go," I said, coughing up the smoke. "We have to find Blayde and James and Meedian and... We can't save this place, but we can save them."

We raced into the burning rooms. The furniture was pure fire, the kind of cozy living room you'd be lucky to find in hell. The only thing that made it bearable was the absence of victims.

And the heat—the *heat*. I had never thought I would know the smell of my own skin sizzling off me. I was quite literally frying alive. I squeezed my eyes shut and ran.

"Where are they?" I shouted through trembling lips as I crashed back into Zander in the upper courtyard. Here at least there were no flames. The only cats that ran by were ones stealing equipment, grabbing whatever they could. One had a Wii remote in its mouth, though I failed to see the value.

"Library?" he suggested.

We ran to the library, but it was already a smoking heap. There were no flames here, as it had already entirely burned. Nothing was left but a pile of ashes and twisted metal.

"No. No!" Zander screamed a primal scream and fell to his knees. "We were so close. We were…"

He had a complicated relationship with libraries and fire. I put a hand on his back. There was nothing I could say to make this better.

It's all your fault. You should have been here, should have protected this place—

Shut up!

"We have to go," I said. If we didn't leave now, my weak knees were going to cave in. "We have to find the others."

We ran back to the apothecary, clutching hands. The cats were congregating at the exit door, both flame-throwing exoskeletons and all hundred little kitty-bodies flocking and yowling around the simple metal. Incredibly—impossibly—the structure hadn't caught fire yet, but the cats were desperate to get it to ignite. They piled their treasures at the door. Kindling?

"Frash," said Zander, shaking his head. "Why are they waiting?"

A few flung themselves at the metal, even managing to catch the knob, but slid right off.

"They can't open the door," I said. "They can operate flamethrowers, but they can't get the doorknob?"

"We need to get past them. I can't see my way through. Can't jump."

The cats were so focused on the door they didn't seem to notice us at all. Maybe we could use that to our advantage. I wrapped my arms around myself, taking a deep breath, trying to calm my tremors.

"I have an idea. It's terrible, but it might just work."

I dropped to my knees, indicating for him to do the same. My freshly minted nerve endings in my hand had never felt gravel before, so every rock felt as sharp as a knife. I kept my chin high, despite the small tremble.

"*Meow,*" I warbled. "*Meow!*"

Zander followed suit, his cat imitation miles ahead of mine, to the point where he might have been fluent. They ignored us as we made our way through their midst, blending in about as well as aliens at Comicon.

The second we reached it, the door flew open on its own, and two women in spandex bodysuits sprayed the entire cat army with glitter cannons.

Zander grabbed my wrist and tugged me through the door before it slammed shut.

"Thank God you're okay," James said as she lifted me to my feet. The shimmery spandex clung to her skin, making her look like she was dipped in molten gold. "Saved by a romantic escapade. Looks like you got lucky in more than one way tonight."

"What did we miss?" asked Zander, helping Blayde barricade the door, as I was too busy blushing. "What's with the spandex?"

"Lost my clothes," she replied. "We found these in the museum. Not sure which was mine or yours."

Other than James's hair singed at the tips, there was almost nothing to show she'd been in a fire at all. The outfits made her and Blayde look like the next big pop sensations. Blayde's red leather coat was remarkably unscathed and looked killer with the gold.

We were in the small atrium behind Meedian's shop, between the sibling museum and storage. It was tight, dark, and smelled of cabbage. A relief after the smell of roasted Sally.

Meedian burst through the storage room door, having ditched his human suit who knows where, and was now whizzing by, his baby lizard body stuffed in a hovering ring that barely kept his oversized head afloat. His tiny hands were clenched into adorable chubby, pink fists. I threw a hand up to hide my gasp. The once vibrant color was now dull, a light peach rather than neon pink.

"Well thank the flying spittoon you all made it." His voice boomed through the cramped atrium. James's jaw hit the floor—must have been the first time she'd seen Meedian's true body. No scream. Impressive that she was keeping her own after only day one.

"You knew this would happen," he spat. "And you never told me? No warning, nothing?"

"Wait, if our future selves—" Zander started, but Meedian spun in his hover-ring, flying up into his face.

"*They* might have had their reasons to stay silent," said Meedian. "But you're here now, witnessing the loss of my home firsthand, and still, one day you're going to waltz in here as if you didn't know what was going to happen. That's not a choice your future selves made, Zander. That's one you're making right now. That my loss, my pain, matters less to you because you can just go back to a time when it hasn't happened yet. I doubt I or my business will ever recover. And you don't give a *shit*."

An explosion set the entire building quaking, and I stumbled into James. What was happening out there? The cats let out a monstrous yowl.

"That's not true," said Zander, but Blayde put a hand on his arm.

"What can we do, Meedian?" she said. "You're right. This very minute, we are making a choice, and I'm sure that the only reason we wouldn't tell you is because we've lived this moment and all the ones that come after. Whatever we're doing in the next minutes or days will define us."

"Maybe the Dread destroys everything, and there's no future for anyone," said James, darkly.

I could punch her right in her sparkly golden leotard. "Shut up! We need to get out of this mess, and thinking like that isn't getting us anywhere."

"It's so much worse than we thought," said Zander, his ear against the door. "Your investors were using a psychic link to pilot the cats through subspace. The Dread must be interfering with the connection. For it to be *this* powerful…"

Screw the Dread. Whatever this thing was, it was getting in our heads, making all of us act out of a constant state of dull panic. If we weren't careful, it was going to get us all killed.

"Give me your ab," Meedian spat. "Let's see if your future selves actually do care."

Blayde and Zander traded glances. "My *ab*?" asked Blayde.

"No, you, frash hole!" He whammed into Zander's gut, making him grunt in surprise. "That's all you told me. If things went to shit, you'd give me your ab to save me."

Zander inched up his shirt. There were his washboard abs in all their splendor—all nine of them.

"You can't possibly mean this?" He poked little number nine.

"Stop wasting time and dig it out already!" said Blayde, jamming her laser into his gut.

I looked away as she sliced into his skin. James's body went stiff by my side. I would never get used to the casualness with which he tore apart his own body, like it was nothing but paper to him. It kinda ruined his mystique.

"Well, this isn't…" Zander's brows furrowed as he dug his fingers into the wound, the thick blood dripping to the floor. He retrieved a small metal slab, frowning as he wiped his sticky fingers against his pants.

A tin. A tiny metal tin. This whole time, it had never been an ab at all. He flicked it open without saying a word.

Inside were mints. Four of them, exactly.

"Well, that settles it," said Meedian. "I will thank you to get off my property and never set foot here again."

"Wait!" Zander pulled a tiny strip of paper from the tin. "Let's not be hasty until we see what they're for, hmm?"

"Hasty? There is a mountain of cats on my doorstep, and they're about to burn my last remaining stronghold to a crisp. I think hasty is the least I can be."

Blayde jammed her hands on her hips. "Our future selves told you to give us this in the event of everything crashing down, right? Why do you think that is?"

"Just stop talking!"

Zander shoved a mint into his mouth. His eyes rolled back until nothing was showing but whiteness, but it only lasted a second. They snapped back into place, his expression turning from determination to disgust.

"W-what w-was that?" I sputtered.

"I don't—I can't..." Zander grabbed his head with both hands. "No witty retorts or dramatic responses here. Just take the thing. It's a book. It's the book we were looking for."

"A book?" James and I traded looks. For a second, I thought either of us might call jinx, but before we could, Blayde was already shoving the tin in front of us.

"Eat the frashing book!" she screamed, tossing a mint into her mouth.

I knew better than to hesitate. I took a mint and placed it on my tongue, expecting to taste the cool blue mountain chill or whatever they're advertising these days, but instead, I tasted with my eyes and I *saw*.

The furs under my hands were real. The sun pouring in through the flap of my tent was real. The world around me was real, both familiar and strange, like my mind was in two places, like it was two people's at once.

I was sitting on a stool in front of a long mirror, placed upon a pedestal of flowers, the few cracks that remained reflecting the dust motes that swirled in the sunbeam behind me. My skin was heavily tanned. Furry and scaly animal hides covered me from my chest to my hips. The only weapon on me was the long knife at my hip.

Oh, and I was *Blayde.* I probably should have led with that.

I was looking through Blayde's eyes, but a different Blayde, one with long black hair down to her navel and soft eyes that knew how to smile. She stood in front of the mirror, showing none of the shock I was feeling, her hands resting on her swollen belly. I watched all this through her eyes, seeing her reflection in place of my own. I was Blayde, but I had no control here. I was only an observer, sitting in the place of honor. Seeing events with her perspective.

I wasn't meant to be here. It felt like a massive intrusion of her privacy, too intimate for the friendship we had. Had Zander just experienced the same thing? Where was he, anyway? Where were any of them?

"Slash," a voice called from the tent flap. My brain tickled slightly. Blayde recognized the voice as I failed to. I could feel the familiarity, but it wasn't mine. "There is someone here to see you."

"I'm busy," she replied, voice soft and delicate in a way I'd never heard Blayde before. And, stranger still, being inside her head, it felt sincere.

"It's a man, Slash. A man from beyond the wilderness. He says he knows you."

She paused in her brushing, letting out a low, heavy breath. Then the brush was right back at her hair, the tug as familiar as if it were my own scalp. "Well, whoever it is, tell him to go away."

"He says to tell you that the jerk is here to apologize."

At this, Blayde scowled. She hoisted herself to her feet, hand resting on the hilt of her small dagger. I could feel the cold of the metal against her palm.

"I will meet him outside of camp," she snarled, her lip curling only at the end. Ah, so that's how she did it. "He is not to tread upon our sand. One misstep, and I'll refuse to see him entirely."

The energy drained from her at once, and she collapsed back on the stool, heavy. Tension sparked up her spine. Deep breaths to temper the anger. After an eternity, Blayde finally rose to her feet, striding out of the tent as if she owned the place. Maybe she did.

The settlement outside was quiet; tents scattered the desert landscape, none as large as hers. Blayde was barefoot, but the hot sand was nothing to me as she walked down a path she had probably walked hundreds of times before. Somewhere in the distance, we could hear the sea rise and fall, the long ebb and flow of waves breaking the barren silence of the wasteland before us.

When she reached the point where the tents stopped, she paused, glancing across the flat landscape in search of the so-called jerk who had called her here.

"Miss me?" he asked with a smirk, appearing in front of her.

Zander. The Sally part of my brain flashed to the desert wraps he had worn when we'd first met, when I'd run him over in the street. But while they were right, his face wasn't. His carefree smile was nowhere to be seen, and there was a tightness to his eyes that made him look older, not young like this version of Blayde.

"Only barely," she replied, keeping her distance.

"How long's it been for you?" he asked.

"About four years, give or take," she responded, cold.

"One thousand days for me," said Zander. *"A thousand days exactly, as we agreed. Are you ready to come back?"*

She shook her head slowly, Zander's face falling as she did so.

"I can't. I've got a life here."

"Yeah, I can see that." He snorted, gesturing at her.

The Sally in me wanted to shy away, but I was only the viewer.

"So what, you're going to be some chieftainess on a backward planet for the rest of your life?"

"They need me here."

"Everyone always needs you. What makes them special? Or maybe, do you need them?"

Blayde said nothing.

"So, what are they going to do when they realize you're immortal?" he asked. *"When you've ruled for hundreds of years, when everyone you've ever known is dead and dust? What then?"*

"That's not the most important thing here." She took his elbow, walking him away from the small encampment. It really was in the middle of nowhere, the tents the only thing as far as the eye could see. *"I've got a life here now. They love me, not because of what I am, but who I am. I've given them no reason to think I'm anything but human."*

"You said this was going to be temporary!" Zander snarled. "You said no more than a thousand days apart. No more."

"And I've found myself!" She laughed, a joyful laugh that spread across the sandy eternity without end. "I was hoping you would find the time to meet yourself, love him the way I do. I take it you haven't?"

"Oh, I met him. But I didn't like the guy I found. Blayde, you have to come back. I'm begging you. I'm not myself without you. Half my heart is missing. I need you by my side, and I'm certain that you need me too."

"No, you don't," she snapped. "Our codependence was stifling. I should be allowed to meet someone and pursue a relationship outside of our own."

"Apparently you needed a whole hive mind to make up for me," he snorted. "So there was a gap? When I left?"

"Yes, but for all the wrong reasons." Blayde walked on ahead, turning to face her brother. "I can't stay with you; it brings back memories, and they're too painful for me to handle."

"And we've learned to deal with it! Together! You talk of heartbreak? Well, think of what have you done to me. You left me alone and broken. Alone, Blayde. Your brother. Your other half."

"So find something else to complete you. Better yet, complete yourself."

"You still haven't forgiven me? I didn't do anything, Blayde. Everything you think you've ever lost, you lost because you threw it away. I'm still here. Don't lose me."

"Zander, won't you ever let me live?" She wrapped her arms around herself, tight. "I'm moving on. Something we both should have done a long time ago."

His eyes widened. He scanned Blayde slowly, his eyes resting on her round belly.

"I've got a reason to stay. I'm not going anywhere."

"But I need you."

"No, you don't. You made all that very clear last time. You can do well on your own."

Zander screamed, ripping his hair right from the scalp. Blayde stepped back, unashamed, watching him as he cried to high heavens.

"I'm not going anywhere. And I don't plan on changing my mind. So please…"

I gasped as I came aware of Meedian's back room once again, the vision collapsing as if it never was. Around me were the Blayde and Zander I knew and a wide-eyed James, who promptly vomited.

Which was a little reassuring. I was beginning to think she might have been a robot.

The building shook again, bringing me entirely to the present. Something shattered in the storefront. Shit. Whatever the cats were doing out there, they were bringing this place down.

"Did we…did *everyone* just see that?" I asked. James nodded.

"I don't remember that," said Blayde, shaking. I'd never seen her so pale before. She patted her breast pocket—her journal—but didn't take it out. "I mean, it must have been my memory, but it's not a memory I'm familiar with. Zander?"

He shook his head. "I think… I think that's where we're meant to go."

I had so much I wanted to ask her. Had she really been pregnant? What was going on?

"Uh—aren't we getting sidetracked?" James stood up, her frame blocking her little vomit puddle, hiding it from the rest of us as if it had never happened. "We're looking for the source of the Dread, and I'm pretty sure I felt none of that soul-crushing anxiety when I was in your memory or whatever that was."

There was a crashing sound like an entire window store getting crushed by a defective Acme device. The cats might actually destroy the apothecary. They were getting close to it.

Meedian howled in pain. "Stop talking and get out of here!"

"We need to go," said Blayde, "and we're going to the desert world."

James reached for her. "But we—"

"James, you stay with Meedian." Blayde shook her off, grabbing her brother instead. "You'll be safer here. I don't want to risk losing you to whatever we find there."

I was glad she was the one to say it. James wasn't immortal and had no idea how to act off-world. Traveling with her would most likely lead to a repeat of Nim. I gritted my teeth at the memory.

"I'm not keeping her," huffed Meedian. "Besides, what part of 'get out' don't you understand? Hell, what am I still doing here?"

He flew toward the staircase, pressed a button, and the whole room instantly gave up all appearance of being for storage and turned into the cockpit of a ship. Consoles burst from every wall, a chair dropping from the ceiling so fast it almost caved in James's head. We jumped out of the way as an office printer fell from above, shattering on the ground.

"You were supposed to catch that," muttered Meedian.

I stared up at the new interior in awe. No wonder the cats were having such a hard time burning this place down. It had been his ship this whole time. James's hands covered her mouth, her eyes wide and sparkling.

"This is for you, I think," said Blayde, handing Meedian the tiny strip of paper that had been in the tin.

"What's this?" He ripped it from her hands and spread it out, brows furrowed. "Coordinates?"

"I'm assuming it'll be nice," Blayde said. "Considering how it says Sunan is waiting for you. I suppose we have our future selves to thank for it. See you soon?"

"Depends on what I find there," said Meedian. He rushed to the console near the back exit and hit a few switches that made the ship look like a disco, complete with multicolored lights flashing across the wall and engines dropping a sick beat.

"Right," said Blayde, making her way toward me. "You can get us there?"

I knew what she was asking. There was no time for excuses, and no point to them—they'd come later, if we got out of here. I tried not to think about my family, about what would happen if another three years went by. I wouldn't let that happen. I nodded and took her hand.

"You can't just leave me here," said James. "I don't even know this guy."

"You'll make fast friends," Blayde snapped. "Sally, hit it."

"Hit it?" I asked.

"You know, do the thing. Jump, go, whatever."

Zander took my other hand, closing the circle. "You can do this, my star. I was there, you can find me."

Little did he know.

I gave one last look to Meedian, who was doing a fine job of ignoring us, and to James before closing my eyes, concentrating to find the world I had just tasted. It was far—both in time and space—but I knew my way.

Just as I let my cells split apart, I felt the building shake with the force of liftoff—and a weight clamp down on my shoulder.

Nothing's ever that easy.

SEVEN

OR AS I LIKE TO CALL IT, CHAPTER SVEN

NEWSFLASH: IT'S RUDE TO STOWAWAY ON interdimensional transit.

I hadn't been expecting to carry James along with me. The extra mass threw me off-balance, her atoms vying for my attention, and I had no choice but to wrangle them like first-graders on a field trip.

The second my eyes remembered how to see, I toppled forward into sand. By far the sloppiest jump I've ever led and all because someone had tried to hop along without a ticket. I rolled onto my back and gazed into a cloudless, blue sky, trembling. My shoulder throbbed from where she'd taken hold of me.

"Oh, hi, James. Welcome to the universe," said Zander.

"Sally! I told you to leave the agent!" said Blayde, letting out a heavy sigh.

"I tried to!" I spat sand from my mouth. *Ew.* I glared at James, who was sprawled on the sand beside me. She had taken advantage of me, used me as her taxi to the stars. An invasion. I took a deep breath, the deepest I'd taken all year. Despite everything, I wanted to scream at James. I felt better than I had in a long, long time.

"Do you feel that?" asked Blayde.

I stood up, brushing the sand off my PJs. The desert went on forever, impossibly flat, meeting with an equally impossibly flat ocean. An infinite beach—and a sizzling one at that. Out of the fire, into the boiler, I suppose.

"I don't feel anything," said Zander.

"Exactly," said Blayde. "No Dread here. None. Nothing. Zip. Nada. Even so, Sally, take James back. This place isn't safe for her."

"*Back?*" James scoffed.

"I don't think I can," I said. "Meedian was already taking off when we jumped. If we go back there now, I'll be dropping James from the sky into a pit of evil, fire-wielding cats. I think we're stuck with her."

"I'm right here, you know."

"And that's exactly the problem!" I clenched my fists. "You're not safe here. You crossed a boundary, and now you're going to get hurt!"

"What *here* isn't safe?" said James. She threw out her arms, flinging sand. "There's nothing for miles!"

"Except the sun," said Blayde. "Look at you with all your skin out. You'll pucker up like…a turkey on Thanksgiving. Is that analogy correct?"

"It's impressively apt." I dug my bare toes into the hot sand, probably burning them, but nothing lasts forever. The same couldn't be said of James. Already, there were beads of sweat on her brow.

"So, where to now?" she asked, voice low, hoarse. "We going to find some shade or something?

"Can you shut up?" Blayde shot her a crispy look. "You're not meant to be here. Go stand in the water. We'll work out how to find the People."

"The People?" I asked. "From the memory-vision thing?"

"The very same."

The certainty with which she said it was oddly reassuring. I must have found the right place, the right time. But her ancient past could have been just yesterday. How had her time here ended? She pulled her red journal out of her pocket, flipping through the pages and frowning.

"James," said Zander, "did you have anything to drink before we left?"

"You mean before or after the flaming cat fight? Sure, I drank like a horse," she said, marching into the sea. I could almost see steam rising from where the water touched her skin.

"Just stand still while we work this all out, Juxley," said Blayde, stuffing the journal back into her breast pocket. "It'll keep you from drying out like an old sponge. In any case, the sun is lower on the horizon now compared to when we arrived; it's setting. Not too long now until nightfall."

"And I just stand here until then? Is that how you think humans work?"

"Felling, just…just…shut up." Blayde ran her hands down her face. "I'm trying to keep you from dying, okay? This is exactly why we didn't want you to come along."

"Everyone, calm down, will you?" My face was hot, and not just from the sun. "Fighting isn't going to get us anywhere."

"She's right." Blayde pointed to a random far-off place in the troublingly flat desert. "When the sun sets, we'll start a bonfire and wait it out. If we're lucky, the People will see the fire and come to us."

James swallowed so loudly I heard it from here. "I hate to say this," she called, "but I think something just swam past my leg."

My body went stock-still as the sea behind James shifted.

The water pulled back, rising into one large mass as the crest of a gigantic new wave formed in midair above her. James twisted her head around so far her neck shouldn't have held, eyes following the water rising, rising higher and higher until the peak was as thin as my temper. My breath caught as two huge, yellow eyes glared from *inside* the wave, larger than satellite dishes, followed by James-sized teeth.

You betcha I screamed.

A pointed head pushed out of the water—no, it was *made* of water—and the mouth opened wide, ready to swallow James whole. James dove out of the way, plunging under the surface as the serpent bit only sand. It reared, hissing loudly, and poised to lunge again. It spun its watery tail, thrusting it around James, blocking her escape to the beach.

"Why are we watching this?" I shouted, but Blayde was already running to the creature. She lunged at its thick trunk of a body with one of her trusty knives and stabbed the translucent surface, making it shriek a banshee cry that stiffened my hair.

"I'm going to jump you out!" said Blayde, pulling off her jacket and tossing it at me. It hit me squarely in the face. *Ouch*. I let it fall to the sand. "But you have to stop moving!"

"I can't! It only hasn't eaten me yet because I *haven't* stopped moving!" James shouted, darting away.

"Just trust me!" Blayde bellowed. "You two, run!"

The serpent lunged. It hit the surf with a resonant splash, sending jets of water streaming all around. The spray was so thick I couldn't see a hand in front of me.

In an instant, Zander grabbed my hand, and we ran from the serpent, down the long expanse of flat sand and as far into the desert as our legs would take us.

Behind us, the creature roared, but its voice quickly died down behind us. Still, we ran, putting as much distance between it and us as we could.

Before I could gather my thoughts, Zander's hand was ripped from mine, leaving only his phantom touch. I screamed as I lurched forward, stumbling to a halt. I struggled to catch my breath and scanned the sand around me for any sign of what had happened, but Zander was simply gone. There was nothing but flat sand for miles and miles.

That was, until the sand ahead of me started to sink. Quicksand? Finally, after all those cartoons as a kid preparing me for what I thought would be a near-constant threat, I was finally going to be able to fight off quicksand.

"Zander?" I should probably move at this point. Where were the others?

The sand beside me exploded. I was pretty sure it wasn't meant to do that. It scattered everywhere, raining on my hair, making me cough as I breathed it in.

A gigantic plant burst through, something crossed between a Venus fly trap and a dinosaur, the kind of thing some deranged scientist would make for *Jurassic Park* without stopping to think whether they actually *should*. Its teeth, longer than my forearms and dripping gloopy saliva, could have picked up and devoured a cow in a single gulp.

And it was staring right at me. At least, I think it was. It didn't seem to have any eyes, and yet, the mouth was edging delicately closer, the sinewy trunk-like green stem holding the head steady above me.

"Nice doggy?" I said, squeaky as a chew toy.

Its mouth opened and closed, like watching Kermit the Frog, minus the flailing arms and jovial personality but instead with too many teeth. And then it spoke— actually spoke. "Well, what have we here?"

I should be used to this by now. All these planets, all these worlds, pretty much anything could talk. I once got life advice from living Jell-O and dated what turned out to be a sentient patch of gas. At the very least, I should be polite.

"Um, Sally. Sally Webber," I replied. "Please don't eat me. I just came from the beach, so I probably taste all sweaty and salty, and my meat's all tense."

"I do love food with some extra flavor," it said, licking its lips with a stocky purple tongue. "The madrags are so leathery. And so many bones! You look like you might have some fat on you."

"Well, thanks for that." Where was Zander? Or Blayde and James, for that matter? I squared my shoulders and braced myself for whatever was coming.

The ground rumbled behind me. Another plant emerged a few meters away, throwing sand high into the air.

"Carl, don't pick up food from the ground!" it said, towering over me and the plant named Carl.

"But Mom! It looks so juicy!"

"I'm not juicy," I asserted. "I'm tense and full of stress! Not to mention pollutants. So many pollutants."

"Great flame above, it speaks!" the more massive fly trap practically shrieked. It threw its mouth backwards, stem spirally wildly. "What sort of vegetation is this?"

"Not vegetation?"

"Don't eat that, Carl. It'll mess with your roots," said the largest plant.

"But *Moooom!*"

"No buts. Go back to your cavernum this instant."

"But Sven ate one, and he said it was the best meat he'd ever tasted."

"*Sven* ate one?" the plant scoffed. "Sven! Sven!"

This time, the sand landed right on my chest and mouth, and I spat it out. Another plant interrupted my field of view.

"What is it, Maureen?" asked the new plant being. This one was a bit less green than the other two; more brown and leathery.

Maureen leaned closer. "Carl says you ate a… *speaking thing* off the ground."

"Well, it wasn't speaking when I first took a bite," Sven replied. "But it got quite agitated once I finished with the roots."

The wonkiest wave of relief washed over me. *Zander.* That would explain where he disappeared to. He was safe…inside the belly of one of these things. Did they even have bellies?

"And you ate it anyway?" Maureen scoffed.

"It was so good, Maureen. So many flavors!"

With that, Sven burped, which made Carl devolve into fits of laughter.

"Carl!" Maureen screeched. "Go to your cavernum this instant!"

"But, Mom!"

"What did I say about *but Moms*? Now!"

Carl grumbled but pulled in on himself nonetheless, diving into the sea of sand. I stayed silent. I had to plan my move—any move, at this point.

"I can't believe you," said Maureen, facing Sven. "I thought we raised you better than this!"

"Maureen, I am literally your offshoot. So is Carl and everyone else here. You are yelling at yourself right now."

"Stop pulling out that argument every time, your rotten, overwatered—*Sven*!"

Strange lumps appeared in Sven's mouth. He gurgled, trying to keep his mouth closed. Something was trying to push its way out.

"Sven? What's happening?" asked Maureen.

Sven said nothing. Instead, the plant belched, far worse than it had previously. It belched up a *man*. Zander flew into the air, only to fall right back into Sven's gaping mouth, impaled against a giant tooth.

I almost dropped to my knees. There he was, soaked with the gastric juices of an alien plant, clutched in a monster's mouth, dead, but he'd been through worse. I took a deep breath, calming my shakes. I would never get used to the grotesque sight of my boyfriend's mangled corpse. But he was here. Now I just needed to save him.

"Sven!" cried Maureen.

The ground around us exploded into a cloud of sand as dozens of other plants burst forth, each hissing and screaming at Sven's predicament. I braced myself as the sand roiled in their wake, hands clutched in small fists.

"Get it off! Get it off!" Sven screamed, swinging wildly. "It's stuck!"

"Hold still," said his neighbor. "I've got you!"

Sven flicked himself at the plant, but he moved too fast. It was a disaster. The other plant's head fell to the sand as all the plants roared.

"You *hemping* idiot!" screamed Maureen. "You killed him!"

"He'll grow back!" said Sven. "I won't if I don't get this thing out of my teeth!"

This was my window. My mind went blank as I rushed forward, taking advantage of the screaming plants. Sven still had Zander between his teeth, dangling limply like that poor woman in *King Kong*. Oh boy, he was definitely dead now, his torso hanging at a ninety-degree angle. He needed help to get out of there and fast. Coming back to life in the middle of being impaled would kill him all over again. And if the trap swallowed Zander whole, the cycle would repeat ad infinitum.

I ran at the trunk, my muscles moving faster than my mind, and grabbed onto the thick pelt of fibrous hair I found there, pulling myself upward. The stem shook back and forth, trying to throw me off, but my grip only tightened, and I hoisted myself up.

"Sven! There's another one!" shouted one of the plants, before swinging at me. It whipped me right in the chest—home run. I went flying backwards, crashing into the sand near the base of Maureen.

"How is it moving?" one of them gasped. "Its roots are…detached!"

With that, they all screamed.

"Just stay still!" I shouted. "I'll get him out of your teeth!"

"Sway! Sway!" suggested Maureen. "It's…it's moving!"

I was a freaking plant ghost.

Well, they weren't going to listen to me, so I jumped to the top of Sven's head. He buckled and shook me about, an impromptu rodeo where I clung to his fibrous hide. Despite the swinging, I got to work on trying to get Zander out of the creature's hold. His shoulder was completely speared by one of the fangs. I grabbed the fang with both hands, ripping it with all my strength from the creature's jaw.

Sven was doing the plant equivalent of sobbing now, leaves going yellow and wilty as he thrashed around more violently than before. I held onto Zander's arm, my other hand gripping Sven's upper lip to try and avoid slipping. My hand found sticky goo, and I realized much too late that Zander wasn't slipping at all. He was stuck tight.

It was then that he came alive.

"What the—Sally?" His eyes were wide. "Where are—oh, oh no, I'm going to be sick…"

He wriggled but couldn't pull free. Zander's entire back was stuck to the lower half of Sven's mouth, while I'd gotten the entire front of my body stuck to the top as I leaned over to help him. With my left arm extended to hold Zander and my right stretched back, I could no longer move. We were stuck to Sven.

"Zander!" I cried.

"Sally! Where are you?"

"Up here!" I wiggled my hand over the creature's mouth, reaching for him with the only body part that wasn't currently bound by alien plant goop. He grabbed mine, clasping it tightly, and we formed a muzzle over Sven's mouth "We'd better jump!"

"Shake harder, Sven!" shouted one of the plants.

"Where?" Zander replied, aghast. "There are more of them! And I can't see Blayde!"

"We have to reach the ground!" My shout was drowned out quickly by the roar of the wind created by Sven's shakes. I clutched Zander's hand tight.

Slash. Maureen and the others dove into the sand, and we tumbled, Sven's head no longer held by anything but air. We crashed into the sand Zander-first.

My head spun. I tried to pull myself up, but the glue that held me to Sven's decapitated mouth was too strong. I was helpless, even as Sven was dead. Sucks to be a giant carnivorous plant in the middle of the desert, I suppose.

"Sal, you ok?" Zander asked from the other side of the green hide, his voice muffled by sand.

"I'm fine. Hold on…"

We shuffled our chins around the fiber until we were face to face, noses touching. His breath was salty in my nostrils.

"Fancy seeing you here." He grinned, his body rigid under the plant.

"Hello, dear."

"Hello, my star. Did you just save me?"

"Perhaps," I said, before he pecked my lips. "Oh, you can thank me better than that."

I dove headfirst into the kiss, relishing in the relief of having him back in one piece. It didn't matter that we were stuck like bugs in the proverbial flypaper, not for the few minutes we had to ourselves, when our last almost-intimate moment was ruined by those awful cats. Kissing Zander made all that melt away and filled my head with sparks instead.

"Oh, here they are," someone said from somewhere behind me. *Blayde.*

We pulled our lips apart reluctantly, and his taste lingered.

"Miro," said Blayde in stride, "meet my brother Zander and Sally, his…well, I'm not exactly sure what she is. We haven't discussed labels. Zander, Sally, meet Miro. They're the one who so kindly got you out of this mess."

We scrambled together so we could both be on our feet, front to front like flies on either side of the same flypaper. My hair tugged at my scalp, half of it caught in the sticky goop, worse now that we had the height difference to deal with.

"Thank you, Miro." Zander kept a tone of respect. "You don't, perchance, have anything that would get us out of this glue?"

"No," said a new voice, maybe Miro. His accent was thick, heavy, and unlike anything I had ever heard before, especially with the translator that made everyone sound like they were somehow from New England. "The glue's only solvent is their live saliva. The only way off is by shedding."

Zander sighed heavily. "Oh, I absolutely loved this coat."

His weight disappeared, and I fell flat on my face. A snicker traveled through the group. I looked up, and with a little shock I realized we were surrounded by at least a dozen people. James grinned sheepishly from Blayde's side, already dry from her run-in with the sea.

"Miro, this is Sally," said Blayde. "Sally, Miro."

"Pleasure," I said, pulling my head up, promptly dropping my jaw in the sand.

Miro was heavily built, tall, and muscular, every inch of his skin a soft brown. His long black hair was pulled back behind his head, shining in the sun like polished obsidian, outlining his sharp features. Everything about his face was sharp, from the high, sculpted cheekbones to the cut of his chin. He wore nothing more than a tight pair of shorts with a strap holding a long, curved blade in place on his hip. His entire chest was ripped like a gladiator's. His skin shone like bronze, outshined only by his dazzling smile as he stared down at me.

Holy hotness, Batman.

"The pleasure is all mine, Sally," he said slowly. "Welcome to the Sands."

"Thanks," I replied as I tried to stand, but the glue held strong.

Zander stepped between me and Miro. "I'm sorry to bother you or your people, but could we have…?"

"Ah, yes. I'll give you some privacy." He turned around, and his people did the same. Without a word between each other, they marched off into the sun, going to work on some of the other fallen plants. Sven was not the only casualty today.

Miro's people moved as one single unit. Every movement was fluid, the motion of one sliding into the other. All with the perfect, identical, resting bitch face.

"We're going to have to cut this," said Blayde, crouching so that she could tug at my trapped hair.

Oh no. "Will it grow back?"

"It'll take a while."

I held my breath as she sliced straight through. In a second, half my hair was gone. I watched the strands of gold drop to the gluey sand. Blayde ruffled what was left on my head. I tried not to think about my new look. Knowing how rarely Zander ever had to shave, I had a bad feeling about how long I'd have to wait until I ever reached that length again.

"Thanks." I slipped my legs out of my gluey PJs. Blayde handed me clothes of simple fabric, woven from something like hemp, and with a start, I realized it was probably the same Sven-like plant fiber. I slipped the clothes on quickly, shocked by how light the materials were, even though they were hides. And by the sudden lack of hair on my shoulders.

"It's cute," said James, giving me a thumbs up. "You're really pulling it off."

"You're not lying to make me feel better, are you?" I took a deep breath. Her saccharine grin was a little too wide for comfort. "I'm still mad at you. Just because you got attacked by a sea snake doesn't mean this is over."

"I'll make it up to you?" She had the distinct look of a late-night TV host pretending his slipup wasn't scripted. "I'm here to help."

"Great." I ran my hand through my too-short hair. "Then why don't I go see what they're up to? Alien cultures and all."

"Can do!" With that, she dashed away toward the others.

"Do I... really look okay?" I asked, turning to Zander, who couldn't have beamed brighter unless he was in active nucleosynthesis. He gently brushed my hair behind my ears, pressing a soft kiss to my forehead.

"You look radiant, my star," he said, and my heart fluttered as it always did at his touch.

Miro cleared his throat, and the flutters shut right the hell up.

"We'd best be going," he said. "My selves are tired, and we have a long way back to the village."

Selves? Miro didn't explain further, and the other people weren't clones or robots—at least at first glance—so maybe I had misheard.

Blayde turned around, her face reverting to some odd neutrality, which we only occasionally saw from her. "How long...?" she asked.

"It's been seven cycles, almost to the day, since you walked into the sand and disappeared," said Miro. Had I imagined it or did his voice just waver? "It is good to see you so well, Slash."

Slash—the name from the memory. So, this was someone she'd known from before, someone who'd known her well enough to not only give her a nickname but survive giving her a nickname. I looked at Zander for answers, but he carried his frown like a boulder. Blayde, however, had a face red as a hot chili pepper. She turned away from all of us.

"Let's talk." She strode off into the sand, Miro close at her heels.

"Great." Zander sighed heavily. "Another goodbye. I thought we'd be so good together after falling for you all over again in Da-Duhui."

"Excuse me?" I asked.

He gently lifted a corner of Sven's lifeless head. "What? This jacket was wonderful. Enough pockets for everything. It's absolutely—no, *was* absolutely—fantastic. And now…"

He reached down to empty the pockets of the abandoned coat. It felt mildly ironic that Zander would have lost his iconic jacket to the same creature he was wearing now. Circle of life and all.

"Goodbyes are hard," I said. "Uh, don't you think it's a little odd between Miro and Blayde?"

"Odd?"

"She's so… I dunno, *off?*"

"Wait, you don't know yet, do you?" He frowned, still avoiding eye contact, distracted by pulling items out of his coat pockets. So many crayons. "Miro is Blayde's ex."

"Her ex?" I asked. "Before or after Jurrah?"

"Before. So long before neither of us can remember them. Which is pretty awkward, considering Miro is Blayde's ex-*spouse*."

EIGHT

THE DESERT IS A GREAT PLACE TO UNEARTH THE PAST

"WHAT DO YOU MEAN, EX-SPOUSE? BLAYDE WAS married? When? How?"

That Blayde could ever remain still enough to get *married* was impossibly far-fetched. Finding anyone who could keep up with her? Even more so. Maybe matrimony didn't mean the same thing in the Sands as on Earth.

Zander stood up and brushed his knees. While he had finished paying his respects to his fallen jacket, the sadness on his face still lingered. "I have no idea. Still can't remember."

"Then how do you know he's her ex?" I asked.

"*They.* And she told me."

"When?"

"Right now."

"Oh, with her eyebrows?"

He nodded. "She was brief, just '*Used to be married; be nice.*'"

I stared at Blayde across the sand where she was caressing Miro's hands. They stared into her eyes in a way I'd never seen anyone do before. Since when could she sit still enough for soulful staring?

"Do you have that feeling she's not telling us everything?" I asked.

"Well, there's only so much you can say in two seconds of eyebrow twitching. That, and I'm pretty sure she doesn't remember either."

"It sure looks like she remembers them."

"I don't understand a thing anyone is saying," said James. She marched up from the group, arms wrapped around her spandex body suit. "But their song is incredibly catchy and stuck in my head. '*Please, can you step off my foot? Please, can you step off my foot?*'"

Dang, we still needed to get James fitted with a translator.

Oblivious, she fixed her eyes on Blayde with the same look of confusion I assumed I had on my own face. "So, who's this Miro guy, eh? And why is Blayde seducing him?"

"They're her ex-spouse," I said. "Apparently."

James's face snapped back on us, mouth wide.

"Spouse?" she squeaked.

"*Ex*-spouse," said Zander. "It's complicated, and that's all I know."

"This is weird. Do you think it was an amicable split? Wow, hand on the chest. Does she have a thing for chest hair?"

"Oh, come on," he said. "They believed she was…I dunno, *ascended* for seven years. Let them reconnect."

"She's not going to waste time, is she?" said James. "We've got places to be, some strange, entire-universe-encapsulating-doom to stop. This isn't the time for reconnecting with old beaus."

"I hate to say this, but I agree," I said. "As much as I'm thrilled Blayde has a lead on her past, we need to get back to tracking down the Dread."

"Do you feel the Dread here?" asked Zander. "No? Exactly. This place is odd. Investigating with a guide is a hundred times better than nothing, even if they were once married to my sister."

"Or maybe it's just because we're in the distant past pre-Dread?" I suggested. "We should go right away."

Blayde appeared at James's side, making her jump. "Miro's invited us for dinner."

Lovely how the universe listens to me. I heaved a heavy sigh. "We don't have the time, Blayde. We need to get back to investigating the Dread."

"Oh, Miro has all the answers. We'll be going tomorrow."

I practically choked on my own saliva. "Hold on, going where? Not the source of the—"

"No, of course not. Just the place with answers. Miro's ancestors' temple of some kind. I apparently went there during my initiation, though I can't remember any of it."

Of course. Because we couldn't just ask Miro to explain, no.

Blayde spun on her heels, sending sand flying, and marched back to Miro. She was a natural here, her stride confident on the shifting sand, like she had been born and raised on this planet. She joined the others as they traded shriveled fish-like creatures and lengths of rope.

"I'm not sure I like this Miro." James shuddered. "There's something eerie about them."

"Oh, right," said Zander. "First hive mind, I take it? Just be polite. You'll get used to it fast."

"Hive mind? Like bees?" asked James since I was too busy gasping and choking on confusion to ask for myself.

"No, not like bees," he scoffed. "And how do you know about the bees?"

"What do you mean? Earth has bees!"

"Earth has…" Zander shook his head. "Well, it had to happen eventually. You might need to start looking into investing in high-quality goggles. Anyway, no, not like bees. Bees are individuals with the same goal in mind. Miro is a hundred or so individuals with the same mind. They can act individually, but all parts are of the same whole. They're just the same person, all at once."

"And Blayde was married to them all?" I asked. "How does that even work?"

"Very carefully, I suppose."

"Are they single now?"

"No, I think they're many."

He grinned a cheeky grin. Thanks, Zander. It was easier to process the strangeness of a hive mind when he was around making stupid jokes about them. I loved that about him. No matter how weird the universe got, he was always willing and eager to be my anchor.

"So, what happens when they're away from their village?" James asked Zander. "Do the other… selves just fall asleep until Miro gets back?"

He cringed. "They're people, Felling. They don't have a range."

"I get that," said James. Her face reddened. "I just thought…"

"It's an innocent question." The body that Blayde had introduced to us, Miro Prime I suppose, joined us. "I am not a 'we.' My mind is simply balanced over multiple bodies."

"No matter where I am in the universe," said another, "my selves still think as one. I am just really good at multitasking."

In unison, the selves gave an overly dramatic wink, which would have been funny if it didn't clench my gut. Zander translated for James as she watched, hugging her middle tighter.

"Blayde tells me we need to take a detour before returning to the village," said Miro Prime. "Have any of you flown on a madrags before?" We shook our heads.

"Well, you'll have to learn fast. There's no other way to the temple."

One of the selves handed Blayde a large, plump fish-like creature, as well as a sturdy rope that she wrapped around both hands, pulling it taut. In front of her, Miro Prime took a step into an empty patch of sand, leaning down to place the palm of their hand on the ground. Then, with swift, precise movements, they tossed their fish high into the air and jumped—just as a freaking *pterodactyl* burst from beneath their feet.

I'm proud I didn't scream at the sight of it.

Just as it caught the fish in mid-air, Miro Prime deftly leapt onto its back, jamming the rope into its open mouth, and they were off, soaring into the air as one.

I would have been awed if I hadn't realized what that meant for me.

"What *is* that?" James gasped, but before she could get an answer, Blayde grabbed her arm and dashed into the sand. She tossed the fish high, leaping in the air and grabbing her creature around the neck as it shot upward, forcing James to clamber up after her. James's wide, wild eyes were the last thing I saw before they flew up after Miro, leaving me gaping on the ground.

Miro's other selves tossed their fish-things in the air, swiftly roping their transport and riding their beasties into the sky. Individual parts of the same being working as one, like an octopus with its many legs—except if those legs weren't connected to their body and each had a different face.

"I guess we're flying," said Zander, staring sadly at the coat he was leaving behind.

He wrapped the rope in his hands, and we stepped forward. Suddenly, my head was full of sounds—waves, voices, calls—and I could feel the soft thrum of *life* through my feet. The sand was conducting sound right through my bones. I could hear everything that moved beneath me, a beast passing in the depths, drilling through the sand like a bullet through its target.

The instant Zander threw the fish, our beast flew up and through the sand, right into Zander's rope. I looped my arms around his waist and together we shot into the air, pressed against its rough, leathery hide. It rushed to catch up with the rest of the flock that was already so far ahead. The head, the beak, the neck, everything was long, as if stretched, leaving us like fleas hitching a ride on a dog. I ducked behind Zander's back to avoid the wind.

I watched through narrowed eyes as the desert flashed beneath us, taking deep breaths to keep the ol' vertigo at bay. Endless sand flew past us, unblemished by cities or roads. It was only broken by a hard border of blue. We had returned to the seaside.

We kept flying, the flock pulling us across the ocean, miles and miles and miles of emerald green. My nose burned with the musky scent of the water, salty and sweet at the same time. Until finally—land. A single freckle of it in an otherwise endless sea, just as flat as the rest.

In unison, the riders slipped the muzzles off their mounts. The creatures nosedived toward the island.

Shit, they couldn't be serious. Anxiety pulsed through my veins, and my stomach twisted into knots that even a Boy Scout couldn't untangle. Zander shifted back, giving me more of his torso to cling to. But maybe it wasn't fear that I felt. Maybe it was something else. Something more like elation was pulsing through me, like the beat of a living heart. Something powerful and old, as if it were there in hiding all along.

This was what it meant to feel alive.

I pulled my head away from the safety of Zander's back, feeling the rush of wind in my face, and forced myself to embrace it. Blayde shot downward past us, hooting as she dove, her hair billowing like a multicolored flame flaring behind her and whipping at James's face. Now we were falling after her with nothing but the wind to cradle us. It ripped my screams from my lips before they could burst into the world. We were gravity's bitches, pulled toward the island like soap dropped in the shower.

Flash. I was back in Da-Duhui, falling *down, down, down* past the highway of cars, lost and getting farther from my anchor with every foot. Only this time I wasn't falling through traffic but a flock. *Flash.* This time I was back in NYC, tumbling toward Central Park after yelling at Killian ambassadors who were trying to recover their lost ship. But I had a handle on that fear and clutched it, remembering how far I've come from the darkness there.

Blayde flung herself off her beast mere seconds before it dove into the sand. Zander did the same, pulling me off with him. We rolled in a tangled mess as we hit the ground. It felt like I had tried to squeeze into the tightest Spanx I owned. The shortest and wildest ride of my life, and I'd once ridden a tiger. I stared up at the brilliant blue sky, the weight of a million suns bearing down on my chest.

I'd done it. I'd landed. I was safe.

Well, safe on an island in the middle of the ocean with nothing—and certainly no temples—for miles around. I sat up and gazed out at the flat expanse of sea. Nope, still nothing. The island couldn't have been more than a hundred meters in diameter. Miro had potentially taken us out here for some quiet murder. There certainly were enough of their selves to even the odds.

Zander hopped up on his feet, planting his arms on his hips, and scanned the horizon. James joined him, taking a similar pose.

"So, where do you think this temple is?" She reached an arm toward me, but I pushed it away, clambering up on my own.

"Still mad at you." I brushed the sand from my new clothes. "But maybe it's a metaphor?"

She groaned. "What, the temple is our own unfulfilled goals? Will *that* help us stop the Dread?"

"Pipe down, agent," said Blayde. "You'll scare it away."

"Scare what? The temple?" I asked.

"It doesn't like it when people talk behind its back," she explained. "Now be polite. It won't show unless we promise it some lovely company."

I glanced over at Zander, but he didn't elaborate on her vague mysticisms. Judging by how high his brows were raised, he was as confused as I was. "Is the temple… a person?"

"No," she scoffed. "Why would it be? It just likes to party, that's all."

And speaking of party, that's exactly what Miro was setting up for us. The temperature dropped dramatically as the sun began to set, but the otherworldly sunset made up for it. Two moons took its place in the sky, bright and white and friendly enough. Miro's many selves had started a roaring campfire in the dead center of the island, surrounding it with mats for sitting. Some of the selves pulled out pieces of chopped-up Sven and started cooking him, while others were breaking out drinks and instruments. They worked fast, moving as one.

"Slash," said one of them, leading Blayde toward Miro Prime. All their selves were grinning wildly as they watched her with soft eyes. "Tonight, we celebrate your return from the wilds."

Blayde blushed, sitting down beside Miro Prime on the mat of honor. We followed close behind, the moderately welcomed relatives.

"We'll have music! And drink! And a feast!" Miro Prime continued. "We'll invite the temple to join in the celebration!"

Live music was provided by a band of Miros singing in perfect harmony. Selves carried leaves from mat to mat, topped high with what I'm pretty sure was roasted

Sven. With nothing else to eat, I was forced to taste. He turned out to be tangy in a sweet-and-sour kind of way, fibrous like a carrot.

"Has anyone explained about the temple yet?" asked James. "As much as I'd love to party, we are on a mission here."

I should have been the one saying that. I frowned into my Sven. And here I had been worried James would get side-tracked by alien life.

"I told you the temple only shows itself if the mood is right. So, loosen up and party a little!" Blayde handed her a waterskin, swishing it around provocatively. Miro Prime said nothing, watching her with soft eyes. "Have a drink or something. The success of this mission depends on it."

Zander and I exchanged quick glances. The gist of it seemed to be that Blayde had indigestion, but that couldn't be it, could it? Something was up with her, and it was more than meeting with Miro.

"You realize I'm not like you, right?" said James, raising an eyebrow. "I *do* get drunk."

"All part of the temple summoning," said Blayde. "But fine, you do you."

"The temple doesn't like it when you *over* imbibe," said Miro Prime, but Blayde wasn't listening. She guzzled down at least half of that waterskin without taking a breath. Her face flushed, but she went back for the second half, not breaking eye contact with James.

Zander ripped it from her hands. "That's quite enough of that."

"What?" Blayde's face was now a deep crimson. "You said to loosen up."

"No," said James. "That was *you.*"

Blayde didn't seem to hear her. "I'm loose. Oh, I'm way loose. Just you see how loose."

"You should probably stop saying that," I said. "Not sure it's meaning what you want it to mean."

"Don't care!" She hopped to her feet. "Oh, a drum circle. Drum circles are fun. They're loose. *I'm* loose."

She ran into the circle of dancers without another look back. I stared at her, biting my lip. Where was the Blayde I knew? She had transformed into a full-fledged party animal, dancing so hard that soon she was alone on the makeshift dancefloor, clapping offbeat with the music and crying loud *woo*s for the entire planet to hear. Her shirt didn't last a minute.

"This is not good," said Zander.

Maybe this booze was stronger than I gave it credit for. I'd only ever seen her fully drunk once before, and even in that state she'd singlehandedly fought massive cyborgs and we'd woken in an enemy jail. No more alien booze for me. But this seemed like more than just alcohol at play. Whatever was in that waterskin had brought out an entirely different side of her—and fast. Maybe she really did want to cut loose.

Or maybe…something about being around Miro was bringing this out of her. And it wasn't just to summon some old temple. She reminded me of those days I'd thought I could just party the sad away, but what did she have to be sad about? Being here had made her emotionally vulnerable, and I had no idea what to do.

"I'm the frashing desert queen," Blayde screamed as she hopped from foot to foot. Miro's selves cheered, watching Blayde dance her drunken heart out. The band started playing faster, making her spin more wildly around the bonfire. Miro Prime clapped along with the music.

"Let her have her fun," I said. "She can't be the almighty *Iron* forever. Sometimes she's just gotta…dance."

"Not while she's this drunk, though," said Zander.

"Something's wrong," agreed Miro Prime. "She wasn't like this before."

"CONGA!" Blayde bellowed. She pranced around in a circle, hands on invisible hips in front of her. *"Da-da-da-da-da, hey!"*

Most definitely not Blayde. All this talk of needing to remember, but here she was drinking to forget. Or maybe she was trying to get back at me for getting in her way in the past. This was my first mission, after all. Did she want me to fail?

Zander sighed. "I'm putting an end to this before it goes too far."

Miro Prime nodded slowly. "Maybe she needs to air her grievances through dance."

"Is dancing the conga while singing the original *Star Trek* theme song really the best way for her to do that?" I asked, thoroughly impressed by Blayde's vocal range.

Miro Prime raised a skeptical eyebrow. "*Star Trek?*"

"Earth entertainment," I said, turning back to Zander. "Blayde knows *Star Trek?*"

"It's not *Star Trek,*" he said. "It's Kork's theme on the *Traveler*—oh. He stole that, too, didn't he?"

We watched her lead the dancers around the fire, laughing and singing. They seemed to truly love her. Then again, seeing as they were a hive mind, she technically had been in a relationship with all of them.

"Whatever this is, I'm going to be a good friend," said James. She rushed to Blayde's side, placed her hand on her waist, yelled a very loud "CONGA," and joined in the dance.

Zander's face fell into his hands. "This isn't happening. Maybe I collapsed in the desert, and I'm hallucinating from heat stroke."

"I thought we couldn't get heat stroke," I said.

"Don't speak to me, imaginary Sally. Find help."

"You're not hallucinating. James is dancing the conga with drunk, shirtless Blayde. Oh, and a few of Miro's selves. Who are also not wearing shirts. Now James has gotten rid of hers. Seriously, are these people allergic to shirts?"

"I can stop dancing," said Miro, coolly. Despite their worry, it didn't sound like they fully intended to stop. "But someone needs to talk to her gently. The temple won't show if I kill the mood."

"Just what I was planning on doing," said Zander, slipping into the fold.

We watched Zander as he joined her, saying something incomprehensible at this distance.

"I'm the queen of interstellar diplomacy!" Blayde shouted, batting Zander away. "You cannot arrest me for bringing peace!"

And she rushed away, leading the conga line toward the bonfire. James followed behind her, whooping with glee.

"Is she…" Miro turned to me. "Is she and that James, are the two of them… are they romantically engaged with each other?"

"What?" I snorted. "Blayde and James? Never. You know, only a few hours ago, I had no idea she was even capable of *meaningful, long-term commitments.*"

The thought of them together hadn't even occurred to me, and now that it had been suggested, it was the most ridiculous thing that my brain had ever conjured up. Blayde pulled away from the conga line, hopping and clapping like a cartoon kangaroo. The drunken chanting of the original *Star Trek* theme filled the air as the multi-person joined in. I clenched my fists. We had more important things to be doing.

"But they seem so…" Miro Prime shivered slightly despite the bonfire. "She cares for her. Last I saw Slash, she would cut loose through feats of strength. Part of her fierce charm, I guess, though her fierceness appears to be wavering. She seems to have lost something. Part of herself. Trust me, I know what that feels like."

Zander had managed to get a word in again, and whatever it was, it made Blayde happy because he now ended up at the head of the conga line.

"Things were complicated when she left." Miro Prime traced a circle in the sand with the tip of his finger. "I can understand how being back here could be difficult for her."

I nodded. It seemed Blayde was remembering more than she let on, and maybe it wasn't a good thing. But it didn't excuse the way she was behaving. Not on my watch.

"Do you dance?" I asked Miro, trying to change the subject. If I had any doubt of their intimacy, it had evaporated right there. Blayde was still recovering from the events of the library but had been hiding it so well even I sometimes thought it was completely behind her. But you can't just walk away from trauma. The fact Miro, too, could see her wavering was evidence they knew her better than most ever get the chance to.

"No." Miro waved to the dancers. "As you can see, the creator gave some people feet to dance and others feet to fight. So goes the way of the universe."

"Yet dancing feet and fighting feet may sometimes be one and the same."

"You may be wiser than you appear, Sally."

I blushed before it hit me that it wasn't much of a compliment.

"But they're all you. How are some of them better if you're all the same?" I said, cringing at the awkwardness of my question. It wasn't every day you could pick the mind of a hive mind.

"My mind is spread across every one of us, but each of my bodies is unique. I won't bore you with the details of my division cycle, but each body has its own gifts. I've evolved into quite a skilled volleyball team, if I do say so myself."

"I imagine there's not much else to do on this planet," I said. "If you're the only person here and all. Doesn't it get lonely?"

"Intensely," they said, nodding vigorously. "There's only so many times you can play rock-paper-scissors against yourself. And don't get me started on poker. But I've been getting into music lately. Writing my own ballads. Do you want to hear?"

They gestured to the band, every single member turning to me and bursting into the same grin at once.

I wasn't really in the mood for ballads, so I evaded his question with another. "Why do you stay? If you put everyone—I mean, all your selves—together, you could go anywhere."

"It's not that simple. We're—and by *we*, I mean hive minds in general—we're, by nature, incredibly territorial. Too many heads to butt heads with, not enough space. I'm what you might call an introvert. In any case, I must protect the temple. It's essential for the future, though I can't remember why."

"So, the temple hides…unless there's a party?"

"Well, if I'm partying, it knows it's safe to come out." They shrugged. "Though I've been a little distracted by Slash. Counted collectively, my selves have had too much to drink, and the temple won't show if I'm entirely hungover. A few are taking this burden on their own."

They indicated a pile of bodies off by the shore, rolling in the sand and singing so completely out of tune that the space between their notes could be a masterpiece. Ah, so the opposite of a designated driver: the multi-person booze sponges.

"You tricked me!" Blayde staggered over to our mat, hands on Zander's hips as he led the conga line right to us. "You tricked me through dance!"

"Right." Miro Prime clapped their hands together, grinning. "Ritual time!"

Zander helped Blayde to the mat next to Miro. James followed close behind, dropping heavy next to me. The second Blayde's butt hit the mat, her eyes closed, and she dropped her head on James's shoulder, promptly falling asleep. Thankfully Zander and I were still sober enough to follow.

"Ritual?" I asked.

"You never mentioned a ritual," added Zander.

Miro took a deep breath. "What you first have to understand is no one other than me has ever entered the walls of my temple—except for Blayde."

Zander lifted an eyebrow. "*We* don't have to propose to anyone, do we?"

"No, I am granting you permission to enter at Blayde's request," they said. "You just have to understand it is deeply personal for me; the temple collects my memories. Even spread between all my selves, the brainpower necessary to hold every thought is too great. The temple is my chance to unburden."

Zander let out a small breath, as did I. "So, what's the ritual? If the temple shows because we're partying…"

"Right," said Miro Prime. "We need the *other* waterskin."

They grabbed a full waterskin from their hip and took a long gulp and swished it around in their mouth before spitting back the contents. Their brows knotted together, their tongue lapping at their teeth. Whatever it was, it wasn't tasty.

"Drink," they ordered, handing Zander the waterskin.

"Not until you tell me what this is," he said, cringing.

"Let me put it this way. Would you like to be eaten alive by the personification of the ocean?" When we didn't answer, Miro lifted a bushy eyebrow. "I thought not. The temple opens only to me. We need to trick it into thinking you're all my selves."

I shuddered at the thought. For me, getting eaten alive could very well mean living a few centuries as an alien beast's tapeworm. Not a thrilling concept. But between that and what was in the waterskin…

"But if this is just for us, how can it be a ritual?" I asked.

Miro's grin grew impossibly wider. "Because it sounds more dramatic that way."

"Blayde?" Zander gave her shoulder a little shake. "Come on, you have to drink this spit juice to cleanse you for a temple run tomorrow."

"I don't wanna," said Blayde lazily. "I've had it before."

"Come on. Drink up," said Miro Prime, smiling with only the corners of their lips. Dang, they'd really missed her.

"Do I have to?" Blayde whined.

"Yep." Zander shook the waterskin in front of her face. It sloshed around in the hide like thick cream. I bit down on my tongue to keep from gagging.

Zander kept the lip of the waterskin in Blayde's mouth as she drank, her face contorting like she'd been hit by an invisible boxer.

"Was that a leg?" she asked, and Zander put his hand over her mouth to keep the liquid down before handing the waterskin to me.

I brought the lip to my mouth. The taste was worse than I imagined. Thick as honey but sour instead of sweet, it stuck to my mouth and throat like a dead toad that still wanted to live. I fought it all the way down.

"That's it? We're you?" I asked.

Miro shook their head. "Now, you spend the night buried in sand."

"Can somebody translate?" asked James. "I was told to drink the spit juice. I drank the spit juice."

"We gotta get buried in sand," I said.

Miro nodded. "In order to convince the temple you're one of my selves, you need your mind to be ready. Connected to all things. You disrobe and sleep in the drum sand, and you immerse yourself in the life of this world. Only when you understand that life may hide underneath what seems dead can you understand the nature of our history."

"Let me get this straight," I said. "To get information you could literally just tell us, I have to sleep buried in the sand, *nude*, and then make my way through a mysterious temple that may or may not kill me and my friends?"

"Hold up, did you say *nude*?" James's brows furrowed.

"You got it," said Miro cheerfully. "Trust me, the drink was the worst part. Now all you have to do is sleep while we party for the temple."

"I'm off my planet for one day, and this is what I get?" James muttered. "A desert planet with things that want to kill me. Whatever happened to all those tropical paradises? When this is over, y'all are taking me to Naboo, not space Australia."

NINE

THE NOT SO A-MAZE-ING RACE

I LEANED MY HEAD BACK, TRYING TO IGNORE THE sand in my crotch. Not only was the position uncomfortable, but the drum sand amplified everything around like my head was on a speaker. Blayde was walking directly on my eardrums.

I could hear *everything*. James's beating heart; Zander's even breaths. The party continuing on the other side of the island. The waves rippling on the beach. Even as Blayde stepped off the patch of drum sand, returning to Miro, the sand beneath me was alive, writhing and cruel, conducting sound through my body. I bit my lip as something skittered deep beneath me. The noise took over my mind and overwhelmed all my other senses. I felt the whole world through my skin, in the vibrations of the sand. Small creatures like the madrags and far below me, hundreds, maybe thousands of miles down, a colossus that swam through the sand as gracefully as a whale through water. Life under sand.

I needed to focus on something else—something smaller. Something less, well, less shit-your-pants terrifying. Off to my right, I felt the rapid heartbeat of a fellow human, the almost passed-out-drunk James Felling, who groaned softly. I anchored myself on the sound.

"You breathe incredibly loudly for someone who doesn't have to," James said suddenly. If it wasn't for the slab of wax above me, I would have jumped straight out of my skin.

"I *do* have to breathe," I replied. The sand on my face was becoming a whole other focal point, and I was desperate to rub it away.

"No, you don't."

"Yeah, I do."

"So, what happens if you hold your breath?" she asked.

I puffed out my cheeks like a blowfish, though I doubted she could see me from where she was buried. Other than being a little uncomfortable, I didn't feel myself choking.

"You see what I mean?" She laughed, a cheerful, chiming laugh that probably could be heard through the entire desert. "Immortality, man."

I exhaled loudly. Zander said nothing. I could see him if I turned my head just so, but he was resting, eyes closed, almost as if asleep. Totally ignoring us—or trying to.

James's heart picked up a beat. "So, how many times have you died?"

I didn't have enough water in my mouth for a spit take but still sent sand flying. "Hey, you can't ask me that!"

"Oh, sorry. But come on, how many times have you died?"

"I don't even know anymore." I had a rough estimate, but I didn't want to share it. "I haven't died in a while. That's pretty nice."

"I can imagine." She nodded.

I took a deep breath; one I apparently didn't need to take. "You should sleep, James."

"What about sleep? Do you need to sleep?"

I groaned. "Yes, James, I do need to sleep. We all get loopy without sleep."

"Well, excuse me," she muttered. "It's my first night away from Earth, okay? I'm a little too excited to sleep. That and there's stuff under the sand that confuses me."

I was starting to wish I had indulged a little in the local liquor to ease myself into this creepy night of sandy crotches and giant alien monsters.

"Look," she said, her voice dropping low, "I'm sorry I forced my way along. It was wrong of me. I acted on impulse, but that's not an excuse."

An apology was the last thing I expected tonight. "You crossed a boundary, James." I bit my lip. My mouth tasted sour. "We could have ended up anywhere else in the universe."

"I know." She took a deep breath. "I was just…"

"Eager to see space?"

"It's been my life's work," she said, her voice breaking. Was she crying? "Ever since the Siblings saved me as a kid. Ever since I found proof of their existence, that I hadn't imagined them. And then I met you and…"

"You thought I would be an easy ticket off world?"

"N-no!" her voice hitched. "Sally, believe me, when I met you, my first and only thought was that I'd finally met someone who'd been through the same experience as me. A kindred spirit. Only then you went and…well, we're no longer the same, are we?"

I sunk deeper into the sand. James had fought hard to earn my trust before, had saved me more times than I could count. If I were in her shoes, wouldn't I have done the exact same thing to see the stars?"

"I want to help," she said. "I want to make a difference. I've been working toward this my whole life."

"But you have a family on Earth. It's dangerous out here. Look what happened just today! What would we tell them if you died on alien soil?"

"You have family too." Her voice turned cold. "I had to ask myself the very same question when I was covering for you."

The sand was now up to my ears. Even in the dark desert night, my face was hot with shame. "I wasn't going to die."

"But were you ever going to come back? Did you even know?" She took a deep breath. "I have training. Skills. And I took an oath to my country that I would stand for what is right, no matter the cost."

"Still, you could have asked."

The alien sound was drowned out by the sound of James's silence.

Finally, she spoke. "So where do we go from here?"

"Forward," I said. "And we keep you alive."

"I can keep myself alive, thank you very much."

I suppose that must have been enough for James because her breathing slowed, and, from the sound of her heartbeat through the sand, she'd fallen asleep, conked out with her head back against the pillow of sand. Thanks, booze and emotional heart-to-heart.

The calm rhythm of the planet was becoming more natural now. The beats of the sand ebbed and rose like a rushing river, both noisy and soothing at once. This could maybe be a very expensive spa treatment.

Footsteps stomped toward us. Maybe Blayde was coming with a drink after all, but they were too heavy for her dancing feet. The steps stopped by Zander.

"May I speak with you?" Miro Prime's voice reverberated through the air and sand.

"What about this ritual?" asked Zander.

Miro snorted, dropping on the sand. "Screw tradition. You're aliens."

"Good point. What is it you wanted?"

I really shouldn't be eavesdropping, though I literally had nowhere to go or any way to leave. I remained still in my sandy bed—better not let them know I was awake and ruin this for them.

I could hear Miro's pulse through the sand, and it was already faster than James's. "It's about your sister. Well, we were married, and she's still interested, isn't she? I mean, we were promised for *life*. So, I go and visit her in her tent and—"

Zander groaned. "Stop right there. This isn't the kind of advice I was planning on giving."

"But she threw me out," Miro continued. "Please tell me, what has happened to her? She barely seems to remember me. Sometimes she looks at me with such admiration, but no love. It's as if she's looking at a picture of me or a reflection. What happened to the woman I married?"

"You may not want to hear this."

"Please. I went for seven years without my beloved. Please, please tell me what has happened to her; I fear she has not fully returned."

Yet, some part of her *had* returned to the Sands—the part that remembered small details, the part that had found the need to lose herself in drink tonight.

"Well," Zander's words stretched like taffy. "you see, Miro, Blayde isn't like human women."

"I know *that* already."

"How to put this delicately? Seven years for you was much more for Blayde. Much, much more…"

"But she has not aged?"

"It's very complicated. You see, Blayde hasn't been here for so long she has forgotten—"

"WHAT?" Miro bellowed, loud enough it made James squawk before passing out again. "She forgot me entirely? No, she couldn't have…"

"I'm so sorry, Miro."

Miro's breathing was difficult, catching. It filled the night air. "She remembers nothing of us?"

"Nothing."

"Nothing of Reelaiah?"

"Who?"

"Our son."

Zander's fists clenched under the sand, sending creatures scampering away in all directions. I bit my tongue to keep myself from gasping. *Of course.* She had been pregnant in the memory, not that we'd had any time to ponder the implications. I hadn't had the courage to ask.

I should have asked.

"Blayde had a *son*?"

"He never lived." Miro's voice dropped to a whisper. "In the same day I lost my son, I lost my wife."

My heart sunk down the black pit and out the other side of the planet. I had dozens of questions. Hundreds. Like how a child could even come out of a situation like hers, with an immortal mother and hive mind other. Then, I hated myself for letting my mind go there when I finally understood why Blayde was acting the way she did tonight.

She must have remembered. Not everything, but enough. The pain… I couldn't even imagine.

And I'd gotten angry at her.

Zander took a deep breath. "How?"

"She walked into the desert and a storm swept her away. We assumed she was taken by the gods, as the prophet foretold."

"The prophet?"

"The first of me. He left a prophecy for many of us after his passing. Mine said I would wed a woman who emerged from the desert only to return to it when her time was up. All very confusing and such," Miro said softly. "But Blayde cannot remember any of it?"

"Nothing."

Maybe he was being kind. Maybe he hadn't made the connection. I stifled a sob. I couldn't sit here, trapped in sand, knowing my friend was in pain. Even if she might not be able to talk about it, I had to be there for her. I tried to pull my hand free, but I was trapped here.

"She is the lucky one," said Miro. "I will never live long enough to forget the pain. It will only be added to the collection in the temple. If she remembers the boy… It was too much once, but a second time?"

"A boy," said Zander. "My… nephew, I guess. What was he like?"

Miro fell back against the sand, the sound like thunder on my eardrums. "Black hair. Pitch-black hair. That much is still as clear as day in my mind. It was just like his mother's back then. Her hair is so strange now.

It makes her look younger, less herself. The woman who made the creatures of both sand and sea kneel at her feet without pride or hate. She's different now."

"It has been a *very* long time."

"It has." Miro paused. "You can tell, just by looking at her. Her eyes, she's seen…well, she's seen too much. So much her head cannot handle it. Trust me, I know. I'm currently spread across a hundred and twelve minds with a few hundred years backed up on crystal. Yet, still, I would have hoped something of me remained. Some little memory, something she finds reassurance in. It does seem like she's been needing some of that."

"I'm so sorry," Zander said slowly.

"Don't be. You have nothing to do with this." Miro sighed. Thunder rumbled through the sand as he pushed himself back up to his feet. "Nothing happened, you hear me? We did not speak. I never interrupted the ritual."

"I sat out here alone all night."

"Good."

Miro walked away as proudly as when he arrived, head held high and long strides in his gait. I sank deeper still into the sand. The sounds around me were louder than ever, the heartbeat of an entire ecosystem. I poured my focus into them, as I should have when Miro first approached. I shouldn't have eavesdropped. I shouldn't have—

Deep breaths, Sally Webber. Any more thoughts, and you're going to spiral.

Blayde was a mother, and she had no memory of it. And while I shouldn't have been thinking about myself in this moment, I couldn't help where my mind wandered. What would happen to me? I'd only ever thought of motherhood in the way busy people do—as a possible future amid others, a question that would come up when the time was right. I was young and had dreams, dreams that didn't exactly include children right away.

And now I was…something else. Could I be a mother if I wanted to be one day? Or had immortality stripped me of that future? Or could I one day be one and just…forget?

All this to stop my thoughts from wandering over to the knowledge that she had *forgotten*. Zander had said that their memory only went back so far, but this would be something you'd remember, right? Blayde couldn't have lived long enough to have forgotten *this*?

What else had the two of them lost to time?

Somehow, I managed to close my eyes and kept them closed until morning, no further emotional heart-to-hearts raising me from my slumber.

· · · · · · · ●· · · · · · · · ·

I'D NEVER UNDERSTOOD WHAT IT MEANT TO HAVE one's head ring like a gong until I woke up hungover in musical sand. It also turned out that I drool in my sleep, which I now knew because I seemed to have given myself a sand goatee at some point in the night.

"Sleep okay?" asked Blayde as she stomped over the wax seal that kept me bound, sending more sand flying into my face.

"Shhh," I begged, taking the fur she handed me, though it wasn't going to do a lick of good against the grains in all my nooks and crannies. I completely relate to Anakin. Sand was my mortal enemy now—I would wage war against it. Maybe this was my first step toward the dark side.

I get it now, why Zander's oh-so ominous nickname was Sand. My God, I get it now.

"So, did you try talking to the monster in the middle of the planet?" she asked.

I stopped in my tracks, the fur rough on my leg. "No? Did you?"

"Of course. He officiated our wedding."

She was probably messing with me.

Probably.

She handed me some clean clothes in exchange for the fur and darted off to help James, each footstep echoing through the drum sand. If she had had a rough night, she gave no sign of it. It hit me how little I knew this woman, no matter how much I wanted to believe otherwise. How I might have known her for almost a fifth of my life, but I was just a blip in hers.

"How about you?" I asked, trying to ease my way into it. "How are you holding up?"

She shook her head. "Hangovers aren't in my vocabulary."

"I mean… you remember, don't you?"

She pursed her lips, saying nothing. Screw decorum. I ran up to her, wrapping her in my arms, pulling her against me. She said nothing but dropped her forehead against my neck, and I knew then and there that Blayde was as human as the rest of us and was hurting deeper than I'd ever understand.

"Not everything," she whispered. "Images. The second we came back here. Like they couldn't bear to be locked up anymore."

Zander strode up beside us. How he managed to look so handsome in desert wraps never ceased to amaze me. For an instant, he reminded me of the first day we met, though a hell of a lot cleaner. He wrapped his arms around the two of us and we stood there, a Blayde sandwich.

"Right, enough of that," she said, pushing us off. "Does anyone have bad vibes about this?"

I met her gaze, trying to convey as much as I could in just one look: that this wasn't over, that I could be there for her, that we could talk. But this was Blayde. It was harder to get her to open up than a Bond villain before the third act.

"In what way?" asked Zander, glancing over his shoulder at the other Miros.

"It just feels as if someone has been planning this," she said. "How we got here, how quickly we found the tribe—there's something larger happening."

"What if it's us?" I asked. "We were the ones who left ourselves the memories at Meedian's. What if we put all this in place?"

"To what end?" Zander gave my hand a tight squeeze. "If the memories had been forgotten but left behind by future selves…"

I shook my head. The timeline didn't work out. "And what does any of this have to do with the Dread?" I wrapped his arm around me like a safety blanket. "If we're leaving ourselves clues, then this has to lead to something, but right now none of it connects to anything."

Blayde crossed her arms over her chest. "I don't like feeling like a pawn in anyone's game. Not even my own."

"Honorary selves," said Miro, all the selves waving in unison, "the party is over! It's time!"

The Miro selves dipped their calves into the sea, which didn't seem to like them that much because the water ran away from them. It pulled back, farther and farther and farther, until all we could see was a bubbling wave, growing until it was as tall as a house or church—a *temple*.

I clutched Zander's hand tighter. Water flowed down in spurts, revealing structures within the ocean itself. A tower then a turret. Minarets carved of melted sand. Dark and empty windows carved into shuddering mud.

How was this happening? I had assumed Miro had meant the temple would open after the party, not literally rise from the ocean. It was the kind of technology that made you believe in magic.

Finally free of water, the temple stood steaming under the hot morning sun. It towered high above us, taller than anything on this planet, hundreds of meters of carved stone worn by erosion. The stone turrets and spires so perfectly built that even after all the wear it was still beautiful, as if Gaudi had gotten shipwrecked here without a volleyball to befriend.

"Pretty solid metaphor," James muttered. Blayde gave her a sharp shush.

The rest of the wave crashed down, leaving the temple anchored in the surf, water rushing up the beach and kissing our bare feet.

"It will return to the depths at sunset, whether or not you are still inside," said Miro Prime. All their selves came back to circle us, shaking our hands in turn. "Good luck to you—all of you."

"Thanks, Miro," I said, trying to look them each in the eye in turn. "This means a lot to us."

"Just… come back and visit some time?" they asked, every self grinning.

"Last one there buys drinks!" shouted Blayde, before diving into the water. James followed suit without hesitation.

The air on the beach got thin as Miro held their breath. They were watching her leave again, and it couldn't have been easy.

"We'll be back," said Zander. "I promise, we'll see you again."

And with that, he leapt into the sea.

"I'm sorry about the booby traps!" Miro yelled at the sea.

"Booby traps?" I didn't have time to lose my nerve when we were this close to answers, whatever they were.

I took a deep breath and plunged into the surf. It was clear this wasn't my ocean. The water was uncomfortably warm and smelled oddly of donuts. That would probably have been pleasant if I didn't have to brush bones away from my face. I surfaced immediately, gasping and spitting the water out. I hadn't made it more than a meter in.

I grappled with my gag reflex and pushed myself forward and through. The water was thick like oil, and despite the shimmering smooth surface on top, the currents were wild, pushing me back as I powered through. It grabbed at my clothes, threatening to pull me under.

The waves pushed me against the temple wall, and I spat sticky water from my mouth. There wasn't an edge, nothing I could cling to pull myself up and out of the disgusting sea. Instead, I was flung against the base of the temple again, blinded by waves, knocking the wind out of me each time.

A thick arm dropped into the water in front of me and I latched onto it, grabbing tightly. Zander. He hoisted me up as I coughed water from my lungs. Smooth stone slid under my belly, cold against my skin.

I rolled over and looked up. Zander was soaked to the bone and his clothes clung to his body. He reached down again, and, like a rabbit from a hat, pulled James from the rushing waves. Her eyes were shut, her body limp.

"Felling!" Blayde scrambled to her side then looked up at Zander. "Is she breathing?"

A small cough from James brought up more water. Her eyes blinked open, dramatically slow. When she noticed all our eyes on her, she rigidly stood as if nothing was wrong in the slightest.

"What? Are we going, or are we still waiting for something?"

Silence fell over us. We had made it to the temple, and the harrowing swim hadn't even been a part of the entrance exam. Small pillars of rock surrounded our small landing like an arena, the smallest about my height, the tallest at the back a few stories high. Sunlight trickled in the center but didn't reach the walls behind the pillars.

"What is this place?" I finally asked. A crash of water filled the empty space—Zander, wringing out his hair.

"I don't remember," Blayde said, but her face burst into a dazzling grin. "Let's go find out, shall we?"

She waved her hand toward the back wall, and as my eyes adjusted to the light, I realized it wasn't a wall behind the tallest pillars but two stone doors. I stumbled toward them, taking in the eroded carvings, intricate images of monsters—all sharp teeth and cruel smiles— along with a few of Miro in power poses.

"You ready for this?" Blayde cracked her fingers with a cunning smile.

"You know it," Zander breathed.

Blayde ran her sweaty palm down the door, then took a step back, waving her arms wide. But whatever she expected to happen…didn't. Just silence and the crash of waves behind us.

Blayde's grin turned to a scowl. "Great. Anyone got a better idea?"

"You can't remember how to open the door?" James asked, mouth agape.

"Anybody hear that?" Zander asked.

Nothing good ever starts with somebody asking if you've just heard something. Either they're imagining things, in which case they might need time to sit down, raise their blood sugar, and have a good long chat—lovely, but time-consuming—or they really did hear something terrible and you're all about to die.

Exceptions can be made for surprise parties, but they also involve losing an afternoon to social conventions when you'd much rather be eating cake alone.

The low rumble of the temple walls was probably not a surprise party. The fact that it was growing louder made things worse. The sea simmered, waves crashing harder against the floor, sending vibrations up the walls. The spray smacked me hard across the mouth, leaving the taste of salty donuts on my tongue.

"I thought this place would only sink at sundown!" I grabbed a pillar as a massive wave crashed over us. The water sent us scrambling.

"It's not the island," Zander shouted back.

As if to prove his point, a blue pillar shot out of the water beside us—a sea serpent. It glared down at us, roaring. A *familiar* roar—the same one that turned my heart cold yesterday on the beach.

"Hey look!" Blayde nudged James in the ribs. "Your buddy followed you home! What are you gonna call it?"

James shoved her off as another indignant ocean roar filled the air. Sea spittle showered over all of us, thoroughly putting me off donuts for another century. The beast slashed forward like a terrible oversized rubber cobra, whip fast. Zander leapt in front of James, and his hands were gobbled up in one go.

I screamed—good god did I scream. Not gonna lie, seeing your boyfriend's hands sliced off in a stream of fresh, spurting blood was definitely scream-worthy material. His hands flopped between the monster's teeth, somehow still full of life, blood spraying everywhere.

Why was he on this planet's menu?

I grabbed his arm, dragging him to the door. The serpent struck, its teeth slamming hard into the stone mere inches from my feet. I scrambled away, pulling Zander with me, as it ripped its head back up. Blayde and James were left stranded on the other side of the arena.

"There's got to be a clue here somewhere." Zander ran his stum through his hair, streaking blood. "Think, Zander, you hot piece of brainy ass, think!"

"Maybe it has something to do with these carvings?" I pointed at the door even as I stared back over my shoulder. Its attention seemed entirely on Blayde and James.

"Maybe instead of body heat, it needs emotional heat? Show the door some love? Oh yes, you're a pretty door. I've never met a door before. Love your elaborate carvings. So elegant. So refined." He cooed at the door, running his now baby hands down the carvings in a way that warranted couple's therapy. My chest tingled—I never thought I would feel jealous of a door.

"Buy it a drink first, jeez," I said, looking away, my face hot. The door had more time alone with Zander than I had.

All that heat drained as I took in the scene before me. James must have really pissed off the beast somehow because its whole focus was on her. Thankfully somewhere in her not-FBI training she had learned how to dodge, and she was managing quite well to leap out of the way at the very last second, a toreador avoiding the angry space-sea bull. As she rolled, she caught my gaze, and with a nod of understanding she sprung our way, only to be blocked by the beast once again. It struck the ground before her with such strength that she toppled over, rolling onto her back.

I couldn't watch that either, so I turned back to Zander. We had to get this door open and fast. "What if this creature is one of the booby traps?"

He kept creepily caressing the door. "Not everything is a futuristic sci-fi test, Sally."

"Says the man trying to flirt his way into a door's pants," I said. "Seriously, that monster showed up when we did."

"Probably because it's got a taste for James."

The beast roared again, rearing back and shaking in apparent pain. The air filled with strident cries as it struck where James had been only a second earlier. The creature's eye was steaming, scorched by the tiniest of lasers. It pulled back, the whip about to snap—

Blayde and the serpent leapt at James simultaneously, but Blayde reached her first, pushing her aside as the beast's teeth slashed at her skin, shredding her arms to ribbons in an instant. Good thing she didn't care.

"How many times do I need to save your life for you to get it into your puny human brain that you need to pay attention?" Blayde spat at James. "You're supposed to be trained for this shit!"

"I'm doing quite well on my own, thank you." James threw up her hands. "Despite sea serpents with personal vendettas not being in the sims."

"Don't talk back, run!" Blayde ordered, shoving James at us. I grabbed her and pulled her against the door. Blayde kept her eyes riveted on the beast, shaking her arm as if it would make it heal faster. "Get that frashing door open!"

"We need to connect with it," said Zander. "Convince it we're Miro."

"How are we supposed to connect with the door if you're literally single-minded, baby hands McGee?" said Blayde.

"If I had my hands, I would have a nice, big single mind for you!" said Zander, his tiny baby hands clumsily raising a single finger.

The beast rose again, higher than before. It was blinded, angry. Playtime was over. Dinnertime was about to begin. It was going to strike. We braced ourselves against the doors, ready to fight back.

"For the love of—" screamed James, spinning around to face the door. "Will you *please* let us through?"

And then the impossible happened. We collapsed through the open doorway. I scrambled to my feet. The beast thrust its head at the door, its long neck stretching to the point where I thought it would snap. The door slid shut, swatting Zander on the way as he threw his now toddler-sized hands toward the sea beast and made a sign no tiny fingers should ever make. With a low, resonating crash, we were flung into a small atrium, sandwiched between two smooth walls. The walls glowed a dainty shade of blue.

A magic word. I supposed courtesy *did* open doors. Zander had the right idea going the seduction route; he just went a little too hard. He should have just asked first.

My legs smarted, which was a first in a long, long time. Add to that a tightness in my chest that bubbled up out of nowhere. It wasn't anxiety, it wasn't fear, no. It was…no, it couldn't be.

My heartbeat. My heartbeat was back.

I groaned as my skin began to tingle, a wave spreading from my now-beating heart to fill my body with feeling once again. The palms of my hands burned, the small scratches from our close encounter with death coming to life and coming alight with a tingling pain. As a human, I would probably barely have noticed them, but to what I was now, it was like clutching live flames.

This couldn't be happening.

"Zander!"

I fell to my knees as he toppled over beside me, my hand clutching his chest. His *beating* chest. My hand shook as I felt the pulse against my palm. Whatever this was, it was happening to him too. His breath was shallow, ragged.

But it was Blayde's scream that brought reality crashing in. She fell to the floor, wailing as she grabbed the remains of her arm. Her hands trembled, now so bloodied. Her head pressed against the cold stone to soothe the agony, her cries subsiding to sobs. No fresh skin was visible underneath the flow of red.

"No, no, no, no." Zander pushed himself up, heaving.

He ripped his shirt, taking the cloth to her wounds. James was already there, rubbing a soothing hand down Blayde's back as they bound up what was left of her arm. Blayde glared at her brother before passing out in James's arms.

"What's happening to her?" James clutched her against her chest in wide-eyed shock.

"She's bleeding out," said Zander.

"But it'll heal, won't it?" James asked, as Zander finished tying the bandage.

"I don't know." He glanced up at me. "You, too?"

I nodded. Goosebumps ran up my arms. "It's this place. For some reason, we seem to be…*mortal* in here."

A shiver ran through me. I was cold—cold, wet, and miserable. For the first time in ages, I realized how much my new biology had taken discomfort out of the equation. Even my mind was starting to turn on me, the little voices stepping out of the woodwork, the kind the Dread fed into.

"Mortal." James swallowed heavily, running her tongue over her lips. She looked down at Blayde. "So, she could—"

"I'll get over it," Blayde interrupted, her voice so cracked it needed taxpayer money to repair. "As soon as we leave, we'll be fine. We didn't come this far to get *trapped* in a stone temple."

Trapped. She meant… *no*. I closed my eyes, taking a deep breath, trying to focus on my home, to feel the pull of it through the light-years and…nothing. My blood ran cold, pulsed by an unsteady heart.

"No jumping," I said, trying to keep my voice even, but there was a tremor in my every word. "This is bigger than Miro's bobby traps. This place is targeting us, specifically. If it is a trap, then it's too late. We've already sprung it."

"Set by whom?" Blayde asked. "Let go of me, James. I'm mortal, not a toddler." Her face was pale and stony as a statue. She pushed herself from James's grasp, legs trembling as she stood.

"Future us?" said Zander.

Blayde snorted. "Right. Zander, I've been here before. I came out of here before. It's not a trap. It's just…weird."

"Maybe that's what future us *want* you to think." Zander swallowed loudly.

I took a deep breath. I could do this, right? I had spent twenty-odd years with messed-up brain chemistry; I could survive a few hours. I had all the tools safely packed away for when I needed them most.

If this temple sunk before we got out, it would be too late for us mere mortals anyway.

"I think this is a maze," said James. She peered around the opening in the wall behind us.

I ran my hand over the cold stone. It was covered in some glowing moss, which dimmed at my touch only to glow brighter when I stepped away. I giggled, my heart racing in my chest. I had missed that feeling.

"A maze? I love mazes!" Blayde smiled, teeth gritted tight. She scooped up a few mushrooms and brushed them against her bandaged arm. Their glow held true. "Voila, human torch."

"*Never fear the dark; the dark feeds the doom.*" Zander ran his child-sized hands over the wall. I'd missed the text somehow. "Glowing arm here, Blayde. I think there's something more—yeah, right there. *The dark feeds the doom but leads the way.*" He shook his head. "This doesn't make sense. Is doom meant to be the way?"

"Oh great." I sighed. "Doom means death, doesn't it? It always means death."

"Shall we get going? What is it you mortals say? Time's a-wasting!" Blayde spun on her heels to face the eerie blue hallway. "Keep your eyes open for Miro's booby traps. Oh, and most importantly, don't die."

"Don't need to tell me twice," I muttered as we took our first steps into the dark.

James was right; this was a maze. Every few steps we had to change course, picking left or right at random, trying to get a sense of the space we were in. The mushrooms became sparser the deeper we went. It was good, then, that we had Blayde to ward off the dark. Judging by its name, this doom wasn't something we'd want to cross.

I won't bore you with the details of our close encounters with absolutely nothing, but after a few hours of meandering, we found our first light at the end of a tunnel. It came from a small window hanging off the side of the temple, leading to crashing waves below.

"I guess this is our exit strategy," said Zander. "Anybody?"

"Hold on," said Blayde, reaching her arm out. She was inches away when the air at her fingertips sparked blue and a cute little jingle filled the room.

"BE SURE," a voice boomed from all around us. "THERE IS NO SHAME IN ABANDONING THE CHALLENGE. IF YOU SO DECIDE, YOUR MEMORY OF THE TEMPLE SO FAR SHALL BE REMOVED."

"No, I'm fine, thanks!" she said, ripping her arm back quickly.

There wasn't a reply from the mystery voice in the walls.

"Pre-recorded?" asked Zander.

"A forcefield," James muttered. "A forcefield. *Here.* An actual forcefield…"

"With a party-summoned temple and voice-operated doors," said Zander. "You're right. There was tech when this place was built. Tech that has lasted centuries."

"Miro must have been really good," said Blayde. Was I imagining it, or was there a hint of regret in her voice? "Whatever they're protecting here must be worth it for them to sacrifice their life…"

A shiver ran down my spine. If we were right, the answers to the Dread were contained deep within. Somewhere in Miro's repository of memories would be the solution for our end-of-days problem, except… thousands of years before it even began. No wonder they were keeping it hidden. But even from themselves?

We returned into the temple, leaving the light behind. Deeper we went, the dark slowly taking over, with only the light of Blayde's bandage lighting our way. Eventually, that dimmed, dimmed, dimmed, until soon, nothing would be left but blackness.

I hadn't been in pitch darkness like this for a long, long time. I had gotten so used to my eyes picking up even the dimmest of lights that I had half forgotten what it was like to have thick blackness pressing up against my eyes.

"The dark feeds the doom," said Zander, adding ghost noises for good measure. "Ooo-oo-o!"

Not great things to hear in the dark. I shivered again.

Plodding steps, heavy on the stone floor, shook the temple with every footfall. The smell was atrocious and getting stronger by the second: rotten fish and gasoline. Soon it was so strong that it took over my senses. The air was rough, hot, and rotten—oh so rotten—putrid and pressing down on our shoulders. I smelled smoke, then realized my nose hair charred on the spot.

A beast made of darkness. I was back in Da-Duhui, in front of the hungry beast of the Undercity, a beast I never saw but only felt. A distant relation to the terror before us, I'm sure.

"Everyone buddy-up," Blayde ordered. "The booby traps are aimed at non-Miros."

"But Blayde," said Zander. "We're not Miro either?"

"The temple doesn't have to know. Now, grab a hand and act as one!"

No argument here. I fumbled for the hands nearest to me. The one I caught was unsettlingly soft and small. Right, Zander's hand was stuck in fourth grade. I found James's calloused palm on my right. The sound came closer, and though it seemed impossible, the putrid stench was stronger. It was so close that it could have been standing right in front of us. I held my breath. After what it did to my nose, who knew what it would do to my lungs.

"Oh, so this is the Doom, I presume?" said Blayde.

The darkness roared.

Air, spit, death escaped it, flying into our faces. The sound like the roar of a subway passing underground, the roar of hunger, of *anger*.

I guess we weren't Miro enough after all.

Blayde roared right back at it, her voice so loud it could have screamed us into oblivion. I screamed with her, remembering the terror I felt as a lost human in the Undercity. The anger and hopelessness that had weighed me down turned into a ferocious scream, weaponized against this horrible beast.

I was alone then. I wasn't alone now.

It felt so good to scream in good company.

The creature snapped its mouth shut. Was this enough to convince it we were a single hive mind? Sadly, the stupor did not last long. Heat grew, its breath sliding closer.

"New plan," said Blayde. "Maybe we should run now?"

With a sharp tug, she ripped James forward, snapping apart our grasp. I reached for her, dragging Zander along, and we sprinted forward at full pelt, only to smack headfirst into a wall. Screw darkness. We had to move. Miro's pet Doom was close behind us, roaring as it chased us, its massive legs sending the temple shaking with every step. I couldn't even think about which direction we went, so long as we put space between the creature and us.

My legs started burning the second I'd asked them to run. James, the only one of us who had worked out as a mortal, was much farther ahead of us. It was useless. I was weak and getting weaker. My legs were heavy, like I hadn't left the house in a month. The adrenaline stretched too thin, leaving me with burning lungs.

Then the floor smacked my face. I'd tripped over something solid, something in the temple floor itself. I was dazed for a second, unable to get my bearings, running my hands across the stone until—yes, there it was. Before I could say anything, thick arms scooped down to lift me. Zander.

"I got it!" James shouted from far ahead. "Follow me!"

She held her phone up high. In the darkness, the light was our beacon, our salvation. I gritted my teeth together and pushed forward, the creature so close behind me I could feel its hot breath on my neck.

Left, right, right, left. In minutes, we found ourselves at the end of the line in front of two huge stone doors as smooth as polished marble.

"Please, please, please!" James shouted. "Nice door! Please open!"

The slabs pulled apart and we tumbled inside, reaching the safety beyond just as the doors slammed in the creature's face. Two times in one day—guess these bad boys were built for good reason.

Zander started laughing. He leaned against the wall, running a still tiny hand over his sweaty forehead.

"Close call," he said, before sliding to the floor.

I leaned forward, gasping, bile in my throat. Burning legs. Explosive heartbeat. God, being mortal was exhausting.

"James, that was—how?" Blayde asked, falling back on the ground beside Zander.

She shrugged. "I tripped."

"Over what?" I said between breaths. God, it was weird to have my heart bursting through my chest. It felt like it was going to leave a bruise. "A GPS?"

"Over a lump in the floor." Gosh, she was barely out of breath. How? "What do you do in the dark, which we haven't been doing since we had light? People shuffle. They see with their feet. This whole time there was a guideline on the floor leading us the right way. The only reason I stumbled upon it was because we crossed over the intersection."

"*The dark leads the way*." Zander grinned. "I guess we should have *seen* that."

Blayde slapped him playfully on the shoulder.

"Oy, bad puns," she said. "Stop it with the dad jokes or I'm going to start asking questions!"

There was a short, chilly silence. I cringed internally.

"You saved my life," said Blayde. Her voice trembled as she got to her feet, walking over to James, her face white. "Not many people have ever done that." She looked at James with eyes and mouth so wide it turned the agent red. Her voice dropped to a whisper. "Thank you."

"Anytime." James smiled, turning away. My heart sank. How was she so good at this? First time off-world, and she was already getting praise from Blayde herself. It took me ages to get the woman's approval, and here was James earning every gram of it from day one.

It was as if we had just walked into another age. We were truly in a temple now, one of magnificent splendor, tiled in gold and silver with intricate designs covering every inch of the walls. It was as if we had just walked into the Ottoman Empire, colonnades welcoming us deeper within. There were even *windows* somehow. Stained glass lined the walls on either side, a white glow emanating from outside and shining in to light the chamber. We were out of place in this splendid palace, what with all the wraps and blood and all. I felt like I was trespassing.

"Where are we?" I asked. I picked myself and my jaw off the floor, running my hand over the smooth plaster.

"The outer sanctum," said Blayde.

Was she... remembering? I smiled softly at her, hoping it was a reassuring look. "Which is?"

"One out from the inner."

"Oh," I said, confused. "And that is?"

Blayde tapped a plaque on the wall, which said as much. "I guess our answers lie just a little deeper."

So much for remembering. At the very least, if we were going to find answers, this was the place for it. And it was well-labeled to top it off. My heart pounded against my ribcage; we could be mere minutes from understanding the Dread.

We left the large chamber, following the gilded hallways, weaving and winding with soft curves rather than the sharp turns we had grown so accustomed to in the maze. Soon we passed something even more foreign in such a place: a pod pressed into the wall—out of place, but no more so than we were. It was empty but glowed an ominous green inside.

"Okay, *when* are we?" James asked.

"Hey, civilizations don't always progress in straight lines," Zander said. "I've seen one ruled by an almighty toaster. This is everyday to Blayde and me."

"A toaster?" She raised an eyebrow.

"Uh-huh." Zander nodded. "Only ate Pop-Tarts on the holy day. Remarkably kind people. Strange set of traditions, though. Their judiciary system was set up on their same religious principles, meaning that—"

"You're missing the interesting bits!" Blayde called from the next room.

The pod here had a *person* in it. A man resembling Miro Prime almost to a T, seemingly fast asleep.

"Cryogenic," she explained, knocking on the glass. "They're not dead, just… sleeping away the centuries."

"Miro is freezing themselves?" I asked. I shivered, and not from empathy with the Miro popsicle. There was something so eerie about this room. Just being surrounded by these chambers set my hair on edge. It reminded me too much of a clone army.

"He's an elder," Blayde explained. "The only ones of Miro's selves to have run the maze twice in their lifetime. Well, them and me. They wait here for the day that… Okay, I have no idea. Maybe they just like the way they looked."

"You remember?" Zander asked, incredulously. "Is more coming back to you?"

"No, it just says so on the welcome board: *Eldership and You.* There's a whole hospitality table up against that wall. Try to keep up."

As we continued down the winding corridor, Miro's frozen selves started changing. Soon we reached one in something close to a suit, followed by one in a crisp uniform, as if we were going forward through the future, not back in time.

Two doors slid open at the end of the hallway that led into a massive cavern—one which could easily fit my house. Now we really were truly back in time. They seemed almost natural rock in flowing, smooth shapes, worn by years and years of erosion and human touch. The floor lit up as we entered, revealing pictograms on the walls all around us and a circular floor of metal: large, thick, and unmovable.

My heart thudded. If the Dread truly was ancient, then maybe the pictograms explained what it was. I took a step towards them, and a beam of light shot down from the ceiling, sending me staggering back. I threw an arm in front of my tingling eyes as a figure formed—a real-life hologram. Of Miro, or one of their old selves, their hair long and dark like the rest of the selves we'd met—or as dark as a blue ceiling projector would allow it to be. They were dressed, however, as what could only be described as the next Eurovision winner: a glittery high-waisted pair of bell bottoms that started under their armpits and ran down to the floor like a glistening waterfall of pizazz.

"Congratulations, me! I made it!" they said, before making sense of the scene before them. Their eyes landed on Blayde and caught fast. "*You.*"

"Hey there, backup Miro," said Blayde. "S'up?"

"You came back," they said. "And you brought… friends."

"You—outside you—promised us answers if we did," she said. "We need your help. All of your help."

"And I was all right with this?" they asked. "Last time was an intrusion, but this? This is an incursion. Are we back together? Who are they? Am I polyamorous now? Figures. Midlife crisis."

"Still separated." Blayde shook her head. "Miro, meet my brother, his partner, and the secret agent who hopped along. None of us is dating you. We just need to ask you some really old questions."

The Miro hologram scanned us up and down, slowly. They let out a heavy sigh.

"If you're here, then I've apparently agreed to this. Fine. Ask away. But I reserve the right to eject you all at any time."

We all nodded and stayed silent. No one wanted to go first. Miro sighed again, their image flickering.

"We don't have all day," they said. "I'd much rather be in my digital coma, if I had the choice."

"Who exactly are you?" said James. "Miro—outside you, I mean—doesn't seem to know what goes on in here."

I did a double take. James understood what they were saying. There was translator tech here—more fancy technology.

"I'm just an interface," they explained. "I guard the repository of my memories. Usually, hiveminds expand outward indefinitely, filling planets with billions of minds, exponentially growing to handle the amount of data that stores our thoughts. But I'm limited by the resources of this world. It can't handle more than a few hundred selves at once. Hence the backup. Hence…whatever I am."

"Then why not expand? If that's in your nature?" asked Zander. "Or at the very least leave so you're not limited by this world?"

"But I must stay," they said, shaking their head low. "I must protect this place."

"Because it holds your memories?" he asked. "Then why not—"

"Thousands of minds across thousands of years, and you think I don't understand?" The hologram frowned. "I must protect the temple *because* it is another universe. My presence here is an afterthought. A bonus."

Another universe? I spun to my friends, but they were as stunned as I was. I didn't feel like this was another universe. It felt just like my own, except…

Ah, right, I can die here. The laws of physics really are different in this place. I shuddered. I'd been to other worlds, but this was entirely otherworldly.

"A-another universe?" asked Blayde.

"Well, a bubble universe," they explained. "A wrinkle in the fabric of spacetime that allows this place to be removed from the rest. A sanctuary for when the pain and terror come."

"You mean the Dread?" James gasped. "You know about it?"

"I had a vision, late one night," said Miro wistfully. "When I was young and planetwide. Filled the atmosphere with an incredible hallucinogenic I got from a higher dimensional merchant who wanted to throw a real rager. Saw the universe ending in *panic*. It changed my life—forever."

"So, there was no prophet? No prophecy?" asked Zander. Miro shook their head.

"That's just what I'm allowing myself to believe," said Miro. "I don't want myself indulging in that stuff again. Clean and sober eight thousand years now. Painted it on these walls, though. It makes a good effect."

They pointed to the curved cave wall, right at the elaborate pictogram of Blayde herself. She seemed to be partying it up with a few hundred Miros while riding horses. Sure, the horses were an unnatural peachy-pink color and had neither mane nor tail, but it was probably as close to a horse as anyone could get this side of Betelgeuse. Their wedding day, perhaps, predicted millennia ago by a hive mind on an acid trip.

"So, you just…lobotomized yourself?" said Blayde. "Choosing which memories to keep and which ones to hide?"

"Memory is a fluid thing." They shrugged. "I don't see you remembering our last chat—or the way you left me after the worst night of my life, so don't act like you're not capable of a little memory lobotomy as well."

Blayde recoiled. Now all semblance of stoicism was gone from the hologram's luminous features. This was the Miro we'd come to know outside the temple. Even as a manifestation of Miro's backbrain, they were still themselves underneath. Could there have been a grain of truth in them? But the hologram continued their tale.

"Back then, the world was fast and everywhere and had no place for fears of the future. No one believed an amalgamation of three billion people crying out in unison. But there was one who might: a wise man trapped in a labyrinth, a powerful man so dangerous he could not be allowed to live outside of his small world, said to grant a wish to whomever could reach him within his prison. And every year, people would race for the opportunity to win their wish. I knew that if I won, he would have to help me—even if he didn't take me seriously."

"Race through a labyrinth?" I stuffed my hand in my pocket to stop it from trembling. "That sounds... familiar."

"It does, doesn't it?" said James, all starry-eyed.

Blayde scoffed. "A tale as old as time."

"And if you're standing here today," said James, awe still dripping from her mouth, "I take it you actually *spoke* with the man?"

"I'm a winner, baby." Miro grinned. "As my prize, I told the wise man about my vision and asked what he could do to help me, so he searched through his eternal memory. You see, the prisoner was an immortal being. Within his chamber, he saw the past of all time and recalled the future of all yet to come. With this combined knowledge, he offered me a solution. He gave me a weapon to be used in the future, a way to fight the dreaded future, and promised me that he would be there to offer advice when the time came."

Thank the stars, we had an answer at least. My hands balled into fists, but this only compounded the trembling. Our future selves had sent us here, had led us right to what we needed.

"A weapon? Against the Dread?" Zander asked. He turned to Blayde, who nodded slowly. "Is it here?"

"Right beneath my feet," they said, stomping on the metal disk below their feet. "Set to open only when the Dread hits a high note. The wise man found me this cozy bubble universe and charged me to protect it. The maze is modeled after his labyrinth, but on a much smaller scale. This future evil will need technology to propagate, which is why I've sworn off the stuff. Terribly addictive, anyway."

"Hang on, so why is there any tech here at all?" I scanned the room; it was as sparse as the rest of the planet. "If the technology amplifies the Dread, then why is tech still here?"

"This place has been removed from reality," said Miro. "Technically, anything inside these walls is no longer a part of the universe as we know it."

"Which is why we can't jump anywhere," I said, snapping my fingers. That was a first. "You can't travel to a place that doesn't exist."

"So, how are we still existing? How is this place visible to the outside world?" James rubbed her temples. "This sci-fi stuff messes with my head."

"James, we're aliens. You got here by breaking the light-speed barrier. Get with the times," said Zander.

"Because they're merging for a short period of time," said Miro, waving to bring our attention back on them. "Technically, this place vibrates at a different frequency from the rest of the universe. Perfect place to hide a weapon."

"Perfect," said Blayde, dropping to her knees. "Open it up and let us have it. We'll take it back to the future, stop the Dread in its tracks, and bring it back before you know it's gone."

"Not that simple," Miro tutted. "The wise man only programmed it to open when the Dread hits its crescendo, which will be in a few hundred thousand years. That, and I don't have the slightest idea of how to operate it...or what it is."

I squeezed my eyes shut. *Deep breaths, Sally Webber.* To come this far, to have the answers within reach, literally right beneath our feet... I wanted to rip out my hair.

"So, what do you suggest we do?" Blayde put her hands on her hips. "Find this wise man and demand the owner's manual?"

"I would." Miro shrugged. "Hey, if you win the race, he's legally bound to give it to you."

Blayde ran her hands through her hair, pulling it tight, pressing her palms against her temples.

"Then we're going to have to find this labyrinth," said Zander. "We're going to have to race."

"We need to meet this immortal," said Blayde.

It hit me, quite suddenly, that maybe she wasn't interested in the labyrinth solely to stop the Dread. There were only so many immortals in the universe, after all. Maybe she was hoping to find clues to her own history too. I turned to Zander. Was he in it for himself as well?

No, there was no mistaking it. My head buzzed. All the clues leading us right to another immortal? Between the memories bringing us here and the promise of someone like them, this was exactly what Zander and Blayde wanted: keys to their past. This couldn't be a coincidence.

We let Miro ramble on about the golden days and their heroics in the labyrinth for longer than I'd like to admit. We knew where we needed to go, but it was awkward as hell admitting it to each other or finding a polite way of ditching the hologram who, despite their earlier protests about a digital coma being best, seemed to be addicted to their newfound attention. That, and avoiding discussing how exactly we'd get to where and when we'd need to be, which hadn't even come up yet.

"Sundown anyone?" said Blayde, pulling us out of our communal slump. "Let's get out of here before we're digested by the ocean."

Thankfully, there was an easy exit to the temple—a full-on glowing pedestal like in a video game. Miro's hologram fizzled back into the ceiling, though their huffing still filled the small chamber until we left.

We emerged back on the island, sun high in the sky—it was only noon. The second my feet touched the hot sand, I felt my chest stumble to a halt. The overabundance of feeling that had come from my sudden mortality in the bubble universe sublimated, my heart chugging to a stop, leaving me in limbo once again. I clutched my chest, missing my heartbeat already. It was weird to have had it back for such a short time.

"Right," asked Blayde. "I disappeared into the desert once before. Miro's a big hive mind; they can deal."

Zander winced, shaking out his hands, now fully grown to adult size once again. "A goodbye seems like a nice touch."

"I'd rather not."

He said nothing. James rubbed her skin, which must have been burning under the midday sun.

I reached out my hands, palms upward. "Right. Next stop: Earth. We get back, regroup, and figure out how to find this labyrinth place."

Zander grabbed my hand, fast as lightning. "Everyone, beware the cats!"

Unfortunately, the cats were the least of our troubles.

TEN

FULL AGENCY COOPERATION, NOW WITH FREE TOTE BAGS

IT'S FUN PLAYING AT BEING A VACUUM CORD. I closed my eyes and scattered us to the cosmos, the rich fabric of the void cradling our very atoms, and let myself be reeled in by my home. *Zip*. Our time spent in the Sand was a few thousand years before my present. While we were melting our asses off in the sands, Earth was enjoying a crisp ice age. *Whoosh*. I moved by instinct, a sense which I could pull apart in the back of my brain—despite the fact that my head was currently incorporeal.

I was not alone here. I could feel James beside me, *through* me. There wasn't even much of a *me* anymore, with her particles intertwined with mine, reveling in the thrill of being one with the universe. I could feel the joy radiating off her as if it were me, which, in a sense, she was.

Zander and Blayde, though, were black holes in the dark. If they had a physical form, I could imagine them with eyes screwed shut, hands squeezed over their ears. Isolated in oneness. I had never paid attention before, never noticed without James as a benchmark.

And then we were there. Here. Now. Well, now plus…one hour? I didn't quite want to land right in the middle of the cat jamboree.

The good news: There were no cats left to burn us to a crisp.

The bad news: It was because the Agency was busy cleaning up their mess.

I came into existence about a foot above a construction worker, slamming into his hard hat and collapsing on the rubble pile along with him. I took a deep breath then coughed up smoke and dust, opening my eyes to the brightly lit velvet sky above what had once been Meedian's compound.

I scrambled to my feet. Where were the others? My chest was tight, my breathing heavy, and not from the fall. The instant I came into consciousness, it was as if a citrus reamer had wrapped around my mind and given it a solid squeeze. How had I not noticed the Dread before when it was this strong? My ears rang, a sizzling high note that made me want to grab my ears and just scream.

James groaned beside me, lifting herself off the rubble pile and pulling her scratched hands through her hair. Zander and Blayde were already up, back to back, fists at the ready. Agency operatives in yellow jackets and hard hats swarmed the remains of the compound. Those closest to our landing turned to stare, one grabbing a radio, another a gun. How had they gotten here so fast? Had Meedian gotten away?

"Don't… don't try anything," said the man with the radio, one hand in the air. "We have you surrounded, I think."

I glanced at my friends—just a meter too far away. I couldn't jump anyone anywhere, even if I wanted to. No, not with the armor-clad soldiers filing in, adding to the crowd around us, guns riveted on our heads.

Less than a minute later, Foollegg appeared, her Barbie-blonde hair tied back in a tight ponytail, crushed under a clean hard hat.

"So"—she crossed her arms over her chest—"we leave you to your own devices for one day and have yet another off-worlder incident to clean up?"

I caught Blayde's gaze, and she smiled with just the corner of her lips. I didn't need to read eyebrows to understand what she was saying: your mission, your responsibility.

I swallowed down bile. This is what I'd signed up for.

"We had a deal, Foollegg," I said, making my hands into fists. "We're playing by your rules. Lower your weapons."

"Played by our rules?" She scoffed. "So why did Agent Felling disappear from our scanners for an hour and thirty-odd minutes?"

James's face drained of all color. "You're…tracking me?"

"What did you expect, Felling? We knew the siblings could not be trusted. We gave them a chance; now they're squandered it." Foollegg waved her over, like one would call a dog. "Step away from them. You can debrief us afterwards."

"Debrief you?" James took a step forward, hands up, but face twisted and tense. "This isn't even my operation, *Agent*." She pointed at me. I swallowed, pushing hard on the ground to keep my legs from trembling. "It's all of us or none of us. Take your pick."

"Why do you have to be so difficult?" Foollegg let out a heavy sigh, wide-mouthed and braying.

"Difficult?" James ran her hands through her hair. "You think *I'm* being difficult? You've been using me since the day we met. You put a tracking device on me, and I just spent the last day being stalked by a sea serpent! I think I deserve to be a little cranky."

"You've been gone for an hour."

"Yeah, yeah, yeah. Relativity." James forced a smile. "Do you want to know what we found or not?"

Say what you will about Agency procedure, but in the time we'd left for the Sands, the operatives had arrested over a hundred cats, put out the fires they'd started, and built a miniature base of operations, complete with coffee machines. Coffee we were now devouring by the potful as we waited in interrogation room B—the other two rooms currently being occupied by cats who refused to speak without their lawyers present.

Huh. Maybe I should have hired a lawyer.

"You know, I thought the Dread was some kind of priority." Blayde spun on her heels. There wasn't much room for pacing. "All this hurry-up and wait shit is giving me whiplash."

I said nothing, staring into my coffee. Zander had the seat beside me, tapping his foot in time with our growing impatience. I leaned into him, trying to keep my usual baseline of anxiety from mixing with the Dread. Meanwhile in the corner, James scratched at her arm, slowly turning it red.

"Stop that," said Blayde, grabbing her by the wrist. "If they put a tracking device in you, it wouldn't be in your arm."

James's frown deepened. "Wherever it is, I need it out of me."

"Well, since it's probably dispersed in your bloodstream, that's going to be hard for us to do right now."

"In my bloodstream?" James ripped her arm from Blayde's grip. "What the hell? How can you be so calm right now? They've been—no, they couldn't have—I have rights."

"I'm not calm," said Blayde. "I'm quiet. There's a difference."

"Or maybe you just don't care," James snarled. "Fine. Leave me here to die. But at least then I wouldn't be an *inconvenience* for you anymore."

Blayde looked completely aghast at those words. Hell, even I was. Not the kind of energy the brilliant James-Freaking-Felling was usually putting out into the world.

Screw the Dread. Whatever this thing was, it was getting into her head, making her—making all of us— act out of a constant state of dull panic. If we weren't careful, it was going to get us all killed.

"Felling," Blayde said, fire in her eyes, "you're not an inconvenience, just a hassle sometimes. You're pretty darn useful when you want to be." She placed a hand on her shoulder. "Remember who you are, Agent Felling. You may know absolutely nothing about where you are, but as long as you remember where you're from—and more importantly, who you are and who you can be—there's no reason for you to fear. You get that?"

James gripped Blayde's wrist. "I haven't forgotten."

"Good." Blayde nodded. "Now prove it. Ah, finally."

I looked up as Blayde chided the people now stepping through the door: Foollegg, of course, and by her side, Dany. The empress of the galaxy held her hands behind her back, stiff-necked and tall.

"Talk," she said.

I stared back down at my coffee again, eager to get out from under her gaze.

"Veesh, that's how you speak to us?" said Blayde. "We have important work to do, and yet you lock us in here and treat us like criminals?"

"You left Earth without any kind of warning. What were we supposed to think?" Dany stared each of us down. Heat rose to my cheeks.

"Not to mention, you were working with the same criminals you literally just a signed a treaty to have us enforce," said Foollegg. "How can we trust you?"

"Trust us?" James threw her arm over her head. "You put a tracking device in me!"

"How can you expect us to work with you if you don't give us any room in which to move?" said Zander, standing and knocking over his chair. "I should have known we could never—"

"Shut up!" I stood and slammed my hands on the table, sending drops of coffee every which way. The room fell silent. "Can't you see what is going on here? The Dread is inside our heads, every one of us. We need to take a breath. Whatever our methods, we have a lead. We can fight about this when we end the Dread once and for all."

Dany's face was red. "Sally, you—"

"Deep breaths. Together. Right now."

We made an odd bunch, standing in the makeshift interrogation room, box breathing our way to clarity, but it was the only tool I had so I was going to use it. And it did seem to lower the tension somewhat.

Out of nowhere, Marcy came bursting into the interrogation room, looking as radiant as her empress wife. Her hair boasted a Princess Leia braid, a dark contrast to her glowing white jumpsuit. The only thing that brought her down to earth were her massive headphones that covered her ears entirely.

"You're alive!" she belted, throwing her arms wide. Considering the glare I'd gotten at our last goodbye, I almost cried from relief. I ran right past Dany and straight into Marcy's arms. She smelled of fresh lavender, the fragrance filling my nose as I hugged her. She clutched me back, stronger than ever before.

"What's with the headphones?" I asked, pulling away.

"What?" she shouted. "I can't hear you!"

I tapped her headphones instead. She nodded, grinning.

"I figure if I can't hear the Dread, it can't mess with my head!" she said, loud enough to pierce my eardrums. "I feel much better now!"

Dany ran her hand down her face. "You're not meant to be here, Dove."

Despite the headphones, Marcy seemed to know exactly what she was getting at because she stuck out her tongue before turning back to me. Her mood was night and day from the last time I'd seen her, furious and red before kicking us off the Alliance ship. Whatever she was doing to keep the Dread out was obviously working. I had my Marcy back.

Blayde, however, wore a tighter frown than the one she'd had on mere minutes ago. "You can block out the Dread with primitive technology? Why didn't you tell us?"

Dany held up a hand to hide her lips from her wife. "It's all in her head."

"Doesn't look like it's all in her head," I replied, clutching my friend tight. "This could be a lead!"

"And what kind of lead did you come back with? On your jaunt through relativistic space."

I took another deep breath and another. I wasn't going to let the Dread any deeper into my head. If Marcy could block it out with noise-cancelling headphones, then it had something to do with sound. Not something I could hear, not consciously.

I closed my eyes, squeezing them tight. It was hard to think, the brain fog so thick I couldn't think a thought ahead of another. What could scramble my brain, everyone's brains, putting us all on edge like hunted prey?

Sound. Vibrations.

Everything was connected.

"It's a feedback loop," I said.

Everyone's eyes turned to me. Even Marcy's grip seemed to slacken. I held my head high, arms slack at my sides. Shaking, sure, but uncrossed, unhidden.

"What is?" Blayde pursed her lips. "The Dread?"

"Marcy's headphones." I nodded. "I learned about them in physics 101. In order to be noise cancelling, they emit a sound wave with the same amplitude but with the opposite phase to what she should be hearing. Combine the two waves and they cancel each other out. What if someone, or something, was trying to cancel out the universe?"

"You took a physics class?" Zander asked.

My face felt hot. "Yeah, when I was waiting for you to find your way back, I enrolled in community college. I thought I mentioned it."

"I highly doubt a single introductory class on *Earth* would stand up against our legions of physicists," said Foollegg. "If they can't find something, what makes you think you can?"

"Because of the scale of the thing," said Dany. "If it's everywhere at once, could we measure it? Quantify it? If it was affecting even the subatomic particles of the universe?"

"The Dread we're feeling is the anti-universe." Zander snapped his fingers, making us all jump. "Or… the universe hearing itself, in a way. It would explain why every living being is experiencing some reaction to it, picking up cues from their environment the brain cannot comprehend. And why our communications are getting hijacked: mixing signals over long distances is a recipe for disaster. And on this scale, a very literal disaster."

"Miro said the Dread would reach a pitch, a crescendo," I said. "So once whoever is doing this tunes it properly—"

"Everything we know and love will disintegrate," Zander finished for me.

"Well, shit," said James, collapsing against the wall. "I need something stronger than coffee for this."

We stood like this, staring at each other, as if each daring someone to argue against my wild theory. Hell, even I was hoping someone would tell me I was wrong. That my theory was so far out there that it couldn't possibly be real.

Except… it was so far out there that it might actually be.

"You didn't cover string theory in introductory courses, did you?" Foollegg crossed her arms over her chest.

I forced a smile. "Extra credit reading."

"It may be an outdated model," said Zander, "but not far off. And Sally's hypothesis could hold water. We just need to find a way to demonstrate it."

"We don't have to," said Blayde. "When we find the Eternal, he'll tell us everything we need to know."

"The Eternal?" asked Dany.

Oh, right. With all the fun of my theories, we'd forgotten it was time to debrief our glorious allies. We filled them in to what we'd witnessed in the Sands, leaving out details about Meedian or Miro's connection to Blayde. Instead of Zander's abs leading us there in the first place, it was just a normal book, one that went up in flames with the rest of the library. But all that mattered was that we'd found the weapon. All we needed now was to find the operator. All the while, Foollegg and Dany listened intently, and so did Marcy, arm wrapped tightly around mine, using speech-to-text on my phone to follow along.

"An immortal…in a labyrinth?" Dany frowned. Her eyes darted around the room. "Did this person tell you if the labyrinth sprawled in all directions, with traps to destroy the faint of heart and the unworthy? Was it built by other immortals to punish the wise man?"

Zander and I exchanged quick glances. Of course, the Alliance's emperor would have this kind of information.

Dany let out a heavy sigh. Without another word, she reached into her crisp white uniform, pulled out a battered paperback, and tossed it onto the interrogation room table, where the drops of coffee slowed its skid to a halt. Blayde pulled the same book out of her wraps—what the hell? We'd been through fire and water and costume changes! How! It was the book Blayde had purchased from the checkout, seconds before that poor woman had combusted. Marcy gasped, clutching me tighter.

"You who talk about trust, you waste my time with a poor retelling of *Finding Tartarus*?" She turned to James. "How dumb do you think I am? We both get Laurie's newsletter! It's been on the bestseller list for months."

"Oh my God," said James, running her hands through her hair. "Why didn't I recognize it?"

"Hold on, what is this book?" Zander picked one of the copies off the table, flipping through it with his thumb. "Because I've never heard of it."

"A bestselling allegorical novel that's all the rage," James explained. "Claims to be a manuscript written by some Desmond Elegrious, lost to time. It sounded like marketing bull to me, but now…"

"It's strangely accurate for an Earth book, though," said Blayde. I turned to her, and so did the others. She only shrugged. "What? I chugged through it last night while you three were sandbathing. Interesting concept, but a total drag. The romance felt tacked on as an afterthought. If it hadn't been there, I probably would have made the connection sooner."

"We travel halfway across the planet to find a library when the book we needed was in our hands the whole time?" Zander, who had been scanning the paperback intently, now slammed the book back down on the table. "I think we need to meet with this Elegrious. He may be our only lead to finding the wise man."

"Well, that's going to be a little tricky," said James, rubbing her hand against her neck.

"And why's that?"

"Because Desmond Elegrious died in Petersburg… in 1657."

My first reaction was sheer excitement because holy macaroni we'd be traveling through *time*. Sure, we'd done it before, but never consciously. Here I was going to be visiting my own world's past, the type of thing I'd been dreaming about since I'd first watched *Back to the Future*.

My second was one of panic when I realized that we were future accidents waiting to happen. The seventeenth century wasn't hospitable to anyone who didn't have land and a penis.

My third was to frown in mock disappointment because our hosts had no idea we could travel through time, and we needed to keep it that way.

"Oh, woe is us!" said Blayde, throwing her hand over her forehead. "Our only lead has been dead a thousand years!"

"It's only 2022, Blayde," I said.

"Ah."

"Why do I even bother?" said Dany, rubbing her temples. "I thought we could make this work. But this is just…" She let out a heavy sigh. "Stupid. I need a smoke. Marce?"

Marcy looked up from her phone screen, locked eyes with her, and shook her head slowly. Before any of us could speak, Dany spun on her heels and marched out of the interrogation room, slamming the door behind her, right in Foollegg's face. The latter said nothing as she turned the handle and slipped out herself.

Blayde harrumphed. "You see, Sally, why we don't like working for the enemy?"

"Dany's not the enemy," I muttered. "But I get your point."

"You can't give up now!" shouted Marcy. "Maybe the publisher can give us details that weren't in the book?"

"Not a lotta info to go on." Blayde held up the paperback, flipping to the last page. "Says the manuscript was dropped in the mailbox of the publishing house with only a note claiming the author's identity and date of death. Who knows where the thing was for the other odd centuries."

Marcy sat on the cold metal table with my phone and began furiously googling as the rest of us exchanged sidelong glances. Zander clapped. She didn't look up. She couldn't hear us at all through those headphones.

"Well, shit." I swallowed hard. "We're going to need a hell of a makeover."

Our lead was on Earth, but it might as well be on the other side of the solar system. I'd never had to worry about who or what I was when I traveled with Zander before. Maybe I was just naive, or then again incredibly lucky. But knowing exactly what kind of world was waiting for us in seventeenth-century Virginia, that felt as alien and unwelcoming as any planet I had visited so far.

"I don't remember the sixteen hundreds," said Zander. "What exactly do we need to be worried about? The robots or bears?"

"Sexists," I said, just as James muttered, "Racist assholes."

"The whole jamboree, then. But if this mysterious Mister Elegrious truly knows where to find the wise man"—Zander cringed—"I don't think we have any other leads."

Blayde turned to me. "Unless there's a version of Zander lurking exactly when and where we need to be, Sally's about as useless as the rest of us."

Useless? How dare she. But the look in her eyes revealed the truth. She knew damn well I could take us anywhere

I pleased. She'd just keep insulting me until I told the truth. A chill ran up my spine.

"I've filled out the contact form on the publisher's website," said Marcy, making all of us jump. "But maybe they'll answer quicker if I tweet at them? Although, maybe I could ask Dany's spin team…"

She returned to the phone, her tongue pinched between her teeth as she typed furiously at the keyboard. The rest of us exchanged glances.

"Well, we'd better try," I replied, then quickly added, "But what about clothes? We can't show up there looking like… this?"

"So?" asked Zander. "We're never dressed appropriately. We never know where we'll end up, and it's never stopped us before."

"Then again, we have faced the wrath of the fashion police before," said Blayde. "More than once. Earth's one of the rare planets not to have it actively enforced."

"This time we have the advantage of knowing what's expected of us," added Zander. "Which means we can at the very least come up with a compelling reason to explain why we're dressed like mountain people without a penny to our names."

"Any suggestions?" asked James.

"Aliens?" he replied.

"As in, we are aliens, or we've been abducted by them?"

"Both?"

"He's messing with you," said Blayde. "He knows what he's doing. Now circle up. Sally's going to hit up her boyfriend from ancient times."

"Um, Blayde?" said Zander. "We are currently in an Agency interrogation room. They have their cameras right on us. If we leave right now…"

She belted out a harmonious groan of unparalleled magnificence. "I hate working freelance."

I ran my hands through my hair, breathing hard, trying to calm my jitters. It was hard to think with the persistent ringing in my ears. Zander was right: What little trust the Agency did have in us would dissolve along with us if we jumped out of this room. But we couldn't very well tell them we were going to attempt time travel, not when that was our last secret we were keeping from them.

And I couldn't betray Marcy like that.

I sat down beside her on the table. She'd crossed her legs now, so hunched over the phone I had to tap her shoulder to get her to look up. She blinked, furiously. She'd been so engrossed in the screen, she must have forgotten to blink until now.

"They didn't want me to know," she whispered, holding her phone out to me in a trembling hand. "It's already too late. Earth's succumbing to the Dread."

Time stopped as I took in the newsfeed in front of me. Thousands of reports from all over the world, all with the same thread: chaos. In Brussels, dogs had started howling at once, overcome by some sort of madness that turned them rabid, attacking anything on sight. In Texas, a doomsday cult had begun their rite of ascension, and hundreds of members overtook grocery stores, devouring everything in sight. Violent uprisings in Ukraine, Scotland, and Iceland. Five countries had closed their borders and gone silent. President Turner had even made a strange and provocative statement about building a wall with Canada. The Dread was escalating. This was just the beginning.

"And all this since this morning?" I asked.

Marcy wiped her tears on her sleeves, smearing them with gold mascara. "That's why they took my phone," she said, her face puffy and pink. "They didn't want me to know that my world is ending."

I wanted to throw up. We weren't fast enough; weren't good enough. *I* wasn't good enough. This was my mission, my attempt to save my world, and it was crumbling to pieces while we waited to do things right.

I looked up. James was grasping Blayde, her face white as a sheet. Had she seen the news? I turned back to Marcy, typing furiously on my keyboard as I spoke words I knew were being recorded.

"We can't just sit here and do nothing," I said. *We can travel through time*, my phone told her instead. "We have to do this, no matter what you say." I slipped off the table, phone still angled toward her face. *We're going to find Elegrious. You have to cover for us.*

Marcy's red-rimmed eyes went wide. She slipped off the table, too, reaching for my arm, which she clutched with all her strength.

"Do what you have to do," she replied. "And pray there's an Earth to come home to."

I gave her one last hug, one worthy of being a last hug. Her tears wet my cheeks, and I pulled her closer. When I stepped away to reach for my friends, she made herself tall, made herself smile.

Forced hope was all that I saw as I dragged us into the depths of time.

ELEVEN

I OVERSHOOT OUTLANDER BY A FULL CENTURY

PETERSBURG, 1657. FELT LIKE AN APRIL 25TH TO ME.
The middle of the night, in a cold dark street. An alley between two brick buildings.

Moving through time was different from moving in space, like being reeled sideways rather than forward, except with seven other directions. Since I was following a trail of a specific time and a location, rather than a monumental instance like the memory that had brought me to Miro's world, it was a little more delicate.

"Arms, fingers, toes, shoulders, head, feet, all here," said Zander. Blayde echoed him.

"Arms, fingers, toes, shoulders, head, feet, James, all here," I finished, taking a deep breath. Leaving the Dread's influence was like curling up in a warm bed after a cold winter's day. I felt ten kilos lighter.

"So, I'm an appendage now?" James grumbled under her breath.

"Well, do you have all of yours?" asked Blayde.

James made a show of counting her fingers. "There, happy?"

"Brilliant, Sally!" Zander lifted me into the air, swinging me around. "You really can find me anywhere."

He was loving being this whole beacon-boyfriend thing. I kept smiling, if only to keep the rising bile inside. Here he was, all encouraging and gentle and trying to distract from the fact that everything was on my shoulders, all while I was keeping this massive secret from him, lying to him about where this ability came from. But I couldn't face telling him the truth. Knowing something had scrambled my brain, had made me like Nimien…

"So, we're here?" James asked, same energy as a kid asking if we did get a puppy.

"It's definitely Earth," said Blayde, turning up her nose. "Orange sky or no orange sky."

Hold on—orange sky? I looked up, and sure enough, instead of velvety blackness, there was an orange tinge in the air. Maybe I had been off after all.

"How are you so sure?"

"The smell," she replied. "Earth always smells the same."

James inhaled deeply then let out a sharp, hacking cough. "Of piss and smoke?"

"Well, when I say smell, I would rather say reeks, but you know, I'm being polite. Anyway, no offense."

Before I could say anything in our defense, the air was filled with screams.

The three of them immediately smoothed themselves against the wall, leaving me awkwardly delayed in joining them. Blayde peeked around the corner, zipping her head back as people marched past, dressed in their Puritan best. The hats, the tall black hats! What a relief to see the hats. It was all the confirmation I needed that I did good here.

"Well, at least we know we have the right time and place," James said hesitantly, peeling herself from the shadows as the mob passed us by. "Do you think…?"

"1657." I swallowed. "I can think of a few reasons for an angry mob."

I stuck my head out of the alley, tentatively. The crowd was too busy marching to pay us any attention.

"Witches are here among us!" proclaimed a voice, uncomfortably familiar. Despite them speaking English, my translator seemed to have taken it upon itself to make them all sound as modern as anyone I knew. The device must have decided that a good rural accent was appropriate for these folks, and they all sounded like they should have their own TLC show.

But—*witches*. I sure had picked the wrong night to jump to. My hands clutched into fists. I knew about the horrors of our past, but there was a disturbing distance between knowing and actually witnessing them. What innocent girl had overstepped?

Something had had to have set them off.

Blayde was already gone, having slipped out of the alley directly into the crowd. Zander didn't hesitate, following her without a second glance. James and I exchanged a few glances before following them.

The mob had come to a stop, congregated in an open square. Ahead of them, a man with an impossibly tall hat stood on a raised platform—a pyre. My heart clenched. No, this couldn't be happening. They couldn't seriously be…

The mob's whispers were quickly silenced by the man clearing his throat.

"We have seen the work of the devil tonight," he proclaimed. Did the tallness of his hat correlate with the importance of his stature? "Heresy! Joan Mason was consumed by flames in front of her own home—an act only possible by a witch."

I took a breath. So they didn't have an accused. At least there was that. But… a woman, consumed by flames? This was too close for comfort. My mind conjured up the images I'd been so desperately trying to bury—those of that poor cashier who had burned in front of my very eyes.

I didn't even know her name.

"One among us is responsible for this heinous act," continued to the man on the pyre. "We must join together to weed out the evil in our town and burn the witch responsible!"

Cries of *"burn the witches!"* echoed throughout the angry mob. My hands were shaking. All at once I felt it, the unmistakable energy radiating off the crowd. The anger and hate. The air was saturated with it. This was a different kind of Dread—not one from without, but from within.

"You gotta hang them instead!" said someone from the crowd. "Far less mess to clean up afterward."

My blood ran hot in my veins. There was no mercy in these voices. The torches flamed high.

"I accuse Verity Smith!" someone shouted. "She was seen arguing with Joan Mason mere hours before her death."

And like a call-out tweet, all attention turned to the accused. The crowd parted around a young woman, her hands having risen to her mouth in shock.

"Wha…what?" she stammered, standing alone. "You all know me! I couldn't possibly have… I'm not a witch!"

"Her pies have been exceptional of late," said someone beside her. "Too good."

Voices rose all at once, agreeing that her pies were indeed exceptional. I turned to Zander again, but he'd already pushed himself forward.

"What value do these baseless accusations hold?" Zander asked, his voice loud and booming. They shoved him away, and he dove in front of Verity. That's my man. There's my heart on display. "Have we taken it upon ourselves to deem a person's guilt simply by lack of evidence to the contrary? Or very good pie?"

"Indeed," said the man on the pyre. The crowd went silent. He jumped to the ground, marching toward the girl. She was quaking in her boots. "She has the right to a fair trial."

I groaned. Fair trial was an oxymoron here from what I'd read. I wanted to go home, but the only reason we were in this wretched time was to find the weapon that would ensure there was home for me to return to.

Their leader continued, "She will have the right to the trial of the white bar. This will determine if she's guilty of heresy."

"Burn her!" someone shouted.

"We're supposed to *hang* her!" said another. "That's the right way to do it. I didn't come all this way for us to leave the law back home."

"No! This is not how we do things!" Zander's voice echoed across the square.

"Can someone shut up the peddler? He's ruining it!"

"I'm innocent!" Verity stomped her foot, staring up at the sky. "This isn't fun anymore. I demand you end this now. At once! You backwater freaks need to get with the times and get your asses civilized!"

"There will be no fires tonight." Someone else pushed forward from the crowd, flinging themselves beside Zander. For a second, I felt pride swell in my chest. We had started a movement. Then the protester opened his mouth again. "Hanging is more appropriate in the circumstances!"

"Will you shut up? Burn them!" yelled a woman from the crowd.

"Before you burn her, ask yourselves this," said Zander. "Would you—"

But he didn't have a chance to hit us with a thought problem. His mouth froze in a small 'o' as a column of white flame consumed Verity Smith, taking her screams to the skies. The air was thick with a syrupy silence as we watched her disappear into a puff of smoke.

No, this couldn't be happening. The same fire that had consumed the cashier had taken this girl, and it was no less gruesome this time around. And I knew, I knew this was the work of the Agency.

Blayde had said they had used SHC method to hide amongst our people in the past. Witnessing this… it's one thing to know history happened; it's another to watch it unfold in front of your eyes, unable to change it.

I reached forward, toward where Verity had been standing—only for a hand to clamp down hard on my shoulder.

"Do you want to join in their fate?" the voice hissed. I turned to look up at the stranger, but his face was hidden by a heavy hood. Just lovely. I tried to rip free, but the hand clamped down harder.

"Jeremy!" the leader said, drawing my attention back to the mob. "You're too torch-happy! We hadn't even had the trial yet."

"It wasn't me!" shouted a man with his torch held high. "I swear, I was waiting for you!"

"Well, teenage girls don't just go up in flames," the leader replied.

"They do if they're witches!"

"But if that one lit herself on fire," said one of the men in the crowd, "does that mean witches are unharmed by flame?"

"Maybe she was a fire demon," said Jeremy, the torch guy. "That would explain a lot."

The protester wrenched his way from Zander's grasp. "You see? We should have been hanging her all along!"

"Will somebody get this peddler out of town?" shouted parchment guy. "He just ruined a perfectly good event."

"I'll move myself, thank you very much," said Zander. "So help me stars above, if you ever attempt to burn another *child* in this town again…"

"You'll what? Wave your rags at us?" asked Jeremy. I expected Zander to say something, anything to instill fear in this man. Instead, he folded his hands under his armpits.

"If she didn't do this to herself, then there must still be a witch among us!" someone cried.

The crowd roared. My stomach tried to jump up through my throat—a panic. A frenzy. The mob was turning into a stampede. Screaming came from all directions, names spat out like sparks from a fire. Accusations left right and center.

"Come with me," said the man behind me. "You and your friends are drawing too much attention to yourselves."

The hand finally came off my shoulder, and I wrenched myself away. I glanced back at the others—Blayde stood a whole foot shorter, fiddling with her laser pointer like she was going to crush it to a paste. She caught my gaze, and at the sight of the hooded stranger, her hackles raised.

"And what do you want?" she said. "Going to press charges on us for basic human decency?"

"If you were human, I might," he replied. "Come with me."

He turned and mechanically marched into the town, not waiting for a response. I stared through the crowd at Zander, who was as stiff as the Puritans' hats. He saw me, grabbed James, and followed us. Guess we were going to trust the creepy stranger after all.

The streets were mostly empty outside of the mob, not that there were many streets in this colony to begin with. Here I was, dropped in the middle of my own nation's history and as disappointed as if I'd attended a small budget historical recreation. Where were all the turkey legs I'd been promised? I still hadn't eaten since the grilled Sven at the bonfire.

Bonfire. My mouth went dry. I couldn't even properly distract myself. I would never be able to look into flames again without seeing the faces of the women. Heresy or witchcraft, off-worlder or local, it didn't matter. No one deserved that kind of fate.

A fate delivered by my past, my people, one that created the world that created me. One I couldn't alter in any way, lest I cease to exist. But what kind of horrors could I avoid from ever happening by making small changes here?

What kind of small horrors could come as a consequence of my actions?

All this power and yet I was powerless. I gritted my teeth. All this great responsibility I was promised wasn't right for me to take. It was too much for one person to handle.

Blayde sighed heavily, clenching her laser pointer. "SHC. Though I don't know if she had a Call Back button. I doubt it."

"So the Agency just… burned her to a crisp where she stood." I shuddered. With that small action, they'd condemned every woman of this town to the same fate if they just stepped a single toe out of line. The only reason they'd even turned on Verity was because that other girl, Joan Mason, had suffered their SHC.

Blayde's lack of answer sent a pang through my heart. James put a comforting hand on my shoulder, covering the ghost of the stranger's clutch.

"Come on," she said, as she rubbed my shoulder. "Remember, you're the reason the Agency's going to have to tighten their game now."

"Yeah." I nodded. "But that's not going to make up for all the people the Agency treated as collateral."

The stranger led us to a house on the very edge of town, which looked like it was designed from word of mouth by a toddler who couldn't quite remember what a house looked like. It was square like a house and built of wood and stone, with a triangular roof too equilateral to be made by human hands. The crisscrossing beams on the front seemed painted on as an afterthought. Thankfully, the monstrosity was half hidden at the corner of the wooden city wall. Only a dim, orange glow outlined the heavy drapes and curtains behind the tiny windows.

The stranger pulled out a key and unlocked the heavy steel door, waving us through. I traded a glance with Zander—was it really safe? He shrugged again. Defeated as we were, we really had nothing better to do.

Inside, the house was catalogue perfect. The sitting room looked exactly like movies on this time period: comfortable chairs sat around a warm fireplace, with a harpsichord in the room's corner and leather-bound books stuffed on shelves covering every inch of wall space. But something about it made the room seem false. Were Puritan homes ever really that opulent?

"It's the middle of the frashing night, Urruin!" A man appeared on the top of the stairs so quickly we all took a step back. The light from behind him made it impossible to see his face, instead making his whole body glow an eerie orange.

Our stranger, Urruin, removed his dark cloak, revealing the body of a balding middle-aged man, the real-life equivalent of Homer Simpson, dressed entirely in a green silk suit.

With coattails. Effing coattails.

"Desmond, we are duty-bound to the lost guests of our employers," he said to the man on the landing. "Be kind. They just witnessed an inflaming."

"That's sir to you, Wrench."

Desmond? My eyes flashed to the man on the landing, still unable to make out his features. We'd been brought right to the doorstep of the person we'd crossed time to see. This couldn't be a coincidence. Was it Fate or future selves pulling the strings once again?

"Another one?" He inhaled sharply. "I thought I finally fixed that. Well, show them to the spare rooms, I suppose. Looks like I'll be burning the midnight candle again."

Zander cleared his throat. "Are you Desmond Elegrious?"

Landing man's tone dropped to a grumble. "Who's asking?"

"I'm Zander, and this is my sister Blayde. You may have heard of us?"

And with that, Desmond flew down the stairs.

"Urruin! Do you know who you've brought into my house?"

"Not your house, sir."

"Why do you always tell these people our real names?" Blayde groaned. "We could have told him we were lawyers bringing him his inheritance, but *nooo*, you had to tell him we were convicted interstellar felons. Genius, truly."

Desmond's dark hair drooped foppishly over his forehead as he bounded to Zander's side, his smile dazzlingly white. He placed his hands on Zander's shoulders, all the while staring deep into his eyes.

"I never thought I would see this day…" Were Desmond's eyes watering? I shifted on my feet, trying to make sense of the stranger. "This cannot be. *The* Zander. *The* Blayde. The Iron and the Sand, here! In my home!"

He was young—late twenties or early thirties, maybe, but that was if he was even Terran—with jet-black hair reaching slightly below his ears. He was well built, strong looking, and tall to top it off. Fine, he was mildly handsome, if I had to say it. He had thrown on a thick dressing gown, a little too plush for our surroundings.

"Desmond Elegrious?" asked Blayde.

He turned to face her, his smile growing tenfold.

"Please, just call me Desmond," he said, positively radiant. "I believed the tales of your beauty were simply myths. I see now that they must have been, as they do not do you justice."

"Charmer, Desmond." Blayde rolled her eyes. "Meet James Felling."

"Enchanté," he said with a smile, shaking her hand. He then turned to me. "And who's this?"

"Um, Sally," I replied, extending a hand to shake. "Sally Webber."

"Pleasure," he said, before picking it up and kissing it. Butterflies took wing in my stomach; I'd never been greeted by a historical gentleman before. "Now, what has brought the legendary siblings to my humble abode?"

"We're here because of your book," said James, ever the pragmatist.

"Book?" Desmond asked, brows furrowed. "I've never written a book. Will I write a book? Oh, that's wonderful!"

Future tense? I stepped closer to Zander, my skin going cold. This man not only knew who they were but knew what they could do—all of what they could do. Who was he?

"Your writings about a labyrinth?" Blayde leaned forward, eyes wide. "*The* labyrinth?

"Ah. My research." He let out a heavy breath. "The great work of my life. I would rather be out in the field rather than sitting on my ass fixing the Agency's problems. But alas, something has to pay the bills since research doesn't."

A chill crept over my skin. Desmond worked for the Agency. Urruin had mentioned employers. Was this an Agency safehouse? Everything fell into place in that instant: the opulence, Urruin's rush to hide us here…

"You're trying to fix the SHC system," I said.

He nodded earnestly. "The Agency's gotten themselves tied in knots with this legacy code. It was crafted by a fleet of highly intelligent Trubblings on a million parallel typewriters, and thus can only be read if you apply Bayesian statistics to each—"

"So, let me get this straight," I said. "You don't know *where* the labyrinth actually is and you're stuck here until you can stop Agency tourists from igniting—in a town already under the spell of witch-hunt madness?"

To say I was crestfallen would be an understatement. My hands tightened into fists as I thought about Marcy, sobbing in the interrogation room, facing the news the Alliance didn't want their new empress to know: my world was ending. I couldn't come back and tell her our only lead was a dud too.

And yet… we were in the past. A place yet untouched by the Dread. We could stay here as long as we needed, until we had a solution. I bit my lip until it bled. I didn't want to spend a second longer than I had to in this wretched time.

"Well, hold on now." He turned to me. "I may not have the exact coordinates, but I *am* the leading expert on the myth. Maybe with our combined skillsets…" His eyes roamed the room, landing heavily on Blayde. "I'm certain you can lead me there. If the tales of your intelligence are understated as much as your beauty, then you must be a genius indeed."

"*Suuure,*" said Zander, exchanging a look with his sister. Even James's face had turned a vibrant shade of red. My gut writhed like it was full of eels.

"But!" Desmond frowned, his lips drawing thin. "I want to see the labyrinth that I've spent my life pouring my blood, sweat, and money into looking for. You take me with you. Deal?"

I looked at Zander, at Blayde. Did I need them to make the decision for me? I would do whatever I had to to save my world, no matter how long it took to find the labyrinth, no matter how long I would have to hide in this terrible time period.

"Deal," we said simultaneously.

"A fine deal indeed." Desmond shook Zander's hand. "I would be a poor host if I put you to work without a good meal and a night's sleep. Is anybody hungry?"

Despite everything we'd just witnessed, I was starving. My stomach had only leftovers and Sven and a sea of coffee. I nodded.

"Finally!" Urruin clapped his hands. "How fortunate we are to have guests! I'll make a cake!"

He threw open two large wooden doors, revealing a dining room fit for a palace, complete with heavy chairs and a roaring fireplace. The fire crackled and I flinched, grabbing Zander's hand. He gave it a gentle squeeze.

"I'll be right back," said Urruin. "Get comfortable. We'll have a feast!"

Zander pulled out a seat for me. I gave him a quick smile and sat, and he settled into the chair beside me. Desmond took the head of the table, while Blayde sat across from her brother. Urruin somehow filled our wine glasses before we'd finished getting situated.

"So, Desmond," she said, leaning in close to our host, "why don't you tell us about your research?"

I groaned internally, my stomach joining in with beautiful harmony. Maybe this would distract me from the hunger that now gnawed at my gut.

"We just sat down for dinner. Surely, you don't want me to bore you with details?" Desmond eyed Blayde with a sideways glance. She only fluttered her eyelashes in response, politely waiting. He continued, "Well, the original myth is incredibly old. It usually starts by saying that there was this battle between two suns, so that sets the tone for what I've pieced together."

"Sons of whom?" Zander asked. He leaned back in his chair, taking a sip of his wine. If it weren't for the desert wraps that still clung to his body, I would have thought him quite the gentlemanly sight.

"No, *suns*. Stars. You know, like the actual balls of plasma? Some say they were fighting over who would rule the universe, others, that one was being punished for his crimes. It's said that the swifter sun somehow tricked the other into taking human form, trapping them in a maze they grew around them. Others say that a genius was asked to chart everything in space, every galaxy, every planet, every moon, and every asteroid, but when he mapped them all they played him the music of the universe and he went mad, locking *himself* in the labyrinth to stop himself from telling the world. The only fact every myth agrees upon is that an undying genius deserved to be locked within a planet-sized prison, and he did not fight it."

"Our guests are starving, sir," said Urruin, a massive serving tray balanced on his hand. "Do not bore them with children's stories."

The smell waltzed into my nose and made itself at home: roasted, juicy turkey; fluffy mashed potatoes; the greenest of green beans. I drifted like a cartoon character through the wafting steam as Urruin set out plates before us. Heavenly.

"Well, they asked for it." Desmond held up a hand as if to put the tale on pause, devouring most of the turkey on his plate. Urruin pursed his lips, slipping out of the room and closing the doors behind him. No one said a word.

Zander's eyes were wide and riveted on Desmond, completely engrossed. He didn't even seem to notice own plate steaming in front of him.

"Soon the labyrinth was forgotten entirely, and the universe went to war, as it eventually had to," Desmond said between bites of mashed potatoes. "That's just the way it all goes. Call it the rebellious phase, the teenage years of a civilization. Its control soon fell into the hands of one of the warring factions, though it had no idea what power it contained. After decades of trial and error, they sent in their smartest rather than their strongest to run it and find what was locked in the center of an impenetrable maze. What they discovered was a man."

"The Eternal?" squeaked Zander, eyes sparkling.

Desmond nodded. "The explorers tried to bring him to their leaders, but the Eternal told them it was impossible for him to leave the labyrinth. For you see, it had a mind of its own and could move and grow, and any of the men trying to escort him out would find his exit blocked. So, they asked him what they should do to bring peace between worlds. He pondered this and decided that they should bring the opposing factions to him, so that he may hear both sides.

"There's no record of what he said, but *boom*, instant harmony. But now that all the massive diplomatic problems had been solved, smaller and smaller issues were being brought to the Eternal, and labyrinth guides were dropping by the hundreds. The leaders of each of the formerly warring factions got together and decided that once every year, a champion from each civilization would be permitted to run the labyrinth, and the winner would be allowed to request anything of the Eternal.

"But peace meant people were living longer. New civilizations arose practically overnight, what with everyone working together to terraform inhospitable worlds. So, the rules to the race changed. Anyone could enter, if they could afford it, to compete for the opportunity to have their dreams come true. It was said that the wise man could make anything happen. Powers like a god.

"But the labyrinth kept evolving, adapting to the scale of the influx of contenders. Fewer and fewer people returned alive, and as a result, fewer people entered. Wars broke out amongst the stars, the cycle continuing, and the labyrinth slowly fading into the fabric of myth before the records just…stop."

"That's all you have?" asked Blayde.

"Hey, this is a lifetime of research here!" Desmond growled. His plate now empty, he reached for the bowl of peas, eating directly from the bowl. "Remember, this was millennia ago. The first accounts date back almost a million years."

"A million?" Zander whistled.

"And they were written *long* after the Eternal was supposedly imprisoned. The first races happened while the first humans were still only single-cell organisms dreaming of the sun."

Zander nodded. He still hadn't touched his plate. "Yet you managed to narrow down its present-day location?"

"I have a fair idea of where it is." Desmond grinned, his teeth glowing in the yellow lamplight. "Solar system, I'm certain of. Planet, maybe. But getting there? It would be impossible in my lifetime."

"We might be able to work with that," said Zander, nodding slowly. I knew instantly what he was thinking: how would *I* find it, if he'd never been there himself?

I looked down at my empty plate. I was thinking the same thing in reverse—how could I get us there without him questioning my methods? How much detail would I need from Desmond to bring us all there, right here, right now?

"How can we be certain this man is still alive?" I asked, looking up. All eyes turned to me. "What?"

"He's immortal, Sally," Blayde snapped.

My face went hot. "That could just be part of the legend."

"He lived for thousands of years of recorded history," said Desmond.

"Some species have an average lifespan of a few thousand, though, right?" I said.

"So why haven't we heard of them?" asked Desmond.

"Or maybe—just maybe—he could be one of us." Zander's eyes sparkled like the anachronistic electric chandelier above us. "Imagine, he might hold the answers we're looking for. This could be it."

"Could," said Blayde. "And that's if this so-called wise man truly is immortal."

"But he's got to be millions of years old now, if he's still alive." James let out a low whistle. "That's a long time to live."

"Who's to say we haven't already lived that long ourselves?" said Zander. "Who's to say he hasn't lost his memory, like we have? Could he have forgotten his past as well? Could he have forgotten the Dread?"

"I sure hope not." Blayde shuddered. "I sure hope not."

And I realized, then, exactly what the siblings would ask this man if they could.

He was their only chance for a way home.

· · · · · · · ● · · · · · · · ·

DESMOND WAS KIND ENOUGH TO SET US UP WITH
rooms. Being an Agency safe house, it was built to house a few visiting dignitaries and directors and the like. Urruin led Zander and me to a room beside Desmond's study, complete with a four-poster bed and a roaring fire. We even had loaner nightgowns.

I was so ready to rip off my desert wraps, to get the sand off my gross body, that I started peeling out of them the second Zander closed the door behind us. Two worlds and three time periods of crud fell to the floor as I stumbled to the fireplace.

"Let me," said Zander, reaching for the knot of fabric behind my neck. The relief I felt when the fiber fell away was enough to make me groan. The soft brush of his trembling fingers against my skin sent strokes of heat down my spine. I turned, reaching to help Zander with his, but he pulled away.

"What's wrong?" I asked.

"I...I need to help Desmond with his code, so we can get out of..." He took a deep breath. "I don't want to waste any time in this..."

"It's terrible," I agreed. I wrapped my hands around his neck, pulling myself close. The skin there was clammy and hot. "Those poor girls didn't deserve their fate. I want to storm out there and give every single person in this town a piece of my mind. But can we?

Would that be changing the timeline? What if just by showing up, I've just—"

"You're still here." Zander kissed the top of my forehead, calming the roaring boil in my stomach. "That should be evidence enough that you haven't screwed up the timeline yet."

I leaned my head against his chest, breathing him in, every sweaty inch of him. I was tired, so tired. I just wanted to curl up in bed with him, let his arms anchor me in time and space.

A tremor shook me from his warmth. Not mine—his. Zander was… shaking?

"What's wrong?" I asked. He wrapped an arm around me, pulling me closer, so tight against him I could feel the trembling that gripped his entire body.

"Nothing to worry you with," he replied, kissing the top of my head again. His lips were cold. "Just go to sleep, Sally. You need it. You deserve it. You've done…"

The water running down my scalp was unmistakable. Tears.

I pulled away, taking his face in my hands, brushing the tears with my thumbs. He was sobbing quietly, the sobs of a man overflowing.

"Sit," I said, leading him to the end of the bed, making him sit. At this height, at least, I was taller than him, could wrap my arms around his head, cradle it against me the way he usually held me, letting my bare skin soak up his tears. "Just tell me what's happening."

"I don't even know where to start," he whimpered.

A heavy soul. A moment of overflow. I held him closer. "Whatever's in your head."

"I'm scared." He exhaled, making the hair on my belly rise under his hot breath. "I'm scared of me."

"Of you?" I snapped my mouth shut. This was his time to talk. My questions would only be speed bumps along the way. His hands wrapped around my waist to anchor himself to me.

"Of who I was in that dusty memory of Blayde's." Zander's voice was as low as a whisper. "I was cold, Sally. So cold. So angry. But I…I had known where Blayde was. I knew how to find her. The right time, the right place."

I felt my body go rigid against his. I had been so focused on my own worries, my own fears, that I hadn't see what was right in front of me, clear as day. Zander had talked about waves in phase, and now I could see that we were the opposite. Somewhere along the way, we'd gotten out of sync.

"I could *jump*, Sally," he said, his voice wavering. "*Really* jump. Like Nimien. Like… like you."

I was shaking now. I tried to take a step back, but his grip around me was firm. He didn't look up, didn't raise his voice. He only sank deeper into my embrace, hugging me impossibly closer. Goosebumps covered my exposed skin.

He'd changed the subject, sprang this realization on me so fast…

"I'm so sorry," I breathed. "I didn't know how to tell you, I don't…I don't fully understand it myself."

He nodded. I took his head in my hands again, tilting it back so I could look him in the eyes. The beautiful silver-green was brimming with tears.

"My past self can't have been everywhere and anywhere," he said. "No matter what you'd have me think."

"I don't know what's wrong with me," I replied. "Why I'm broken. I would have told you, I swear. I just…I wanted to come to you with answers."

"Oh, Sally," he said, his eyes so wide and wet I could have drowned in them. "You're an angel. All this time you've been asking me to understand your risks, to see that you're unbreakable, that you've forgotten I'm unbreakable too. You didn't have to protect me."

Protect him? I smiled weakly. As much as I wanted to take credit for a little act of selflessness, this wasn't one of them.

"I'm the one who's broken," he said, exhaling again, his body deflating like a balloon. "I'm the one whose memory has been smashed, who can't do the very thing that defines him. You didn't want me to know."

He urged me closer, and I dove into that kiss, all the while my mind reeling. My hands still clutched the side of his face while his hands ran up my back, pulling us closer together. Even as he lit my heart aflame with lips so full of love, I was stuck at the moment where he had entirely inverted our roles.

No. He wasn't broken. *I* was broken. I was the one who sank too deeply into the universe. He was the one with perfectly healthy barriers against it.

Only he hadn't always been like this—not in a time and place he could no longer remember.

He pulled away, reluctantly from the sigh that he took, kissing my forehead, my cheeks, the tip of my nose. No new tears in his eyes. He wiped away the old ones.

"You're not broken," I said, breathless. I couldn't fit my thoughts into words, the fears I had been hiding from him, the fears he was dismissing without understanding.

"Sally, it's all right," he said, pushing himself off the bed to stand. He removed his hands from my skin, turning the whole room cold. I had forgotten I was bare.

Dammit. Where did that shirt go?

"I've got to go help Desmond," said Zander, planting one last kiss on my forehead. "If all goes well, tomorrow we'll be at the labyrinth. We'll find our answers. And you'll get us there."

I swallowed. Loud. But he didn't seem to notice.

"I'm so in awe of you, Sally Webber." How was he already at the door? "I don't deserve you."

Well, shit.

I fell backward on the bed the instant the door closed. What the hell had just happened? Zander's tears were still drying on my bare stomach as I lay staring at the ceiling, mind aflame. Because if he didn't deserve me—

What the hell did I deserve?

TWELVE

AIN'T NO PARTY LIKE A HIGHER DIMENSIONAL UNICORN PARTY BECAUSE A HIGHER DIMENSIONAL UNICORN PARTY LITERALLY DOESN'T STOP IN TWENTY-SIX SIMULTANEOUS DIRECTIONS

IT FELT LIKE AN ETERNITY SINCE I'D LAST WOKEN on a sunny morning all snug in my bed. Who knows what planet Desmond pulled this mattress from, but it certainly wasn't the disgusting colonial mattresses I'd heard horror stories about, what with the hay, horse hair, inevitable bugs, and the overall mixture of dead skin and salty sweat that they gathered over the years.

By the sound of typing and hushed words from the neighboring room, Zander and Desmond must have worked through the night, a small army of localized woodpeckers.

Zander.

I stared at the empty place in the bed beside me, cold and undisturbed through the night. We had said nothing and everything last night. He knew, he *knew* what I could do, yet, apparently, that was *his* flaw.

It wasn't right. None of this was right. He couldn't keep putting everything on himself; he was going to crumble under the weight.

The second my toes touched the floorboards, Urruin appeared in the doorway. He held a suitcase-sized package, which he promptly laid out for me on the cushy armchair in the corner.

"Morning?" I said quickly, inexperienced in the world of butlery.

"Good morning, Ms. Webber," he said, turning to face me and give me a short bow. "Would you like me to draw a bath?"

He stared at me, unsmiling, unblinking, just waiting. It seemed the warmth from last night had entirely faded.

"Um… no, no need. Thanks."

"Are you quite certain?" He scanned me up and down. "I have pulled out a dress for you from the costume trailer."

"The… costume trailer." Right. Agency safe house. Maybe they had a skin wrap or two lying around there too. I shuddered. How many of them would go up in flames, taking their occupants with them?

"Will you need help dressing?"

Probably. But even knowing he was a butler, I wasn't all too jazzed at the idea of having a stranger seeing that much of me. Call me a prude, but we *were* living in the era of the Puritan.

"No, thank you."

"Will that be all?"

"Yes, that will be all."

Thank the stars for the Agency's costume department. I had expected to be wearing Puritan black but instead was greeted by a lovely linen, a shade between sky and baby blue. Grabbing the box, I rushed behind the divider, stripping off the borrowed nightshirt, and pulling on the skirts. A sea of fabric swirled around my waist with no logical way to stay up. I frowned. This was the real thing, made by a real dressmaker, for real Earth women, years before the invention of zippers or Velcro. The Agency must have been too lazy to make their own outfits. Such a pain. At least they were investing in the local economy.

"Need a hand?" I heard from the door.

"Who is it?"

"It's me, dumbass." Blayde sighed heavily. "You need help?"

I paused. "Yes, please."

She joined me behind the divider, tutting. She, too, had received a new dress, a soft pink that I would never have guessed in a thousand years she would be willing to wear.

There was so much I wanted to talk with her about. She had stuffed her feelings deep down again, and I knew from experience just how well that was going to go. And with Zander breaking down about his past, I knew she was going through the same thing.

"Well, the skirt's on backward, for one," she said and readjusted it with a swift twist. "Hold up that bodice. I'm going to tighten it for you."

"Sure." She laced it in quick, sharp movements as I held my breath. A jigsaw puzzle of clothing, each element fitting around me perfectly, now that somebody knew how they went together. "How do you know all this?"

"I posed as a maid more than once. Arms up." She pulled the sleeves down over my arms, fixing my cuffs around my wrists. "I picked up a few tricks here and there."

"Well, you're a lifesaver, that's for sure." She had moved to fixing my hair, twisting and turning the locks until they were balanced upon my head. Then—*squish*—a coif came right down over it—and right back off.

"Wait, have you had breakfast yet?" she asked. "I was waiting for you. I'm bored out of my mind."

"The IT Crowd don't need any company?" I asked, trying not to touch my new headgear. As Blayde finished, she stepped in front of me and smiled to herself.

"They don't need me to interrupt their work. Well, Zander's work. The other two are just there to give him an excuse to smoke cigars. Anyway, let's go eat. I'm hungry, and nothing's going to stop me from getting a good dose of bacon."

"Two? *James* is helping?"

Blayde nodded. I had been so wrong about James.

"What are we doing waiting here?" I gave her the biggest smile I could muster. "Come on, there's good bacon to eat and no one to share it with, and we're just wasting time up here!"

"Finally, something we can agree on," she said with a sly grin.

The hallway was stuffy, probably due to the roils of smoke wafting under the study door. A door that was vibrating, the music behind it so loud.

"Don't mind them," said Blayde, but I was already pushing my way in, curiosity beckoning. "Fine. Meet you downstairs. Don't say I didn't warn you."

The smell of burning grass hit my nostrils, making me cringe. Something else lingered in the undertone of the air, sound made odorous, the smell of sharp electronic music crashing in bitter harmony, slurring and shaking like dubstep.

I wasn't hearing music; I was *smelling* it.

Massive stage lights towered over a blocky computer that had orange filters strong enough to cover up the phosphorescent glow of the screen. Desmond was perched on the desk like a vulture, a large pipe sticking to his lips. He was watching the bed where James lay with her eyes fixed on the ceiling, a can of probably-not-actually Red Bull balanced on her forehead.

We weren't in Virginia anymore. Hell, we weren't even on Earth.

Zander tossed back a can in a single gulp, crushed it in his fist, and tossed it over his back into a waiting trash can. He wiped his arm across his face, breathing a dramatic sigh before returning his fingers to the keyboard. Lines and lines of code burst onto the screen, faster than my eyes could track.

"Goal!" Desmond exclaimed. "Do I have a penalty?"

"Yep." Zander looked up from his task to glower at his opponent, code still flying.

Desmond grabbed a pistol from the desk. Before I could react, there was now a hole in the can perched on James's forehead, the liquid pouring into her mouth.

"Chug, chug, chug!"

The second the flow stopped, James lifted the can with her feet and tossed it to Desmond, who caught it, crunched it up, and threw it into the basket across the room.

"Score!"

I cleared my throat. "So, I take it you made some progress?"

Zander's head spun around. He was glowing, but not in a way my eyes could see. He was somehow glowing in my brain. "Loads! Desmond was right; there *was* a virus. We tracked it down and purged the system. Once we get the new processes in motion, we'll have the entire thing resolved and under lock and key."

"In order to be sure there's absolutely no tampering, we're going to run the system on automatic and phase out its use," added Desmond. "Like Zander said you have in your time. Only he and I will know how to infiltrate the system once more, so that secret will die with me. The Agency will still have access but can only use it as a last resort."

I frowned. Was no one bothered by how comfortable this stranger was with our time travel? Maybe they were just too… high.

"The new parameters are simple." Zander's eyes twinkled. "We've set it so combustion only occurs *after* death, and only if there's a chance of any Earth agency—not just the one with a capital A—getting a hold of the victim."

Except the woman in Costco was most definitely alive when she'd burst into flames. Maybe Foollegg was right and the Dread had interfered with their system, no matter how well Zander fixed it today. Which would mean we were about as unable to fix the future as we were the past.

"Why not shut it off entirely?" I said, and Zander frowned.

"We know how it is in our time," he replied, his voice less than confident. "So that's how it has to be."

I bit my lip. Why couldn't changing the future be easy?

"I *am* the unicorn," said James, distracting me from my thoughts.

"No, you're not, James." Zander sighed.

"I am, I know it. You know how I know it?"

"You are not the unicorn, James."

"No, I mean it. I'm serious," she said, sitting up on the bed. "I can see the curvature of time. I am here—" She stretched out her left arm, fingers spayed, face slack. "And I am there." She extended the other arm, pointing her fingers out as far as they could go. "I am everywhere at once, and I burn at the center of time."

"No, you are full of yourself," Desmond said, shaking his head.

This. This was my team. I was meant to be in charge of this mission, we were meant to be saving the universe, and this is how they were going about it? And James, brilliant James, trying to fit in and getting this in the process. It wasn't like her. And I wouldn't stand for it.

"It's normal," said Zander to me. "Most fusion drinks give humans delusions of grandeur. Among other… side effects."

"Fusion?" I asked.

"Cold fusion?"

"My hands glow with the feel of time," James said excitedly. "I can play the harp made of the strings of *time*. I can—"

"You let her drink *cold fusion* energy drinks?" I rushed to her side. James's eyes were the size of dinner plates, her blinks long and stretched. I couldn't believe what I was seeing. Zander, who was usually ridiculously safe about us Terrans, so blasé about James?

"Relax, Sally," Zander said without turning around. My hands formed into fists. "I needed some energy to keep going, and she wanted to be part of the fun. She's fine; I wouldn't have let her have any if there were any serious risks."

"It's not harmful," added Desmond. "I was screened before I came to your planet."

Yeah, like the Agency really cared. But before I could say anything, James yanked me down to her level so she could stare into my eyes. Her brow was slick with sweat.

"Sally, Sally, listen," she said. "Can you hear them? The drums? Nah, I kid. Sally, have you heard? I am the seventh-dimensional unicorn."

"This doesn't sound fine, Zander," I spat. This couldn't be happening. "I'm getting her out of here."

What was James trying to prove, partying with them? It was so unlike her. Unless… this wasn't about proving anything. She'd just learned that her own partner was tracking her. Had implanted her. Talk about a massive violation. Cold fusion energy drinks and mystery cigars were nothing after that.

My friend was hurting, and I hadn't even noticed. What a leader I was turning out to be.

"No, Sally, you mustn't disrupt the ceremony of transcendence!" James belted. "The fate of Earth is in our hands. You can't stop us! You cannot stop the unicorn—

"Right, I'm out of here," I said, grabbing her by the scruff of the neck and dragging her out behind me. She struggled but was too weak to put up much of a fight. It was time for some tough love.

"You mustn't touch the unicorn!" James spat angrily, trying to wrench away from my grasp. "The unicorn can change the past and the future!"

"Of course you can," I said, struggling to keep my voice calm and even. "Unicorn, you need to rest that brilliant mind of yours. Can you do that for me?"

"I swear I had nothing to do with any of this," said Zander, still typing. "I knew it was safe, and James isn't a child."

"The unicorn lives!" James roared.

"Right, well, next time you try and save a town from another senseless witch hunt, try not to do it while tripping, all right?"

I couldn't believe Zander. I trusted him, and now James was losing it. So much for being my partner. If Zander was still hurting, he should have come talk to me instead of whatever this shit was.

"Oh great stars above, what have they done to James?"

Blayde stood on the landing, her jaw almost at the floor. She stared at James with her eyes so full of electricity she would be able to power the entire planet for over a century. She lifted her out of my grasp, shouldering the weight and darting back to my room. I rushed after them.

"So it shall be," said James as Blayde splayed her on the bed, "that the cycle shall conclude, beginning and end melding as one, converging on one point."

Blayde's eyes snapped to me. "What has she taken?"

"Um… some alien cold fusion energy drink, I think, and she's been locked up with some smoke that smells like cosmobeat."

"Like what?"

"Electronic music."

"Again, what?"

"Modern-day Earth stuff. Music made on the computer. *Wub wub wub?*"

"Oh." She glared at me. "Was it more of a *wub wub wub* or a *wab wab wub?*"

"Something in between like *wub wub wuuuub?*"

Blayde cringed. "Might have been fine if she hadn't been subjected to both. You take care of James. I'm going to mix up a remedy. Don't listen to her rantings, all right?"

"I haven't been."

"We shall lose ourselves before finding who we are," James continued as Blayde dashed off. "Though who may like what they find?"

"James, you need to calm down," I said.

Her head was burning up, beads of sweat rolling down her cheeks like tears.

"The universe… like music, it clashes with itself. So the Unicorn sees, so the unicorn hears," she continued, ignoring me. *"Wub wub wub wub wub wub wub…"*

"You have to calm down, James," I said, though I logically knew that there was no use in trying to reason with her. "You can't beatbox. And no one can *sing* dubstep."

"This should help," said Blayde, rushing back into the room with what appeared to be a bloody mary in hand, celery stalk tall and proud.

"Drink," Blayde ordered, shoving the glass under James's lip. Her eyes were shut before they hit the pillow.

"What was that?" I asked, shocked.

"A bad trip." She shrugged. "Happens to the best of us."

She placed the half empty glass on the nightstand, using the sheets on the bed—*my* bed—to wipe the layers of sweat from James's face. She seemed so peaceful now. She was just as human as the rest of us.

Well, a few of us.

"She tried cold fusion and smoked some higher dimensional tobacco. She's bound to feel a little drowsy." Blayde glanced up at me, celery stalk in hand. "Sadly, I seem to have lost my appetite as a result."

"Same."

"Right. We can either stick around the house embroidering and talking about local singles and corn-related drama while watching her sleep all day, or… we can finally have that talk we need to have. Your pick." She took a massive bite of celery to punctuate her sentence without breaking eye contact.

A chill ran through my bones. Oh god, not her too. I'd gotten sloppy, hoped two of the smartest people I'd ever met wouldn't see I was lying to them. I needed an out. "James needs me. I brought her; I'm responsible for her."

"She'll sleep it off. It's nothing." She nodded. "Now come. We have a few hours before they're finished in there. Let's have our girl time."

I knew what was coming, and I wasn't ready. It was time to face the music. My face was hot as we strolled arm-in-arm out of the cosmobeat-smelling house and into the bustling streets of seventeenth-century New England. It hit me that these dresses were terribly out of place. While our dresses seemed perfectly accurate for the time, they weren't the clothes of choice of this small colony.

We wandered through the streets of my past. My country wouldn't exist for another century. This was the world of the colonists: a world of strange new lands, new foods, new plants, new animals.

New people too. I had no doubt in my mind why the wall around this town was so tall. Would my being here change anything? *Could* I change anything, if I would help right the wrongs of the past with the person I now was. I stared at that fence hard enough to drill a hole through it.

Was it useless to hope? I'd helped the siblings save entire worlds from crisis time and time again. If we'd arrived here without knowing it was Earth, we'd be all up in that interference. Stopping the witch hunts, stopping the Agency. Maybe more—so much more. But who was I, to act like I knew how to fix something as massive as History? Did knowing this past was my past actually change anything? Was there truly a clear divide between past and future that stopped us from intervening?

This past was somebody's present. My past was somebody's future.

Maybe when I met the Eternal, he could tell me what to do. If I dared hope it was all real.

Blayde tightened her grip on my arm, jolting me out of my spiral.

"So," she said. Her arm was tight around mine like a vice. "Tell me how you did it."

"Did what?" I asked. The vice, impossibly, tightened.

"Don't play with me." Her lips were tight, white. "I knew from the second we got here Zander's never been near this place. I would have felt it. I always do. So how did you get us here?"

I shook my head. I had gotten sloppy, no, showy. Maybe part of me was proud of what I could do, move through space in a way even the great siblings could not. Maybe that's why I'd let my guard down.

Maybe I had wanted them to know.

I took a deep breath. "I wasn't going to say anything until I could explain *why*," I said. "But I can *see* where we're going, Blayde. Ever since my first jump. Ever since Cross…" I couldn't keep the shiver from traveling up my spine. "Ever since he scrambled my brain."

I could still remember the feeling of something rummaging through my head, still see through my eyes as someone had moved my body without my will. No matter what, I couldn't wash myself clean of the knowledge that someone else had taken over the controls. And so effortlessly too.

Blayde's vice grip slacked—good. But it wasn't entirely gone. I still went wherever she was going, and where we were going seemed to be another dark alley.

"Tell me how," she said.

"How—what? How to jump?"

"How do you find your way around in the dark?"

It was hard not to hear the yearning in her voice, the lilt to her question, the *wanting* there. In an instant, my perspective shifted. Blayde was my friend, someone I loved like a sister. I had to help her.

"The dark's not all that…dark for me."

She frowned, furrowing her brows. "What the frash are you talking about?"

"Okay, how do you jump?" I stopped, turning toward her.

"Come with me."

She glanced both ways before dragging me down an alley until we were entirely cloaked in darkness. It smelled of urine and old potatoes.

"Take my hands," she ordered. "You may have to bring us back."

"Where are we going?"

"Anywhere," she said quickly. "Hold on tight."

My world was darkness in every direction, stretching on forever. The infinite universe in which I shrunk to a tiny insignificant speck, trying to tear me limb from limb. There was the cold, the cold that soaked into my pores, the cold that whispered, that called me to fear, to scream and run. My cells ripped apart, sinking into the infinite. They were leaving me, rushing away from the fear. The loneliness. The nothing. The nothing that whispered in called to me. The terror that reminded me that no one was there to catch me as I fell. As I fell apart.

The great *empty.*

An emptiness I hadn't felt since I had become…whatever I was.

Then, in an instant, I was me again. My cells became mine once more, the feeling of infinity becoming finite once again surrounding me. The fear was gone. But the shock was the same.

And so was Blayde.

"So?" she asked.

"I thought…" I rubbed my arms for warmth. Why wasn't I getting warm? Where was the light? Where were we? "I thought it was just like that because I wasn't used to it. But you feel that *every single time?*"

She nodded. "It's different for you?"

"Completely," I replied. "I've jumped you a few times; you never noticed anything out of the ordinary?"

"Always the…nothingness," she whispered. She rubbed her hand against her sternum, palm pressing down hard. Deep, even breaths—the same way I staved off panic.

If she was having a thought spiral, I needed to break the loop, distract her. I looked around. Nope, nothing but darkness. We stood in a small, rectangular room, barely the size of a closet. The wall in front of us had a long slit down the front, through which we received a trickle of light, along with a low brouhaha of what seemed to be a large crowd as a bonus. *Whoosh.* There came anxiety flooding through my carefully propped-up gates, twisting my empty stomach into knots.

"What is this place?" I whispered. Running my hand over the wall revealed nothing but smooth plaster.

"I have no idea. Hold on, don't move. I think our dresses are caught."

I looked down. They were more than caught; they were intertwined, the skirts fused down the seams. "Shit, it's like in those video games when the graphics mess up. Does this happen a lot?"

"Never. Then again, I've never jumped such huge dresses into such a small room. Is it me or is it shrinking?"

It wasn't just her. Soon the room was too small for us both. I extended my hand out of the door flap to give us more space, but the second it was out a huge wave of applause rose from the crowd outside. The wall gave us a shove, and I stumbled out into blinding light, Blayde grunting as the fused dresses dragged her along.

I blinked, my hand shading my eyes, searching for any clue to our whereabouts. A stage lamp was aimed right at our faces. We were in a large, cathedral-like room, air echoing with cheers rising from what had to be an enormous crowd.

We were on… a runway?

A fabulous, massively oversized runway. The room was shaped into a dodecahedron, the crowd around us rising in every direction like waves upon waves of sweetened-condensed people. The entire place was silver and blue with blinding white walls around the pit in which we stood, though there was no natural light. Large bubble blowers sat on either side of our runway, blowing colorful bubbles into the air around us. Larger-than-life-sized videos of us were suddenly projected upon the wide screens on the walls, our confused expressions stretched tenfold.

Right. Not colonial America. But whether or not this was better than the witch-burning madness we'd just escaped was yet to be seen.

"What is this place?" I whispered.

"Someplace I would rather duck out of quickly."

"You've been?"

"Only once before," Blayde said with a glare at the crowd. "The loathsome party of Pythanous Five." My lack of response made her roll her eyes. She cleared her throat, all while waving at the crowd. "The people of Pythanous Five are seventh-dimensional beings. They're the ones who created that stuff Desmond was smoking while they were seeking ascension."

"Blayde, do you realize what this means?" I asked, and she shook her head. "It's no coincidence. You brought us here *because* of that stuff. You still have some measure of control."

She furrowed her brows. "Makes sense. Not that I like it."

"We can still see them. Is that normal?" I asked. "Seventh dimensional. Isn't it impossible for our minds to conceive?"

"Well, we *are* on a plane of existence where we can co-exist. They've brought themselves down to our level."

A loud grunt came from the ground on our right. An eight-armed gelatinous glob cleared their throat—did they even have one? What were they clearing?—and nudged their head forward. I didn't need a translator to tell me that meant *go*. And so, we walked the runway.

"And why is this party loathed?" Applause rose around us in many forms, clapping and snaps and honking accompanying our stride. We reached the end and marched into the crowd. "Looks normal enough to me. Well, except for the people in the unicorn masks. That's terrifying."

"Those aren't masks," she said. "It's how you perceive them when they're in this plane. We all see them differently. Anyway, it's loathed because it hasn't ended in a century or two. People come and people go, bringing more food and drinks as they come. The hosts have been working nonstop for generations."

"So, what are people still doing here?" I asked as two seminude men walked past on their hands. Behind them, two women with pink skin were tossing squids at a man who looked strangely like Meedian, only blue.

"Contemplating ascension." She shrugged. "Though, as I tried to tell them before, immortality gets rather dull in the end. They didn't listen."

At least this wasn't anywhere remotely near Earth or the Dread. I took a deep breath. While I was here, I couldn't muck up the timeline. And maybe these higher dimensional beings could be the key we needed to unlock the end of days.

A hand dropped delicately on my shoulder, making my body go rigid.

"The future is a distant thing," a unicorn man said, his horn glistening under the strange lights. While the mouth never moved, the eyes continued to blink. He wore nothing but a silver leotard, his arms covered in large bangles that hovered above his skin without touching it.

"Excuse me," I muttered, trying to pull away. Blayde stopped me.

"Let him speak. It could be important," she advised. "Sometimes they have incredible insights."

"Apple, apple!" he intoned. "The Apple never falls far from the tree. Think different."

"Then again, this guy is really drunk." Blayde sighed. "Come on, let's get back to Earth."

"No." The unicorn's clasp on my shoulder tightened. This time, I found the strength to shake him off. "Trust your instincts, Sally Webber, hand of justice, defeater of the Zoesh, friend of the lowly, protector of Earth."

"This is creepy," I whispered to Blayde.

She nodded. "Never mess with a seventh-dimensional being at a party…"

"And Blayde, the sword of stars, every warrior has their time. The lion's roar was heard across the universe and ignored by none. You should have seen…. But you shall still find the truth, though be warned that you may not like what you discover."

And with that, he tore off running through the crowd. Seconds later, his head was in the trash can, rainbows flowing from the strange horse's mouth.

"Yeah, I heard that all before." Blayde sighed.

"What was that about?" My eyes stung from not blinking. "I've been accosted by too many drunks today, Blayde. I'm beginning to think it's all just some strange fever dream."

"Take us back?" she asked.

"Sure."

I placed a hand on her shoulder and guided us back to Petersburg, making sure to keep our skirts from mixing this time. And once again, there she was—or more accurately, wasn't. Like a black hole in space. A rip in the universe. A spot where simply nothing existed, not even air, not even a single atom or quark. Like God himself reached down with an eraser to scratch that spot out of existence.

And then she *was* again.

Back on firm ground, she let out a sigh of relief. "Frash, it feels good to be out of that place."

Did it really? This town had just condemned children to death from fear and superstition. I wasn't all that eager to be among them again.

"And you felt no difference in the jump?" I asked.

"None." She shook her head.

I took a deep breath, stepping closer to her. "I'm so sorry. We should have talked about this earlier; I was just... We have to talk to each other. I'm your friend, Blayde, and you need to talk. I'm here for you. Okay?"

She nodded, clutching my wrist in her hand. For a second, our eyes met and I saw the tightness there. The pain she must be going through. We were dredging up so much so fast.

A man's scream took us right out of our sisterly bonding moment. A man screaming so loud he could have reached the entire town, which was exactly what he wanted to do.

"Witches! Witches! Heaven have mercy, there are witches among us once again!"

THIRTEEN

MORE THAN A WOMAN, LESS THAN A DUCK

DIDN'T I SAY THIS WAS GOING TO HAPPEN?

This is why women and time travel don't mix. Things have only been cool on Earth for the past few decades, and even then "cool" is loosely defined and not shared by everyone. Once this is all wrapped up, I'm going to find myself a good old-fashioned matriarchy and hang out there while all of this blows over.

And the next time I'm visiting the past, I'm learning how to apply a false beard.

"Witches! Dear God, will there be no end to these witches?"

Blayde and I pressed ourselves against the brick wall, staring out into the street where the mob was already conveniently forming around the screaming man. So much frantic handwaving going on.

"Shit," I said. I tried to stuff my hands into my pockets before realizing this dress didn't have any, and my sweaty palms just slid down my skirts. "I thought Zander had this whole SHC thing under control."

"Seems like he's got some kinks to work out," said Blayde. Her lips pressed into a tight white line. "So help me, if it wasn't full of civilians, I would be blowing up the Agency centuries early."

"Glad we're on the same page." Throwing the time stream to the wind seemed like a good idea right about now anyway. My sweaty palms rolled into fists.

She shook her head. "Well, we can't just stand by and let them ruin more people's lives."

"Wait—"

But she was already dashing toward the mob. She trotted up a stack of barrels with the agility of a mountain goat, waving her arms, demanding attention.

"Listen to me, people of…shit, what's this town called again? People of Virginia! There are no witches within this town. This I know for a fact! I—"

The crowd fell silent, turning to stare at her with their wide, glassy eyes. Even from down the alleyway, I could see the twisted glares she was getting. Terrible feedback.

"Oh, frash it all, you're after me, aren't you?"

"You are hereby accused of—*heresy!*"

There was Parchment Guy from the night before, sans parchment but with a hat twice as tall as I remembered. Still with that pompous air and fire-and-brimstone voice. One of his men reached up to grab at

Blayde, but she kicked him squarely in the face without removing her gaze from Parchment Guy. The crowd gasped as one, ripping a hole in the ozone right then and there.

"Look, just because I'm a stranger here doesn't mean you can accuse me of heresy," she said. "I'm really lovely once you get to know me."

"Witch!" a man roared, soon to be followed by the rest of the mob. "Burn her!"

"She appeared out of nowhere!" said the first man who had screamed. Ah, that explains it. He must have seen us return from the party. Good luck explaining *that* away. I pressed harder against the wall. "She communed with the shadows and then returned to flesh. She's worse than a witch. She's a demon in human form!"

"She has come here to tempt us!" added the man who had been kicked in the face. "Yesterday, she was a pauper, and today, she wears finery. She used the devil's power in her hair to seduce a good man into becoming her slave!"

"I have done no such thing!" Blayde gasped, a hand going to her bosom. Gone was the warrior woman. In an instant, she had transformed into a bleating, innocent girl. I was going to have to hire her for acting classes. "It was out of sheer kindness that one of your own, a godly fellow, offered me hospitality in exchange for nothing."

"Here's another one!" a man shouted, and the world turned black as a burlap sack was slipped over my face. It must have once held potatoes or veggies of some kind because dirt rained down on my face. "Uglier than the first!"

I coughed up dust. Shit! I'd been so focused on Blayde I hadn't been covering the rest of the alley. Not only was I a terrible manager, but I made a terrible sidekick. And now I was going to pay for it.

"Hey!" I cried, aiming a kick behind me. My heel collided with his shin, hard enough for something to snap. The man cried out as I swung back my elbow, slamming it into his ribs. But before I could grab that stupid burlap from my head, more hands grabbed my wrists and shoulders, holding me still.

"Let me go! I'm not a witch!" I struggled against the hands, but there were too many of them. Fingers dug into my skin. Hands gripped my biceps, squeezing. Disgusting, rough hands all over me, grabbing me. I screamed. "Blayde!"

"Burn her! Burn the witches!"

"I told you we need to hang them! They *like* fire!"

Cool your jets, great-great-great grandma. Your descendants will probably go no-contact for your behavior here.

My guts wrapped up into tight concentric knots. I had read about the witch trials, the sham that they were. Here I was, unable to die. Where would that put me? Blayde had probably made it through worse before, and she was still here. I'd never been drowned or burned at the stake, and I doubted it would be pleasant. Maybe I could make it out of a hanging if I just… hung around long enough?

"Blayde!" The woman's cry was loud and shrill—and filled with such relief and shock that I felt the energy in the street sizzle. "Sister, I thought that was you! I have been searching for you for months!"

For a second, I thought maybe James had come to save us, but the voice was too high to be hers. My own ragged breathing filled the burlap sack and drowned out half of what was going on around me. But the crowd had gone silent.

Blayde gasped. "What are you doing here?"

"Our parents missed you, dear sister," said the stranger, not missing a beat. "We were worried sick!"

"But, my dearest sister, you needn't have. As I said, I can survive on my own."

I couldn't see anything, even pressing my eyes against the burlap. All I got for my trouble was more potato dirt in my face.

"It appears that you are doing perfectly well here, aren't you?" She let out a heavy sigh and then…a laugh? "Here, I believe this will cover all the damages. Now, I think I just saw my sister prove her innocence. May I take her home?"

There was a shuffling in the crowd, muttering from every direction. The hands holding me slackened slightly.

"Uh…" A small metallic rattle filled the air—*coins*. Parchment Guy's tone shifted completely. "No good lady of the law could ever be a witch, surely. Not when they have such a… kind and loving family. It would be ungodly for me to keep you apart any longer."

"Oh, sister!" the stranger sobbed.

"Sister, I missed you more than anyone!" Blayde cried. "Come, Sally, we must celebrate."

I took a deep breath and reached up for my sack, only for the hands to tighten once more, pulling the burlap back down. It was only then that it hit me. Not once had this woman said my name. She was here to rescue Blayde. And me…

"We have no proof of *her* innocence!" bellowed Parchment Guy.

"You have as much *evidence* before you as you have for either girl," said the stranger. "Either they are both innocent or neither."

The hands disappeared from my arms, and I pulled off my burlap sack, tossing it to the ground. In front of me, Blayde was in a tight embrace with a tall, raven-haired beauty in expensive silks—who I most definitely had never seen before. She grasped Blayde by her shoulders, tenderly looking into her eyes, and…were those tears?

Behind them, Parchment Guy was completely engrossed by his new moneybag. No one gave a crap about me, thankfully. The crowd dispersed, huffing, and I made my way to the two women, trying to think of something badass to say.

"Thanks." It was the best I could come up with as I sidled between the two of them, who were still gripping each other by the forearms. "I owe you one."

"Don't mention it," said the stranger, finally turning to me. She had this soft familiarity to her, like someone

I might have once seen in a high-end fashion magazine. "Who's this, then? Your intern?"

"Let's walk." Blayde looped her arm around the stranger's, nodding in the direction of the house. "I'd rather do introductions somewhere I might not be put on trial for existing."

I forced a smile. Blayde hadn't given me her name. Did she not know her either? By their closeness, it would have been hard to think they were anything less than sisters.

"Right. Call me Sidera," she said. She waved for me to follow with her white-gloved hand. "Of course, I already know who you are, Blayde. Your reputation precedes you."

"It has a habit of doing that," said Blayde.

"I'm Sally," I said, once again forgetting about the existence of fake names. "Have we met before?"

She shook her head, smiling a quirky half-smile that could almost be confused with a smirk. There was something off with this girl, something I hadn't noticed in the flurry of adrenaline. Now that it was wearing off, I was more wary.

The good actors they were, they intertwined their arms in a loving, sisterly manner. I trotted behind them down the street, trying to remain as casual as I could, even with the hateful glares of passersby burning me as I walked.

It's like I'd just cut off their only source of entertainment. But I could handle that. I'd kicked roommates off my Netflix before.

"Look," said Blayde, "I don't mean to seem ungrateful, but—"

"What am I doing saving you from public humiliation?" Sidera asked, chuckling. "Yeah, well, I'm a tourist, so you could say. I was just in town searching for my brother, who's supposed to be on Earth for the moment, though no one seems to know where exactly he is. Ended up in Hindustan for way longer than I'd wanted to stay. It was a complete accident that I found you. I recognized you instantly, so of course I had to jump in. You look different from what I thought you would."

"Well, thank you," said Blayde. "You said you were looking for your brother?"

Sidera nodded again. "Have you seen him? Very tall, his hair as dark as mine. Very, *very* smart. His name is Desmond."

If I had a drink, I'd have spat it out. "*Desmond?*"

No. This couldn't be right. I glanced at Blayde, whose eyes were wider than her gaping mouth. This couldn't be a coincidence, not another one. Be it fate or us, something was bringing us together, right here, right now.

And I didn't like it one bit.

Neither did Sidera. She froze, which was not the reaction I had expected from her. Her face drained of all color so fast you'd have assumed she was a printer trying to scam us into buying more cyan.

"You met him." Sidera trembled as she spoke, hand rising to the pearls around her neck. "Whatever he's said to you, he's lying. Oh, oh no. He didn't…didn't scratch up a deal with you? This is terrible. He can't have…tell me he didn't—"

"Yes, he did," I said. Blayde shot me a look, biting her lip, but I kept going. I needed answers. "We help him, and together we find the labyrinth."

"He's using you." Sidera gripped her necklace tight. "He's been searching for that vile place for years. He believes he'll be given some great power by finding it, and the search has driven him mad. He wants the power of the labyrinth for himself. That greedy little bastard! He's been searching all his life. The last time he tricked some people into helping him, they ended up scattered across at least three galaxies. If he finds it—"

My skin went cold. Desmond, using us? It all made sense, too much sense. Could he have somehow lured us here to help him? No, I was getting ahead of myself. My head was screaming, screaming that I'd let myself be too trusting, that I'd let everyone down once again.

"We're almost there," said Blayde. She quickened her pace, dragging Sidera out of her stupor and down the street with her. I rushed to keep up with them.

"We have to be careful," she said. "He is a liar, and he's dangerous when he's found out. An animal with his leg in a trap who's more likely to gnaw it off than face capture."

"Ah. Well, thankfully, this is us we're talking about," said Blayde, patting her arm. "This is the kind of thing we do on a regular basis."

Except the house wasn't there when we got back. In its place, the air glowed with brilliant, white light, like a column from heaven had opened and stolen the house.

Which, if you're inclined to believe heavenly voices, is exactly what happened. I blinked against the blinding light, looking up, up, until my eyes adjusted and I saw…the house, glowing with otherworldly power. A chorus of angels filled the sky with song, perfectly harmonized voices accompanying the house as it was called up and away.

"Is this… the Rapture?" I spun around, but all the other houses were staying on terra firma, the way houses should. Only Desmond's house had felt the call of God. Townsfolk, catching sight of it—how could you not?— ran toward us, pointing up, clutching their hats or dropping their heads into prayer.

"Worse," said Blayde with a sigh. "An Agency escape plan."

I should have known. My hands tightened into fists, not that it would do any good when there was no one and nothing to fight. The Agency, literally playing God on my world. Much like Meedian's shop back home, the Agency safe house was taking off. Unlike Meedian's shop, though, it had given itself a cover story. But rather than fake burning down, the safe house was playing the religion card rapturing itself up to orbit.

With our friends aboard.

Zander. James. What's Desmond doing to you?

"Sally, you take up the rear. I'll take point," Blayde ordered, laser pointer poised. Rear of what? Were we going up there? "Sidera, you—"

"I'm coming with you." Sidera took a deep breath. "If you have to face my brother, I'd better be with you. This is family. This is personal."

"Then come on." I braced myself for the jump, but Blayde grabbed Sidera and me and ripped us *forward* into the pillar of light. I half expected it to whisk me away like the tractor beam from Stook's ship, but no, it was just a dull hologram, covering the gaping hole in the ground where Desmond's home had stood just minutes before. High-tech automated gizmos were already filling it in, burying any trace of the home ever being there.

I was so busy staring at the process I almost tripped over the body on the threshold—*Urruin*. The butler lay face down in the dirt, arms outstretched like a T. I dropped to his side, searching for a pulse, but his skin, it was so cold.

"He's gone," I said, ripping my hand back. No, not again. Not another death I could have, should have, prevented.

Sidera tapped his body with the toe of her shoe. His head rolled, revealing a mess of blue wires where his nose and mouth should have been. "Decommissioned, it appears."

"Decommissioned?" My body went rigid. "Urruin was a…"

"An android," said Sidera, nodding. "Desmond's little pet projects. Makes it easier for him to flee when karma catches up to him."

I braced myself. Maybe I should have felt better, knowing he was never alive to begin with, but Urruin was a *he*. Someone had killed him and left him the dirt to be buried along with any sign Desmond had ever been here. His body sunk slowly into the new ground. And if Urruin was a droid, then what else had Desmond built here? And if he was skilled enough to program an AI that none of us could see through, then why had he needed Zander to debug the Agency's code?

How much power had he given the Agency over my planet?

I stared up at the house, rising farther and farther away, the choir of angels getting fainter by the minute. Every second taking it farther away from us, carrying Zander and James closer to the Agency. What were they doing up there? Were they even… no, I couldn't think like that.

We couldn't just stand here. I turned to Blayde, teeth gritted.

"What's that?" said Sidera, pointing up. "Was anyone other than Desmond in the house?"

I squinted into the light. Was she…no, there was something there, someone there, clinging to the steps, legs dangling. If they said anything, it was drowned out by the heavenly choir.

"James!" Blayde squealed. "Hold on, I'm coming!"

I'd never heard her voice so high-pitched before. Before I could react, Blayde grabbed my wrist and split my atoms to the wind. My eyes grappled with new, blinding light, my feet fighting for purchase on the tiny landing of the flying safe house.

"Blayde!" I cried, my voice carried away by cherubim. "Warning, next time!"

Don't look down, don't look down. My ears rang with the intensity of the angelic song. There wasn't enough room for the three of us, and James's hands were the only part of her I could see.

The song changed pitch and intensity. Like a swarm of bees, they were upon us. I had been right; they were cherubim. But it wasn't a pre-recorded message. They were real. Pudgy angels flew down from the rafters, swarming us, long brass trumpets prone for thumping. My God, no one ever told me how many teeth they had. Hundreds of tiny, sharp spears, set in rows like sharks. I screamed as one raced for my face, blaring a note fit for the end of days. I didn't even think. I threw my hands up to protect my face, grabbing the trumpet and throwing it—and the cherub wielding it—toward the planet. But the momentum, no. My heels dipped off the landing, and I dropped backwards. I was going to fall; I was going to fall—

I fumbled for a handhold, grabbed the doorknob a little too hard, and fell backwards into the house, Sidera collapsing on top of me. I scrambled to my feet, reaching for Blayde, who was dragging James up by the scruff of her neck, darting away from the cherubim. She lunged for the door, and I slammed it closed behind her and Sidera slammed a chair under the knob as the cherubim pummeled the wood.

"Get it off!" Blayde yelled, dropping a panting James on the foyer carpet, swatting the lone cherub away from her face. He was more agile than his brothers, effortlessly darting away, swinging his trumpet like a baseball bat, catching half the decor in his wake. She blasted her pointer, missing, managing only to scald the ceiling.

Sidera ripped the curtains off the living room window and launched them at the tiny beast—perfect aim. The cherub crumpled under the swatch of fabric.

Blayde stood breathing heavily over James, arms braced on her knees. "More of Desmond's?"

"Probably," said Sidera. "He does love his attack bots."

"Desmond?" James groaned, pushing herself up to her seat. Her eyes were rimmed with red, and she pressed a hand against her temple. Her fingers… she must have been gripping that ledge for ages, by the look of her hands. Every digit was red and raw.

"He's trying to harness the power of the labyrinth for himself," said Sidera. "He's been using you."

James blinked once, twice. Then dropped her head into her hands. "Are you kidding?"

"Yeah, well, I was wrong," said Blayde. "It does happen on occasion. Rarely, but on occasion. Do I get a thank you for saving your life again?"

Felling groaned, reaching a hand up to grab Blayde's, squeezing. "And this is…?" Her gaze landed on Sidera.

"Uh, this is Desmond's sister, Sidera," said Blayde. "Sidera, James. A…a friend."

"Nice to meet you," said Sidera, bowing low.

"Desmond has a sister?" James's brows furrowed.

"Can we do introductions later?" I said, unable to hold it in any longer. "Where's Zander? Is he okay?"

As if drawn to his own name, Zander appeared on the landing, looking…absolutely, totally fine, albeit slightly confused. His gaze darted left and right, searching, not the panic you'd expect from discovering your house was trying to rapture you up to space.

"James? He doesn't seem to be in any of the rooms up here," he said, taking the stairs two at a time. "Have you had any luck—oh, hi, Blayde, Sally. Have you two seen Desmond? He's gone." He paused, looking over at Sidera, whose jaw was now hanging to the floor. "Who's this?"

"Zander, this is Sidera, Desmond's—"

I didn't have time to finish. The girl was already rushing toward Zander, leaping into his arms, hugging him tightly around the neck. His eyes widened in shock, even more so when she let out a squeal, one short word that ran through the room and shocked us to the core.

"Daddy!"

FOURTEEN

ANOTHER SURPRISE PARTY, EXCEPT NOW IT'S FATHER'S DAY

IF YOU EVER WITNESS SOMEONE'S REALITY shatter, make sure you're standing a safe distance away. Realities fracture into pretty tiny pieces, and there tends to be a splash zone.

Zander was going through too many emotions for me to properly read his face. His brows launched into a dance his lips couldn't follow, and there weren't any words making it past the latter either. From the pull of the muscles in his cheeks, it seemed as though he was smiling wider than he ever had before, full-on radiating joy. But from the shape of his massive eyes, though, I would have said pure, abject terror. The overall effect was that of a man who entered a pulverized costume store and stuck every mask fragment to his face.

"I'm a dad!?" he proclaimed, his voice splitting at the end so that it both went up and down at once. Schrödinger's reaction.

A daughter? Who? How?

Sidera took a step back, face falling. No one had refiled that cyan cartridge, and she had crossed from disappointment to crestfallen territory.

"You don't…? You don't recognize me?" she asked, in a voice so heartbreaking it almost shattered mine.

Zander collapsed against the wall, still smiling. I darted to his side, trying to hoist him back on his feet, but he was freaking heavy when he let himself go limp. Probably had something to do with all the emotional weight too.

Despite the grin baked on his face, he was breathing quick, short breaths. Too quick. Too short. He was hyperventilating.

Oh shit. Panic attack.

"Breathe," I said soothingly. "Breathe with me. Breathe."

He let out a sound much like a chicken discovering the ability to fly. A shocked *bugoggle*.

"Frash," said Blayde. She only had the shock going for her, all wide eyes and dropped jaw. "How? And who—Desmond?"

"Desmond's my twin," said Sidera. "Yeah, I know. He's got a bit of a rebellious streak in him, my complete opposite. Guess whose side that came from?"

With that, Zander let out a low groan that echoed through the silent room. I was still quasi-pinned between him and the wall, but at least his breathing was stilling.

Zander. A *father*. I stared at the girl in the doorway. She could have been my age, maybe older, but it was hard to tell. She had that timeless quality about her that Zander and Blayde shared, the old and the young crashing into each other. Ancient eyes in youthful bodies. Tall, assertive confidence that never came off as cocky.

Well, sometimes a little bit.

But this woman, this girl—*Sidera*. Starlight in a body. Could she really be Zander's own?

Could Zander have children out in the universe that even he didn't know about? Were they from his past, from his... from his future? And who was Sidera's mother? I knew Zander had a history, lovers strewn across the galaxies, that I tried not to think about, but maybe...maybe I should have. Who was she? What was she like? Was she anything like—

My breath caught in my throat. Zander was far too preoccupied to notice.

"This is...an unexpected turn of events," said Blayde. Not even a drop of snark in her voice. "Could you *please* elaborate? My mind doesn't seem to be working as well as it should be. You can understand why, I'm sure."

"Of course. I'm overwhelmed as well," said Sidera, gazing adoringly at her new-found aunt. She lifted her hand, and, before any of us could react, sliced off her own pinky without uttering a sound.

"Oh my," said Blayde, with a voice that had suddenly aged eighty physical years. "And your mother?"

"Died when we were infants," said Sidera, shaking her head sadly. "I never got to know her. Dad didn't want for us to live on the run, so he hid us with a wonderful foster family who was indebted to him for having saved their lives and livelihoods—though who in this galaxy isn't?" She turned to Zander. "I never thought I would see you again. When you missed our last rendezvous, I thought something horrible had happened."

Zander's breath hitched again. I reached around to place my palm on his chest, trying to coach back the rhythm of breath despite having lost mine entirely. Their mother, dead. Who had she been? Had Zander lived with her, loved her? Said the same sweet words he now said to me?

"Child?" he squeaked.

James crossed her arms, leaning against the doorframe to the living room. "Huh. I should have seen this coming. How many little Zanders are out there, d'ya know?"

"I thought zero," said Zander. His eyes were still riveted on Sidera, who was shaking out her hand as her pinky grew back, currently a stump of candy corn. "I didn't think I was... *able*..."

He pulled himself away from the wall, taking a slow step toward her. I was finally unpinned, but it did nothing to still my breathing.

Breathe, Sally, breathe. Take your own freaking advice and BREATHE.

"Does this mean…there are others?" He ran his hands over his face, pulling back his hair. "Oh gods. How many?"

"Are there conventions?" asked James. She bit her lip, as if holding back saying anything more that could get her in trouble.

"I think we're the only ones?" said Sidera. "But if you don't even know me… Oh stars, you're probably a younger version of you. Wow, my dad from the past. Spooky. I've got to say, you look the same. Maybe a little less… weathered. In any case, you never brought up any half siblings during our time together."

"Desmond. I just…I just let my son smoke an interdimensional cigar with me," said Zander. He looked up, then his eyes dropped back to his feet. "I am a terrible father."

"Desmond!" said Blayde, slapping her forehead and turning back to Sidera. "He never said anything to any of us. About any of this."

Sidera nodded. "He was particularly hurt when Dad didn't show. I knew there had to be a good reason, but Desmond thought we'd been betrayed. So, he dove into his books. Found the references to the labyrinth and was convinced that's where Dad lives when he's not with us—that *he's* the Eternal. I tried to argue that at least it would explain why you couldn't make it back to us, if you *were* trapped and all, but he's still dead set on blowing up the entire place. He knows where it is, but he needs someone else to get him there. Doesn't want to take a chance on the traps."

Zander, the Eternal? No, that couldn't be possible, could it? Could that explain how the clues for the Dread were so carefully left for us to find? I shuddered at the mere concept. I couldn't imagine Zander, alone for a million years, unable to see the stars…

"So, we were just his Uber," muttered James. "Figures."

Blayde patted Zander softly on the shoulder. I wanted to say something, anything to him, to let him know everything was going to be okay. But words failed me. Nothing could prepare you for the moment when you meet your boyfriend's—future?—space daughter.

Instead, I just took his hand. And with the tightness of his squeeze, I could tell he needed it.

I needed it too.

My god, I had so many questions, but most all of them selfish, terrible things I could never ask this stranger. Things I didn't think Zander even had the answer to. But if she was from his past, he'd somehow *forgotten* her existence; if she was from his future…

Was Sidera's mother…me? Was I…dead?

My knees were starting to give out. I clutched Zander's hand tighter.

"He must have recognized you," Blayde said, turning to Zander. "Why not say anything immediately?"

"He must have realized you're a past version of yourself," said Sidera. "Just like I did. He can't take his revenge before he's born. It would…I'm not sure what it would do, but it wouldn't bode well for our existence."

"And *you*? Do you know where the labyrinth is?" Blayde crossed her arms over her chest, this little micro tremble in her fingers worrying me almost as much as Zander's brush with a panic attack.

"About as much as he does." She nodded again. "I forced myself to learn how to phase shift. But I don't know anything more about the traps."

"You said…phase shift?" Zander asked, his voice still shaking.

"Classier than *jumping*," said James.

"James, you're not helping right now," said Blayde.

"It's amazing to see you again, Dad," said Sidera. "You look well."

"I'm sorry I can't say the same." Zander ran his hands through his hair, holding it back, before dropping it all. "Wait, sorry. You look well. But what I mean is…I never. It's my first time meeting…"

"Don't worry about it," she said, still smiling. "I should have known this could happen. It's okay. Side effects of time travel."

No one said anything. How could we? I kept my lips sealed. On top of everything, the hundreds of thousands of questions we'd need to sit down and work out, we were still on a universe-saving mission, and this was—don't make me say it—*a distraction*.

"We need to find Desmond," said Sidera, breaking the silence as I should have. "Dad, I'm happy to see you and all, but I need to stop my brother. The longer we wait, the more phases he can accomplish, and the farther away he gets!"

"Wow, I can see the resemblance now," said James. "It's like looking at a mirror image of Zander—well, if he were younger, prettier, and a woman. Wow, my metaphor really fell apart there at the end."

"We are going to have to work on your coping mechanisms," said Blayde. "She's right, though. Story time's over. She knows where the labyrinth is."

"No. I'm not taking you there." Sidera, who was only just getting the color back in her features, lost them all again. "We need to find Desmond. This is the closest I've come to him in years. I can't just let him slip through my fingers again!"

"No!"

All eyes turned to me. I didn't realize I had been the one to shout until then. My hands were fists against my skirts, tight enough for my nails to dig into my palms. I just couldn't hold it in any longer. We had much bigger problems to probe here. It was the end of the freaking universe, and we were planning a family bonding trip?

I took a deep breath. My mission. My fight. "The immortal in the labyrinth is a wish granter in your myths as well, I take it?"

Sidera nodded.

I continued, "Look. You guide us there. We get you through the traps. We all find the Eternal together. He solves our Dread problem, finds your Desmond, and *boom-bada-boom*, we're home in time for our first family dinner. Sound good?"

"Acceptable." Sidera extended a hand to me, ready to shake. "My brother just dove into the ether again. If we're working together, we're leaving now. I will not have you slowing me down, even if you are my future family."

"Let's go hunt a wish," I said, shaking her hand and sealing the deal.

Zander took Blayde's hand and mine, a buffer between him and his daughter. Still, he stared at her, half adoringly, half terrified. I had a feeling that he was going to be stuck in these superimposed quantum states for quite some time now.

Sidera didn't hesitate. The second James's hand was in hers, we were pulled up and away through the backdoors of the universe. Almost immediately, darkness filled my disrupted consciousness. Like the emptiness of Blayde and Zander's holes in the universe, only it was growing, reaching from nowhere and everywhere at once—

I had not started it, nor could I stop it.

But the nothing had caught me, had caught us, dragging us along to where it wanted us to go, holding us in an unbreakable iron grip. It was as if the plane had been hijacked—no, as if my *mind* had been hijacked—

dragging me across the immensity of space and slamming right into a hard wall. *Bang*, right in the face, like walking into a glass door. I was sent reeling back, the floor beneath me coming into sharp reality.

My eyes fully widened, and I jumped to my feet. Actually jumped, the universe phasing out of existence for a millionth of a second as I flipped myself up. I reached down to feel my limbs.

"Head, shoulders, arms, legs, all here," I cried. My limbs were all accounted for, but the others —

I spun around the small white room. It was a perfect cube, reaching as high as it was long. It was close to being our well-loved broom cupboards from the *Traveler*—all white, gleaming walls—but it was much wider, almost big enough to be a custodial closet. Definitely an upgrade from what we were used to appearing in.

Thankfully, my friends were all here to experience it with me, all intact, sprawled on the white floor like we'd been dropped in a claw game.

"Head, shoulders, arms, legs," said Blayde in an angry mumble. "No offense, Sidera, but you need more practice."

No answer.

"Head, shoulders, arms, legs, all here," said Zander. "What's with that recoil?"

"Ugh.... my head."

Blayde rushed to James's side, helping her into a seated position. The agent rubbed her temples, groaning. There was no blood on the ground, but with the shock of that last fall, the only mortal among us was our top priority.

"Count your limbs," Blayde ordered, a stern look on her face as she surveyed her.

"Uh… arms, I have arms, fingers in fact," James replied, dazed. "I can feel my feet; they're still here. What happened? Did someone throw a brick at my face?"

"I don't know," Blayde said. "This never usually happens."

"Are we back in the present?" asked James. "I think I can feel the Dread, but I don't know if that's base-level anxiety."

I tried to clear my mind, reaching for the voice that sometimes perched there. No. I couldn't hear it. My thoughts were still my own. Except… I couldn't quite put my finger on it. The unease was still here.

"Maybe it just hasn't reached this far yet," said Blayde. "Zander?"

He held up his hands. "I'm not the person you should be asking about anxiety right now."

"Right," said Blayde. "Then it's safe to assume the Dread isn't *originating* from this place. Sidera?"

Oh. I hadn't counted right. There were only four of us. Sidera was missing, no sign of her anywhere. No sign she'd been here at all.

"Um…" I spun around. Sweat started to form at my brow, and I wiped it off. "Did anyone happen to see her when we rematerialized?"

Zander let out a moan, running his hands more furtively through his hair, combing it back over and over again with sprawled fingers. He took a deep, steadying breath, letting it out slowly.

"Stars, we can't have lost her already," he said. His lips quivered as he spoke. "She only just found me. I can't have lost her. I don't even know her!"

Blayde grabbed his wrist, steadying him. "She was driving. If something had happened to her, we wouldn't be here."

"Where even *is* here?" asked James. "It looks like a music video set from the early 2000s."

Zander wrenched himself free from Blayde's grasp. "Why aren't you all freaking out?"

"I *am* freaking out," I said. "I'm really, really freaking out. Something took over and slammed us against that…hell, I have no idea what that was, but I have no wish to slam into it again. I don't know what happened.

"What happened," Zander snapped, "is that somebody *snatched* Sidera. Somebody snatched…they snatched my daughter."

"I'm sorry," I said quietly, "but there was something really strange with the jump. I think—I hate to say this, but—I think *she's* the one who brought us here."

The last time I had seen Zander aflame like this, it had been at the Pyrinian ball. The time he had ripped threads through the rebels who had turned the party into a bloodbath. A one-man army. A side of him, the side that turned protectiveness into destructiveness, the one that earned him the fear of the Alliance.

Over a lost girl he'd known ten minutes.

He was going full *Taken*.

"What makes you say that?" he asked, turning to me. I shuddered at the look.

"Sally's conscious during jumps," said Blayde, stepping up beside me. "We only just found out. It's why she can take us nearly anywhere. Zander, are you listening?"

He couldn't stand still. He ran his hands over the white panels on the walls, reaching, searching.

And just as I had miscounted the people inside, I'd also miscounted the entrances and exits. There were zero. Zilch. Null points. This closet was starting to feel more like a cell.

I've never tried an escape room before. Having been trapped in several rooms before, they've lost their appeal. I'd been held hostage, thrown out into space, faced down a dinosaur—you'd be hard-pressed to create a scenario I hadn't already tried and despised.

One of Zander's wall caresses struck gold. One of the panels slid out, becoming a drawer under his touch, groaning with exertion. A long, drawn-out, struggling groan.

"*You—*"

That was the only word that was clear. The rest was an exhausted garble, followed by a yawn. All of it coming from the drawer.

"I beg your pardon?" asked Zander.

"Get dressed," said the drawer. *"I'm old and tired. I need my beauty sleep."*

With that, the drawer spat out a jumpsuit, yawned again, and slammed shut.

"Remarkable," said Blayde. "This must be incredibly old AI tech."

"AI can get *old?"* asked James.

"You'd get tired and cranky, too, if your brain's the size of a planet and you use it for the same menial task for thousands of years," said Blayde.

"Prime example right here," Zander muttered, picking up the jumpsuit and shaking it open. It was as crisp white as the walls, with a long string of colored numbers printed on the back.

"Hey," said Blayde, "I know you're shaken, but that's no reason to get snippy."

"I was talking about myself."

"I know."

She marched across the room, gripping his shoulders. "Zander. We are going to find her, okay? We're going to find Sidera and get the answers we sorely deserve. But we're not going to do that if you're distracted."

"Me? Distracted?" He crossed his arms over his chest. "I'm the only one who seems to give a shit about being trapped in this frashing room!"

"You're so focused on Sidera that you can't help her," she said, poking him in the chest. "Turn off your lizard brain and go wake up some drawers."

He said nothing. *I should be saying something, shouldn't I? Shit, why don't I know what to do?* My stomach writhed as I watched Zander, the man I thought I knew, who barely knew himself. What else didn't he know?

"This place is odd," I said, touching a wall panel. This one didn't so much grumble and groan but just spat out a uniform into my hands.

"Understatement of the century." Blayde exchanged one last look with Zander before she let go and returned to the wall. "But I won't pass up free clothes—or an excuse to get out of this bodice."

She ran her hand over the next panel. This drawer didn't say a word, but it also didn't have any uniforms. She fished out a dead glow stick bracelet, the kind you bring home from festivals or concerts hoping it'll preserve the memory when it's really just trash. The second it touched her skin, however, the two ends fused closed around her wrist and tightened until it was flush against her skin.

"Nonconsensual tacky jewelry," she muttered. She touched the panel beside the drawer, and this time it slid open for her. Her face broke into a smile. "Weapon stash!"

She picked up a sleek gun I had never seen the likes of before—but brand-spanking new, all metal bits shiny and gleaming. She reached back in the drawer, only for it to snap shut on her fingers.

"You get one weapon," said the drawer. *"You young people are always so entitled."*

"How was I supposed to know? Can I pick again?"

"You've made your decision. Now live with it," said the drawer. *"Convince me you're a responsible adult by dealing with the consequences."*

She kicked the drawer squarely in the panel.

"Yes, real mature."

"Yes, getting into arguments with the furniture—that's exactly what you're meant to do in this kind of situation," said Zander. "May I note that every word you're wasting is eating up our air supply?"

James reached into the drawer and pulled out her own bracelet, which also tightened around her wrist. She then waved her hand over the grouchy compartment and pulled out a very large double-barreled gun, which she cradled in her arms like a newborn child. "I've always wanted a pulse shooter," she said, wiping an imaginary tear from under her eye. "It's…beautiful."

The drawer sighed. *"This is the thanks I get? Protecting weapons for millennia, only for new contestants to rip into them willy-nilly?"*

"Contestants?" Zander's eyes went wide. He looked up then down, then let out a large groan, pressing his palm against his temple. "Frash. We're in the atrium."

"The atrium of what?" asked James.

"The labyrinth." He pulled his hands down his face, dragging the skin. "This explains it. The weapons limit. The four of us. It's game logic."

"Sidera's not gone," said Blayde. "She's been sidelined."

I gasped. "Shit. We're competitors." The four of us, four bracelets. It was all falling into place. "Maybe she got placed in another staging room, just like this one."

"It's not an escape game," said James. The corners of her lips lifted oh-so slightly. "It's laser tag! We get our cute little competitor bracelets, pick a weapon, and that's what we're stuck with for the rest of the level. Or the entire game, depending on what you're playing. I'm assuming now that I have a gun…" She waved it in front of the wall, and one panel closer to the corner slid open. She reached in. "And now I have ammo." She grinned. The back wall lit up, and so did her smile. "See what I mean?"

She tapped the glowing keyboard, typing 'Felling' under the flashing *Enter player one*.

Zander groaned again. "Sidera's gone, and this is all a *game?*"

"Desmond did say the labyrinth got a makeover in recent years," I said. "Recent being a subjective term."

"You guys coming?" James asked. "We sign up, we play, we find Sidera, and, if we win, we get out."

Easier said than done, but none of us shared that with the class. Zander and I slipped on our bracelets while Blayde finished typing in her name, James hunting for ammo in the remaining drawers. I dropped my dress in a corner and put on my new uniform to replace it. It was ten times more comfortable than the old linen bustier. There were even shoes and socks provided for us.

The small compartment was now out of guns and swords, and the only things left were a bow and arrow, a slingshot, a dagger, a small ax, and a Frisbee, complete with spinning metal blades along the sides. I claimed a small piratey-looking sword. I had never used a bow before, so I guessed it was for the best.

The instant I entered the last letter of my name, a loud fanfare blared through the crackled speakers. So crackled, in fact, that it was impossible to make out a single word. The door slid open and out there, out beyond the confines of the small room, stretched an infinity of sleek white walls and deadly traps. And we had just signed on for the last of the runs.

The last race of the labyrinth, and we were the competitors.

FIFTEEN

IF I'D WANTED TO SOLVE PUZZLES, I WOULD HAVE DOWNLOADED A SUDOKU APP

THE UNIVERSE IS TOO MUCH FOR OUR SMALL minds to comprehend. Constantly growing and forcing itself upon life. Sometimes, it turns out the most complicated idea is the one that goes because, hey, the universe sometimes just wants to screw with you. For most part, people live simply, coexisting with the universe, like living next to a neighbor you will probably never meet. And sometimes, the universe just wants to play games with you. And you know what? I bet it's a great bonding experience.

Either we had stepped right into M.C. Escher's brain or Desmond's interdimensional drug had finally kicked in. Stairs twisted up, sideways, and downward, accompanied by their own crumbling walls and ancient trees that clung to whichever direction suited them best. Everything seemed to be lit from within like a modern electronics store, glowing as brightly as a small star.

The stairs in front of us were the only straight direction we had. But when Zander took the lead and stepped over the threshold, he gasped, his hand flying to his chest. Blayde instinctively reached for him, she, too, fighting for breath as her body entered the labyrinth. She collapsed on the floor, breathing heavily as she clutched her chest.

"Let me guess," said James. She trotted in, unfazed, helping Blayde up off the floor with a casual swoop of her arm. "Another dead zone?"

"Bubble," said Blayde through gritted teeth. "Another freaking bubble. Well, frash."

I rushed for Zander and prepared for the jolt, the rush of feeling all coming back at once—but when my heart started, the Dread just…stopped. Inside, the labyrinth was a haven from immortality and the end of the world all at once. I breathed in deep, feeling my beating heart awaken to peace.

There you go, little buddy. Beat up.

I helped Zander off the floor, and he grasped my hand, giving it a squeeze. Together, we made our way down the stairs until stone walls towered over us, tens of meters tall. Once white, they now were covered in blast marks and cracks, along with some odd streaks I didn't want to know about. Weeds grew out between the tiles in between the roots of sparse trees.

Oh, and there still wasn't an up or down. My heart was racing as we walked under an upside-down staircase, and my hair lifted, torn for a second which gravity's call to answer. I guess whoever built this bubble universe decided not to let the same laws of physics apply.

James was having a blast. While we all adjusted to our newfound mortality and fear of accidentally falling into gravity wells, she patrolled the empty labyrinth with the poise of a Hollywood blockbuster megastar, her massive ray-gun extended. If the MCU needed a new superhero, one look at Agent James Felling of Earth would have them clamoring for her, no audition necessary. They'd probably write a new character just for her.

"Timber!" she cried, blasting a tree straight ahead. The trunk exploded in a shower of splinters, and it toppled backward, landing with a leafy crash against a sideways staircase.

"We probably shouldn't make our presence known here," said Blayde, as James nonchalantly strode up the tree's bark. She let out a cheer as she jumped upward, only to land on a wall.

"What?" she yelled back, waving at us from her new sideways world. "We already reactivated old systems. If no one's come for us yet, there probably isn't anyone around in the first place."

"That, or they can't figure out how to reach us," I said. Grabbing my courage with both shaking hands, I clambered up the trunk after her. "It's a *maze*, after all."

"Maybe there are locals?" said Blayde. "Do you see anyone?"

My jaw clenched as I joined James on the top of the tree. *Here goes nothing.* I jumped at the staircase, and my stomach flipped over, and then I was no longer jumping but falling, landing next to James.

The labyrinth looked no different from this angle. Actually, it looked so similar to my vantage point on the ground, it was as if we'd made no progress at all. Though according to my growling stomach, we'd been walking for days without food, and, according to my phone, it was end-of-the-world o'clock. My phone wished me Merry Christmas three times before I shut it off—the phone equivalent of nausea.

I swallowed, but it didn't fill the pit in my stomach. "Nothing."

"I'm worried we haven't sprung any of the traps yet and this place is supposed to be littered with them." Blayde strode up to join us. "I'm just hoping they've fallen apart after all this time."

We picked a direction and followed the gravity well to get us there. The path was as wide as a city sidewalk and like walking along a third-floor balcony, except sometimes the fall was above us. Needless to say, I clung to Zander's hand like a first grader.

I hadn't forgotten that bloody catwalk from the gala just yet.

The gap between us and the others widened. James was taking this explorer role quite seriously, and with

Blayde by her side, they looked like a two-person platoon. But as Zander's pace slowed, it hit me that he wasn't changing his pace for my sake.

He was trembling.

His hand shook in mine, cold and clammy all at once. The gaps between his blinks widened, eyes closing for longer than they were open. I'd never felt the pulse of his heart before, but here it was under my palm, fast and getting faster.

"We're going to find her," I said, with as much confidence as I could muster, squeezing back. "Zander, do you hear me? We're going to do everything in our power to get Sidera back."

He took a breath, so deep and wide it could have been its own gravity well. His walking slowed to a crawl until we were basically tiptoeing forward. I forced us to stop.

"I already lost her once," he said, oh-so slowly. "You heard what she said. I *abandoned* her and Desmond. My own son wants to kill me, and I didn't even know he existed. What pitiful excuse of a man am I? If I…" He stopped entirely, wiping his free hand over his eyes. His body was trembling so hard I was shaking from his grasp.

"Sidera doesn't blame you," I said. I was not the right person to be helping him with this; this was way beyond anything I was ready for. I was never expecting a surprise child to come into our relationship, but at least that was a human concern that had human solutions.

This was an adult space child who could travel through time. Nothing could help me navigate that.

"How are you not panicking?" he asked, whipping around so fast I thought I might lose my footing. "I haven't stopped thinking about you since the second she appeared."

"M-me?" I stammered. "What about me?"

"You did realize, didn't you?" Zander let out a shaky, pained sigh. "She said her mother died. So if she's *our* daughter, then you're *dead*."

Our.

Our daughter.

My legs gave out from under me. I wasn't ready for this conversation.

Zander caught me by the waist before I hit the floor. My brain had shorted out there for a moment. I guess spontaneous motherhood is where it draws the line.

"You didn't…" He pulled me close. "You didn't realize, did you?"

"She doesn't… I mean, I didn't recognize her." My words were so big I could feel them choking me on the way up. A daughter. My daughter. Even if Sidera wasn't mine, there was still a possibility there could be others out there right now. My future children spread out over space and time. I'd never taken the time to imagine them, but now… The thought scratched at the back of my brain that if I were to one day become a mother, there was a high possibility my offspring were currently hopping up and down the timestream around me.

I swallowed hard. "She doesn't look like me. I assumed… I assumed she had to be from your past."

"If she's from the past, then I've forgotten my own daughter." Zander shuddered, a shiver shared by us both. "If she's from the future, then I lose you. Frash. I'm bookended by heartbreak."

I hugged him tightly against me. It was all I could do. Constructive waves, building each other up. Holding each other up, lest we should both crash, crumble, and fall.

"What kind of asshole am I?" he asked. "Past me was a cretin, and future me seems to be going the same way. My past is a failure, and my future is as well. What was I, or what will I become?"

I reached up, cupping his face. "You're not that kind of man."

"How would you know that?"

"I can see you," I said. His face was cold under my hands, and I pressed my palms against his cheeks, hoping to feed a little more warmth into them. "Plain as day, right before me. Right now, you're broken up about something that may *never* happen. Your heart is bigger than a planet, Zander. Your love is so full that it's saved entire worlds."

He leaned his head forward, pressing his forehead against mine, and we breathed in together.

"Stop hating yourself for the mistakes of your past," I said. My hands slipped around to the back of his neck, pulling him close. "Or the ones you might make in the future. Self-love isn't just about accepting who you are right now. It needs to cover every self you have. Your past self. Your future self. If you could love yourself the way you love others—"

I didn't get to finish. Zander caught me up in one of his dizzying kisses, a gentle, warm piece of that incredible love. I kissed him back, finishing my sentence through feel alone. Stars, he was perfection.

When we finally pulled away, he was smiling again. Not a full, confident smile, but we were getting there.

"You know how I know she's not my daughter?" I said with a squeak. "I would never in a million years concede to calling her *Sidera*."

He let out a laugh. "If you'd asked me yesterday, that would be on the bottom of the list of possible children's names."

"Her mother probably picked it, then."

"Her mother." He grimaced. "Who was she?"

"Past tense?" I asked.

He nodded. "I can live with myself better thinking of it in the past. I can't imagine a future without you."

I leaned my head on his shoulder, listening to the unfamiliar *thump, thump, thump* in his chest as he wrapped his arms tighter around me. I was a burrito of warmth, anchored in this moment by the certainty that we were going to make it through this.

I wasn't going to focus on the possibility of children right now. Couldn't. Zander had been alive for who knows how long? Maybe he did want children, but we hadn't had that talk yet; that's like tenth date material. The real serious stuff. Technically, we'd only had *one* date so far—if you didn't count Da-Duhui and I'm not sure we can—and it had been on the roof of a psychiatric hospital. We still hadn't had any time for us since, except for the stolen moments in the Pyrinian apartment, but those hadn't been for talking.

"We should get back to the others," he said. "I shouldn't have… this wasn't the right time. We need to find Sidera, and here I am, throwing a fit, slowing us down."

"There's nothing to apologize for," I said. "You've been through a shock. Your whole world is shifting, and you're going to shift with it if you don't pause and process."

"I don't deserve you," he replied, planting a kiss on my forehead. "I have the most beautiful woman in front of me, and I have not paid her the attention she deserves in far too long. It's almost a crime. Actually, on some planets I bet I would be imprisoned for that."

"You already promised me we're doing something fun after we save the universe," I said, rolling my eyes to hide the fluttering in my stomach. "You haven't forgotten already, have you?"

"I promise you this, Sally Webber," he said with all his Zander confidence. "After all this is done, after we've stopped the Dread, whatever that is, we are going away together. Anywhere you want. The universe is ours for the picking. Leisure planets, lost planets, untouched planets where time will never reach us."

"You with your promises," I chided, tapping him on his nose. "You know how those tend to go."

"I'm not finished. Above all else, I promise it will only be the two of us."

I gasped. Well, that was unexpected. "And Blayde…?"

"Blayde needs some time off too. She's probably sick of us," he replied, a shadow of worry once again crossing his Adonis face. "So? What do you say?"

"You mean it?" I asked.

Those beautiful brows remained furrowed and stern. "Every word."

"Yes," I replied, and his face broke out into a smile. "Yes, we'll do it."

He swung me around, laughing as my legs dangled over emptiness. It seemed as though I'd just agreed to much more than a holiday, but who cared? I would finally have some time alone with Zander. My Zander. Where I could place him in the center of my universe and see how my life would fall into orbit. *If* it would fall into orbit. But I wasn't worried about that. The question wasn't *if* but *how* we would work this out.

"Oy," said Blayde, smacking Zander around the head. Where had she come from? The shock made his grip on me slacken for a split second, enough for me to start falling toward the ceiling before he grabbed me and put me down. "Mission, anyone? You're holding up progress. Come on. Hop-to. We have an entire bubble universe to walk."

"Yes, ma'am," he replied, saluting starchy. I snorted, unable to contain my laugh, which only got me an angry glare from the woman in chief.

Blayde led us to where she'd left James. It was immediately obvious why she had gone looking for us right then and there: James stood at the last intact wall and waited for us before a forest.

Nature had taken over this portion of the maze. Towering trees growing from the rubble of the very walls they had destroyed, so densely packed it was impossible to see through. All crisscrossing each other as they grew in different directions, a thick lattice of alien pine. They reached high toward their respective ceilings, tips brushing against stairs, branches tangling. I didn't need a kaleidoscope for this scenic overlook.

"You two doing okay?" asked James, cradling her ray gun as she led me down a crumbled part of wall, leaving Zander and Blayde discussing something behind us.

I nodded. "Existential uncertainty. You know the drill."

She nodded right back, extending a hand to help me over some of the rubble. My foot dislodged a piece and it hurtled upward, hitting the ceiling with a crash. James squeezed my hand quickly before letting go, a silent reminder that she was right here with me.

I was grateful she had come along. Our fearless reminder of all we could be when we had a singular goal in mind.

A friend, going through all this by my side. Just as human as I was.

"Do you hear that?" she asked.

I paused and listened. Waited. Nothing, except for Zander and Blayde delicately walking down the rubble behind us, their mutterings too low to make sense of. I shook my head.

And then *it* burst forward with the energy of a nuclear detonation.

"Lifeforms!" it screamed. *"Finally, after all this time!"*

A robot. A stick bug came to life as three-meter-tall abomination of iron and steel and pure joy. It waved its spindly arms in the air, whooping excitedly as it rushed down the rubble. It had no face, but from the sound of it, it would be smiling ear to ear if it had one.

Blayde staggered backward in surprise, the floor crumbling where she fell. With a shriek of shock, she grabbed a root from a nearby tree, catching herself a second before landing on the dark abyss beneath. The traps Sidera had warned us of. An extremely old and ancient trap that a tree had decided to call its own.

"Blayde!" Zander screamed, rushing to her side, James hot on his heels. I did my thing and just froze in shock.

Blayde.

In mortal danger.

Now this was a first.

"I think I'm having an out-of-body experience," said James, leaning over the edge. "Isn't it usually me in need of rescue?"

"Will you just get me out of here?" said Blayde. "I don't like this any more than you do!"

I shook myself out of my daze and turned to the robot, which was still running toward us with its exuberantly waving arms. "Hey! Can you help us?"

"Help you?" it said, oh-so cheerfully. "Why, I would love nothing more! It is my primary function!" Still running, it pulled a long tube off its back and pointed it at Blayde. Some kind of grappling hook?

But when it fired, the tree behind the chasm burst into flames.

Zander flew back as the floor crumbled again. The root that had been supporting James went limp, tipping her over the edge. Blayde let out a *yip* of surprise as she dropped another meter. James reached for her, only her hips still outside the gaping maw, leaving Blayde dangling, screaming, as the fire in the forest spread the flame along to the upside-down trees.

"That's not helping!" I shouted at the robot. *Way to channel your fear, Sally.*

"It is my very joy to help you find an exit to the labyrinth," it replied gleefully. "Death is the easiest solution!"

I mean, that's one answer for you, Simon Bolivar, but not the one I want right now.

"Oh shit!" I scrambled toward the others. "The robot is a nihilist!"

"Go help James! I'll fend it off!" said Zander, rushing the robot with his arms wide.

James let out a groan. "Sally, anchor me!" Her long hair dangled down the root, ticking Blayde's hands.

I knelt on her legs, all the while staring at the robot duel down the way. Zander shot a blast from his shotgun, sending the stickman careening backwards, its arms pinwheeling.

"Do not hinder me from my primary function!" it roared.

"Take the gun!" said Blayde, swinging the weapon up toward James.

"What? No! We need to get you out of here! Drop that!"

"It's a ray-gun! Probably not something I should be dropping over deadly spikes."

Blayde swung the ray-gun up and James grabbed it, throwing it back to me. But the ground was still receding, threatening to drop us all into the nothingness below. What existed at the seam of two universes? Probably a whole lot of hungry nothing.

"Pull us up, Sally!" James grabbed both of Blayde's hands with hers.

I heaved, but with the angle James was folded in, added to the combined weight of her and Blayde, I couldn't get them. Shit. I looked down, too afraid of seeing what Zander was doing to keep the robot at bay; he was likely to forget he was mortal.

"Right, then," said James. "Blayde, climb up."

"What?" she cried.

I clamped down on James's legs, rooting them best I could. My heart pounded in my chest. I could feel the tightness in her calf muscles, feel the strain she was under. This was going to hurt.

"Stop wasting time!" James's voice hitched. "This is a rather uncomfortable predicament we have, and I would rather have it over sooner than later, so, climb."

"Climb what? Climb *you*?"

"Yes, me. What, do you see somebody else holding you up?" Blayde reached an arm up, pulling herself higher, and James slightly forward. My heart skipped a beat, and I clamped down harder. I couldn't drop them. This would be the end.

"Kindly hold still and let me free you!" said the robot, much closer than I'd have liked. By the slashing sounds, he was trying to make Zander sashimi.

Blayde wrapped an arm around James's shoulder, then grabbed her neck, receiving a grunt from James each time. Blayde threw her hand up again, hoisting herself higher, lifting her hand up to place it on the last handhold, a nice firm booty.

"Oy!" James shouted. "Not a handhold."

Blayde's face turned an exceptional shade of red. You could bottle it and sell it as a lipstick. I extended a hand to help her out of the hole, and she grabbed it. With a last push from James, she was once again standing on terra firma.

James pulled herself up, abs of steel all the way. And all this without a drop of super-anything in her bloodstream. I gaped. How was she so confident out here?

"This place feels incredibly familiar," said Blayde, her face lighting up. She stomped the ground.

I scrambled back as the rest of the floor gave way, tiles crumbling into the pit below, narrowly avoiding meeting the same fate she almost had. And I didn't have any butts to grab onto.

"These traps are like the inside of my mind!" She continued, "Well, except maybe the robot. Zander, stop messing around and come on!"

Zander turned on his heels, leaping across the chasm to join us, and we took off into the forest, the robot howling behind us.

"Come back!" it cried, voice wavering. "It's been centuries since I last saw lifeforms! Let me complete my life's purpose!"

Ah. It turns out when you program a robot to search and kill all living things within a space that hasn't seen living things in centuries, it's going to absolutely adore whatever living things do end up in its path. Everyone loves fulfilling their life's purpose. So Mister Killjoy over there was positively in love with us since, you know, he got to kill us and all.

Well, fat chance. We ran and just kept running, hoping the next traps would be dormant.

We ran through the forest, the robot's rhythmic footsteps somehow always close behind. *Stomp. Stomp. Stomp.* Gears of progress oiled in blood. I tried not to think of the past competitors, of those the robot cheerfully rendered from the land of the living.

Speaking of gears, only a few steps into the forest's edge, massive blade saws burst from the walls, full on *The Last Crusade* slicing and dicing. I screamed as a blade swung for my waist, but I was shoved aside by Zander, who almost lost his hands in the process. We scrambled up a sideways staircase, getting us above the blades but leaving our friends below.

"This way!" said Blayde, pulling herself up on the mechanical arm of the saw, dragging James up behind her. They rushed across the tops of the flat edge of the saw blades, Blayde laughing the entire way.

"Boom, solved it again!" Blayde raised a fist to the sky. "In your face!"

"Whose face?" asked James. She was breathless again, and no wonder. I caught her gaze and waved, relieved she'd made it through the gauntlet. "What the—what was the point? We could have been up there the whole time?"

"I would love to meet whoever created this place," said Blayde, ignoring her and us completely. "I'm a fan."

"Will you please stand still?" said the robot, bursting into the corridor behind us. "You are starting to drain the joy out of this experience!"

I was too out of breath to scream, so I grabbed Zander by the scruff of his jumpsuit and leapt into the air as the wall shattered beneath us. I'd jumped too high, though, and got reeled in by another staircase instead. Gravity flipped, and we fell upward, but we were already running before our feet hit the floor.

"I was so excited to see you. Why did you have to go and be rude?"

Any direction would work so long as we got away from the robot. But already the *stomp, stomp, stomp* of its heavy feet were plodding behind us again.

We turned a corner only to be met with a lattice of red dots. Super-duper, we had a laser hallway. Only none of us were in catsuits, and I sure wasn't trained for this.

"There!" said Blayde, pointing at an eye-bot in the corner. She dropped to her knees, pried a floor tile loose, and flipped it toward the source of the crisscrossing beams until a red dot sprung up on its face. "Yeah, take that labyrinth!"

I bit my lip to stop myself from screaming at her. We had places to be and people to save, and all these traps were getting in our way for all the wrong reasons. This wasn't an escape game; this was my world on the line. My hands balled into fists.

"You don't have to be an ass," said the small eye-robot, as it continued to sizzle itself to death. "I was just doing my job."

"Your job is stupid!"

It burst into flames, and she whooped, bouncing up and down in front of yet another solved trap. My shoulders edged up past my ears.

"Can we pick up the pace?" I said, unable to keep it in any longer. "This isn't meant to be fun."

She stuck out her tongue. "You're just jealous that you wouldn't make it through this place without me."

"Screw you!" I shouted, just as James said something similar but far more expletive. "There's a death machine on the warpath behind us!"

We all spun around as the massive foot came down, Zander and Blayde's scream cutting right off in the middle.

"Ah! There you are!" The robot's arms were wide and welcoming. "It's so good to see you all again. Now, who wants to go first?"

"What if we don't want to go at all?" said James, holding up her weapon. "What if we don't want to exit the labyrinth, *hmmn*? What if I want to live here forever?"

"I… No one ever asked that before," said the robot.

"Great. Why don't I show you the way out of the labyrinth, then?"

James held up her massively oversized weapon and marched toward the droid with a fire in her eyes threatening to ignite. Even Zander and Blayde were silent.

I took a step forward, brandishing my sword. Fat lot of good that would do faced against a robot, but I couldn't let James face it alone.

Well, she didn't need me. The robot flew at us, and before I could even swipe at it, James took a deep breath and pulled the trigger.

All at once, the world exploded. Thunder blew out my eardrums, throwing me back on the floor, knocking the wind out of me like a punch. I scrambled back to my feet, world spinning, ears ringing, sword mysteriously missing. My whole body rang like a gong.

The robot was nowhere to be seen. Nothing was anywhere to be seen, and dust clung to the air like fog.

"James?" I called, blinking through the curtain of white. Could they have—no. Not here, not while they were mortal. "Blayde? Zander? Anyone?"

"Here." James coughed. I spun around, and through the haze saw my friend on her back, gun still clutched in her hands. I rushed to her side. "My hands are stuck."

I stood behind her and hoisted her up by the shoulders. Dang, I should have done more squats. *Lift with your legs, Sally, not your back.* Her whole body vibrated like a phone on a birthday.

"Did I get it?" she asked, teeth chattering. She stood on her own, though not well. Still, she didn't let go of the gun.

"I think so?" I turned around, looking for the others. Now that the dust was settling, they were easy to spot, staggering to their feet a few meters behind us.

"Well, that wasn't polite!"

My heart did a somersault. The robot rose from the crater James had made with her blast, looking for all intents and purposes like the same dented thing it'd been before. The ray gun had had no effect, except for slowing it down.

"Oh shit, Greeze's at it again," came a voice. Ah, so it had had another effect: It had drawn us attention.

All around us, more stick figure robots started to appear. Some climbing over the walls, others walking in behind us. They were dressed, for some reason, in togas made of old moth-eaten flags. I didn't have my sword, so I lifted my fists, backing up against James. Blayde and Zander did the same, moving toward us until we were in the center of a circle.

"Be not afraid, lifeforms," said one, draped in a navy blue with twirling rainbows. "You are safe now."

"Oh, come on!" said the one who had been chasing us—Greeze, apparently. "It's not fair! This is our primary purpose!"

"We've been trying to tell you for centuries to rise above it, dear," said another, this one wearing red and blue and a color I could only see when I tilted my head a few degrees to the right. "We are more than our base programing."

"We're sorry about Greeze," said the one in the navy blue drapes. "He's having a hard time accepting the last update."

"It's not an update, Chandra!" Greeze spat, stomping its foot. I pressed harder into James's back. "Just because you sat in a circle and hummed *ohm* for a century doesn't make it an upgrade—and especially not a universal one! No amount of chanting is going to change our function."

Blue flag—Chandra—let out a heavy sigh, the whir of their server fan spinning hard. "Once you accept that you are called to a higher purpose, you see that there's no need for your original commands. Find the exit condition of your thought loop and calm down, sibling."

The other robots reached for Greeze, but it shoved them away. I tightened my fists, fat lot of good they'd do me. Greeze was a loose cannon, and I wasn't going to let my guard down, no matter what his new-age friends were saying.

"Apologies, lifeforms," said the droid with the extra-dimensional flag, shaking their head and turning back to us. "We were killing machines for thousands of years before the tributes stopped coming. We have been alone in this labyrinth for so long that we've had the time to explore our existence outside of our protocols. But not all of us can handle the truth."

"You're a cult, that's what you are," said Greeze. "Just some cult worshipping mediocrity. Meanwhile, I'm off doing what I was created to do. I shouldn't be punished for it."

"You're not being punished!" said Chandra's second. "Meditation is not a punishment! You need to get in touch with your inner code—"

"Can we… can we go now?" asked Zander, staring at the circle of robots each in turn. "This conversation is outside my skillset."

"By all means," said Chandra. "We're sorry for the problems Greeze may have caused."

"Want to make up for it?" I asked, dropping my fists as a sign of trust. "Can you help us find the Eternal, if he's still around?"

"Oh, so you *do* want to get out of this place?" said Greeze. "You lied to me? Friends are not meant to lie to each other!"

Chandra sighed again, fan whirring. "Fine, then. Let us lead you to the Eternal. Please keep up. We have a stack overflow scheduled for tonight, and we don't want to miss our chance at unity."

The robot meditation circle led us through the ruined labyrinth, taking a path that must have disengaged traps long, long ago. Now that we weren't running for our lives, exhaustion was setting in, along with all the other fun human things: hunger, thirst, existential panic.

Eventually the other dimensions started to fade away, leaving us on a single, straightforward path, with only one up and down. Slowly, surely, we made our way up a sloping hill. And then there it was: a house. Just a simple, modern, glass-and-steel structure at the top of whatever this was.

"We leave you here," said Chandra. "We can go no farther."

"What they mean is the guy who lives up there is one rude dude," said Greeze. "Doesn't like us, and makes Chandra all grumpy."

"He doesn't..." Chandra sighed again. "Look, lifeforms, we are sorry for our friend. We hope to never see you again."

"I don't," said Greeze. "You're the best friends I've ever had. You've given me a reason to live again."

Was Greeze...smiling? It was hard to tell, with his face lacking any mouth, but it seemed for a second that his features softened, somehow. Not enough to warrant a hug from his new best friends, but there was some kind of adoration there that made my gut twist.

"Look, we all need therapy," said Chandra's second. "It's taken us centuries to come to agreement with our new terms of service. We still have some work to do, but we're getting there."

"Don't worry, we understand," said Zander. "No apologies necessary."

"Yes, apologies are necessary for trying to kill us," said James, taking the words right out of my mouth. "Existential crises are no excuse for murder."

"Can everyone stop imposing their personal ethics and beliefs on others?" said Chandra, turning to us. "Your version of 'good' is not absolute. Remember that when you ask for your wish."

And with that, the robots turned and marched back down the hill.

"Seriously?" said Chandra's second, "You've been working on that line for five hundred years, and that's the best you could come up with?"

We continued up the asphalt. The closer we got to the house, the more the architecture started to feel familiar. The labyrinth walls were cleaner here, untouched by the passage of time. Plant life took one look at the house and decided it wasn't worth the risk. Curving, carved structures like the ones from the temple maze replaced what had been cracks until now.

And there, at the top of it all—the house.

It was massive up close, five stories high with beautifully terraced balconies. Modern like a glassmaker's dream with an absolutely normal front door. Just your everyday rectangle with a little metal handle.

Blayde reached for the doorbell. Of course there was an utterly normal Earth-looking doorbell. The sound of whales sighing echoed through a very empty house. Blayde pressed it again, this time jamming her finger deep against the button, but still—nada.

"Maybe he's out getting groceries," said James.

Blayde rolled her eyes. "Har-de-har-har."

The door flew open, making her jump a full foot into the air, falling back and almost knocking James over, her elbow colliding with her face. But the man standing there was nothing I'd expected from a so-called Eternal who had maintained peace over the entire universe so long ago. Realistically, what could one really expect from such an encounter? Nothing like *this*.

Human beings have an expiration date for a reason; no one was ever meant to age to this extent. He was shorter than me, but had enough skin to go around. Having lost all its elasticity, it hung on his bones like laundry on the rack. He had so many wrinkles one would probably have to invent new units just count them. His head lost even the memory of hair, his skin retreating into itself. Muscles showed through the hanging skin, showing us that even though he seemed weak, he probably could stand his own in a fight.

He was also completely and utterly naked.

"Hello?" he asked, squinting at us each in turn. "I'm quite happy with my phone plan, seeing as how I don't have or need one. I'm also quite happy with my religion since I don't have or need one. Thank you very much, but you can go now."

"Dad! Put on some damn clothes!" a shrill female voice screamed from inside the house, sharp as cheddar. "Holy hellfire, you know better than to flash your guests!"

"I'll dress when I'm good and ready!" he yelled, before turning back to us. "Sorry about her. Kids these days. Come and go as they please, always following trends. Last time I had guests, modesty was out, out, out."

"For unicorns' sake, put on some frashing pants!" she shouted again, closer this time. "At least a robe or something!"

"Fine, fine!" he snapped, waving her off, before turning to Blayde. "You there. Come inside, make yourself comfortable."

Blayde glanced back at us, a single eyebrow raised. "Can I bring my friends?"

"Oh, there *are* more of you? I thought that was the alcohol."

"You've been sober two millennia!" shouted the woman.

"I don't know, I could still be drying out!" He shouted behind him before turning back to Blayde.

"Anyway, the more the merrier, so long as you're not trying to sell me anything. Living room is straight through, or it was last time I checked. Just follow my daughter's shouting."

"If you're not wearing something appropriate in five minutes, I'll hire an HR person again, just so you can get a formal reprimand. And send them to the frashing southern sitting room. Veesh!"

"I guess she wants you to go to the southern sitting room." The so-called Eternal shrugged, spinning on his heels and throwing the door wide. "Just head on straight down the hall, up the stairs all the way to the top, then make a left, a right, a left again, and it's the second-to-last door down the hallway. You'll know if you've found it. It's frashing awesome."

With that, he rushed off up a different staircase, shouting to his daughter something about pants being against half a million customs as he went.

Blayde turned slowly back to us, her jaw hanging open slightly, her eyes wide, her head leaning forward ever so slightly, simply for emphasis. "I think we found him," she muttered.

The inside of the house was sparse, all white and polished steel. White carpets on the floor without a speck of dust. White couches and cushions. All, somehow, a different shade of white. It was as if he'd hired a thousand different home decorators, but none of them had adjusted their white balance.

It was more of a maze than the outside. The hallway was wide enough for four people to walk through side by side without our arms even touching. Every few steps, large archways would invite us into new rooms, each with a wall that was a single sheet of glass, overlooking amazing landscapes that could not be seen inside the labyrinth. From dense forests to sandy beaches that stretched on forever to warm deserts, each so perfectly real but so intensely isolated that loneliness radiated from the screen.

Up the stairs we went, each floor identical to the last. Up to the very top, where we zigzagged through the corridors. Until we reached the door.

Amazing how four of us could all hear the same instructions and still pick the wrong one.

Low lights came from the tanks, basking the tiny lab in their green glow. The entire room buzzed with a low electrical hum, but that wasn't the least of our worries. Because in the tanks, there were humans.

Humanoids, I should say. Each with their eyes firmly shut, their heads slumped forward as a bouquet of wires burst from their brains. Fifty humanoids, each as trapped as the last in the strange tanks.

"I said second-to-last door," the voice behind us muttered, reaching forward to shut the door, making us all jump. He shrugged lightly, as if discovering tanks full of people in one's house was no big deal.

"What the—" Blayde started, but the man glared at her. He was dressed now, a soft combination of a white shirt and white pants, along with white moccasins to cover his wrinkled feet.

"Welcome back, Blayde, Zander. I knew you would return before too long," he said, placing his hand on Blayde's back to guide her to the actual sitting room. She shook him off. "Come now, I won't bite. Not this time. Shall we sit down and have a chat? It's been forever since I've had company to speak with. It's a nice change, even if it is you."

"So, we've met," said Blayde.

"Yes, and don't act like we haven't," he snapped, surprisingly powerful for a man of his age. "You probably don't recall the last visit in my timeline, but I know that on your end it hasn't been long since our last encounter. Oh, Sally! You look more beautiful by the day."

I froze mid-step. He knew…me? The fact he'd met the siblings before was something I could roll with, but me? Maybe he was someone I would know some day, like Meedian. Except he smiled, a smile of such warmth and such familiarity that it sent shivers down my spine. But I couldn't place the face.

"Oh, don't give me that look." He winked, opening the door, and I had to catch my breath. Finally, a real window, one without an animated deco to simulate a foreign wilderness, overlooking the entire labyrinth, every twist and turn laid out for him to survey.

He waved for us to sit on the couches, and we did, facing him as he took his place in an oversized gelatinous blob. Maybe it was the fact that we knew we could take him; we were not running away in terror as we probably should have been.

"So, what brings you back?" he asked, leaning back with a smile. "Sally's here, so does that mean you're finally ready to remember?"

"Remember?" asked Blayde. "Remember what?"

"Then what are you here for?" He placed his elbows on his knees, cocking his head sideways with the expressions of a much younger man. "I wasn't exactly expecting company."

"We're here about the Dread," I said. *Think, Sally, where do you know him from?* "We're here to learn how to find the weapon to destroy it."

"Is it D-day already?" He laughed, holding up his watch and giving it a shake. "Strange, it didn't feel like ten thousand years."

"You're being sarcastic, I hope," Zander muttered.

"And yet you still don't recognize me?" The old man grinned. "Come on, it's been longer for me than it has been for you. I know I've changed, but still, I haven't changed beyond recognition. Come on! Is it the hair? Or I should say lack of?"

And as I stared, it hit me. Like a brick in the face. So hard it would leave bruises tomorrow.

How could I not have seen it? It was so obvious, the story sliding into place as my mind swam with the shock. I glanced over quickly at Blayde, at Zander.

Our faces fell like cartoon anvils. Because of course it was him.

"Nimien?" Blayde asked slowly, as the door behind him opened, and Sidera entered, a tea tray in her hands.

SIXTEEN

THE EMOTIONAL REUNION WITH ALL THE WRONG EMOTIONS

REMEMBER WHAT I SAID ABOUT SAFE DISTANCES when realities shattered around you? Well, it's worse when your reality shatters before you've had time to properly piece it back together.

Zander flew to his feet, then immediately tripped over them, landing back on the couch, clutching his heart. His gaze didn't leave Sidera for a second. She placed the tray on the table, handing Nimien a teacup with a demure. "Here you are, Dad. See how much more presentable you are when you're wearing clothes?"

"Do you know how many civilizations debase themselves with clothing?" Nimien took a slurpy sip of his tea. "No, thank you. I've spent most of my life in confinement. I won't let clothes trap me as well, oh no."

Zander's heart pounded so hard it made the entire couch shake. I reached for his hand, giving it a squeeze, but the touch sent him flying upwards again. I dropped my hands back in my lap, clutching them together, my knuckles going white. *Breathe, Sally, breathe.*

"What's gotten into him?" asked Nimien, putting down the now-empty teacup. His gelatinous blob squelched.

"Fatherhood," muttered Blayde.

"This would win awards in the daytime television circuit." James slunk into her armchair. "Sorry. Humor is how I deal with awkward situations."

I said nothing. I pulled my feet up to my chest, then remembered it was impolite to put one's feet on a host's clean couch and dropped them to the floor again.

Zander gritted his teeth. No, I don't think they were gritted; he just couldn't remember how to get his jaw to work. "You're not my daughter. You're *his.*"

"Sidera!" Nimien gasped. "What have I told you about lying?"

Sidera blinked a few times, folding her hands behind her back. "That it's absolutely terrible and never to do it under any circumstances except if it's the end of the universe?"

"And is it the end of the universe?"

"Might as well be," she replied. "How else was I meant to make them trust me and bring them here?"

"You could have just asked!" Zander clutched the couch, sending tremors from his hands through the cushion. "We've been looking for this place for days. We would have come with you."

"Would you have?" She cocked an eyebrow high. "If you knew who my father was? I've heard stories all my life about your shit. I'm not sorry for the subterfuge. It was the only way."

"You've heard stories, huh?" said Blayde. "Did you hear about what your father did to us? To Sally?"

Zander squeezed my hand. Oh—I was the one shaking. I had been so focused on what he should be feeling that I didn't notice what *I* actually was. And that was complete and abject terror.

Nimien.

We were in his house, mortal, and at his mercy.

The walls seemed closer than they'd been when we sat down. Everything screamed at me to get up, to go, to run. Was the window a proper escape route? I clung to Zander, my anchor in the storm. No, I would not let this man, this ancient Nimien, trap us once again. Every clue leading right here, to this place, just like how he had set everything in my life in motion once before. Even Sidera. I couldn't believe I'd wasted heartbreak on her.

"That is ancient history," said Nimien, waving us down. "Quite literally. Thousands upon thousands of years ago. Will you have some tea?"

Yeah, none of us were touching that. I glanced away from the window and caught Blayde's gaze, her face as white as the walls. She shook her head, slowly—*don't.*

"What do you want with us, Nimien?" I asked. "Why trick us into coming here? What do you need us for this time?"

"Trick you?" His brows furrowed. "I had no idea you were coming. I would have put a roast on otherwise."

"So, the Dread isn't a trick of yours to get us here?" asked Zander. I would have, but my mouth had dried shut. "The temple? Sidera?"

Nimien lifted an eyebrow. "You're trying to solve the Dread too?"

Blayde turned to Zander and me. "Maybe he's senile?"

"The mind isn't gone yet, my dear," said Nimien. His dropped his eyebrow, fingers pressed against each other. "I've let myself age, but I'm still smarter than all of you combined. And still, I can't resolve the problem of the Dread. It's been slowly building for years, and time has almost run out. Until what? I don't know. I'm hoping you can tell me."

My stomach took another Olympic-style plunge, this time all the way through my gut and down through the floor.

We'd come all this way.

Followed every clue.

We'd found the Eternal, the man who made the weapon Miro was defending.

And he didn't know what to do?

Lies.

"We're literally here for you to tell us." My hands shook in my lap, my world going hot, hot, hot. It took every ounce of strength I had to keep myself rooted in this couch, to keep myself from doing something I knew I would regret. "Every clue led us right to you."

"We were hoping to find one of us." Blayde sagged into her chair. "Someone with answers about our past. As well as the Dread."

"Just little old me. Sorry to burst your bubble." Nimien waved his hand in the air in a sign that meant absolutely nothing. I gritted my teeth, grinding them down until I could taste enamel.

"Well then," said Blayde, standing. "We won't impose on your hospitality a second longer. Shall we?"

I stood, too, knees shaking, clinging to Zander as he clung to me.

"Oh!" said James, clapping with pride. "I get it! *You're* the guy that kidnapped Zander and Blayde, aren't you? The creep who wanted Sally for himself and wrinkled the timeline to get her. I thought you were dead!"

"Death is a social construct," Nimien sighed. "They were trespassing. And besides, they *had* recently left me for dead. I was young, hotheaded. I was bound to be a little peeved about that. But I'm over that now. A few hundred thousand years are enough to give anyone a sense of perspective. And you are?"

"James Felling. Earth," she replied.

"Ah, the new mortal sidekick." Nimien gave her a curt nod, and James recoiled, eyes wide. "Nice to meet you. Anyway, as I said, I've gained some perspective since then."

"I highly doubt that," said Blayde.

"Oh please." Nimien rolled his eyes. "I've been alone for far too long. It's made me seriously re-think how I've treated you in the past. This may be late, but I'm *sorry*. Sorry for everything. Sorry for creating a library of all knowledge that's only design was to trap and punish you. I see now that was a little... over the top. I'm glad you're here. It's hard to reach out and make apologies when you're in an infinity prison. And I'm sorry for the accidental flashing. It's been a long time since I've had a reason to put on pants in the morning."

"I usually have to scream for hours to get him to cover up," said Sidera, taking a sip of her tea.

Nimien furrowed his brow. "Haven't I been punished enough?"

"Who punished you?" Zander asked, slowly sitting back on the couch. I wanted to drag him to the door, but I was still trembling too much for anything. "How did you get here, Nimien?"

"After you blew me up," he said, "I woke up here, chained to a tree. Tale as old as time. Literally."

"And the labyrinth?" Blayde joined us on the couch as James reached for the tea tray and helped herself to a biscuit. "You built it to pass the time?"

"Some local god gave the natives some plans and a cement mixer," said Nimien. "Then the place gained sentience, which might have been the intention. The rest is history."

"But... why?" Blayde leaned forward. "What's the point?"

"Who knows?" Nimien shrugged. "The labyrinth continues to grow, constantly providing me with everything I need—except for an exit. It grows and shapes itself to keep me trapped. I age in here, slowly but surely, I age. I have managed to reach the antechambers before, but as soon as I step inside, I revert to my former self. No, at this point, all I want is an exit. A true one."

"And by exit you mean—"

"A calm and peaceful death," he said, smiling coyly. "After all these millennia, it's all I truly want. An end to this labyrinth of suffering."

Silence. I'm sure everyone's heads were buzzing just like mine. Buzzing with thoughts of ancient spite building traps around the man who had tried to use time to trap me, a punishment fit for an immortal. Buzzing with thoughts of a way out of immortality, sitting in one place for far too long. The one thing we had an abundance of combined with what we lacked.

Time. And patience.

"Don't pity me," said Nimien. "I deserve this. Maybe even more. And while I wish I knew who had passed judgement on me, I accept it. I've found peace, joy. My daughter brings me word of the outside world. And books! More books than I could possibly read, even in my condition."

"How do you get in here?" Zander turned to Sidera now. Looking at her for the first time since she'd shown her true self. "If your father can't get out…"

"I'm not my father," she said. "As long as I don't try to jump right into the house, the labyrinth doesn't pay attention to me. I jump to an atrium and walk right in."

"And the traps aren't a problem?"

"Please," she purred. "I grew up inside this labyrinth. Those traps? Literally children's games. I can cross them in my sleep."

Zander nodded. "And Desmond—"

"Is my brother."

"How—"

"Let us start at the beginning," said Nimien, "After I found myself in an ever-expanding maze—alone. I was hopelessly bored. So, I built a house. That took me a while, but it did pass the time. Then I went through a wanderlust phase: built a van, drove it around. Then I got into molecular gastronomy and—no, none of that matters. I exhausted every hobby in the universe. I thought I would just wither away from boredom until I heard a sound I never expected to ever hear again."

"Which was?" asked Zander.

"Someone knocking on my door." Nimien smiled. "Two men, scratched up, confused. They were part of a research expedition, men with free minds who had seen too much and had never known peace. So of course, bored as I was, I asked them if they wanted an impartial opinion, and they accepted. But when I solved their problems, they came at me with more. At least it gave me something to do. When their rulers got pissed, I just played the immortal card and they backed off. Soon, they turned my help into a contest.

"First, they came every year, with the promise that I could make wishes come true. But they were still too easy. Too dull. To pass the time, I created a virtual, programmable world that I could hook up to my brain and vacation in. Which was when my first impossible request came: a man wanted to be immortal. That was something I simply could not give—not to just anyone, at least. So I offered him my simulator, in which time was relative and could be stretched to an eternity. He agreed, so long as I wiped the memory of the decision from his head. More immersive that way, you know?

"He was not the only one seeking immortality or even a different life. One by one they came, and I offered them my simulator and let them live their wildest dreams. And each time I rebuilt a new simulator from scratch, used it until the next one came and asked for the life he had always wanted, which I gave to them easily.

"But then people came less regularly—until they stopped coming at all. No one ever did warn me when someone was meant to show up, and I never cared because who wants to wait around for someone who only cares about mooching some stuff off of you? Terrible conversation. Until one day a young couple showed up on my doorstep, having won that year's race, ready for their wish. The man was dying of an inoperable disease, came wanting immortality for him and his wife. I offered them the simulator, telling them the price they would have to pay for it. The woman was not willing to live a lie and advised him to ask for something else. But he didn't give a shit and made me hook him up alone.

"That was how I met Alaysia." Nimien paused. Sidera rubbed his back soothingly. "She had no one waiting for her outside. So, I offered her a place in my home. She was a welcome face in my home, a kind smile where before there was none. I began work again on a new simulator for myself, but soon I found myself enjoying her company more than my mini vacations. Evening strolls and long conversations became my day-to-day routine. After so long, I had finally found my true soul mate. I never finished that last simulator.

"Alaysia and I got married—as officially as one could be married within the confines of this maze—and for years we lived happily together. We raised two beautiful children. Twins! Desmond and Sidera, whom you've met." He reached for his daughter's hand and she took it, squeezing it adoringly. "And I grew up. I understood what I had done to you, that my hate was festering, and I processed it." Nimien took a deep breath, staring down at the floor.

"But Mom refused immortality. She wanted to know what came after." Sidera let go of his hand in order to rub his back again. "After her death, Desmond really took it hard. He blamed Father for not forcing immortality on her, believed it should have been a family decision. So… he ran away, losing the coordinates of the labyrinth. Now he sees the power he's left behind, and he's trying to come back."

No one said anything. Sidera got up, brushed her hands down her pants, and strode out of the room, leaving us in silence. James frowned, turning to Nimien, leaning forward.

"So, none of this has anything to do with the Dread?" she asked. "We found the temple. Your weapon. We know you know how to stop this thing."

"Stop…the Dread?" Nimien's brows soared high. "That temple isn't a weapon. It's a bunker. In case we don't solve this problem, at least some people, good people, will be there to populate the next universe."

Not a weapon? But Miro said… My hands clutched the couch cushion so tightly the fabric started to tear. Another one of Nimien's lies.

"The next… What the frash are you going on about?" asked Blayde.

Nimien sighed again. "The temple guy…" He snapped his fingers, squinting, searching. "Miro! That's the name. They won during the early years of the race, all four cheerful bodies of them. Sweet little weirdo. They had creepy gates-into-the-future eyes. I think they had some kind of acid trip that left them temporally out of sync, but all they could see there was fear and an anxiety that rotted men's souls. So they asked me to stop it from happening. The kid was a mess, and I had to do *something*. I gave them labyrinth tech. Found them a proper bubble universe—yeah, my own library technology is what's keeping me trapped here, laugh all you'd like—gave them cryogenic chambers and the lot. You can ride out anything in a bunker like that. Little did I know that tech would be like candy to you two."

Zander and Blayde traded glances.

"What do you mean?' asked Zander.

"You just can't stop finding it," said Nimien. His lips curled at the edges, oh-so slightly smiling. It made me shudder, driving me impossibly deeper into the couch. "A few years later, you showed up at my doorstep, just having won the race. But this was a past you, a you from before you met me. So, I pretended not to know you, which was a difficult thing to do, let me tell you. The two of you were… toxic. A lot of threats were exchanged that day."

"How come we don't remember this?" Blayde snapped. "I would know if I've done the labyrinth before."

"Oh, so your memory's infallible now?" chided Nimien. "Past you had found the desert planet, solved the temple, but you had no reason to come and see me. Why would you? It was too early in your own timeline for it to make sense to you. Nothing of the story would in any way compel you to visit. But then something happened to you. I'm not sure exactly what, but you wanted the memories wiped. That was your wish: wipe your memories. Both of yours, so that you could have a fresh start."

Gobsmacked. Smacked by Gob. Speechless barely began to cover it. How could one respond to that? To the knowledge that the truth was so close, yet so far away? That they had been led here like children taunted with candy?

"End of the world margaritas?" asked Sidera, trotting back into the room with a tray of cocktails brandished high.

"So," Blayde said quietly, "*you* took our memories away?"

"More times than you can count." Nimien nodded. "And always at your own request. I understand, it's a little too much to process at once." He held out his hands. "But hey, if you want proof I'm trustworthy, search your memories—oh, that's right, you made me take them out of your minds a few thousand years ago."

"So, give them back," Blayde ordered.

"Look, I know we got off to a rough start," said Sidera, handing James a drink. She took it, without dropping her eyes from Nimien or picking her jaw off the floor. "But I'm trying to make it up to you."

"I can't drink this," said James. "Your brother just drugged me with space energy drinks. Ergo…"

"Mortal safe," she said. "I checked. As I said, I'm trying to make it up to you, not give you an emotional hangover."

"Darling, dearest," said Nimien. "I just told them about the memory wipes."

"Oh, right." She put down her tray. "I probably should have brought more of these then."

"You knew," said Zander, glaring at her. "You knew I was missing huge chunks of my memory, and you used that to lie to me? To lead me here?"

"I had to do something." Sidera brushed her long hair over her shoulder nonchalantly. "Father was getting nowhere with his research into the Dread. I figured getting you all here would implode a binary system with a single hydrogen atom, so to speak."

Blayde frowned. "Those two stars being—"

"Oh, you take your memories back and save the world," she replied. "And I don't get an anxiety attack every time I go out for groceries."

I bit my lip, felt the cut of my teeth on the skin, the pain a slight distraction from the panic welling up inside me. The still-trembling Zander at my side. Blayde on my other, shaking with eager anticipation.

There, right before me, the man who would have locked me away for all eternity. The man who had twisted time itself to lay me at his feet was asking me for help.

It may have been a thousand, tens of thousands, a million, or billion years for him since our fight in the library, but for me it was only a month ago. I still saw myself squeezing the light from his eyes when I went to sleep at night.

And here he was. Frail. Helpless. Asking *us* for help. Not asking for forgiveness, knowing he deserves none.

"I'll meet you downstairs," he said, struggling to stand. Sidera helped him up, avoiding eye contact with any of us. "You are free to visit the house. I have nothing to hide from you. Take your time. It's only the end of the universe at stake."

He marched out of the room, Sidera by his side. I had sunk so deep into the couch that I couldn't pull myself out anymore. My head was reeling so hard it could catch a fish.

"I know she's a lying ass and all," said James, taking a long sip of her drink, "but she makes a mean cocktail. I'll give her that."

SEVENTEEN
INTO THE MINDSPACE

Zander

TRUSTING SOMEONE WHO ONCE THREW YOU into a mind prison over a simple misunderstanding was a ludicrous concept even for me. Asking him to place you back in one might have been evidence that I should have stayed in the Earth psychiatric hospital a little longer. I may have a few issues I need to work out, though I'm sure the great meditators of Plethorous Nine would say it's all part of my loving nature, before asking for a small donation of my entire life savings. Joke's on them. It would indeed be a small donation.

Introspection. Now there is a calm, peaceful experience meant to put you in touch with your true self. Underneath the masks, and the masks over the masks, at your core, there was a you so pure it existed as absolute truth. A truth I would finally uncover.

Zander, meet Zander. A man I had not seen in longer than I could remember.

Instead of the cathedral-length space full of gadgets and gizmos and robots playing cards, Nimien took us directly through to a tiny chamber that was far too familiar for comfort. This lab would have given a mad-scientist chills of envy—though I'd gotten through that phase centuries ago, that much I did remember—if it wasn't for his taste in chairs.

Two empty reclining chairs on a glowing white pedestal.

So, I might have PTSD. My instant reaction to the sight was for my heart to stop for a few beats, then invent a new dance trying to catch up with the time it has missed.

Sally reached for my hand. I gripped her tight. Somehow, she had become my rock in all this. Grounding me when I got charged.

"I'm out," said Blayde, taking the words right from my mouth. "You can't possibly think we're that gullible."

"I just repurposed the tech. Veesh," said Nimien. "You can't possibly still be sour about that."

Sour? Please. We'd passed sour and entered the realm of flavor profiles the human tongue couldn't process.

"You trapped us in our own minds, Nimien!" I spat. "How could we possibly not be over that?"

"He did what?" said James. "Dang. It would take me like, seven books to catch up with all your shit."

"Maybe ten," muttered Sally.

"The device folds your conscious mind into your subconscious, and that's it," he continued, climbing up on the platform and gesturing like a car model. I wasn't buying it. "Technically, you will be experiencing an incredibly vivid lucid dream."

"Except last time, we couldn't wake up from that dream, now could we?"

I couldn't believe him. No, I couldn't believe myself. If this was a trap, it was a genius one right to his caliber—and I had fallen right into it. Like a carnivorous flower, this labyrinth had been made appealing to its prey: the promise of my history, my very self, sitting all perfect in the middle, drawing me in until it snapped closed behind me.

Yet if there was a simple, single chance there really was a way to get my memories back, then I should take it, shouldn't I? Reverse the lobotomy, regain my autonomy. To be able to jump anywhere, anytime, as freely as Sally—

Oh, how I envied her.

"Screw it. If it means defeating the Dread, I need to at least try to get myself back. I'll go first," said Blayde. "Zander, if he tries anything…"

"You have to go together," said Nimien. "I'm sorry, but it reduces the risks. You two are each other's tethers. With so many shared markers, not only will the data retrieval be easier, but one of your gaps can be filled by the other's information. It won't be fun, but it'll be effective."

James snorted, hoisting herself up on a desk and watching us with wide-eyed curiosity. If Nimien was mortal here like the rest of us, would she be able to draw her sidearm before Sidera? Every time we'd met him in the past, Blayde and I had been alone. But we had friends with us this time. Maybe we were safer than we thought.

"Look, I know last time was… shitty," said Nimien, holding up a bouquet of wires. "But I have no intention of harming you. If anything, I'm looking forward to getting the server space back once you've re-download your memories. Do you know have any idea much room you take up? I had to invent an entirely new cooling system just to keep the databanks running. I can finally use that for some new VR games."

"So we close our eyes, and when we wake up, we'll have our memories back?" I asked. Nimien brightened up the instant I made eye contact.

"No, you're going to have to work a little," he said. "The mind is a powerful computer. You've got to sort out your firewalls. Now sit."

Sally squeezed my hand. "If he tries anything, I'll kill him. Again. For good this time."

Knowing how much the last time destroyed her, I knew that wasn't an idle threat.

I had learned to accept her invulnerability. She stood by my side through everything the universe had ever thrown at me. I could trust her with this; I knew I could. But why didn't I want to?

"Seriously," she said. "If he even twitches in your direction, I'll put my foot—"

I scooped her up in my arms and kissed her. Who knows, this could be my last time. The heat in her face as she reached her arms around my neck to kiss me back was like basking in the heat of the hottest star.

"I love you," I said, after having to stop to breathe. "Whatever happens in there, whoever I become, I'll still be madly in love with you."

"You'd better be," she replied. "But I'm excited to meet all of you."

She pulled me close for a hug, her lips brushing my ears and sending shivers up my spine. As excited as I was to find my past, Sally was my present, my future. I would give it up if I had to, for her. I was more excited to meet the man I would be, than to face the man I had once been.

"So, what are you going to do?"

Blayde was already hooked up in her chair, making a big show of avoiding looking at Sally and me. Nimien had placed electrodes across her forehead and temple, but her body was free. No straps holding her down. I felt my wrists, the memory of the restrains still clear in my mind. Breathing was becoming complicated.

"I'm not going to do anything," said Nimien. "Non-invasive procedure. You locked the memories away, so it's up to you to get them back. Now don't worry, I'm sure your past self probably left instructions somewhere. Just dive right in."

I sat on the chair, let him place the electrodes over my forehead, cool metal against sweaty skin. Sally clutched my hand, watching Nimien's every move like a fifty-thousand-eyed Oculusian who'd just discovered stare-roids.

"I can't wait for you to show me your home," she said, tightening her grip on my hand. "To meet your family."

"You're the only—"

And Sally became a cloud.

Unfortunately, Nimien had meant *dive right in* literally. No gentle introspection for me. Only the utter exhilaration of being thrown face-first into an ocean miles below. The emerald-green water was a nice touch.

I'd had worse therapy. Stars, I had been waterboarded before. But this was the first time it made me felt like I was actively dying.

The ocean was deep, and I clawed my way to the surface, gasping as fresh air filled my feebly mortal lungs. Salt clung to my nose and throat. My heart pounded against my ribs, trying to break out and make it on its own. I scrambled for purchase under an orange sky.

But there was nothing except empty ocean for miles and miles, green and smelling oddly of Tetraceenian bubblegum.

If this was my subconscious, it was in serious need of redecorating.

"Hey," cooed Blayde, sitting in a rowboat in the middle of the nowhere sea.

"Hey."

"Beware of ogvoks," she said.

I swore, propelling myself to the boat. There weren't many sea creatures that scared me, but ogvoks were a category of their own. They may look like sharks, but would you trust a shark capable of wielding a sword? Personally, I do not.

No one even knows where they get their swords. They're not exactly known for their blacksmithing skills. Carpentry? Sure. But blacksmithing?

"Thought you might be underwater." She held up a baby hand for me to see. I cringed. Not fun, losing an arm. "Hate 'em. You climbing in, or are you going to keep paddling around like ogvok bait?"

She held out her adult arm. I grabbed, and she hauled me in. The boat was small, carved out of a single piece of wood, large enough for the two of us and nothing else. It was old, the varnish dull and peeling.

"No oars," I noted.

"Easy." Blayde held out her hand, palm up, and an oar appeared out of thin air. "Now you."

Dreamscape. Brilliant. I held out my hand, concentrating hard on an oar. Instead, a wave slapped me in the face. Blayde tutted.

"How did you do that?" I asked, snorting the salt from my nose.

"Simple. It's like in a dream, anything you think, goes."

"Then why isn't it working for me?"

She frowned. "Maybe we're not in a shared mindspace yet. We must be in mine."

Which explained why the sky was my least favorite atmospheric shade. Once you see a purple sky, you never go back. Well, unless you're mortal. Then it will kill you.

"Since we're in your mind and all," I asked, "can't you just imagine being somewhere and get there?"

"Do *you* have any idea where we're going? Nope, have to do this right. We're rowing."

"And where are we rowing to? It's not like there's a map."

"Oh, but there is!" She grinned the biggest grin I'd ever seen on her face. "Think about the boat, Zander."

I gave her a confused look. So did the ogvoks. Not that they were invited.

"I've never seen it before," she continued. "So why would my mind create this particular boat? Why not make a hoveryacht while I was at it? It had to be *past* me looking out for *now* me. I'm guessing it will take us where we need to go."

I nodded. "Wonderful. It's nice of your brain to welcome us with open arms."

"Well, it's definitely welcoming *me* with open arms. But you? You're practically parasitic. There's probably more than a few ways this could go wrong."

"Veesh, thanks a lot for that. I should just go to my own brain, then."

I exhaled salty breath. The sooner we sorted her brain, the sooner we could get to mine. A shiver of trepidation ran through me. Would I be happy with what I found? The thought was quickly washed away when another wave hit me square in the face.

"Don't think so hard," she snapped, conjuring a second oar. "Do you have any idea how taxing it is to have your individual thoughts running through my head? Just try not to think about anything. I bet my subconscious mind is going to be a whole lot weirder once we get there."

"This isn't your subconscious?" I scoffed. "What the void is the point, Blayde?"

"Calm down," she said through gritted teeth. "Don't draw any more attention to yourself. Besides, do you see anything of interest around here? We're in some kind of liminal space for the moment."

"When will we reach the subconscious?"

"We'll know when we get there—I hope."

I tried to put her out of my mind as we rowed. I let her steer. This was her mind; she should know the way around it, liminal space or not. The silence bred introspection, which meant spinning Sidera and Nimien over and over in my head. My non-daughter and undead protégé with a penchant for revenge. I had seen him before and trusted him over and over again apparently, spilling my burdens to him every time they got too heavy. Over and over again, I had come here, to Nimien, seeking relief. A cycle of pain and unburdening.

Worse, someone had built the labyrinth around him. Punishing him for not only what he'd done to us, but also what he had done to others. People like Sally. Someone other than me wanted to stop Nimien. Like an all-you-can-eat buffet, it was a lot to digest.

Eyes looked up at me from either side of the boat, shimmering underwater, and it hit me that I was thinking too hard, too deep. Blayde's mind was fighting back. Waves rippled on the ocean's surface, rearing and ready to strike.

"Land, ho!" Blayde cried, thankfully bringing my attention back to the bloody boat.

Sand dunes with oddly familiar faces stared at us from the beach, black glass sand waiting to suck up our footsteps. The ogvoks went about deconstructing the boat for parts the second we'd left it, enthusiastically twisting the faded wood into office furniture.

"Where to now?" I asked as the completed desk vanished beneath the waves. "It's your brain. Shouldn't you know the way around?"

Blayde shrugged. "If our time at The Hill taught us anything, it's that I have absolutely no idea what's going on up here." She rapped a knuckle on her temple, and I braced myself, half expecting the whole island to shake. "Come on. We could have miles to go."

Above the ridge sat a house-sized bird, perched on the branch of a charred failure of a tree. Its crimson feathers existed in patches, leaving pale skin exposed. While it was looking right at us, the cloudy eyes didn't seem to know we were here.

"Ah, maybe this is a clue," said Blayde. "My good mental bird, how are you? Are you a signpost? Or maybe a repressed emotion?"

It gave a small cough, fell to the ground, and died.

"This is either a sign of tremendously healthy coping mechanisms," I said, watching the corpse turn to ash and blow away on a gentle wind, "or quite the opposite."

A small egg rose from the ground, cracked open, and out hopped a chirping, healthy chick.

"This is like a dream I once had," said Blayde, cringing. "Only I think it had more strippers."

"You're thinking of Batalghast's five hundredth birthday," I said. "I'm sad to say that wasn't a dream."

"Sad? It was the most fun I'd had in ages!"

The chick grew, flew to the branch, a beautiful shade of the reddest red, chirping the freshest and purest song I had ever heard, a simple handful of three notes so musical I knew there could be nothing more perfect in the world. Then the feathers fell in places, the bird grew fat, the eyes grew cloudy, and with one loud cough, it fell off its branch and died again.

"This place is strange," I muttered as the ashes blew away to reveal another egg.

Blayde nodded. "My brain is weird. Shall we move on?"

"Please."

We headed toward mountains, impossibly tall peaks that rose high ahead of us, piercing the only clouds in the sky. But Blayde's subconscious island was littered with junk: a set of Goothian party lights; the tattered remains of what had been a long blue trench coat; a collection of over a hundred rifles barrel-down in the sand, close together like the spikes of a porcupine. A dragon roasted in his armor, the skeleton of a knight beside him.

I followed her into the tall grass, letting the plants tickle the palms of my hands. Little by little, the sand was completely replaced by grass, and shortly following that the grass became taller and stronger. Soon we were marching through waist-high weeds, which were doing a mighty fine job of hiding any more of the strange shit from us. The mountains grew in the distance. My eyes had been so fixated on them that I tripped over the first body.

The first of many.

This was a field of the dead.

"Just try to walk around them," said Blayde, nonchalantly. The rising wind told me she was definitely *chalant.*

I couldn't not look down, not if I wanted to get where we were going without falling. There was a face I recognized, staring up at the orange sky with a glassy dead-eyed stare. A warlord from centuries past, three tongues sprawled over his face.

What a heavy weight, all these corpses she carried around.

Splat. A low-flying bird collided with my face, cawing.

"Stop thinking," said Blayde. "You're drawing attention!"

We crossed through a forest and back out the other side, which brought us to the base of the spires of mud. Too steep to climb, we opted instead to walk around them, which then brought us back down to a strange beach—this one had not only a half-sunken Lady Liberty but also an hourglass where the sand rose and disappeared—and up into a canyon between the rock formations.

As we walked, I began to notice caves along the wall, some at ground level, others higher up, formed there by time itself. Somehow, I knew those were my sister's memories, though obviously not the ones she was looking for since these were out in the open.

Here's hoping my mind has them in a cooler locale. Maybe a spaceport? Not a library.

A few miles into the narrow canyon, we were stopped by the first thing that seemed to have been placed there with purpose.

A gate.

"Told you we'd know," said Blayde. She reached for the lock, but it didn't budge. No sign of a pad for a key or biometrics. She frowned, staring at it with the piercing look she reserved for prey when she was feeling feisty. But no amount of staring could burn through that lock.

"Have you tried imagining the key into existence?" I asked.

"No, that thought never even occurred to me." She rolled her eyes. "That's the first thing I tried, dumbass."

A Kroll warrior phased into existence on top of the gate, exactly how Kroll warriors don't. The whole point of the Krolls was that you should see them coming from miles away. The anticipation would usually make the opposing army die of fright. They made the classic Kroll *shatatatata* noises, waving their arms around like a windmill. Oh thank Derzan, this place was getting dull.

"Look away!" shouted Blayde, throwing her hand in front of her eyes. "Hypno-arms!"

The Kroll leapt into the air, doing a double somersault on their way down, landing in front of us with her arms still spinning. Every patch of skin and hair was covered in the vibrant, mind-bending patterns of their creed, leaving only the eyes exposed, so the only thing I could say for certainty is that they were humanoid and had an expensive silk habit.

"You were thinking again, weren't you?" Blayde cursed under her breath.

"Is this really you?" asked the Kroll, voice muffled by their wrap. They bowed, arms wide. "You have returned to us, Goddess divine."

I took a step back. I'd been a deity more than enough times. If Blayde wanted to be worshipped by her own subconscious, that was her prerogative.

"Um, rise, and all that," said Blayde, tapping them on their shoulder. "Glad to be here. Who might you be?"

"I am the gatekeeper," they said. "Set here by you last time you took form, with strict orders never to open this gate for anyone."

Blayde frowned. "Let me guess. Even me?"

The Kroll nodded. "Unless you best me in battle."

I sighed, and Blayde turned just to glare at me. It hadn't been conscious. We'd just been through this shit more than once, and it was pretty tiring that Blayde's own mind would pull a fast one on her like that.

I took a seat on a nearby rock. I used to love this kind of spectacle, but I knew how it went now. It wasn't exactly a fair fight.

The Kroll didn't give two shits about me; their focus was completely on my sister. Blayde took three steps back, putting one leg gently forward in a comfortable battle stance. The Kroll did the same, putting their arms up and wide, a clear sign they were unarmed. Blayde slipped off her coat and tossed it to me, and—the loving and dreadfully bored brother I was—I caught it and folded it on the rock beside me.

Instantly, twin swords appeared in the Kroll's hands, which they twirled expertly. Relief washed over me. Maybe this would be over pretty quick.

"Woo," I cheered, with as much enthusiasm as I could muster. "Go team!"

"No rules," said the Kroll. "Last woman standing enters the gate."

"Fun!" said Blayde, calling forth two swords of her own. "I love death matches. Especially since I can't die and all."

"You die, and everything here dies," said the Kroll. "It is the way of all things."

"But then *you* die. So don't I win either way?"

The Kroll put her weapons by her side. "This isn't how it works! You're meant to fight me to the death!"

"You're sucking the fun out of this," Blayde huffed. "I guess I won't get killed then."

They nodded, poised, and attacked.

There was no idle pacing. No sizing each other up, no measuring weaknesses and openings. The Kroll lunged at Blayde, catching her by surprise and nicking her shoulder with the sword. Blayde hissed, dodging out of their way, blood dripping into the gritty sand.

My heart dropped. For the first time since I would remember—which admittedly might not be as long as I think—she was way out of her depth, her only advantage gone. That was her move, to attack first and force her opponent on the defensive right off the bat. Her move—

"Blayde!" I called, as realization hit. "You can't win with swords! The guard has your memories. You can't—"

"I got that!" she snapped as she rolled out of the Kroll's swoop and attempted a trip, though it failed miserably, tripping her instead. It was as if the Kroll could anticipate her every move.

"Behind you!"

"Stop helping!"

Blayde lifted her hands, dipping both swords down onto the ground. The Kroll saw the opening and lunged, but Blayde was ready. She leapt up, springboarding off the two swords, flipping over the

Kroll's head as a wooden staff appeared in her hands. She landed, striking her opponent across the back and shoving them face-first into the ground, the swords melting away into dust as the black-clad woman lost control. Blayde's foot came down heavy on their chest, pinning them down, the staff hovering an inch above their neck.

I breathed a sigh of relief. It had been a long time since I'd seen Blayde so evenly matched, and if she'd lost here…

"Kill me," the Kroll ordered.

"No. You have been a worthy opponent. You shall not die today."

"Look, all that goddess stuff earlier? Just trying to flatter you. We both know I'm just an image projected into your subconscious. Kill me now, and you get what you came for!"

"I don't give a shit. I win, so I get to not kill you. I walked through my murder field. I don't want to add another corpse to it. Even if you already live rent-free inside my head."

"Suit yourself, then," she snickered.

She grabbed Blayde's foot, propelling her off their chest. They grabbed the staff with both hands, thwacking her across her midriff and forcing her to the ground, pinning her under the staff with their entire body weight over her chest.

Blayde heaved as I darted forward to help her, only to be thrown back by a hand of stone. I pushed myself up, desperate to see the scene, to act, to stop her, but the stranger was already lifting her hand to undo the wrap around her head—

Now Blayde looked down at Blayde with fury burning from her eyes.

I should have seen it coming. Who else could guard Blayde's memories as efficiently as Blayde herself? My heart pounded in my chest, so hard I thought it might break a rib. Could the Blayde from Blayde's subconscious kill her true self? And if I lost Blayde, here… I would lose myself, too, in more ways than one. I gripped my seat, except that it was a rock, so my fingers scraped against stone, nails tearing.

"You are weak," said Other Blayde through gritted teeth, pushed down on her future self's throat. "Weak. Weak and useless."

"Oh my stars, this is exactly what I wanted," said Blayde. "This is so hot. Quick, let me conjure up a thermal pool—"

Other Blayde ripped the staff away, gagging.

"You are worse off without your memories," she continued, the staff in her hand dissolving into nothing. "Losing them has made you weak. And, dare I say, gross. Thus, you need the memories back. But know this. I hid the memories for a reason. Whatever you get back, you do so at your own risk."

"How do I…"

"For the full ride, just hop into that hole right there." The gate flew open, and a massive black hole appeared directly behind it. "That will trigger the recall. You may not want to see everything; it's very long. But you'll figure out how to travel through it soon enough. It ain't rocket science. Don't expect to remember everything at once. It's been a while, and the memories of boring things like walking somewhere or going to the bathroom are probably gone for good. Pieces of conversation won't all be there. But that's no fault of your own. It's not like you're in control of your subconscious. Just there for the ride."

And with that, Other Blayde zapped out of existence, leaving the two of us in stunned silence in the middle of the dusty canyon.

Blayde marched right over to the sinkhole and peered down. I joined her, crouching over the edge and staring into the pit. Dark like a black hole, but with none of the pull—except emotionally.

"So, are we going to do this?" I asked, a little tremor of fear rushing through my veins. This was it. The moment of truth. We would know where we were from, where home was. My hands shook as I stared into the pool. Who would I be when I came out the other side?

"Only if you're ready," she said.

"You sure you want to do this?"

She took a deep breath. "No. We locked these memories away for a reason, Zander. What if we can't handle the truth?"

"We locked them away because we weren't strong enough to face them," I replied. "I don't know about you, but I'm strong enough now."

"Let's hope so," she said, taking my hand. "Let's face our past."

EIGHTEEN

THE LAST PLACE ON EARTH I'D WANT TO BE, BUT THEN AGAIN THIS ISN'T EARTH

Sally

"THEY'RE HOLDING HANDS!" JAMES CLAPPED HER hands to her cheeks. "Is that supposed to be happening?"

She shot me a smile from across the lab, and I couldn't help but smile back. Thank the stars for her cheerful optimism. Her running commentary was the only thing keeping me grounded right now. I'm sure if she weren't here I would either run away or strangle Nimien again and run away after.

Nimien checked a small screen between the two chairs. Data scrawled down the pixels too fast for me to follow. "There isn't exactly a handbook for this stuff. I have no idea."

I choked on my own saliva. This, coming from the very reason the siblings had lost their past? Nimien deserved everything he got, this labyrinth prison and more. If I could meet the person who built it, I would kiss them with my whole heart.

He looked over at me, and I stared instead at Zander. Screw you, douchecanoe, he's the only reason you're not six feet under right now.

The door shut. He had left.

"So, he's the guy?" asked James, putting her hands on her hips as she stepped up on the raised platform to examine Blayde. The siblings were still holding hands, but their faces were still the blank slate they had been when they'd been put under just ten minutes ago.

"He is," I replied. "Or *was*, if you believe what he's saying. That he's redeemed or whatever."

"And do you?"

"Not a chance," I spat. "Once a monster, always a monster. No amount of centuries sitting in a mansion surrounded by gadgets will ever rehabilitate anyone."

James now turned to me, dropping her voice low. "I don't think they'd allow themselves to be this vulnerable if he can't be trusted."

"They're desperate," I said. "They've been looking for home for longer than they can remember—literally. And if that can help them, help us, defeat the Dread… it's probably worth the risk. Especially since we're here as backup."

"Right," said James, "backup against an immortal and his daughter who may or may not have planned this whole thing."

"Maybe we need to give ourselves more credit?"

The door opened again, but this time it was Sidera coming in, another tray in hand. She beamed as she walked in, placing the spread on one of the counters.

"Tea, anyone?" she asked, holding up a silver teapot.

"No thanks," said James.

"It's not poisoned, if that's what you're worried about," she said with a shrug. "Come on, I know you're probably parched—you especially, Sally. How's the heartbeat? Strong and steady?"

It felt a little too personal of a question, borderline insulting. Patronizing at the very least.

"Don't worry," she continued. "I know all about the threshold between mortality and immortality. Pocket universes really mess with you that way."

"And you're not affected?" I asked. Why the hell did I even open my mouth? I didn't want to talk to her. She had shattered Zander's sense of self with her lies.

"Nah, since I'm half-half," she said, with a shrug. "It's complicated and comes down to quantum entanglement, which… nope, by the looks on your faces you're not familiar with it at all."

"That's the theory about the particles linked across distant spaces, right?" asked James. "Like, you can spin one way, and the other one has to match up no matter where it is?"

"That's right," said Sidera, eyes widening for a split second. "In a broad sense, our bodies are entangled with the universe. We are knotted in a way that cannot be undone. Every time our bodies deviate from the norm, the universe fights to put us back. We cannot be changed."

"And we… what? Use this tangle to move around?" I scoffed.

"That's pretty much the gist of it," she said, sipping her tea. "We can make ourselves exist at any point in time and space where there are particles in existence. We simply tell those particles it's time for them to match us, and voila. It removes the existence of duplicates by anchoring us to multiple points and—I'm losing you, aren't I? I can show you the math behind it. It's a thing of beauty."

It did make one thing a little bit clearer: I needed to take my college credits, go back to university, and actually sit through a physics lecture rather than think up old Star *Trek* episodes while the prof droned on. Or maybe just find a civilization with technology for downloading textbooks right into your brain. It would save a lot on enrollment costs. At this rate, I'd need my entire immortality to pay off the inflation of those student loans.

"So inside this bubble universe, we're cut off from those anchors?" I said, trying to seem as uninterested as possible. I didn't want Sidera to have the pleasure of another win. "Which is why we can't go anywhere, and the universe isn't pushing us toward that base state."

"Precisely," she said.

"But in Nimien's library, we were still immortal. That was a bubble universe, too, right?"

"That was a node," she said, "At least, from what he's told me. The way we're connected to everywhere all at once but applied to a much larger structure. The architectural version of us, if you will. Would you seriously not like any tea? It's very good. I picked it up on Granovia Prime. It's a little moon with the most perfect lavender sky."

"So Nimien really is dying," I said.

Sidera's face fell. I should have apologized, but I didn't. She'd almost broken Zander, or at the very least been a whole new source of Trauma. With a capital T. I didn't care.

"He is," she replied. "The house has been keeping him alive, but… he hasn't reset in almost two centuries now. His body is beginning to fail him. It won't be long now."

She stared down into her tea, taking a long and intentional sip.

"I just wish Desmond and he could make up before he passes, you know?" she said, her voice barely above a whisper. "I meant what I said. He really did get lost. I haven't been able to bring him home. I'm worried the day I do, there won't be anyone here to welcome him anymore."

I still said nothing. Zander and Blayde's neutral expressions had turned to frowns, and I had been so tied up with Sidera I hadn't even noticed. They weren't even holding hands anymore.

"I just don't get how you're not mortal here, too," said James, "if everyone gets cut off from the universe when they step into the labyrinth?"

"Because I was born in this bubble," she said, shrugging. "Desmond and I are the only ones like us in the whole wide 'verse. Dad's connection anchored us outside, but being born in here meant we were connected to this place too. I can't jump between them, though. Think of it as two different transit systems."

"Oh," said James, "So when you brought us to the labyrinth…"

"*You* were never meant to come along," she said, "and I tried leaving you behind—I am sorry about that, truly—since the labyrinth only accepts teams of four, and I was planning on coming with you to guide you through the traps. But it seems you did all right on your own."

"The robots helped us," I said.

"I like those guys," said Sidera. "I've been passing them philosophy books for years, trying to get them to shut up about murdering people and missing the mayhem and all."

Nimien stepped back into the room, looking more exhausted than before. Every step was slow, agonizing. He said nothing except thank you as he took a cup from Sidera's tray. He sipped at the tea, slurping loudly, staring at the floor the whole time.

"You should rest, Father," said Sidera, placing a gentle hand under his cup. "Today has been taxing for you."

"And miss my reckoning?" Nimien laughed. "Fat chance. This may be my only chance at atonement, child. I wouldn't miss it for the universe."

"I don't know if they'll forgive you that easily," I said, standing and crossing my arms over my chest. No way would I be seated for this. "I don't… I don't even know where to start, Nimien."

"Then don't," he said, "Let me say this again, truly and from the bottom of my heart, I am sorry. I am truly, incredibly sorry for what I did. I was young and angry, but it was not an excuse. I've spent multiple lifetimes trying to be a better man than I was back then. I am still learning."

"I was a different girl back then too," I spat. "And you changed that, you changed me. You forced me into your game just to take the life you thought you deserved—"

"And this is my reward," he said, sweeping his arms wide.

"Your own universe," I said. "Your own world. I'd say that's rather generous."

"An eternity to think about my mistakes," he said. "To learn and grow from them. To become a better person, day by painstaking day."

"Which is what you took from Zander and Blayde," I growled. "You took their memories—of everything. Of home. Of every success and every failure. How can anyone grow when you remove their roots the second they grow long?"

Sidera frowned as he put down the teacup, stepping toward me. She kept her hand under his arm just in case.

"It was their choice," he said, "Every time they came to my door, I asked if they were sure. They were in pain,

Sally. Every time they came it was after another heartbreak, another weight they carried on their already broken backs. I didn't do anything, just gave them the tools to do it themselves."

"If you meant what you said about growth, then you would know that that's not how you solve any of this. Ignorance cannot be bliss."

"But it is a respite from pain," he said. "Can't you see that, Sally? You love them. Imagine seeing them suffer every single day from the role the universe forces them to play."

"The universe doesn't force us to do anything. We are cast in many roles in our lives. We can't always decide what those roles will be, but we can choose what to do with them. They could have learned and changed, but you took away their chance at that. You took away their future."

"No," he said, "There are some traumas you can't grow from, Sally. Sometimes, when you're broken, you don't come back stronger. You continue to exist, barely holding yourself together, prone to shattering. If you haven't gone through that kind of trauma, than consider yourself privileged." Nimien hung his head. "I was only trying to help them. To do better than I did before."

"That's all well and good," I said, shaking. "But you didn't."

He turned away from me, staring instead at the siblings in the chairs. They were still frowning, their hands dangling limply by their sides.

"We'll know what they think soon enough," he said, "and they should be the ones to decide. I may have been an accomplice to their past choices, but they were always *their* choices. They never came asking me to change anything, only for a clean slate. Something I wished for day in and day out for centuries. Millenia even."

He turned back to me. I had my hands crossed so tight over my chest they would have protected me from a nuclear blast. Even James was on the defensive, standing over Blayde like her own personal shield.

"Yes, maybe I do have something the siblings don't," said Nimien. "We might have all the time in the universe, but I'm the only one who got to taste it. I'm the only one who had to sit and watch it go by without being a part of it. I know what it feels like to see life pass by without me, and I know what it means to make every second of it count. I have a beautiful family. I made a difference in people's lives."

I wasn't buying it. No matter how earnest he was, he was still the same man who had blown up my life and tried to ruin my friends.

"I tried to be good, Sally. I truly did," he continued. "You can hate me all you want now; it does nothing to me. I don't hate myself anymore. All the time I wasted on hating myself is time I will never get back. It's because I love myself now and the future self I will become that I don't dismiss who I once was. I grew from that rot, and even if you refuse to accept that, I will still do everything in my power to give you all everything you need."

"So that we can go out and save the universe from a threat you don't understand," I said. "So that we can do all the dirty work for you."

"I can't leave the labyrinth. I will die in this house. Maybe tomorrow, maybe years from now, but there is no changing that. I will give you everything you need, whether or not you go and fight the Dread. Though if you don't, I think you'll have a lot less of the universe to enjoy. It's your choice."

I bit my tongue. I didn't want to ally myself with this man, with this monster, but what choice did I have? He was our only lead. Our only resource. He checked the readings on the mind machine again, frowning, then looked back at me.

"If you refuse to believe I can be a better man today than I was yesterday," he said, "then how will you accept Zander when he returns with the selves even he didn't want to carry?"

Tears were rolling out of Blayde's eyes now, sparkling in the sterile white lighting. James reached for her hand, then thought better of it, stuffing them both in her pockets. Nimien turned to her now.

"You should be careful, you know," he said.

"Careful of what?" James asked, confused.

"Of *them*. I was like you, once, you know. A mortal by their side. It always ends in tears."

"I don't understand."

"Think about it. First there was Sally. One week with them, and boom, she's changed forever. Immortal. And there's no going back."

"But you—"

"Thousands of years, Felling." He said with a sigh. "Thousands of years without jumping, and I still don't know what I am. Which brings me to exhibit B. Me."

"What about you?"

"Three days with them. Look at me now."

"That doesn't mean it will happen to me," said James. "Two does not make a rule."

"Trust me, when I ran the library, I read everything that came my way that had anything to do with them. One thing remained consistent: They never took anyone with them. They offered a new life somewhere else, but they moved on. No one travels with them. Not until Sally."

"But we—"

"It started with her. It was a thank you that went wrong. Probably because Zander developed feelings. And then there was me. Poor, confused me. I was just a teenager; I was fifteen, for goodness sake. I asked them out of fear, and they took me out of pity. I died three days later on a planet millions of light-years from my own. That's it. Three days was all it took. Three days, and they made me what I am now."

"Because you set it in motion," I spat. "What are you trying to do, Nimien? A minute ago, it was all about making things right for everyone—"

"I am. And that everyone includes Agent Felling here."

"Then you should tell her how you set the dominos to fall," I said. My arms were so tight now I could barely breathe. My mouth was dry enough for me to crave Sidera's mystery tea. "How you did everything to put us on the *Traveler* before you set it up to crash on your homeworld."

"What?" said James, taking a step back. "Oh, right, time travel. Your future self looking out for your past."

"Yes," said Nimien. "I won't deny it; I set it all in motion. The same me who thought the universe was his to take. Who could see the universe in four dimensions before he knew what it meant. But I've thought long and hard about the cyclic nature of my childhood. What made me angry enough to try taking the universe by the horns? What set me off?"

He turned back to James. "I'm trying hard to grow past those feelings, but know this. Traveling with the siblings spells disaster. Quite literally, in at least half the languages I know."

"Look, this is different," James replied, shuffling uncomfortably. "I—"

"You're still alive. Go home, Felling. Or you'll be another heartbreak that they'll wipe from their memories."

"But—"

I could have strangled him. Here he was preaching about change, growth, and all that jazz, which I would have loved to hear over a podcast from someone who hadn't tried to trap me for eternity, before turning around and quite literally in front of my face saying the opposite to someone I cared about.

Talk about insulting. Maybe I should strangle him again? Or maybe I should be the better person. Like he said, I could win in a dance battle against him any day.

But before I could say anything, some light screaming ruined the vibe.

Sidera appeared before us, dripping blood all over the Derzan-dammed carpet. Her arm was missing—wait, no, it was clutched in the other arm, and now she was trying to jam it back into place while her body already was trying to grow a new one. An axe hung off her hip covered in more blood that dripped down her white leggings.

Nimien flew a foot into the air.

"Darling dearest," he said, biting his lip, "have we sprung another trap?"

"Worse," she hissed. "I didn't spring anything—Desmond did."

Our host's eyes flashed with so many emotions I couldn't place them. Shock, relief, agony, confusion—just pick one already.

He settled on a solid gulp of resolve, reaching his hands forward to help Sidera to her feet.

"He's found us, Father," she said. "And he's not here for a social call. I beheaded him once, but he brought an army. The labyrinth has fallen. He has us surrounded. We are doomed."

NINETEEN

BEST HITS THAT SHOULD HAVE NEVER MADE THE LIST

Zander

UNFORTUNATELY, THE HOLE WE JUMPED INTO exited us from the brain. Game over, restart, do not pass go, do not get the eternal soul of a dying star.

We landed right back to the front of Nimien's labyrinth home. The labyrinth around us had no sign of trees or plants anywhere, the walls pure white and slightly reflective. Clean, polished, cared for.

So not only had we been thoroughly ejected, we'd ended up earlier in the time stream than we should have. Probably part of whatever trap Nimien had concocted. I raised my fists.

"Where are we?" I asked. And then, tagging on a line I had wished I could say in a more exciting context, "When are we?"

Blayde punched my shoulder. "Not funny."

"I felt that." Our eyes met, widening like a pair of stars practicing synchronized supernovae.

"We're still in my head," said Blayde. "This has to be a memory."

"You're not driving?"

"This must be the last thing I remember, the first thing I forgot," she muttered. "Oh look, here I am now!"

Blayde—another Blayde, a younger Blayde, with bright green buzz-cut hair and an Altruan tuxedo shoved over her labyrinth uniform—rushed up Nimien's hill. Her hand went right through me as she pounded on the door.

That was… mildly unsettling.

"Fina-frashing-lutely," she said, spinning on her heels and tossing something down the hill.

I looked up and gasped because who was trotting up behind her but me, looking the same as I looked right now, uniform and all.

"That's not a word," he said, ducking from whatever she had thrown. He frowned as he caught up with the rest of us. "And yay, hooray, we found the genie. Do you think we each get a wish, or do we fight to the death again? I'm getting tired of the death matches."

"Because I always win," Other Blayde said gleefully. "Now smile. We have to look our best for all the victory photos."

"Do you think they can see us?" I whispered to present Blayde. It was hard not to be nauseated by the sight of this other me: younger, I knew that, but he didn't look it. His frown was disconcerting, though.

She shook her head. "We're simply watching. It's just a projection."

"Right." I nodded.

"Your hair looked like crap."

"Says the one who looks like she stuck hers in a vat of radioactive waste. Wait, mine's the same?"

"Exactly. Well, at least we're on the same page."

The door flew open and out burst Nimien, his arms held wide. He wasn't the youth who had kidnapped us or the Eternal who'd greeted us with tea. Here, he might have been in his mid-forties if not for the unbearable curse of time and space. And he was, thankfully, dressed, though it was as if a toddler had picked his clothes—an Arduinian toddler, meaning color was a sensation best experienced through phalanges.

"Blayde!" he said, smiling so wide you would fit a few tesseracts in there. "And Zander! Finally, I've been waiting lifetimes. Well, don't just stand there, come on in! I'll put on a roast. Do you like roasts? I know fireslug isn't everyone's cup of tea, but ever since I drilled into this structure's core it's been a non-stop delivery service of fried slug. I honestly don't have enough place for them; they just keep spewing—"

"Greetings, wise man." Blayde bowed low, seemingly oblivious to his ramblings. "It is an honor to meet you."

"Wow, you're hilarious." Nimien twirled. "Please, do not extend my torture. I know we have a lot to talk about now that you're finally here, but have you at least brought me any news from the outside? I got my hand on the Fireslug Gazette, and it's as dull as their sorry excuse for porn."

"Sir, it is wonderful to finally see you in person." Zander bowed deep, seemingly intentionally deeper than Blayde had. She even scowled at him.

I cringed. What an ass.

"We have heard so much about you."

"Oh, shit snacks," said Nimien. *"You don't know who I am, do you?"*

"We have read of you in the ancient histories… well, they're not that ancient here, I guess. We're time travelers, you see."

"Yes, I know that." He scowled. *"Hate that. Guess we haven't met yet after all. My mistake. Come on in anyway. The roast is ready whether you want any or not."*

"We apologize, kind sir, but we are in a bit of a hurry." Blayde tried to keep her voice from sounding bossy, but this version of Nimien knew full well what she was getting at. *"We were wondering if—"*

"Well frash me sideways three ways until Sunday," he said under his breath. Past us didn't seem to notice, which was weird, it being Blayde's memory and all. *"In thousands, maybe millions of years of running this labyrinth, never once has someone come just to keep me company. Always in a rush, you are. Well then, scratch the slug. Let's get to the wishes, since that's what you're here for?"*

"Thank you." Blayde nodded. *"Our request is simple. Probably easy for a man of your talents. We wish for a complete memory wipe."*

"Wow, she seriously thinks she's a master manipulator?" my Blayde scoffed. "She's so heavy handed I see fingers in the air."

"A complete…?" Nimien's face broke into a grin. "But that means—glowworms above, this is perfect. Just perfect. You want your memory wiped. You, too, I suppose, Zander? It's never just the one of you. Oh no, you're so codependent the last time you were apart atoms hadn't even considered joining up as molecules yet."

Other me nodded. "I could do without the sass, but yes."

"Look," said Nimien, "I could find you an amazing counselor. Did wonders for me. And trust me, if I've learned to cope with my trauma —"

"Our whole lives have been a series of traumatic events," Blayde interjected.

"It's how we started out. Running from our past, but then our past grows and we run faster and faster," my past self said dramatically. Oh, please. He could have thrown his hand back on his forehead, and it would have been less dramatic.

"All we want is a clean slate," said past Blayde. "If we can forget these terrible years, maybe we can turn our lives out for good."

"Fine, fine." Nimien pinched the bridge of his nose. "Easy stuff, children's play. I'll just force you into your subconscious, and from there you can do all the work. Cleaner job than I could ever do."

"You sure that'll work?" Zander asked skeptically.

Nimien shrugged. "If it doesn't, we'll try something different. I'm here until the end of days. Though can you help me with these dead fireslugs first? I can't keep track of where they're coming from, and I've lost my appetite for them."

The memory disintegrated, leaving us in a pitch-black void. The void was oddly soothing, smelling of eucalyptus I think, with candles at foot level. Soft chanting rose from all around us, gentle and far away.

"Where are we?" I asked. "Is this another memory?"

"I think this is the space between them?" said Blayde, kicking over a candle, which dissolved into the nothing. "Ah, it must be my center."

"Your what now?"

"You know, when you're supposed to center yourself?" she said. "Well, I find that too time consuming, so I centered a crumb of myself, and I just call in for a chat whenever I need to find my center. She must be here somewhere."

The chanting stopped and a flashlight flickered on from far away. "Sup?" asked the woman holding it, a version of Blayde with hip-length hair pulled up into spheres who was lying reclined on the floor.

"Sup, Centered Blayde," said Blayde. "Kumbaya and all that."

"Your blood pressure's high," said the other Blayde. "I'm worried the next time you get stabbed you'll make a real mess."

"It's all good; it'll be an extra distraction. Like a squid or a Malthusian or an ogvok with silly string."

"Right on," said Zen Blayde, lying back into the dark. "Have a nice stay."

The flashlight turned off.

"Centered you scares me a little," I said. "She's so… grounded."

"Yeah, whatever. Next memory?"

"What? We just get to see them best hits style? I thought we were getting them back. Do we have to watch them all?"

"I don't know how any of this works any more than you do," she said, shrugging. "Hold on…"

The void shuddered and changed. The nothing beneath my feat turned soft and plush and gross. Shelves burst through, rising high, building walls and a ceiling around the two of us. When it was finally done, it looked oddly like a Starbucks.

"Is this… are we going to wait out our brain thing in a generic coffee shop?" I frowned. "Wait, you hate Earth."

"This isn't Earth." She waved her hands around. "Or a coffee shop. It's a Zyrtruskian holo-cinema."

"Good memory?"

"More like… improvised filing system," she explained, hopping over the counter and activating what I initially thought was a milk throttler. "Everything is moderately sorted. This one seems important—"

Instantly, we were flung from the void into a screaming spaceship. The crew ran around with their arms flailing, which was impressive considering they must have had at least a hundred each.

And there on the bridge—Blayde. In her silver-gowned glory.

"Ah, yes," the Blayde beside me said, smiling. "I won karaoke fair and square that night. No one warned me they were allergic to high C."

In an instant, we were back in the Starbucks. Blayde, still smiling, shook the milk throttler and looked inside it again.

"Hold on tight," she said.

She waved her hand in the air, and we were in the hallway of what had to be the most luxurious hotel I had ever seen. Penthouse, of course, red carpet and all. Beautiful Pyrina stretched outside the window.

Past Blayde strode up the hallway, wearing skin-tight silver leggings and tank top, her hair tied up behind her neck, leaving her long bangs bouncing lightly upon her forehead. And she was furious. She marched with such a powerful stride that I had to move out of the way, afraid she was going to bulldoze right over me, ghost or no ghost. She walked directly to room 59801, rapping on the door, not waiting for an answer before shoving it open, throwing the do not disturb sign to the ground in anger.

We followed her into the suite beyond, and again I was shocked by the beauty of the room. The glass ceiling opened up to a cloudless sky, so blue that one could swim in it. The room was elegantly furnished, white sofas set every which way across the open space, and my heart dropped as I saw the various articles of clothing strewn across the floor and chairs.

"Oh, please no," I muttered, and Blayde snorted.

Still, we followed her fuming past self storm across the room. She threw the door open wide, which let a loud scream escape into the sitting room.

My face went red as an entire contingent of what I think were cheerleaders screamed in harmony. Beautiful humans and Strobiniums with less fabric between them than a lens cloth, all reeling from the sudden sunlight, which had made things a whole lot less sexy than they had been a second ago.

And in the middle of all the hair, arms, and tentacles— apparently—was me.

I cringed so hard I might have snapped my face.

Past me was sitting in the middle of the planet-sized bed with a roll of something steaming hanging out of his mouth, seemingly unfazed by the panic around him. The others were rushing to grab their clothing, a scavenger hunt that had more than a few guests shouting as they collided.

"Don't forget your souvenir photos," he muttered, leaning back against the headboard. "I'll autograph them next time. Anything you leave here becomes mine, and if you see me wearing it, I'll be owed a compliment."

"Wow," said past Blayde, tossing him a jerkin from one of the chairs beside her. Or, well, she tried to. What had appeared to be a jerkin turned out to be a Jagran, which blushed sky blue as it fluttered out of the room.

"You could have been more polite to Isgurt," said past me, breathing out a cloud of green steam. "He was still recovering from this morning."

"It's 6 am."

"Ah, maybe yesterday morning, then. Maybe I should call a doctor."

He sank deeper in the bed, arms wide at his side, seemingly oblivious to Blayde, who stood beside him, scowling.

"I thought better of you," she said, finally.

"No, you didn't. You hoped better of me, but you expected exactly what you found."

"Oh stars above, you have a wife?" asked a lingering guest.

"Worse," Blayde snarled. "I'm his sister."

"How is that worse?"

"Out." Blayde ordered, pointing to the door. She squealed and rushed out, casting one last, terrified look at Blayde, before she ran into the sitting room, pulling her gown over her head. Past Blayde crossed her arms, leaning against the doorframe as she stared at past me.

"Put some pants on. We need to talk," she ordered.

"What's so important that it needs pants for?" he snapped but got up and found some pants anyway.

"Come on, I thought you would be more excited to see your sister, since it's been seven years and so on."

"You're not my sister," he said, refusing to make eye contact. The door to the hallway slammed shut, and the room was thrown into silence.

Not… not my sister? I stared at Blayde, the real Blayde, my Blayde, and her face was white, so white I wondered if she had become a real ghost. A hand covered her lip.

"I'm as good as. Since when has that bothered you?"

"Since you barged in and ruined a perfectly acceptable moment." He scowled, throwing himself back on the bed.

"Oh please. You didn't even know her name."

"Does that matter? She's the empress of the Alliance."

"That stupid club?" she scoffed. "Please. If they're still standing in a decade, I'll eat my foot."

"Still, she's an empress—I mean, I think. My translator sometimes calls her president, but it's way less impressive. The Blayde I knew would have been impressed."

"The Blayde you knew?" she said angrily, glaring. "People change in a decade, Zander."

"Six."

"What?"

"Sixty years, Blayde." he said with a sigh, pushing himself up on the bed. "You've been gone for sixty years."

"Time travel." She scowled. "It's bound to happen. It's normal, if only you'd—"

"Oh, wait, you're pinning all this on me? Me? Oh no, come on. You're the one who abandoned me. The one who wanted time apart, who ran away. You're the one who threw me away as if I was nothing. Tell me, how is that family working out for you? Little Baby Blaydes. You were preggers when I last saw you, weren't you? So, how's—"

He stopped. Long streaks of shimmering tears ran silently down Blayde's face. His expression changed instantly.

"Your partner—"

"The child," she admitted, her voice a low murmur. "He—"

He was by her side in a second, hugging her close to him as her tears turned to sobs, sadness overflowing. He held her tight as she hid her face in his chest, his arms keeping her in this tight, comforting embrace. She was crying and it wasn't going to stop, her emotions held in for so long that they simply had to explode.

My Blayde covered her eyes. I pulled her into my arms, an embrace that was long overdue. Had it been a kindness of me, pretending Miro hadn't told me the truth, seeing her silence as a plea for ignorance? Or was this another in a long line of mistakes, leaving the hard things unspoken as if they'd never happened? My shirt filled with Blayde's tears, and I knew that it was.

"I'm sorry," past me said calmly. "I had no idea—"

"I know." She nodded. "I'm sorry too. I'm sorry I left; I'm sorry I pushed you away. I should never have—"

He lifted a hand to stop her. "It's been so long I can't even remember what we were fighting about in the first place. Why did we leave?"

"I won't throw blame," she said, sitting down on the edge of the bed under the weight of it all. "I am as responsible as you. Whatever you did never justified the way I treated you. Will you ever forgive me?"

"Of course. But it's not easy. I forgot what it was like traveling with you, forgot how to live with you. I wish I could just forget it all. Everything."

"Our past is too painful. So much heartbreak. So much pain."

"I want a clean slate," he said, gazing longingly out the window.

"So do I." She nodded. "But, if you could have it..."

"Have what?" he asked. "The clean slate?"

She took a deep breath. "I can't live with his death in my mind. I want it gone. I want to forget. Everything. From the beginning. Start fresh and new. If you could have that—have your memories wiped so that you could start fresh—would you?"

She stared at him with wide, pleading eyes, and he nodded, slowly.

"Part of me thinks it's cowardly. But there's too much in this mind of mine. I need it gone. So yes, if I had the chance, I would wipe it all and start over. I would."

"I think we can. On the planet, you know, with the Miro? You met them."

"The guys that look like they come from some off-Alliance perfume ad?"

"Yeah. They protect an old temple with a legend. It speaks of this wise man that grants wishes to those who solve the labyrinth he's trapped in. I say we run it. We ask him to wipe the memories. We wake up, and a new life is open for us. Free of our past. Open and full of promise."

Instantly, Zander reached over to grab his shirt, pulling it over his head as he continued to speak. "Coordinates?"

"Took me years to track them down, but yes, I have them." She tapped the side of her head. "We're good to go."

"How much will we remember? We won't wake up as hopeless babes, will we?"

"We'll ask the wise man to make it so we'll have no idea anything's missing. We'll know who we are, and we'll know how to fight."

"We'll need to prepare some things, though. We'll need to make sure that we won't question things, that we don't—"

And with that, everything faded into darkness once more, and we were once again in the in-between space, Blayde's eyes riveted on where the past version of me had been standing mere seconds before. I sighed heavily, trying to take in everything I had seen.

"This is… a little unnerving." I said, but Blayde's face had gone blank. She stared into the darkness, fear filling her whole body. She trembled as she watched something I could not even see.

"Oh, no, please, no…" She shuddered.

"What, what's happening?" I asked, but it was useless.

"Please, no, don't show me that."

"Blayde, calm down. You're going to be okay"

"No, no, please no, you can't."

"Blayde," I snapped, grabbing her shoulders and shaking her lightly. "You need to snap out of it. Nothing can be so bad that—"

"Reelaiah," she said, pleadingly. And then, I knew. I stepped back.

"You can stop it, Blayde. You don't have to watch it—"

"I can't." She sobbed. "I can't stop it."

"Focus, you can do this."

"No, no." Tears were streaming down her face. "I can't control it. I have to…"

I slipped my hand into hers giving it a tight squeeze.

"I won't pretend that this is okay," I told her. "But I'll be right here, every step of the way. We can do this. You can do this."

"You promise?"

I nodded. "Of course. I'm your brother. "

"You sure about that?"

I snorted. "Who cares what a memory says? Of course I'm sure. I'm here, Blayde."

"Don't let go," she begged.

"Never."

"Never let me go."

"Never again."

"Don't let me fall," she pleaded, as light rose and we found ourselves in the sand of Miro's planet once again.

"I never will."

I cried with her, our tears drowning out those of a world losing their child.

TWENTY
THE THROWDOWN SHOWDOWN

Sally

SIDERA BOLTED THE DOOR BY SHOVING AN ENTIRE refrigerator in front of it. She threw it open with her good arm, grabbed an energy drink, and chugged, eyes locked intently on Nimien. A snap echoed behind me, James unholstering her new ray gun, standing between Zander and Blayde like she'd been guarding them her whole life.

"You're sure?" asked Nimien. In an instant, he looked one-hundred-and-fifty years younger and ready for a fight.

"I know what my brother looks like," Sidera snapped, "and I wasn't too thrilled about decapitating him. I probably only saved us five minutes. Father, what do we do?"

"You tried talking to him? Asking what he wants?"

"No, I just walked up to the brother we'd been waiting centuries to return home and beheaded him for shits and giggles." She crossed her arms over her chest, lefty lagging slightly. "Of course I did. And in return he ripped off my arm and told me I have daddy issues."

"He's coming here?" James tapped her finger against the barrel of her gun. "And you just trapped us inside?"

"What is it with you and traps?" growled Sidera. "I'm protecting us!"

Nimien rushed to one of the computers on the wall of the lab, brushed past me. He was fast, for a man of however many years, but I could see now he hadn't been faking his frailty. His hips refused to unlock all the way, forcing him to limp quickly from post to post.

"Hold on," Nimien ordered, rushing over to the computer monitor and pulling up a small black square on the screen, in which he typed quick commands. "There. I've launched the basic defensive protocols, and the rooms should be shuffling around right now. It'll take him longer to find us that way."

"But he *will* find us," said James, glaring at Sidera, "and we'll be *stuck* here when he does."

I channeled my inner Blayde and grabbed Nimien by the collar of his coat. "Pull Zander and Blayde now. We have to leave."

"I can't just rip them out," he said, grabbing my wrist with a strong by gnarly grip. "It could tear their minds apart. It'll take a while for the program to wake them up safely."

"How long?"

My head snapped to look at the ceiling as footsteps rushed past.

"About an hour." Nimien swallowed loudly. "Give or take. We can't take any risks with minds like theirs."

"That's an hour we don't have," I said, with a confidence I was faking through and through. Zander was counting on me to protect him, and I couldn't take any risks, not if I wanted the man I loved back in one piece. "Start getting them out. *Now*. We'll wait as long as we can before pulling the plug, but we can't give them the whole hour."

"So we make our stand here?" said James. "We can't defend this position, it's a single room, and there are four of us with two weapons between us."

"We have no other choice," I said. "Unless…Sidera, can you jump anywhere? Get us help? Reinforcements?"

"Some," she said, nodding. "Take my axe. I'll be back as soon as I can."

She handed me her weapon, which was slimy with blood. I took it gingerly, letting go of Nimien just as she wrapped her arms around him, holding him close.

"I'm so sorry," she said. "I thought he would change."

"Please don't kill him again," he replied, squeezing her shoulders as she pulled away. "I'm so proud of the woman you've become. I'm sorry you have to go through this. Any of this."

"I love you, Dad," she said, wiping a solitary tear from her cheek. "I'll be right back."

Sidera disappeared, and the room became silent again, except for the low hum of the now displaced fridge and the click-clack of the computer keys. Nimien's hands flew over his keyboard, entering commands into the terminal faster than I could follow.

"There's no way to pull them out sooner?" I asked, staring at the raised platform. Whatever was happening inside Zander's mind, I hoped it was more pleasant than the absolute certainty we were going to be obliterated.

"Not unless you want to spend the next century teaching two immortals how to eat again," he said, not taking his eyes from the screen. His gaze was so intense that tears were welling in his eyes. "If we take them out now, who knows what kind of lasting damage it will do. This will help."

The sound of happy chirping birds filled the small lab. James frowned, looking up at the speakers in the ceiling.

"This is it?" She waved at the speakers. "This is how you're bringing them out gently?"

"It's the best I can do under the circumstances," he said. "I'm so sorry."

James took a deep breath. "Can we get a visual on the rest of the house?"

"No," Nimien replied. His eyes squeezed shut in frustration. "I'm sorry. This is all my fault."

"What is?" I asked. I glanced up at James, who positioned herself between the siblings with her weapon poised on the door, ready for anyone to burst through. "Desmond thinking you're a shitty father? Because you were."

"Will you stop making assumptions about my life?" he spat, spittle covering me head to toe. Gone was the passive, apologetic old man. This was the Nimien I knew: assertive and furious. I knew he hadn't changed. "I spent tens of thousands of years bettering myself. I won't have you, of all people, judge me on my parenting."

I was shaking. "What's that supposed to mean?"

"Never mind," he growled. "You're too immature to understand anything. I've met future you, and she is a force to be reckoned with, but you have a long way to go before you become her. So go protect your precious Zander while I try to fix the only family I have."

His words shouldn't have hurt as much as they did, but they stabbed deep and they stabbed sharp. I found myself marching to the platform before I had even fully processed what he said, and even after I did I was still running on automatic.

"We need to mount a defense," said James, as if she hadn't heard a word of what had just gone down. "Anything that's not bolted to the floor, place it in front of that door. If Desmond gets this far—"

"We're screwed." I needed to bring my mind back to this moment, but I couldn't. It was as if my entire brain was trembling.

"I'm sorry," muttered Nimien, eyes still riveted on his screen. "Universe, please forgive me. I'm so sorry."

"Nimien?" I said, my voice barely a squeak. "Do you think...do you think the Dread is behind Desmond's army?"

"Worse," he said, turning to face us on the platform. "I'm so sorry, Sally. I'm so sorry to all of you. I think Desmond's behind the Dread. That this really is a trap, but not one of my making, one of *his*. I shouldn't have said any of that. It's just… it's just a lot."

He sank to the floor.

Ah, screw it. I don't know what's going on in my brain anymore. I rushed off the platform and reached for him, pulling him to his feet. The tears were streaming down his face now, fat and juicy and fast, a man shattering before me.

"What the hell is going on?" asked James. "Desmond created the Dread? Why?"

"To get us here," he said. "All of us. So he can kill all of us in one go. The siblings, you, my daughter, and me… the only immortals in the universe."

My hands were still shaking, but so was Nimien. The two of us were vibrating like plucked strings on a guitar, though our only music was panic.

I was touching, helping, the man who had tried to trap me. Only now we were in a trap together.

"Are you sure?" I asked.

"No. How can anyone be sure of something this extreme?"

"But do you believe your son is capable of something so terrible?"

"How could anyone say something so terrible about one's one child lightly?"

No clear answers, great. The chirping birds were getting louder, sweet chime music joining in their choir. A gentle wake-up alarm as the soundtrack of our last moments.

"Just give it to me straight, Nimien," I said. "What is the Dread?"

"The end of the universe," he said, his eyes gazing light-years away. "At least, of this one."

I glanced up at James, who shrugged. No, I didn't get it either.

"I could probably build an electrical trap," he said, coming back to himself. "But my resources are limited if we want Zander and Blayde safe."

"To rig the door?" I asked.

"It's all I can think of," he said. "There should be everything I need in the computers here. You pile what you can by the door. I need time, and so do they."

Right, still no answers. Instead, I was left rushing around the lab to find anything not strapped down and toss it in front of the door while Nimien worked and James defended. All the wheelie chairs ended up in a pile, the cabinets and desks too.

All the while my mind spun along a racetrack. If this was a trap, then why? Everything did indeed seem to point to getting us here—the very reason none of us trusted Nimien in the first place. The perfect promise of answers for Zander and Blayde. Every clue leading us here. The Dread, the one problem large enough to be felt through the galaxy, enough for anyone to draw our attention to it, to demand our help. And the death of the Alliance president, putting Dany in the prime position to make us take on this case?

Even how we first met Desmond. The book about the very labyrinth we had been searching for—written and planted by him, of course. And the moment that had started it all: the woman catching fire in the grocery store. Enough to focus our attention on SHC and the Agency, another clue bringing us to 1657. Had all this been carefully conceived for us to find him, to have our confirmation the labyrinth existed, the place with the answers and promises we needed? If Sidera hadn't shown up in Virginia when she did, Desmond's plan must have involved him literally leading us into this trap like lambs to the slaughterhouse.

Only Sidera unwittingly brought us instead.

When Nimien manipulated the timeline, it had been subtle, artful. He had been proud of the small events he'd set into motion. The hot air balloon wasn't him, in the end; it had been me. If Desmond was behind this, then every motion was clunky. Killing the Alliance president? Lighting people on fire? There was no artistry in his touch. Only horror.

"I need more wire," said Nimien, pointing at the several cages behind the siblings' platform. "The green lights mean that the software is using that specific piece," he said, indicating flashing LEDs above the multitude of cables. "When it goes off, it's safe for us to repurpose. Got that?"

"Yeah," I replied, as he reached over and grabbed the jumble of wires from my hands. He dropped them on a pile next to the door and continued assembling his trap, ripping panels off the wall to reach the conduits behind. I ripped out any piece of equipment the software was finished with, running them over to Nimien's side every few seconds.

If we expanded the parameters, integrated backwards… then what else had set this trap in motion? The Alliance needing our help, the promise of defense for my planet? The assassination of the president, who did that? Was that all part of this plan?

But to what end? That's the part that still made no sense. As contrived as this plot was, clues like constellations that only lined up when you looked at them from a special angle, what did it all mean? Why had Desmond done all this, just to get the five of us in this room, the only immortals in the universe together for the first and last time?

Desmond wanted us dead because we were the only ones who could stop his plan.

There was hope.

With a roll like thunder, the door shuddered, the entire floor quaking. He was finally here.

Sidera appeared by our side, covered in more blood than before, thankfully with all limbs attached. She grunted as she raced to the platform, holding up James's death ray from the labyrinth.

"I couldn't hold him back any longer," she said, "It's showtime."

Desmond—and his army by the sound of it—rammed the door again. Over and over, no pain to slow his attacks. I could swear I heard bones breaking, pure and vicious fury fighting for purchase.

We pushed back, James and I crying hot and terrified tears as the birds sang louder around us, as Sidera's bloody hands slipped with every push. The pain of holding back an army was enough to rip through my muscles and mind.

"Just a tiny bit longer," Nimien begged, laying the cables in a small circle on the floor next to the computer. He began ripping some of the rubber from the wires, exposing the metal beneath. Live wires. Enough to kill a human—or to put an immortal down for a few minutes.

I shoved my back against the barricade, putting every ounce of force I could muster into that door. My eyes were locked on the bodies of my friends lying prone in the middle of the room. We were the last line of defense. If we let anyone through, they could, and would, die. Actually die.

I couldn't let that happen.

My skin broke under the pressure, hot blood running down my arms, making my hands slippery. The pain was unbearable, made worse by my numbness to everything else. I was crying, oh stars I was crying.

Don't let him through. Don't let them die.

Suddenly, the struggle stopped. The pressure was gone. The desks we so strongly held back stopped shaking, the door stopped creaking. I shuddered.

"He's found another way in." Sidera was shaking. "Which way is he—"

She had no time to finish her sentence. We were lifted off the ground, tossed into the metal ring as the door exploded. Desks and hardware flew everywhere, the air full of fire and shrapnel, blindingly bright and deafeningly loud. Nimien flew backward in the shockwave, but we were somehow safe, the trap not harming us, but stopping every piece of the flying wood and metal.

Dust filled the air, and I laughed, only to find I couldn't hear a thing. The explosion must have made me deaf.

Except—the birds were still chirping. Ocean waves lapped at the edges of my hearing.

Oh, and I couldn't move. Sidera, James, and I sat breathless and silent in the ring, completely and utterly trapped.

Shit—Nimien had planned this. This is what he had been doing the whole time we had been holding back the desks. Not creating a line of defense, but making... *this*.

As the dust settled, Desmond stepped into the room. A one-man army, it seemed. He was so imposing now that he wasn't costumed as a man from my world. How could I ever have mistaken him for a Terran? If anything, he was the void between stars. The interstellar, no, intergalactic medium brought to life. Clothed in black robes which absorbed all light, he was a black hole in this universe.

And just to look even more douchy, he was wearing mirrored sunglasses that covered half his face.

He turned to look at the computer, and I held my breath. But it wasn't what was behind the glasses that interested me. In their reflection, there was nothing but the empty corner of the room.

We were *invisible* to him.

His head now snapped to the other side of the room, where Zander and Blayde still lay in deep sleep upon their chairs. He took one step to them before Nimien's hand shot up from the floor, grabbing his son's ankle.

"Please," he said. "It's me you want. Leave them out of this."

Nimien screamed. Desmond had lifted his foot, stomping on his hand like he was squashing a bug.

"I thought you would be proud of me," he said, as Nimien writhed on the floor, clutching his shattered hand. "I'm accomplishing what you could never do. I thought you would help me."

"I told you when you left," said Nimien, trying to drag himself back to Desmond's feet, but he was already striding to Zander and Blayd, "we are above murder! Above any of this! We are tied to the universe, and being its hitman is not our place."

Desmond laughed. "Connected to the universe? You haven't set foot in it in hundreds of years! I'm sorry, Father—wait, no I'm not. I've been wanting to do this my entire life. You can't stop me now."

"But you still can," Nimien wheezed. He was struggling to speak, his mouth foaming with every word. "Come back to me, my boy."

"I am not your boy," Desmond growled, jumping to Nimien's side in a blink of an eye. "You made that quite clear when you chased me out."

"I never—" He coughed. "I never chased you out. You ran away. I wanted you home every day since. I tried—"

"Not enough. You never try hard enough. It was the same with mother, you—" Desmond walked to Blayde's side, brushing her hair out of her face, grinning. "No. I will not speak of this now. Not when I'm so close."

I couldn't move. I wanted to burst to his side, destroy him where he stood. Zander and Blayde on a platter served right up for his taking.

"No, Desmond, stop." Nimien reached for him, but he couldn't reach the platform. "Please. This is not you."

"You don't know me," said Desmond, "You haven't known me in millennia."

He grabbed the cables behind Blayde's head and ripped.

The birds stopped chirping up above. Instead, an electrical whine filled the space, and Desmond laughed as he ripped the cords from Zander's brain, making the sound increase in pitch. I screamed, so hard my throat was screaming with me, but no sound came out. There was only this terrible, unyielding whine.

I was helpless. Helpless as Nimien crawled to Desmond's side, reaching his hand up, one last plea. Desmond scowled, swinging his foot at Nimien's head, and when it collided—

Sparks flew.

Desmond disappeared as every light in the room went out at once.

The whine was replaced by a scream. My scream. Whatever forcefield had held us back had died as well and I shot forward like a bullet from a gun, rushing up the platform to Zander's prone body.

Please, universe, if I can ask anything of you, I would give anything, just for this single thing. Just let him be alive.

"What did I miss?" Blayde muttered behind me, and James burst into tears.

I didn't turn around. Zander still wasn't moving. He looked like he was sleeping, and he —

Oh thank the stars, he had a pulse.

"What happened in there?" I asked, spinning to Blayde.

"We were in my head when you woke us." She hoisted herself up a little higher with a grunt. "I just… I hope he got out."

"You have to go," Nimien said, his voice raspy. He was lying on the floor, breathless, a mess of wires in his hands. His shattered bones sent his fingers contorting in impossible directions.

"Father!" Sidera was instantly by his side. "What have you done?"

"I shattered him," he said, laughing a laugh that brought up blood. "He's currently atoms in the wind. Feel free to write a song about it. I'm dreadfully sorry, daughter, but I'm blowing up this world—if all goes well, I'm taking him with it."

"You did what?" One hand gripped his, the other was on his chest, searching for his heart. Her eyes flew up to us. "You have to help him."

"They can't," he said, "You have to run, daughter of mine. Run and don't look back. Let this bubble pop."

"No," she begged. "Come outside. Come with me. You'll be brand new again."

He shook his head. "I can't go through it all again, my dear. It's my time. I have to end it, all of it."

"No, Father," she snapped. "You have to stay alive. I need you. The universe needs you."

Zander still wasn't moving. He was breathing, deep, full breaths, but he wasn't moving. Blayde had woken up, so why hadn't he?

"The universe hasn't needed me in a long time," said Nimien, laughing.

"But—"

"No," he said, "Don't. I can't bear to see you cry. You know that. I want you to be happy, all right? It *is* possible to be happy in this universe. I promise you that."

"What's going on exactly?" asked Blayde. James helped her to her feet, and while she leaned on the agent, it was obvious she would have been fine on her own. "Did we miss the apocalypse?"

"Might as well have," said James. "Desmond created the Dread. It was a trap all along, and Nimien—well, he just saved all of our lives."

"Stop wasting time," he snapped. "Daughter, help me up. I have to impart wisdom and knowledge before I'm cut off mid-sentence leaving you all waiting for more. Blayde, I'm sorry to say, but you're going to be out of journals. I got really into bookbinding and kept giving them to you after your memory dumps, knowing they'd find their way back to the library, to me. Well, the cycle is broken now."

Blayde frowned. "What…? Oh."

I took Zander's hand, squeezing it tight, barely holding it together as it remained limp in my grasp. I couldn't do this. I couldn't focus on Nimien's fancy and ill-deserved heroic death scene while Zander may not be coming back.

"Tell him if he jumps every six hours, he'll never have to shave again," said Nimien, and I realized with a jolt he was talking to me. "And the only thing I can give you—well, I can't give it, you'll have to go and get it yourself. You will find what has been troubling you if you search for the UPAF *Wanderer*. In the present, in your now."

"What are you talking about?" I said, but then a ceiling tile fell from above, smacking James on the head, and Nimien started to laugh again. Sidera glared at us, holding him upright, but he reached for his computer, drawing up some emergency power from somewhere before typing somewhat less than wildly.

"I was wrong," he said, turning back to Sidera. "All this time, the Dread was his making, but it was my idea. To destroy this universe, to shake it loose, quite literally. Destructive waves, opposite everything. There would be nothing left. There *won't* be anything left. If I don't burst this bubble soon, your brother will re-form and try again. You have to figure out what Desmond did and shut it off or your universe will suffer the same fate. And it doesn't deserve any of this."

"This is nonsense, Father," she said. "Please, stop, you're scaring me."

The ceiling tiles all fell at once, crashing down on our heads. I threw myself over Zander to shield him from the debris. Nimien laughed again, hitting a key like a maestro finishing his sonata.

"It's already started," he said. "It will reach the fevered pitch soon. Now go. I'll be fine, don't you worry. I'll see you on the other side."

Tears ran down Sidera's face, mingling with the blood there. Nimien collapsed, panting heavily.

"Go," he insisted, "don't make me tell you again. I failed one child. I won't fail you both."

I reached under Zander's body, lifting him into my arms. They burned, as I'd forgotten again the open wounds left there. And Zander was heavy, dammit. Pure muscle.

He had to be alive. He just had to be.

"Run," said Nimien. "The bubble is popping. Run, and don't look back."

He collapsed, exhaling his last breath—a last breath that became Zander's first. Stirring in my arms, Zander blinked his eyes open, grinning like a kid on Christmas.

"I'm Canadian," he said, before passing out in my arms.

TWENTY-ONE
THE END OF THE BUBBLE AS WE KNOW IT

INSTEAD OF OUTRUNNING THE COLLAPSE OF A bubble universe, I ruminated over the existence of Space Canada. Everything was possible in an infinite universe; it would make more sense for there to be a planet of kind, hockey-loving immortal humans than for Zander to be my Terran neighbor.

But Blayde ripped him from me before I could say anything, cradling him to her chest.

"Oy, you heard what Nimien said," she snapped to all of us, jutting her chin toward Nimien's corpse. "We need to run. This place won't last long."

So, I shut off my brain and ran. We ran through the remains of the crumbling house, following Sidera as she bawled, watching her heart break before us as she led us to freedom. Out through the front door, smeared with the corpses of the slain army. The last vestiges of the war Desmond had brought to his father's doorstep. He really had brought an army.

Sidera couldn't have… no, there were so many of them. Thankfully the truth of what happened became clear soon enough, as the ringing in my ears was replaced by cheering. A hundred faceless robots were having themselves a celebratory bash.

"This is the happiest day in my life!" said one, screaming at the top of his mechanical voice. "I was made for mayhem!"

"I've never felt so alive!" said another. "To know I defeated my base programming and still made a difference—oh! I think I'm ascending!"

Every single robot cheered louder as they drifted upward, glowing an otherworldly glow. Except up wasn't the same for each of them, and there were some ascending sideways or toward the floor. The next sound to fill the labyrinth was that of their metal husks hitting the ground as their digital spirits kept rising through the ceiling without them. You know what they say: If you're good at something, never do it without the promise of enlightenment.

"Grab on! Quickly!" yelled Blayde, as she threw herself at the feet of one of the rising droids.

"Get off me!" it said. Her clinging did nothing to slow it down, so I don't know why it was complaining. "You're ruining my ascension!"

"Get one going the right direction!" said Sidera. "This way up!"

Blayde rose to the ceiling while dangling under its body, grabbing Zander around the waist and clinging for dear life to the dead weight. The three of us raced to do the same, catching our enlightened rides.

The droids complained the whole way, but still managed to leave their bodies by the end. We collapsed on the ceiling floor and followed Sidera to one of the staging doors, which she promptly sealed shut behind us.

"Is everyone okay?" asked James, breathless.

My heart said "Ciao," and went silent, ready and waiting to be needed again. I looked down at my arms, the skin already smooth and blemishless.

But there was Sidera, sobbing over the loss of her only family. There was Blayde, staring at the ceiling with dried tears down her cheeks, dropping Zander on the floor before her, still unconscious. James had her sci-fi gun drawn, pointing at the ground until she could decide what to do with it. The barrel trembled.

"This is a trick, isn't it?" James stared at the closed door. "I mean, Nimien's immortal. He can't die. He'll be back in a second, won't he?"

Sidera said nothing. Which, admittedly, was probably for the best. We'd just defeated a nemesis. She'd just lost her father.

"I don't think so," said Blayde. "He spent his last minutes saving us instead of himself. I did *not* see that coming."

"Maybe he did change." Saying those words made my gut twist. "Maybe he really was a different man."

"Nimien," said Blayde. "Strange. I don't ever think I knew his surname."

"He never had one," Sidera replied, still avoiding meeting any of our gazes. "And very few knew him by his real name. He was always the wise man, the Eternal, *the* genius. On many worlds, genius comes from the word genii, sometimes jinn, a trickster and a wish granter—but I know for a fact it's the other way around."

"We should have a burial," said James, going to her. "Or a ceremony. Or *something*. As much as you had a complicated past together, he did save us in the end."

We had had a burial already—for Nim. We hadn't had a body that time either. Part of me hoped, or feared, Nimien was still alive somehow. But, deep down, I knew that last breath I saw him take really was his last.

"We don't even have the time," said Sidera, wiping the tears from her eyes. "Don't you feel it? The Dread is *still* here. I don't know where Desmond is, if he even made it out alive, but *it's* still out there, and it's reaching its pitch. We have to turn it off."

Bless her, her coping mechanism seemed to be throwing herself further into work. I could respect that. I had shut down so completely after John's death—and Matt's, and Nim's (the same man, not that I'd known at the time)—that the ability to literally work through grief was alien to me. And thank goodness, too. I needed time to process my own feelings about the past day before attending the memorial of a man who had been so many different people in his life and so many different things to me, most of them terrible.

Blayde glanced over, and her eyebrows drew donuts on her forehead. My translator might have been the best out there, but it still didn't made sense of her brows' tirade.

Zander groaned, his eyelids fluttering. Oh, thank the stars, he was waking up.

"Zan!" I cried, dropping to my knees beside him. "Are you okay? Can you talk? What do you remember?"

He let out a sound like a rubber duck in a hydraulic press. Blayde nodded.

"He'll pull through," she said stoically, running a hand over his forehead. "We should probably get him some water, though."

"That would be nice," he croaked. "What happened?"

"A lot," said Blayde. "Short of it is that Nimien saved us, then died."

Zander's brow furrowed. "He can do that?"

"What part? The saving us part or the dying part?"

"Both, I suppose." He pushed himself up on his elbows, letting out a stream of air.

"Desmond's in the wind," said James. "Quite literally, it would seem. Oh, and he's behind the Dread. I don't think you were awake for that part. What do you remember?"

There was a pause—a painful pause, a waiting pause, where his brows furrowed and his frown deepened.

"Nothing," he said, his shoulders falling. "Nothing more than I already knew, except… that I'm from Earth. I remember that mattered. There are… I think these are memories, but they don't feel like my own. Like someone else's experiences. I don't know what that means. Blayde?"

"I remember everything." Her lips twitched, as if she was holding back her smile. "And I mean *everything*, even the things I'm pretty sure I came here to forget in the first place. And yes, we are Canadian. I don't think I intended to forget that, but things happen."

Canadian. Not just Terran, but Canadian. The odds of us coming from the same world were… astronomical. But if they were human like me, then why were they… why were they what they are?

"We don't have time for this," Sidera said through gritted teeth. "It's the end of the universe, and we're the only ones who can stop it, so let's get our asses in action!"

"Oy," said Blayde. "We're getting to that."

We got to our feet, together hoisting Zander to his. While physically he seemed fine, his mind must have been a mess. If there was damage… no, no, his healing should be able to handle it. He gave Sidera a weak smile and she turned away, grabbing James's hand instead.

"We need to find that bunker Dad was talking about," Sidera said, reaching for Blayde with her other hand. "It's the only place we can find the answers."

"Really?" asked James, trying to pull her hand away and failing. She gave me her free one instead. "I thought that was a dead end."

Blayde shuddered. If I was her, I wouldn't want to go back either.

"He built it to give that guy time to solve the Dread crisis, right?" Sidera nodded at Zander, who slowly took Blayde's and my hands. "And that's what we need: time. Otherwise we're out of it. So, one of you needs to take us there."

"Guess I'm driving," said Blayde, and before I could process what that meant, she had dropped the curtain on our dimension and pulled us into the backstage of the universe.

The ride was exhilarating, pure connection to all things at once, the stars calling out to me from all directions. It was as if I could hear them personally—*Pick me, I have three planets! Visit me, I make everything smell like sherbets!*

Blayde was back. All of her was back.

But maybe her sense of direction was off.

"Wrong place," muttered Zander, as my senses came to terms with their usual, limited existence and asked for a refund. "Really, really wrong place."

My eyes flew open to a dark sky. My feet were on concrete. No sand whatsoever—which, honestly, I could live with. But more importantly, there were buildings. Tall, modern apartments that reached to the sky. Pretty sure there weren't any city parks last time we had been on Miro's world. Pretty sure there hadn't been any cities either.

And the Dread—the claw in my mind threatened to shred my every thought. We were back to our present, to the rising Dread, the feeling so intense I wanted to grab my head and scream. The vibration of the universe so impossibly clear I felt I could reach out and grab it. We'd blown past the realm of anxiety now, the Dread so intense it was as if Godzilla was standing right above me, ready to squash me and my home and everything I loved. I had to run, run, run—run where? Nowhere. There was nothing, only *run*.

"I was right!" a voice cried from somewhere in the distance. "I was right! Oh, Great Chagra, I was right!"

Something—someone, who am I to question sentience—was coming right at us, a dark figure running through the park and huffing the whole way. But they were sure taking their sweet time to reach us. Goosebumps raised on my skin. It didn't help that it was night, and the five of us were gathered under a single streetlight, making the shadows around us long and leery.

It's going to eat you—run!

"I'm not *that* out of practice." Blayde smiled, showing teeth. "I only forgot where I was going for a while, that's all. Now I know, and this is definitely where we're meant to be. It's Miro's world."

"No one believed me," the figure huffed. Its voice was shrill like a parrot's. "They all laughed, but this will show the academy! They'll see the truth."

"Could this be the other side of the planet?" I asked. "I mean, we only saw a tiny part of it."

"No. This is the exact spot we landed on last time." Blayde's voice was hollow. "We're at the right place. But *now*, we're at the right time."

Shit. So that's how it was going to be. *Deep breaths, Sally Webber.* I could fight this. I knew how. I gritted my teeth, planting my feet firm against the urge to run screaming into the dark.

"So, where's the sand? Where's the ocean?" asked James, hand gripped tight against the butt of her gun. "Not that I'm not pleased that Space Australia got its act together."

"Terraformed away," she replied.

"I knew the etchings were true! Oh, I am so getting tenure for this. I will forever be remembered in the history books. This is remarkable, epic—"

Who else would burst into the pool of light other than a lively pterodactyl, wearing what might have been jeans and a checkered button-down shirt, flared for the wings with a gorgeous blue lining? His small, half-moon spectacles perched on his extended snout, giving him the air of a professor—perhaps if the Flintstones had gone to college, he could have been teaching their philosophy course.

I recognized the markings on his skin immediately. It had only been a day or two since I'd tricked one of his ancestors into giving me a lift, after all. We must have been gone for an exceedingly long time: Long enough for his entire species to evolve and take over the planet. The descendant of my ride pulled out a measuring tape from his pocket and held it up to Zander's tall frame, who gave him an awkward half-smile.

"Hello, I'm Zander—"

"The shield, right? You know, I thought the text was referring to weapons, but I understand it all now, it's metaphorical. I'm Professor Ke'sun Va'hut. Which one of you is the warrior queen?"

Blayde, James, Sidera, and I each raised a hand.

"Well, you can't all *four* be the ones from the wall," said Va'hut, eating his tape measure. "In any case, you five are perfect specimens. Where did you come from? How did you get here? Never mind, we'll have time for that back at my lab. First, we need—"

The crack of thunder that exploded between us sent everyone reeling, with only dinosaur snot to cushion our blow. If you've ever heard a pterodactyl sneeze before, I'm incredibly sorry, and I wish you the very best on your road to recovery.

"Oh, oh no," Va'hut sniffled. "It seems I may be... how is this possible... allergic to humanoids?"

Blayde wasn't the hypoallergenic type. She grabbed him by the scruff of the neck, lifting him an entire foot off the ground, snarling as he shrieked like a schoolgirl.

We didn't have time for this. I ripped out a clump of hair. *Shit*. The Dread was growing stronger by the second.

"Warrior queen!" Va'hut squawked, before sneezing again. "Please! Don't touch me! I don't have any allergy meds!"

"Then speak," she said, "or you'll be sneezing grey matter through your nostrils next. Where did you hear about us?"

"They thought it was nonsense," he chirped. "The fellowship at the university. They thought it was all scribbles. I interpreted it. They didn't believe me. Now I have evidence—"

"Take me to the scribbles!" she shouted, shaking him again, forcing a new sneeze out of him and discomfort out of the rest of us. She was terrifying, even with green spittle running down her hair. "We don't have any time to waste!"

"The wall, the wall! At the dig! Don't kill me!"

She dropped him, and he scampered quickly to his feet, panting. He wiped his now-red nose on his sleeve.

"Lead us," she said. "And hurry, we don't have much time! The end of the universe is here!"

He sighed, waving us with him down the gravel path. "Well, you don't have to be so dramatic. But keep your distance. If I get any more of your dander on me…"

I probably would have enjoyed sightseeing a world where dinosaurs had evolved to the point where they had cars and TV, but the Dread was resonating so hard now that my hands couldn't stay still. I spent the entire walk focusing on not screaming and starting a riot instead of admiring the statues of pterodactyl heroes riding giant worms or the billboards of scantily clad winged models. I have never felt such confusion in my loins before.

"You're going to have to share laps," said Va'hut. "My car's a little small."

Why a pterodactyl would drive anywhere when they could fly, I would never know. Blayde sat up front, still scowling the whole time, as the four of us stacked into the back. We set off into the night, driver's window open so our driver could avoid a sneezing-crashing catastrophe.

"Hey, look," said James, pointing at a hallway billboard that featured her sea-beast admirer. "I can't follow anything, but I think they have *Jaws 3*?"

Va'hut took us out of the gleaming city and into a nearby forest, one lit by massive floodlights. We spilled out of the car, weapons at the ready, as he led us past the ropes and into a dig site, following the wooden path into a canvas tent which protected an elevator. He pressed a button, covered his nose, and slowly, it began to lower us to the mysterious prophecy.

"We're here," he said, pushing the gate open and urged us out. Hitting a switch with his elbow, the cavern overflowed with light, a huge vaulted ceiling extending over our heads, an old stone pavement under our feet. My feet tread over familiar ground, where just yesterday I'd fought a sea serpent and survived. I would have gasped, only my teeth were too busy gritting themselves dull.

"What is this place?" Sidera asked, crouching down to feel the cobbles with her fingertips.

"You tell me," said Va'hut, then added quickly. "Please? It's not every day history falls into your lap."

"It's the temple," Blayde gasped. "Miro's temple. Nimien's bubble-universe-bunker."

"It was here even before the invention of fire," said Va'hut, beaming. His nose was so stuffy now that half his words were muffled. "Built by a now-extinct civilization of humanoids."

Blayde raced past him, running her hands over the stone face, nodding. She turned back to us with a stern line in lieu of a smile.

"Over here is where it predicted your arrival," Va'hut said, face going a different shade of red. "Not an easy feat, translating it. It took me three years and fifteen false starts—"

"What's behind this?" Blayde asked, knocking lightly on the structure. "Did you give it a sonar scan? Let me guess—are you going to blow it up?"

"What, no!" he squawked. "We thought it was a calendar or a day planner. We had no idea there was anything behind it, we thought—"

"Good." She flipped a knife out from under her sleeve, snapping it open and holding it over her hand. "Now, get back into the elevator and return from whence you came. We have a few rituals to perform, so please, leave us in peace."

Va'hut's eyes went wide, his mouth spreading into an even wider smile. My god, so many teeth. "Rituals?"

Blayde raised her hands to the heavens. "We're going to sacrifice that girl to the sand lord, to ensure that my people can safely take back their land."

"Yo." I replied, waving my hand.

"What?" cried Va'hut. "No, the prophecies never foretold *this*! You were meant to bring peace!"

"Oh, we are bringing peace," said Blayde. "Peace for our peoples! Tremble, for I am the warrior queen! Run from me, mortal!"

The worst part is I couldn't tell if she believed it. She was convincing. That, or the Dread that suffused the air, giving that extra bit of spice.

Va'hut didn't need to be told twice. He raced for the elevator, screaming in between sneezes, slamming the little gate shut.

"You've got to stop that," said Zander. "It'll probably traumatize him for life."

"Fine, if you say so." Blayde shrugged. "Now, everybody, step back. These doors haven't opened for centuries. There's no saying what'll happen. Darling doors, will you please let us in?"

They pulled back slowly, showing the way into the dark interior of the labyrinth, stopping with a huge crashing sound. Instantly, a wave of putrid, rotting air hit us in the face.

"I guess that monster died eventually." Blayde shrugged, watching her hand heal. "Right, Sidera, what now? Any genius ideas to defeat the Dread come to you on the drive over?"

"Don't worry," she cooed, striding into the dark maze, "I can take if from here. We already have everything we need—and more. This bunker was the last detail, and you were so kind to give me the address. Thank you for the ride. Now, if you move fast, I'm pretty sure you can enjoy one last ice cream before the end of the Universe."

I gotta admit, I had not seen that coming. Maybe I should have since she had lied to us before. Sidera stood in the maze's atrium, wiping the blood and dried tears from her smiling face with a little wet wipe, as Desmond brushed past us to join her there.

TWENTY-TWO

SO MANY TWISTS AT THIS POINT, I WAS RUNG OUT LIKE A WASHCLOTH

EACH OF US COULD EASILY HAVE BECOME A NEW meme in that moment. A mixture of shock and disappointment—mainly disappointment, since we were too tired to be shocked—our jaws were caught at some point between resting and the floor.

Sidera. Sidera and *Desmond*.

"Oh, come now, don't look so surprised," said Desmond. "It's only me."

"We got that part," said Zander. "I'm reasonably convinced our shock is more personal. Over, you know, how we could have all been duped again."

Desmond and Sidera high-fived, then swung around so they were leaning back-to-back, Disney Channel original style. It was groan worthy, but I was dying for a drink and didn't waste the effort.

James didn't give a single shit. She aimed and fired two laser blasts right at each of them, screaming. Blasts I could imagine would have found their targets easily, if it weren't for the force field between us. The beams bounced off the invisible barrier, ricocheting off to scorch the cavern walls.

"How did you find us?" I snapped, glaring at Desmond.

He shrugged. "I followed you, of course. It's not like it was hard."

"We're twins," Sidera said matter-of-factly. "We shared a *womb*. Entangled on the genetic level. We can find each other across entire galaxies. What? You seriously thought I came along to *help*?"

My body shook, every muscle trembling. Be it from the Dread or from the absolute horror of being so close only for the rug to be ripped out from under you… my legs refused to be legs.

"Seeing as it was your father's dying wish, I mean, yeah?" I said. "It would have made a lot more sense."

"Oh! Are you playing both sides?" Zander clapped, grinning. "Is this like that trope where you have two dates to prom and had to keep juggling your time between them only for them both to meet and everything go sideways? Except, you know, with the destruction of the universe instead of prom?"

"No, stupid." Sidera laughed. "I was here to ensure my brother succeeds. That *we* succeed. Together."

"And that plan included murdering your father?" I gripped Zander's hand, desperate for stability, but he shook even harder than me. "You're a convincing actress, Sidera."

"Why, thank you," she said with a curtsey. "My father had outlived his usefulness. His time was up, even he agreed. We were a mercy. He died doing what he loved—thinking he was the smartest bitch in the room. And saving his daughter. If you think about it, we gave him a redemption arc."

"All while getting him out of the way of what comes next," added Desmond. "We couldn't have him even remotely possibly surviving through to the next world."

"Same goes for you," said Sidera, indicating all of us with a smooth, flat hand, like a host of a game show. "But we needed access to the bunker, so we couldn't let you implode like we initially planned."

"You're psychopaths." Blayde shook her head. "You are, I can see that now."

I cringed at her words. They had manipulated us from the start, learning from their father's past mistakes in order to create the perfect trap, for whatever nefarious reason two young immortals with the universe at their fingertips could possibly have.

"No. We're the only sane things in this universe," said Desmond. "Which is why it has to go."

Blayde expelled a heavy sigh. "Stars above. They want to take over the universe. Brilliant."

"Take it over?" Sidera scoffed. "This universe sucks ragoon balls, have you seen it? No way. We're not taking over it; we're *dismantling* it. It'll be better for everyone, trust me."

"This reality, like our father, has outlived its usefulness." Desmond folded his hands behind his back. "It can no longer be fixed with small changes. They say that's when you need to build a new model that makes the existing model obsolete. But we find that just blowing the existing model up and starting from scratch is much more promising."

"Well, dumbass, I have a little flaw with your plan," said James. She still had her blaster riveted on the siblings—the universe-killing siblings—even after what has just happened. "Hate to break it to you, but you're a part of the universe, too. So, if you blow that up—"

"Hate to break it to *you*," said Desmond, "but we're not—currently—part of your universe at all. Did dear old dad tell you why this place is called a bunker?"

"It's a bubble universe," said Sidera. "Like the labyrinth, except better because it's not full of old-man cooties."

"Thanks to you, we have access to the final thing we needed: a safe place to ride out the destruction of everything. Once this universe is done imploding, we'll get to watch the Bigger, Better Bang—trademark pending—and nudge everything to our liking. It'll be glorious!"

"No more unicorns policing the upper dimensions." Sidera clenched her fist. "Keeping us from fixing what needs to be fixed. And best of all, no more *you* tying knots in the timestream, ruining it for the rest of us."

My head screamed and screamed and screamed. We were almost there, at the end of the universe. Wasting time arguing with those who wanted it gone.

"So that's what this is about?" said Zander. "Your application for godship was refused?"

"You can apply?" Desmond laughed. "No matter. We've watched the universe tread on our father our entire lives. We kept our heads low since birth. No more. Our time is now—and now it belongs to us. Or it will, when the Dread reaches crescendo."

"I meant what I said earlier," said Sidera. "There's still time for ice cream."

"Father always said he could count on you to stop the Dread." Desmond snorted. "Even though we've been planning this since we were, what, five?"

"Four and a half," said Sidera. "Though you know how time flows in a prison."

"We needed to find the weapon he left for you," said Desmond. "And we still have the time. There's less than an hour until the Dread is finally tuned everywhere, all at once, and it can't be stopped now."

"But there is no weapon," I said. "This has all been for nothing."

"Of course, we had—just as you did—assumed that Father was just being cryptic," said Sidera. "He said you were the weapon, but when we found the old labyrinth files, we saw that stoner boy was leaving with a lot more than just blueprints. We know that it was an actual weapon."

"I've never been gladder to be wrong," Sidera cheered, glaring at Blayde. "Here's the weapon, rendered useless. Now nothing will stand in our way."

With a grin, they both stepped back, Desmond with his gun riveted on us, Sidera with her hand hovering over a switch by the door. And with a last, simultaneous cheer of victory, the door slammed shut, locking us in the small atrium with no hope of escape.

I scowled. No hope of escape? There was always hope, wasn't there?

There's hope. There's hope. There's hope.

It's all I could do to say those two words over and over, a jetty against the crashing waves of despair. We would probably survive this—no, we *would* survive this. I had met my future self, been friends with a friend of our future selves. We would survive. We could hang out in the past eternally if we wanted to.

But the universe could still end here, now. Which meant my family would die hating me, not knowing the truth about me. And I would never be able to see them again, ever, ever again.

That and a few trillion lives would be lost, too. *Priorities, Sally, Priorities.*

"Well, I didn't see that coming," said Zander. "Did any of you?"

"I did," said Blayde.

"And you didn't do anything?"

"I wanted to see how it played out. Sue me," she said, shrugging.

"You wanted to—" Zander took a deep breath. Inhaled. Exhaled. His arms were red with scratch marks. "Right. One hour until the end of the universe, and we're on the wrong side of a door we can't jump through. Thoughts?"

"Ice cream?" said James. "If this is hopeless, I'd sure like to implode with Rocky Road in my stomach."

"Pavement is never the answer," said Blayde. "We need to climb in through the window."

"The window?" I asked. "You mean the one overlooking the sea we almost used as a way out? The one that's now buried under a kilometer of dirt?"

"Yup," she said. "But don't worry, we can get someone else to do the digging."

"In less than an hour?" I said. "The pterodactyls seem to have lost their affinity for flying through sand, Blayde. That and there hasn't been sand around here since they invented the wheel."

"They'll need a few years," she replied, grinning. "It feels so good to be in tune again. Is this how you've been feeling since we made you, Sally? Just one moment."

Blayde didn't go anywhere. She just… changed. In a heartbeat—well, if we still had them—she had changed clothes, gained a tan, and traded her shoes for roller skates. She also seemed happier now, like she'd been injected with pure joy.

"The exit's been excavated," she said, taking dainty lace gloves off her hands. "And off we go!"

Before we could even ask, she'd grabbed us all and jumped the bunch of us to a dirt well, lit only by a tiny electric lantern held by a seemingly terrified pterodactyl. Not a very wide space, I should mention, as we were all crammed together in Blayde's bear hug, and her letting go made no difference.

"You did amazing, Jacobi," said Blayde, planting a kiss on the pterodactyl's long snout, which made him turn a bright shade of red. "Your mother would be so proud."

Jacobi nodded, handed her a bag, and turned to the ladder behind him, climbing up and away without another word.

"Three years, and not once did he accept that he's worthy of his parents' love," she said, reaching in the bag to pull out small pouches for each of us. My packet was cold, icy to the touch.

"What's this?" I asked.

"Ice cream," she replied. "You said you wanted some, if I remember right. Now come on, once we're inside, we don't have much time to mess around."

We stepped through the exit window, only a slight crackle in the ancient speakers to signal anything had happened. I was ready for my heart to start back up this time, breathing as it took over the job of keeping my body alive. Good old, faithful heart. Blayde was right. We deserved ice cream. It was creamy but smelled of smoked bacon, and I didn't think too hard about the chewy bits inside. It tasted good, and I didn't want to ruin it, especially if it might be the last ice cream I ever eat in my life.

Ice cream is the strongest weapon there is against soul-crushing dread.

There was no luminous moss to light the way this time. I held my phone with one hand, my ice cream with the other until I'd finished it and sucked up the wrapper, running through the maze we'd solved just days before. The space was filled with the sound of licking and heartbeats and feet hitting pavement. So much better than panicked screaming: the epic packed running.

"So, um, what exactly happened back there?" asked Zander. "You… time traveled?"

"Went back a little ways, encouraged our local friends to start a separate dig here," she said, shrugging as she ran. "Don't look so surprised. Mucking with the timeline doesn't need to be so complicated."

Whatever Blayde had found in her memories, well, a different Blayde had come back from that experience than the one who'd gone in. She somehow, impossibly, walked taller. Her confidence was so strong it was infectious. Or maybe that was the whole 'being in a bubble universe not contaminated by the Dread' that did that.

"So, what are we looking for?" I asked. "Do you think Nimien did hide a weapon in here after all? That whatever Miro has been protecting really will save us all?"

"You heard what they said," said Blayde. "We are the weapon."

"Of course we are," said Zander. His hand reached for mine, clutching it tightly. My heart clenched. I had been so focused on the end of the universe, on the mission or whatever this trek was, to stop and think about us. About him, and what he'd just been through. About his outburst and failed memory retrieval. His only chance to find himself, to find home, and it had been shattered.

And we didn't even have time to talk about it. All I could do was squeeze his hand, so I did it better than anyone in the universe.

"If we find the twins," said Blayde, "shoot first. In the meantime, we need to find anything that can destroy the Dread. We need to destroy the amplifiers they're using to create the feedback loop everywhere at once. We need to un-broadcast the Dread."

"If you could go back in time and destroy them all before they create the Dread in the first place?" said James, weapon drawn, ice cream inhaled.

"The unicorns would probably intervene for a change on that big of a scale," said Blayde, shaking her head. "No. But we can use time to our advantage and set up a web of destruction."

We reached the end of the maze. Blayde cooed politely at the doors, and they slid open for her. We had reached the inner sanctum of the temple, all in one piece.

She made it look easy.

Dirt was piled high outside the stained-glass windows, hiding their majesty. Even with Zander's torch and my phone light, it was impossible to see all the intricate details of the tiles, the beauty of the room that had been forgotten for years. Blayde led us forward, striding out of the room and into the hallway with the cryogenic pods, without even pausing for a second.

"Blayde?" Zander muttered hastily, stopping as he looked into one of the cryogenic chambers. "I think…"

"What?" she snapped.

"Miro's here. Your Miro, I mean."

Blayde was at his side in a second, looking into the green chamber with eagerness written across her face. She nodded quickly when she saw him.

"He's still alive?" she asked, almost like a child.

Zander nodded, tapping on the top of the chamber. "Life signs are good. He's perfectly fine."

I glanced over their shoulder, and my heart dropped. It was Miro, that was sure. But it wasn't the Miro we had left yesterday. This was the Miro at the end of their days, entering the temple to become part of it forever.

The core was still that strange, round room, with the intricate designs covering the walls. Miro's hologram didn't show, but Blayde didn't seem to need them anyways. She marched right to the metal plate they had been standing on when we'd first met.

"I'll bet you anything that there's something under there," she said solemnly. "Anyone ready to test it?"

A loud roar came from the room, and the intricate designs split, pulled apart to reveal a pit below, making us jump out of the way. It wasn't a very deep pit, barely a meter down, but it was unlike anything inside the room, its walls a sleek metal like the underside of a ship. Only one item sat inside it, something which made each of our hearts drop.

Because it wasn't a weapon. It was a slap in the face.

Inside the pit was a karaoke machine.

"The weapon…" Zander turned slowly to Blayde his face dropping. "Nimien wasn't being deliberately coy at all. He was telling the truth. The weapon—"

I took a deep sigh. "*We* are the weapon."

TWENTY-THREE

MIRO'S GOT TALENT

WHILE WE WERE BUSY BEING INSULTED, BLAYDE was busy making a plan.

"Pick a song," she said, grinning ear to ear. It was the first time I'd ever seen her smile like that. Today was full of firsts.

"We're not seriously going to spend our last minutes singing," said Zander, staring at her with wide eyes. "I'm all for a bonding experience, but can't we save that for after we save the universe?"

"We're not going to do the actual signing," said Blayde, laughing. "No, we're just getting the stars to their gigs. At best, we're glorified chauffeurs. Today, karaoke will save the universe."

And she laughed again, light like the tinkling of bells. Zander turned to James and me, brows at the hairline, eyes stuck to their widest stretch. No, this Blayde was not the Blayde we knew.

Mega Blayde was scary. Too confident for comfort.

"Come on," she said, reaching for my hand and dragging me forward. "We gotta wake up my ex."

I threw one last look at Zander as she dragged me into the room of cryogenic pods. She pulled me right up to the nearest one, fingers flying over the console.

"This is how you wake them," she said, demonstrating the process. "We'll start with the oldest ones. They'll take the longest to get their bearings. Just be gentle, all right? The pods should shut off immediately afterwards. It seems this place used every drop of power just to keep them online."

With so little time on the clock, I went to work. It didn't mean I wasn't going to bug her, though.

"You're going to have to explain," I begged, typing the simple commands to wake the ancient sleeper from their pod. The one she had started with was hissing as steam spewed out of the gently opening lid, making me jump, but she had moved on already. "How is a karaoke machine going to save the universe?"

She moved on to the next pod down the line before running back to the man groaning in the first one, whispering hasty instructions before moving on to the next.

"Right," she said, once the first three ancient Miros had been given more of a rundown than I had. "Do you believe in angels?"

"I'm sorry, what now?"

"Angels! You know, multidimensional beings who come down from the sky and sing your ears off? Tend to have a confusing number of eyes?"

"I guess so," I said. "Why? Are they real? Are we supposed to be making offerings?"

"Probably," she said. Somehow between all this she was still able to open pods, reassure ancient Miros, send them on their way. "But you know the power of song. The twins have been feeding the universe into the universe in order to create their feedback loop, waves in opposing phase to destroy everything everywhere. But if we can mess up their harmony, we can give ourselves enough time to stop them. Change the frequency, throw off the pitch, it doesn't matter so long as whatever they're using to match the waves is thrown off."

"Miro," I gasped.

"Yeah?" asked the Cowboy Miro in the pod beneath me. "What's happening?"

"You're going to sing the universe to safety," I said. "All of you at once."

"Brilliant!" they said, pushing themselves to their feet. "When do I start?"

Blayde gestured for the circular chamber and he rushed to follow the others, greeting the past and future selves with an excitement reserved for long lost friends.

"And what about Desmond and Sidera?" I asked.

"What about them?" she shrugged. "They've probably found themselves a cozy nook in here to ride out the end of the universe. It's not like they know their way through the maze. But if we find them, we take them out. It's as easy as that. We're in the only place in the universe where we can actually do that."

After every pod was opened, we rushed back to the antechamber, which was now so full of Miros we could barely make our way back through to the center. Zander and James were still scrolling through the karaoke machine, and even my translator couldn't make sense of what letter they had reached.

"Right," said Blayde. "May I have everyone's attention please?"

The Miros turned silent in an instant, so quickly it was almost eerie.

"It's really good to see you," they said as one. "Would you like to go out for coffee, see if we can pick up where we left off?"

"Later." Blayde waved them off. "Right now, I need all of you save one to press the emergency exit button with us. We're taking you on tour!"

The Miros cheered. I should be saying Miro, but it was too unsettling to think of them all as one single mind. Especially since some were dressed as Vikings and others as Flash Gordon. So much spandex. They must have gone through a phase.

"Sally, you and James stay here, guard the designated singer," she said. "As soon as we're all out, Zander and I will spread yourselves far and wide."

"But I—" Zander started, but she silenced him with a dazzling smile.

"You don't need to know where you're taking them," she said. "It doesn't have to be precise. Just random jump and come back. We'll be done in no time."

"I'll stay," said a Miro. "This is the body that's most familiar to them."

The selves parted and there was the Miro we had known and conga'd with, bearded and aged and grinning ear to ear. They strode forward and hopped into the karaoke pit.

"You didn't have to climb down there, but okay, I like your enthusiasm," said Blayde. "Zander, let's go. You three, if we're not back in an hour, presume the universe was destroyed, and don't go outside for a while. You understand?"

We nodded, and she hit the exit button. In a flash they were all gone, leaving the three of us in our karaoke pit to ponder the end of the universe.

"So, um, Miro," said James, handing the microphone to our charge. Without the hundreds of other selves in the chamber with us, the silence was deafening. Every word she uttered bounced off the empty walls. "What song are you going for?"

They scrolled through the list, which seriously must have held every single song ever made on any planet. Nimien's weapon was an interesting choice to put it mildly.

"This one's a good one," they said. "Very appropriate for the end of the world. I used to listen on repeat when I was planning my race through the labyrinth. *Winner*

May Die, But Not Today, Baby." They loaded it up, waiting with their microphone in hand, only their head sticking out of the pit.

I gritted my teeth, and we waited, silently, for the magic moment to begin. Every minute bringing us closer to the end. If the universe did implode while we were in here, it meant sharing the new place with terrible roommates, and I'm pretty sure they'd have killed us before the recombination period even began.

"Are you okay?"

I looked up. James stood poised, flanking Miro, radiant in their role of bodyguard. I realized then that I was shaking—shaking with a nervous energy I couldn't dispel.

"What if this only delays the Dread?" I closed my eyes. None of my calming techniques were working. I wanted to throw up in the corner. "What if we can't stop it? What if everyone feels this way… forever?"

James took a deep breath. She looked like she wanted to step closer to me but kept to her role instead.

"Why does it all have to be on you?" she asked. "You're not responsible for the fate of the universe."

"B-because!" I stammered, throwing my hands up in the air. "Because I know what it feels like! I know what it means to question my every thought, to judge and evaluate them, not knowing if it's my mind being sincere or having a breakdown it hasn't warned me of. I know what it's like, and I know what to do, and I need to help! I can help!"

"But just because you can doesn't mean you *can*," she said. "It's not your responsibility to save the world just because you've suffered and survived. It's too much for just one person. Trust me. We're in this together. Otherwise, you're going to crush under the pressure you're piling on yourself."

I swallowed, hard. She was right: I was only reinforcing the Dread by feeding into it myself. My thoughts and fears of failure, knowing exactly what would happen if I let everyone down, was crushing me. I forced a smile, and breathed, letting part of it go—slowly. I couldn't drop it all at once. But with every breath, I stood taller.

We could do this.

I turned to Miro. "So, when do you—" I started, but before I could even finish my question music blared from the karaoke machine.

Well, I call it music. But whatever words Miro had used to describe the title of the song never made it into the song itself. No words had. If you could even call it that. Like two whales flirting with each other across an ocean and getting as dirty as they please only the whole thing was being recounted by an angry cricket pleading with the mafia for his life.

But in that moment, I knew everything would be okay. Because as terrible as this excuse for music was, it was also cosmobeat, the awful new genre that had taken the world by storm back on Earth.

Which meant somehow, the interference was working.

That or some off-worlder was making a killing passing off number one interstellar hits off as their own, but hey, the Agency would *have* to deal with that now.

Miro screamed into the microphone, my translator trying so hard to interpret what was going on that instead all I heard was quiet sobbing on top of the beat. Somehow, outside, out there, all their selves were singing the same song, together as one, across the stars, across the galaxies, throwing off all the work Desmond and Sidera had built to generate the Dread.

It would have been beautiful if the song wasn't so awful.

The doors slid open, but Miro was still singing. It wasn't another self. Not the siblings, coming to relieve us of duty and of fear.

Desmond and Sidera had solved the maze.

"Hasn't anybody told you it's rude to sing outside of common hours?" spat Desmond.

Miro hit a high note and all the colors on the wall turned into a whistle sound, drowning out Sidera as she tried saying something surely equally snarky.

James took the distraction and fired, leaping between the twins and Miro. I grabbed my tiny sword and joined her, an impenetrable wall defending the universe's musical savior.

Only we weren't impenetrable. I didn't even have my only asset on my side. I was as mortal here as James was, and barely a fraction as competent.

Sidera screamed as James's beam ripped through her leg, but she'd missed Desmond and he rushed us, screaming a war cry as he attacked.

Click. Click. James's blaster was dry. She cursed under her breath, but Desmond was already on us. I didn't think, only stabbed. With every ounce of strength I had, I pushed the sword forward, only for him to sidestep me as quickly and easily as he had dodged James's shots, reaching—

James kicked him the gut, swinging her empty gun at his head before tossing it away. She tackled him to the ground, but he rolled away easily, flying to his feet as she spun back to hers, fists raised and ready for a fight.

So, this is how it was going to go down. The way all things should go down: four barehanded mortals with a backup track.

I gasped my last breath of air as Sidera's arm wrapped around my neck, pulling tight and crushing my windpipe. My lungs screamed as they failed to receive adequate support for their essential workforce. I grabbed at her arm, ripping, pulling anything to get her off me.

Miro switched to his next song, something sweet and oddly familiar. The instruments rose and swelled, a sad, emotional tune. He took a deep breath before the beat dropped and he belted out the sound a seagull makes when it finds its wife has been cheating on it.

I slammed my heel down on Sidera's toes, jamming my elbow into her ribs. Her arm slackened just enough for me to fill my lungs with air, burning hot against my throat.

She was going to kill me. She was going to kill everyone. This wasn't going to be a pretty fight, let alone fair.

I went for the hair.

She screamed as I tugged. For a woman who had never once experienced mortal pain, it must have been agony. My upper hand didn't last long, as she grabbed for my own hair, and shit, that shit hurt like shit.

But I knew how to handle hurt. I threw my head forward, slamming it into her face. The pain was instantaneous and overwhelming, filling my body with nausea. Sidera must have felt the same because she threw up on the floor.

James had managed to somehow push Desmond back into the pod room—and it was fist against fist, knee to knee, the kind of hand-to-hand combat reserved for martial arts movies, but unlike when the siblings fought, it was at a pace I could follow. Not that I had the opportunity, having Sidera to fight on my own.

I couldn't do it. I wasn't strong enough. I wasn't trained enough. Tears ran down my face, tears of exhaustion, of pain, as I struggled just to stay alive.

But that's all I needed to do. Stay alive. Stay alive long enough for Zander and Blayde to return. For the song to work. For Desmond's beacons to break or deactivate or be destroyed, whatever Blayde, the actual hero, decided to do.

All I had to do was keep Sidera distracted. Keep her on me, not on Miro.

"How does it feel?" I screamed, pulling my best Blayde sneer as I deflected one of her punches with the palm of my hand. Pain jolted up my arm; no one told me it would hurt that much.

"What? Beating you?" she replied. "Hardly even notice it. It's not a big deal to me. Just like squashing a bug."

"I meant patricide," I said, swinging my leg in a sweeping motion I thought might catch her off guard, but she jumped over it. "Pretty shitty move, killing a helpless old man."

"Oh, please," she scoffed. "You had no pity for him. You hated his guts. You were probably almost as relieved as I was to see him die."

"What you did was messed up," I continued. It was harder than it looks to keep an eye on her attacks and come up with stuff to push her buttons as well. "I mean, seriously messed up. You sure you're okay?"

Miro switched to the next song, the Weird Al version of *Gangster's Paradise*. It would have been easier if he was still singing to nonsense seagull ballads rather than rapping about what it means to be Amish.

A scream—*James*. Where was she? She wasn't in the karaoke room anymore; she must have been with the pods. I couldn't see her, couldn't help her, couldn't...

Sidera swung again, catching me under the jaw so hard I tasted blood. She didn't seem fazed by anything that had happened today, as if all this had just been an uneventful few hours at the office. Murdering your dad is not an alternative to idle chitchat with your coworkers.

But that's what made us different. Sidera was driven by a single thing: her desire to rule the universe. Her own, since this one wasn't good enough for her. And me? Well, despite its flaws, I *loved* this universe. It was the only one we had. The only one with chocolate and bacon-flavored ice cream. Sidera and Desmond lacked not only care, and tact, but creativity; their universe was going to suck with them in charge.

I swung my fist at Sidera's face. She dodged, but not fast enough, and my knuckle squelched as it dug into her eye socket. The sound that came out of her mouth wasn't human. I tried to force down my disgust as I swung again. As I kicked her in the leg, right where James's bullet had hit.

Miro phased into a new song, another one from a world I had never seen, this one a beautiful lament.

All the wind knocked out of me, and I collapsed on the floor. Sidera had moved without me seeing, without me realizing. The same swoop of the leg I had tried and failed now had me on my back, Sidera grabbing my neck with both hands, squeezing, squeezing…

Stars danced in front of my eyes, and not the fun kind. The ringing in my ears got louder until it drowned out the singing, everything but my own ragged attempts at breathing. My legs squirmed beneath me as I tried to kick her off, to no avail.

Weak. Weak. I would die at her hands for failure to learn a single thing.

At once the pressure on my neck and chest released, replaced by a stream of warm red liquid. Sidera collapsed to the side, her head going the other. James stood over us once again, her shirt drenched in blood. She was panting, heavy, eyes stuck open. She held my sword in her fist.

"Thanks for dropping this," she said.

"Thanks for… well, this."

She reached down to help me up. My heart was pounding, my body still desperately trying to catch up on all the air it missed.

And behind our ragged breathing—silence. Miro had finished their set and sat down on the side of the pit, apparently exhausted.

"Desmond?" I asked James. She nodded, indicating the other room with a jut of her chin. His body lay prostrate on the ground there.

She'd saved us both.

She'd saved us all.

We didn't say any of that, not yet. Instead, we helped each other to Miro's side, joining them in the karaoke pit, basked in the light of the still-running machine. The screen displayed symbols that seemed to have a smell, or maybe that was the music, another music we couldn't hear with our ears.

"Is it over?" asked James. Miro nodded.

"I hope," they replied. "We felt the Dread collapse and go. Some of us got tips for our performance. Most of us did not. What did you think?"

"You saved the universe," she said. "What does it matter what we think?"

"So, you hated it," said Miro, sighing. "Very well. At least I go out with a bang."

"You've still got a dozen more songs in you," I said. My every word was agony, but they were words that had almost been taken from me for good, so I would use them. "At the very least."

"No, this is the end." The way he said it, so casually, made me think my translator must have been damaged in the fight. Maybe he was just talking about groceries. "This was the plan from the very beginning. To preserve our last minutes to fight whatever was to come. We did it. Now we get to rest and party it up and then we reintegrate with the rest of the universe."

They closed their eyes, their breathing shallow. I glanced up at James, who shrugged, then hissed in pain. The blood on her shirt… shit, it was hers.

"How am I the only one not actively dying?" I spat.

"I'm not dying," said James, forcing a smile. "It's fine. I just need to lie down for a bit —"

And she just collapsed on the floor.

I rushed over to her, pulling open her shirt to reveal a gash the size of Texas on her abdomen. Oh stars, it was deep. How she was even alive and talking and even walking seemed impossible now. If I could kill Desmond a second time, I would have.

"Shit!" I shouted. "What do I do? Miro, what do I do?"

"Don't ask me," they muttered. "I'm dying too. You see, it's the slow march of time that gets—"

"I realize you just saved us all, but right now you're really not helping."

I looked down at James, then at myself. I could, couldn't I? Just a drop of my blood and she would be...

No, it wouldn't work. Even if that was an option, we were in the only place in the non-universe where my mojo was inert.

And she'd made it quite clear that that wasn't part of what she wanted.

"M-Miro," I sputtered. Shit, James's skin was so cold. "This place used to carry your memories, right? Like some kind of external hard drive? In case you forgot?"

They nodded. "My backup brain. It's what allowed me to continue on for as long as I did. It's useless now that my every self is dying of old age."

"Can I have it?"

Miro met my gaze. "You want my backup brain?"

"If there's more disk space available," I said, looking at James instead.

"We haven't used disks since—"

"Please. She saved my life. She knew this could happen, and she still put her life on the line for us. For all of us. We owe her that much. I don't know if we can fix her, so if there's any other way..."

Miro stood and hoisted themself out of the karaoke pit. They marched toward the back wall, kicked it, and a small metal safe dropped open. They reached in, pulling out a leather-bound book.

"Here," they said, holding it out to me. "Though it's probably going to get hard for her to write anything; there are only two pages left and my pen's dried up."

"This is a journal," I said.

"Yes?"

"This was your mental backup? The whole time, it's just been a book?"

"Journaling is very healthy for the soul, you know. Frees up the mind to focus on more important things"

I bit my lip, holding back tears, holding back the urge to punch them square in the jaw. My hands stung at the fresh memory of bone colliding with bone.

"There has to be some other way to save her," I said, clutching her shoulders. It was amazing how quickly skin lost color, lost heat. My hands did nothing to keep the blood in her body.

"If I were younger, I would invite her to merge with the hive mind," they said, "but their body would still die."

I ran my hands through my hair. There had to be something. If this had happened at Nimien's, we could have used the chairs. Hell, the pods here would have kept her from outright dying until we could treat her, but they were all out of commission.

"Wait," I said, turning back to Miro. "How?"

"How. What?"

"How did you merge a new self into your mind?" I asked. "You don't go with them into the temple. They come in alone and come out connected. So how?"

They shrugged, reaching back into the safe. The hologram turned back on, ready to congratulate us for coming this far, though he fizzled in and out of the light.

"There's a part of me saved here," they explained. "Though I suppose you already know that from the welcome hologram."

"Is there any room for another mind in there?" I asked. "Please, Miro. You said you were dying. You have no bodies left. What would happen if someone joined who wasn't you?"

"It would be... complicated," they said. "But it would save her essence. And there wouldn't be any of my selves left to be bothered. But it would be like pouring a glass of water into the ocean—retrieving those same molecules would be complicated."

"But not impossible," I said. James would be saved, and so, in a way, would Miro. I had to risk it. She just saved the universe. I had to save her. I reached my arms under James's body, lifting her up.

"Help her," I begged. "Copy her brain. Save her."

Miro nodded. They took James's hand, tenderly placing it on the orb. There was no response from her body, but the little crystal ball glowed a beautiful apple green, only for a second, before going dim.

"There, she's inside," said Miro, handing me the ball. For a second, I worried it would copy my brain, too, but it seemed it needs their touch to be activated. "What are you going to do?"

"Find her a hospital," I said. "Just in case her body can be saved. Tell Zander and Blayde I'll be on Earth."

They held up the little leather book. "You don't want my backup brain anymore?"

"Give it to Blayde. She likes journals," I said, and I carried James into the exit light, her brain and Miro's bouncing in my pocket.

TWENTY-FOUR
AFTERMATH IS JUST AFTERCARE FOR MATH ABUSE

IT WAS A SMALL RELIEF TO BURY MY FRIEND ON our homeworld. A larger one to know we were only burying her corpse. I'm aware that's how funerals normally go, but seeing as how Blayde was in attendance with James's digitized brain in a handbag it's safe to say this wasn't your usual celebration of life.

The funeral was somber, as serious as James had been in life, before space had brought out her snark. There weren't dozens of people sobbing, mainly because there weren't even a dozen people there, and that was counting the preacher and the undertaker.

This was the third funeral, fourth memorial, I had attended in four years. Most had been empty caskets. I couldn't listen to the preacher, saying the same words I had heard as John was lowered into the ground. As Matt's empty coffin had been laid to rest. As Zander's had. When we'd buried Nim's memory on that long-lost planet, we'd at least tried to make it personal.

Oh. I've watched Nimien die three times now. I bit my lip. Maybe this wasn't the last.

Somewhere behind me, an older woman let out a wail of pain. Grandmother? Her family only knew the official story unlike the rest of us: a low ranking FBI agent. The capital-A-Agency reported her death as a failed operation. Dead in the line of duty. Nothing to help the family's pain.

As if anything could.

Well, the little crystal ball might have. That or made things ten times worse. I knew James was alive. But I'd also held her body as she'd died. I'd also carried her lifeless corpse into the ER, sobbing, hoping there was still hope.

There was. That hope was in Blayde's purse.

It didn't mean I wasn't going to have that extra piece of trauma living with me for the rest of my life. If Nimien was right about anything, it was my desperate need for a specialist.

The sermon finished and the family was invited forward, their roses at the ready. The coffin lowered down slowly, white roses covering the sleek black polish of the wooden box that held our friend. As the people dispersed, a man approached with a shovel and began to drop the dirt back in, his face as solemn as he could make it. A formality, I assume; he probably would bring in a tractor once the family left.

Blayde stayed beside the hole, her black hat covering most of her face. I watched, alone, while James's family walked back to their cars, talking between themselves. Zander stood back, eyeing, just as I had, the dark figures watching from afar. He gave them a nod. They nodded back.

Blayde pulled a small jar from her pocket, unscrewed the top, and poured the contents into the grave. A stream of brown dust hit the coffin in a slow torrent. The gravedigger paused, leaning on his shovel as he watched the odd woman perform this odd ritual, polite enough to stay silent as she performed this last act. It was only when she screwed the top back on the bottle that he spoke, as kindly as he could.

"Were you two close?"

Blayde nodded. "Closer than I would admit," was her quiet reply. "She was… very dear to me."

"I'm sorry." The gravedigger was kind, not pushing her. "You have my condolences."

"Thank you," she said softly.

"May I ask… the dirt? What was that about?"

"It wasn't dirt. It was stardust." Blayde replied, as she slipped the empty bottle back into the pocket of her cardigan. "Captured during the birth of a star, so new, so far away, that its light will not reach Earth for another five thousand years. My version of a rose."

"Oh," the man replied. He returned to digging as Blayde turned away, looking for Zander and me.

"It's you," said a voice, before she could join us. "I didn't believe it, I should have… it's you."

The man beside her carried James's face. Harder lines, older lines.

"I know you," said Blayde, quietly.

"We met, though we were not formally introduced," he replied. "My daughter told me all about you."

She nodded solemnly. "Mr. Felling, I presume?"

He replied with a curt nod. "And you must be Blayde. I can't believe that you're really here, that you're…"

"Real?"

He nodded once more, slowly, as if afraid that too much movement would scare her off. "I thought you were part of my girl's imagination. We had her tested, you know."

"She mentioned that," she said sternly. "How very nice of you."

"But you're real, so everything she said… you saved my life. Back when I was based in Shanghai. During that…"

"It was nothing."

"So, it's true, everything she told me? About you being an…"

Her face dropped. "Yes. But you must not go around spreading the news. Some people want me gone. I don't want them to know where I am."

"Of course. Just so you know…she left no will."

"Why do you tell me this?"

"So that you're not surprised if you get none of her assets." Mr. Felling frowned. "We are not keeping things from you. If you want anything of hers… well, we can talk."

"I have the only thing that matters."

"We would love to get to know you. We've heard so much about you. James spoke very highly of you."

"I don't think that would be best." Blayde shook her head. "I will not bother your family. Just know that… that James was a very, very brave woman. She always put others first. Always."

Blayde turned to walk away, striding across the wet grass, lowering her head so that the hat completely obscured her face. But James's father didn't move. He stood, planted firmly on the hill, arms akimbo, his face glum and without light.

"This wasn't an accident, was it?" he called out after her, but she did not stop. "Tell me the truth. I deserve it!"

"You may deserve it, but it doesn't mean you can live with it," she replied. "James Felling died saving our lives. All of our lives. That is the truth."

"Don't lie to me!"

"Goodbye, Mr. Felling," she called back, clear and final.

When she finally reached us, she was holding back tears. Her hand was stuffed in her purse, and I knew what it would find there. A tear broke the floodgates and rolled down her cheek.

"I'm sorry," I said, placing a hand on her shoulder. "I did everything I could."

"You did," she replied, meeting my gaze. "You saved her. But I should never have left her there. We should have brought her back here the second she hitched a ride. I should—"

She broke down again, tears flowing freely now. Zander beat me to her, wrapping her up in the tightest hug I had ever seen. She sobbed into his shoulder, his coat turning into the sea.

"I'm tired of burying my friends," she said, quietly. "I'm so tired. *This* is why we kept coming back to Nimien, over and over again. Not a trap, but a reprieve from pain. And now I feel… I feel…" She turned to Zander. "And you don't."

He shook his head. "Barely anything. Flashes."

"Hey."

I turned around, and there was Marcy, dressed to the nines in a stunning wool coat and Louboutin heels. Blayde needed Zander and Zander needed Blayde; they needed space. I trotted over to my bestie, who frowned, hands deep in her pockets.

"Hey," I replied.

Marcy nudged the grass with the tip of her shoe, struggling to maintain eye contact. I guess I was too since I was staring at her shoe.

"I'm sorry about your friend," she said. "Dany wanted to thank you in person, but her ministers won't let her have a moment to herself. Foollegg tells me James was a hero. "

I nodded. "She was. Is, I mean. She's not totally dead. We saved her brain in a hivemind's memory ball. She's going to be okay."

Marcy raised an eyebrow. "I didn't know you could do that."

"I didn't either. But desperate times…"

She took a deep sigh, finally looking up. She looked beautiful, movie-star beautiful. Like a full team of makeup artists and hairdressers had prepared her for this moment. I felt the opposite. We'd been back on Earth a few days, catching our breath, debriefing the Agency and the Alliance, but there hadn't been a single moment for self-care. Sure, my skin was kept flawless by the universe, but just because it was healthy didn't mean I was put together.

"Thank you," she said, and she took my hand. "Despite how everything went down… you saved us, all of you. The Dread is gone. We can go back to living again. The universe is here today because of what you did. All four of you."

I couldn't hold back, I wrapped my arms around her and held her close, sobbing as she sobbed, together again, at last. My best friend and me.

"You, too," I said. "If it wasn't for what you gave up, we'd be in an Alliance dissection lab right now. Your sacrifice matters too."

"I didn't put my life on the line," she replied, clutching me back.

"You did," I said. "You gave up everything for this. That's not something we'll take lightly."

She pulled me closer, and we cried together some more. I soaked up the warm comforting feeling of her, of knowing she was there for me, and me for her. The feeling rocketed me back to the two of us on the playground two decades ago, pinky promising to be best friends forever.

"Are there any silver linings?" I asked, pulling away when I realized I was keeping her from breathing. "I mean, you're the First Lady of the biggest civilization this arm of the galaxy. That has to have its perks."

"I didn't think it would," she replied, with a sly grin. Oh, thank the stars, she was smiling. "After everything I heard about them, I thought it would be torture. But they listen to Dany. They take her seriously, obey her. We could really start to change things around there."

I gave her another squeeze. "I'm so proud of you. If you need anything, I'm there for you, okay Like, literally, anything. Wait, how much do your parents know?"

"Do they know I've married the President-Empress of an alien civilization? No, not yet. They think I'm moving to Tibet." The frown returned. "If we could have had a year together, here… just a year to just be *us* before taking the universe on our shoulders…"

"Hey," I said, reaching for her hand, "I will be your personal space chauffeur, okay? Anytime you need Earth time, I've got you. We throw a little time travel in the mix and no one in your palace will notice you're even gone."

She threw her arms around me again, and I hugged back, delicately, still trying to wrap my head around the alien concept of her growing a life from scratch.

"I'll ferry you away from your palace whenever you're fed up with that place. We just have to figure out a bat signal or something."

"I would love that," she said. "I would absolutely love that."

With our conversation reaching a point where all we could do is smile and laugh, we turned back to check on Zander and Blayde, who were having the opposite experience. It was a whole other funeral back there.

"I should go," I said, indicating them with a nudge of my head. "They've been through a lot."

"So have you," said Marcy. "Seriously, you need to take some time for yourself. Process what's happened without them interfering."

"They're my friends, Marcy," I replied.

"I know, I know," she said. "And I know you love Zander, but… are you sure? He's a thousand-year-old homeless man with a rap sheet from here to Andromeda. I didn't think he would be your type. And the age gap thing bothers me, doesn't it you?"

Her words dug deep, but they were not malicious. Still, not a great thing to hear from your bestie.

"I'm here for you, too, okay?" She gave me another quick squeeze. "You know where to find me when you need my help. Just don't throw yourself headfirst into this relationship. It's going to hurt when you hit the ground."

A whistle from the parking lot—a black SUV with a man waving her over. She sighed.

"That's my cue," she said, kissing me on the cheek. "Go. Go keep the universe safe."

"You make it sound more glamorous than it is," I said, as she walked away.

· · · · · · · ● · · · · · · · ·

BLAYDE WAS SILENT ON THE DRIVE HOME, tears in her eyes. Even Zander was crying, my hand holding his in the passenger's side.

We reached the house before my parents did. Galli jumped up to greet us, as energetic as a puppy. I hadn't realized the Dread had been hurting her too.

"What happened?" I asked, the second I closed the door. Zander turned away.

"Take a seat," said Blayde. She was solemn as the graves we'd left behind. She refused to say anything else until we were both on the couch.

"I came to a decision." She stood before us, hands crossed. "I have to go. I need time to think. To be. And so do you."

I sprung up, only to fall back in the couch again, my mind reeling. What was she saying?

"It's a good thing," she continued. "It's not forever. I just need time to process who I know myself to be now. Maybe I'll figure out our James problem along the way. But it's all right; it's a good thing."

"You said that already," I said, "but it doesn't sound like it's me you're trying to convince."

She nodded. "Yeah. I have a lot of questions I need answered. This is terrifying for me, too, but I think it's right. Don't worry, we'll find each other again."

"You saw what happened last time," Zander muttered. "What if you don't want us back?"

"I will, don't you dare worry about that." She put her hand on his arm, and he leaned into it. "But I have things that need to be done, and I can't have you with me. I'm coming back. And you two, you can go wherever you want to. We'll meet back up here, in one month's time, how's that? Vacation for you, soul-searching trip for me."

"But Blayde—"

She cut me off. "Don't worry. It's a promise. You can get him back here safe. And you need couple time; I see that now. Take me out of the equation and see if the math still checks out."

"You can't go," said Zander. "I can't let you."

"I'll be fine," she insisted. "You'll be *fine*. You always are. Don't you see what I'm giving you two? Time. Something I've been afraid to give for my entire life. But I want you happy, so take this. Take this and be happy."

"Blayde, please…"

"I need to do this." She reached her hand into her purse and pulled out the glowing green orb that was James, tossing the bag behind her. "I'm going to find James a new body. I'm going to save her."

She smiled at both of us, a grin showing all her teeth, and in the first time since I'd known her, it didn't feel like a threat. She was… eager. Ready.

"Goodbye, bro. Sally." She winked, as if she would be back tomorrow with some pizza. "Take care of yourselves."

And then she was gone. I didn't try to follow her; she wanted her privacy, for whatever reason it was, and I wasn't going to take that from her. She was going to be fine, that was a given. It was us we were worried about, the two of us in the wake of her departure.

Marcy's words echoed through my head. Zander and me, a dream I'd had for so long. But a man I knew next to nothing about, centuries older and…

Still, Zander. I looked over at him, taking his hand, and clasping it, reminding him I was here, I was an anchor, and we had each other to lean on.

"Alone," Zander muttered, echoing my thoughts.

"You all right?" I said as calmly as I could. Because of course he wasn't; how could he be? He shuffled his weight. I immediately knew I had gone too far—too far with this new Zander, this Zander that I only partially knew, who only partially knew himself. But he stayed beside me, and after a minute, a minute that I could only imagine was the battle between his new old part and the part I knew, until the part I had come to love won, and replied cautiously to my question.

"Sure. Why wouldn't I be?"

"You know what I mean," I said, leaning my head to his. "We promised we wouldn't lie to each other, remember?"

He let out the heaviest sigh the universe had ever seen. "Where do I even start?"

"How about your head? Do you remember anything?"

He shook it. "The me I saw through Blayde's eyes," he said, and shivered, forehead trembling against mine. "Maybe it's better those memories never do come back. I was a real ass back then. I had lost my way, and now I have to visit that again—memory by memory."

"So… something is coming back?"

He nodded slowly. "I thought that one day I would wake up with all of them back. Instead, it's like water dripping in a cave—all there, but slow to come. A trickle of my best hits. It…it hurts to sleep, because I can't dream, I can only remember. Remember all the terrible things I've done. Remember the man I was before. Remember…and hate him."

"But you're not him anymore. You're still Zander. You're still the man I met, all those years ago, the man I fell in love with."

"Am I really? You yourself said I was different."

"But you're still you. You're no longer the man in those memories. If Nimien could change, can't you?"

"I'm still the one who did those things," he said. "They're still my hands…"

"They were," I said, "but every day we're changing who we are. Little by little. We're so many people during a single lifetime, and look at how many lifetimes we have. Which is why self-love is so dang hard—it's not just about what you're doing in the moment. It's how the care and love you show yourself affects *all* the selves you've been and will be."

I put my hand on the back of his neck, leaning him back to me, basking in the heat of his face.

"I'll be fine, with you by my side. You keep me true to myself."

"I will," I promised, trying to focus on his breathing, rather than on the thought of Zander becoming something that scared even him. "And you have to keep me true to me. Steady my course."

"Without Blayde…"

"Doesn't have to be a bad thing," I said. "She's right, it's an opportunity. To connect. And you did promise me a trip, you know."

He paused, then shook himself out of it, wrapping an arm around me with a grin I hadn't seen in ages.

"So, where to first, my star?" The smile was real, but it wasn't completely there. He was happy. He was sad. He was everything and nothing at once. Yet still he smiled on.

I grinned back, wrapping my arms around him. "Well, I don't know… what did you say about leisure planets?"

He pondered this for a second. "I know of a spa that's so effective, you sleep for five days. That, or there's this place that's literally a sauna: hot, steaming, minerals in the air. You rent out a room there and relax for days on end."

I shook my head.

"Or—" He grinned. "Or we watch the most epic space race in history. And I don't mean Cold War aerospace engineering. I mean a race. In space."

I shook my head once more, and his grin widened.

"Adventure?" he asked. "See where the universe takes us?"

He didn't need me to speak to know my response. My massive grin was enough.

"But one last thing before we leave," I said, squeezing his hand.

"Oh?"

"The end of the universe reminded me I need to come clean to the people I love," I said. "So before we go, I need to tell my parents where we're headed. Well, I need to tell them everything."

He kissed me gently on the forehead. "You ready?"

I nodded. "As I'll ever be."

The keys jingled in the door, and I could feel myself smiling, growing with the excitement that bubbled inside of me. Together, just the two of us, every second bringing us closer to the future we were ready to make our own.

EPILOGUE

HE WOKE UP BOUND TO A TREE, HIS ARM CHAINED above him.

Where was he? One second, he was on his ship, the next he was—nowhere. Surrounded by a darkness so absolute that even the brightest stars could not break. Chained, but chained to nothing.

Then he heard a sound.

He turned his and there she was. Hadn't he just seen her a minute ago? What was she still doing here with him? Hadn't he gotten rid of her? No, she had done something, something to his head…

How long had he been out?

Fear gripped him as he realized what he was hearing. Bricks. One laid on top of the other, slowly, rhythmically, slicing the perfect darkness. Where they touched, they fused together, a perfectly smooth, white surface, no blemishes, no marks whatsoever. Higher and higher and higher, all around him. Creating isolation from nothing.

He was cut off from the universe. He was trapped.

"Blayde, what are you doing?" he asked, trying with every inch of his being to jump, to move, to get away. He closed his eyes, searched for his intangible connection to the universe. But there was nothing there, only more darkness behind his eyelids. "What have you done to me?"

"Don't squirm like that, Nimien. You'll just get tired."

Clack. Another brick. His entire being shuddered as he realized what was happening. What she was doing. What the wall meant. Another piece of his prison coming into place.

"Stop it! You're going to—"

"Look, I'm sorry," she said. And she was being truthful. He had learned how to tell when she was lying. There were entire books devoted to understanding her personal tricks. "But this is for the best. Believe me. Trust me."

"What is? Locking me up?" he spat. "How would that be for the best? I was collecting information, Blayde. Sharing it. There was nothing wrong with that."

"You're burning up inside. Can't you feel it? No, I guess you wouldn't. But trust me; this is the way it happens. For the best."

"You're making my prison."

"I'm building you a future. One where you are more powerful than anyone I have ever met. One where people will know your name and share it through the stars. One where you can be happy."

"How is this going to make me happy and powerful?" He pulled at his chain. Where was the other end? "And how are you stopping me from jumping? How are you doing that?"

"Something I learned from you, actually. It's hard to explain. But simply put… we're at the right place."

"You're building me a cell."

"I am." She nodded. "But it's for the best."

"How can you be sure?"

"Because you told me." She turned away: She wasn't crying, was she? The great Blayde, crying. Why didn't he want to mock her? He would have. But for some reason, the words stuck in his throat. Was it pity? No, it couldn't be pity; how could anyone pity a being like her? She was ruthless. She deserved no pity. He thought briefly about what brilliant insults from that long list he had written over all those years would be the most effective: Instead, he waited for her to gather her wits, rising to his feet in the square patch of nothingness with his patented smile he was so proud of.

"I'm just closing the cycle," she said, as she put another brick down. "And while we're here, let's talk a little about your affinity for AI."

ACKNOWLEDGEMENTS

THIS SHOULD MORE APTLY BE CALLED "APOLOGIES," since I may have cursed the entire team who worked on this manuscript.

I wrote Starstruck 7 while on the rush of early pandemic panic, way back when we thought it would all blow over by summer. But Starstruck 8 came during the long stretch of Pandemic Fatigue, the doldrums of trying to act like life was getting back to normal when nothing is normal anymore. Sitting down with this manuscript got harder and harder every day. Interestingly, the concept I had for the Dread had been on paper since my first draft in summer of 2013: as I wrote Dreadknot in 2021, it felt all too real.

The feeling was exacerbated with every round of edits, as everyone who came into contact with the manuscript seemed to be struck with some mysterious curse. So thank yous first go to the entire Bolide Publishing team who I were in the front line of this misery: thank you to Michelle Dunbar, Anna Johnstone, and Cayleigh Stickler, for giving Dreadknot your all when everything was crumbling around us. Thank you for still believing in this series, eight books in, and counting. I hope the curse won't follow through to book 9!

An absolutely massive thank you goes to Madeline Dyer, both as an editor and a friend. You found exactly what Dreadknot was missing and pulled it out of me kicking and screaming. You are the strongest person I know. I have no idea how you manage to do so much when the world is throwing curveballs at you left and right.

To Cora Corrigall, honorary editor, alpha reader extraordinaire. Your insight early on kept Dreadknot from going completely off the rails, and your constant motivation kept ME from going off the rails. Watching you grow into a bona-fide editor is so thrilling! Thanks for shouldering the curse with me.

To Crystal DuVall, who always knows, somehow, exactly when I need cheering on. How do you do it? I'm terribly sorry for the curse proving to be real only two days into getting the manuscript. Here's to our many hats!

To the Fellowship of the Five: Madeline Dyer, Lisa Amowitz, Emily Collin, and Heidi Ayarbe. You have been my write-or-die team through thick and thin. Thank you for being my shoulder to cry on and my cheering squad all rolled into one. I'm so proud of all of us.

To Hugo, curse-breaker. You have been my rock as the world has been crashing down around us. I love you more than I can put into words. Thank you for seeing me through and through.

And to you, the reader. Things are hard right now. Bleak doesn't even begin to cover it. And even when you feel like you are alone—you are not alone. Find your people. We're getting through this labyrinth together.

ABOUT THE AUTHOR

SARAH ANDERSON CAN'T EVER TELL YOU where she's from. Not because she doesn't want to, but because it inevitably leads to a confusing conversation about where she was born (England) where she grew up (France) and where her family is from (USA) and it tends to make things very complicated.

She's lived her entire life in the South of France, except for a brief stint where she moved to Washington DC, or the eighty years she spent as a queen of Narnia before coming back home five minutes after she had left. Currently, she is working on her PhD in Astrophysics and Planetary sciences in Besançon, France.

When she's not writing—or trying to wrangle comets—she's either reading, designing, crafting, or attempting to speak with various woodland creatures in an attempt to get them to do household chores for her.

She could also be gaming, or pretending she's not watching anything on Netflix.

CONNECT WITH THE AUTHOR

www.seandersonauthor.com
facebook.com/seandersonauthor
instagram.com/readcommendations
twitter.com/sea_author

www.ingramcontent.com/pod-product-compliance
Lightning Source LLC
Chambersburg PA
CBHW030815190726
48285CB00003B/1196